Dec. 17, 1992

To Bobette Bird

With my very best

wishes

Joan Schuster

Petroleros

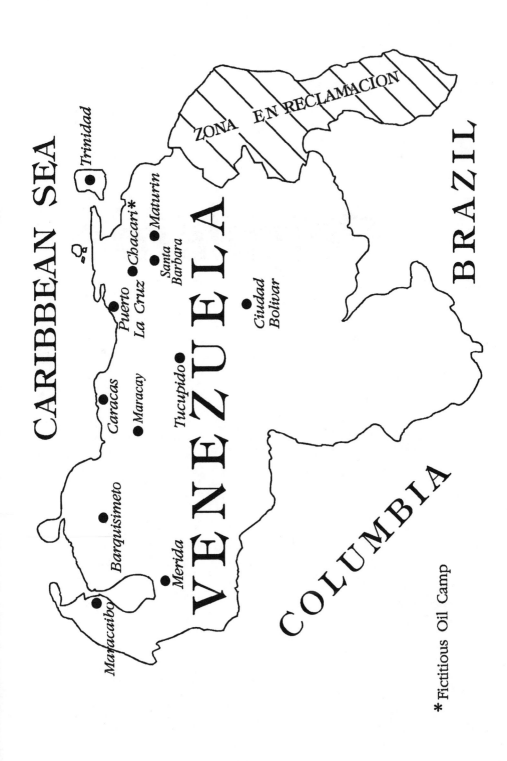

CARIBBEAN SEA

BRAZIL

COLUMBIA

VENEZUELA

ZONA   EN RECLAMACION

Trinidad

Chacari*

Maturin

Puerto
La Cruz

Santa
Barbara

Ciudad
Bolivar

Caracas

Maracay

Tucupido

Barquisimeto

Merida

Maracaibo

* Fictitious Oil Camp

Petroleros

A NOVEL

JOAN SCHUSTER

GoodeNough Press

Published by

GoodeNough Press, P.O. Box 12705, Lake Park, FL 33403

The author wishes to express appreciation for permission to quote from the following song:

ME & BOBBY McGEE
Copyright © 1969 by Combine Music Corp.
Words and Music by Kris Kristofferson & Fred Foster
Used by permission from Kris Kristofferson

FIRST EDITION
Book design by Colleen E. Bohrer

Library of Congress Cataloging-in-Publication Data
Schuster, Joan
    Petroleros : a novel / Joan Schuster.
        p. cm.
    ISBN 0-9631948-0-1 (cloth)
    I. Title.
PS3569.C5555P4 1992   813".54--dc20   92-9196

Printed in the United States of America

10   9   8   7   6   5   4   3   2   1

To
*A*nnie,

who always believed I was a writer.

Acknowledgments

Although I drew on my memories of the years I lived in Venezuela to write *PETROLEROS*, I did considerable research, especially anything pertaining to oil production. *Mil gracias* to Bill Damon who read my research (and many times corrected me!) for his invaluable technical advice.

I also consulted with Fred Latrash, U. S. Foreign Service (retired) and Pedro Rincones, Creole Petroleum Corp. (retired), to verify Venezuelan history and politics. My appreciation to both of them.

To the Bayou Biddisons and Millie & Jack Bluestein for their wisdom and input, thanks for everything.

Jim Espo with his editorial insight was a tremendous help to me.

To all those who helped me remember the Venezuela *de aquellos tiempos* I am most grateful, especially my family — my mother, Ted Cardone; my sister Marie and her late husband, Bill Murnane, Sr.; my niece, Annie Janulis whose knowledge of Venezuela in the 60s was an immense contribution; my nephew Bill Murnane, Jr. and my son, Robert Schuster. And indebted to all of them for their support and encouragement, especially my mother.

To my friends — your interest, good thoughts and prayers are deeply appreciated.

A special thanks to God and His saints.

Author's Note

I tried to make this novel as accurate as possible. For dramatic purposes, however, I used "flash bangs" in a December, 1969 fictitious setting. They were actually used for the first time in the October, 1977 rescue of a hijacked Lufthansa jet in Somalia.

And to those *mambo* purists, I know this dance didn't arrive on the musical scene until the 50s, but I couldn't resist putting it in a late 40s setting. Mainly because I'm a great admirer of Perez Prado and his *fantástico* music. What fun he gave us.

All the camp superintendents' wives I knew were ladies in every sense of the word (they would never have arrived at this position unless they were). My appreciation to all of them for their understanding and sense of humor in my creation of Sugar.

Salud, pesetas y amor
y tiempo para gozarlos.

May you be granted health,
prosperity and love,
and
time to enjoy them all.

PROLOGUE

Maturín, Venezuela - December, 1975

The afternoon sun, still strong, suddenly weakened as if a huge cloud had taken possession of the sky. As she turned around she realized the pale light was caused by the shadow of someone standing behind her. She jumped back in surprise, then stared at the man who had invaded her solitude.

"What are you doing here?" she demanded, the old anger boiling up inside her.

"The same as you," he replied softly.

"Well, aren't you the thoughtful one," she snapped.

"Let's not quarrel," he pleaded. "Not here. She deserves better than that."

He's right, she thought, as she looked down at the only thing they could still share. This is no place for old grievances.

It wasn't always this way. Twenty-eight years ago it was a different story. Her face softened with the memory of better days. Twenty-eight years ago when New York was ablaze with holiday glitter and Ella Logan was singing *If This Isn't Love*, we had a lot more in common than this cemetery on the plains of eastern Venezuela.

A person could drown in a sea of memories.

1

ONE

New York City - December, 1947

Cathleen Joyce gave the financial report her undivided attention, proofing it carefully as she rolled it slowly out of the Underwood typewriter. Before inserting another sheet of paper, she paused to check her pageboy. Most days she wore her hair wound in a chignon because it was quick and easy. With two sisters and four brothers still living at home, claiming the bathroom was a test of never ending cunning. This morning, however, she'd managed to get in and out before the herd began stampeding into the hall, so she'd had time to indulge herself. Satisfied the pageboy was holding, she returned to the report, her eyes never leaving the column of figures while her fingers played a steady rhythm on the typewriter keys.

Then suddenly she realized someone was speaking to her. Looking up, she saw a face dominated by a black mustache and gray eyes. Eyes which took in every detail of her face, nodding in approval as they travelled down to her green jacket and Black Watch plaid shirt. His words came out in a soft laconic drawl, almost as if he were caressing them. Taken by surprise at the man's sudden appearance, thrown off guard by the hypnotic quality of his voice, it took Cathleen a moment to realize he had stopped speaking. Then one of his eyes closed in a wink.

Cathleen, nineteen years old and schooled by the nuns, virginal in more than the physical sense, felt the blood rush to her face. Her insides quivered with a million butterflies. When he asked if her boss was in, she pointed to Barry's office, hoping he hadn't noticed her blush. After he left she struggled to catch her breath, then immersed herself once more in the financial report. But the butterflies returned en masse when Barry buzzed her to bring in two coffees. As she carefully placed the mugs on the desk she felt the stranger's eyes follow her every move. When he thanked her in his mesmerizing drawl, she looked up and saw him raise his mug in a quasi-toast. After which, he winked again. Her poise never abandoned her nor did she blush this time. She walked out of the office carrying herself in the aloof manner which had inspired the office wag to dub her the 'Frigid Digit.'

Shaking, she collapsed in her chair. Mother of God, she cried out in silent bewilderment, whatever was the matter with her? She clung to Danny O'Hara's class ring, hanging on a gold chain around her neck, hoping it would give her the answer. Her work became a disaster; she spent more time erasing than typing. Finally in exasperation, she broke early for lunch and slipped on her black coat styled in Christian Dior's New Look.

"You made some impression on Rylander," Barry Thomas remarked when she returned from lunch.

"Who?" she asked nonchalantly pulling off her long black gloves slowly to still her shaking fingers.

"S. J. Rylander, that long drink of water who was here this morning. I met him last time I went to Venezuela to do the annual audit." Barry was amused by Cathleen's pretended indifference.

"Oh boy, did he flip over you." He knew her remoteness, her 'don't touch' look, hid a shy personality. He was the only one, though, who saw through her mask. The rest of the office thought she was a terrible snob.

Cathleen hung up her coat, carefully brushing snow off the round fur collar.

"I told him to look me up if he ever came to New York," Barry continued. He found the situation hilarious. S. J. Rylander, who had given him a tour of every whorehouse outside camp, had fallen for the Frigid Digit. What a combination. "You'll probably hear from him today," he added before closing the door to his office, regretting the meeting he had scheduled that afternoon. He would give anything to see how Cathleen handled Rylander.

At 4:30 her phone rang.

"Hey, how are you doin'?"

Mother of God, it was him. She struggled with emotions playing hopscotch with her heart.

"Fine, thank you," she replied in her most professional manner. "I'm afraid Mr. Thomas isn't here."

"I don't want to talk to Barry. You're the one I'm callin', Cathleen." She was torn between liking the way he pronounced her name and angry because he made it sound so intimate. There was a long silence as she struggled to think of a reply.

"Cat got your tongue?" he drawled.

"No," she answered frostily. "It's your nickel."

"Cathleen, are all New York girls this tough? I'm just tryin' to be friendly. How about meetin' me for a drink after work?"

"I have plans for the evening."

"I'm not surprised, someone as pretty as you. I'll call tomorrow. But I'll be thinkin' of you tonight." She had the strongest feeling that his words were accompanied by another wink.

Cathleen had nothing planned. Her fiancée, Dan O'Hara, lived in Brooklyn and they saw each other only on weekends. But she certainly wasn't going out for a drink with this stranger. Walking the eight blocks to 42nd Street, she tried to push Rylander out of her thoughts. She liked to walk. After sitting down all day it gave her a sense of freedom and despite her high heels she kept a brisk pace. But today she felt so giddy and light-headed she toyed with the idea of taking one of the red double decker buses, hoping a ride on its open upper deck would clear her head. *Just remember you're engaged,* she reminded herself, and pushed on, walking faster. The crisp December air colored her cheeks, causing more than a few male heads to turn and admire her. The simple lines of her black coat with its mink collar and the mink pillbox crowning her blond hair emphasized her striking good looks.

Making her way through the crowds in Grand Central Station, she kept hearing his voice. When she found a seat in the smoking car, she lit a Lucky Strike, hoping the cigarette would calm her. Cathleen had planned her life to the smallest detail. Working at Palm Oil Co., going to N.Y.U. three nights a week, the train ride to and from work was her study hall. She never socialized with other secretaries at lunchtime, that was reserved for homework. Six more semesters and she would have her degree. Then she would start teaching high school English while she went for her Master's at night. When Danny became a registered architect, marriage. After a few years of teaching, time off to start her family, and when the children were old enough, back to teaching with summers and holidays free for her family. Nothing was going to change these plans. Cathleen believed people could get whatever they wanted out of life by simply taking the time to plan ahead. Then everything would fall into place. Reminding herself she had an exam the next day, she opened her English Lit II book and turned her attention to Shakespeare's sonnets. She memorized the required five, but her eyes kept returning to one in particular.

Love is not love which alters
when it alteration finds

She wondered, would she always feel that way about Danny? The memory of Rylander invaded her thoughts again. It's just the fairies doing strange things, she reassured herself. Hadn't her Irish grandmother told her they liked to stir up things? She reached for Danny's ring, confident it would have the power to eradicate Rylander from her mind. Eventually she stopped thinking about him, but she clung to the ring, sliding it absently back and forth on the chain. By the time the conductor called out, "Harrison, Harrison," she'd finished her English assignment and made a dent in the ancient history homework. She'd have time after dinner to finish studying, wash her hair and wait for Danny's call. Ah, now she felt better. She knew exactly where she was going. It certainly wasn't with some stranger named S. J. Rylander, and most definitely didn't go beyond the boundaries of New York. Perhaps Connecticut if Danny's practice flourished, but no farther.

Cathleen longed for marriage and a home of her own. As much as she loved her eight brothers and sisters, she was tired of fighting for the bathroom, seeing the choicest servings at dinner go to the swiftest, sharing a bedroom with her sisters, Peggy and Beebe. She yearned to be mistress of her own home.

But until she met Danny, no man pursued her. Although she was the prettiest of the Joyce girls, her vivacious sisters were the ones who had the boyfriends. Her reserved manner held too many people at bay. Even at home it didn't go unnoticed; her family frequently referred to her as Princess Cathleen.

She didn't want to hear from Rylander again, yet the next day she found herself waiting for his call. And as she waited, she experienced terrible guilt thinking of Danny. Danny whose understanding had plumbed through the layers of her shyness. *But Danny isn't exciting.* The memory of Rylander in Barry's office, his long legs sprawled over the side of the chair, the lazy way he lit his cigar, kept flashing through her mind. But it was his voice she remembered the most. She found herself comparing it with Danny's, and her fiancée came out the loser. His nasal Brooklyn accent and fast cadence seemed harsh and grating next to Rylander's soft drawl. I'll bet Danny will have a paunch when he's older, but not Rylander; his body will always be hard and slim. Thinking of his body, hers began to experience strange sensations. Exhilaration where her pulses raced and unfamiliar emotions made her tremble. At times she felt close to tears; she couldn't understand what was happening to her.

At five o'clock she put away her steno pad and covered her typewriter. She had an exam that night; just enough time for a quick supper at the Automat. She felt somewhat let down that Rylander hadn't called. Impatiently she waited for the elevator and when it deposited her in the lobby, she walked rapidly toward the exit.

"Hey, how're you doin'?" A hand reached out and stopped her.

Looking up she saw Rylander. She was ecstatic that he hadn't forgotten her, yet what came out of her mouth was a sharp, "Do you always go around grabbing people?"

"Oh, Cathleen, I've been thinking about you all day." His words came out in that soft drawl. "I thought five o'clock would never come."

"And now that it's here?" she asked coolly.

"Why, now that it's here," he grinned, "I'd like to invite you for a drink."

She shook her head. "I have a seven o'clock class."

"Just one drink," he persisted. "Then I'll take you to wherever you're goin' in a taxi."

"Just one," she replied, shocked at her ready acceptance, filled with panic because she seemed to have no control over her actions. But sitting next to him in the skating rink cafe at Rockefeller Plaza, she found herself half liking the way he'd swept her off her feet. She was a romantic who'd seen Judy Garland meet Robert Walker under the clock at the Astor and Rhett Butler carry Scarlet O'Hara up the stairs. Her surroundings enhanced her feeling of enchantment. Couples skated by, hands entwined. At the far end of the rink, the multi-colored lights of the giant

Christmas tree sparkled as if a million gems had been scattered on its branches, giving the entire plaza a fairy-tale atmosphere. She felt as if the pages of a favorite book had come to life and she was part of it.

When Rylander asked what she wanted to drink, she hesitated a moment remembering her exam, then surprised herself again by deciding on a martini. A cocktail she never drank, but which now seemed appropriate for the euphoria she felt. It was such a sophisticated drink. She was aware that Rylander was much older than she was and this added to his attraction.

"And a bourbon and ginger for me," he told the waiter.

Bourbon and ginger ale! She cringed at his choice. It seemed to go with his string tie and boots. Why, nobody wore boots, only actors in cowboy movies. But her critical feelings didn't linger. Mother of God, she was so confused.

"I think I'm in love." The brief moment he paused, her heart started pounding so hard she was sure he could hear it. "With your hair," he continued. "It's like strands of gold. I did a double take the first time I saw you. Felt like I'd died and gone to Heaven."

"What a line, you could hang laundry on it!" The flip remark was something her sister Beebe would come out with, not fitting the cool Princess Cathleen image at all.

"It's no line, Cathleen. But then, you're probably used to compliments."

She wasn't. Danny told her that he loved her. Nothing more. He wasn't one for compliments, nor did he look at her with such adoration. Nervously reaching for a cigarette, she felt his hand brush against hers as he lit it. Inhaling slowly brought back her self-confidence. She picked up his lighter, studying the initials.

"What does S. J. stand for? Stephen? John?"

"Just S. J. My family was so poor they couldn't afford a whole name," he joked. "Most people though call me Ryle."

"Where are you from, Ryle?" The articles in *Mademoiselle* and *Glamour*, which she read religiously, advised encouraging a man to talk about himself.

"Oklahoma. Just like the play." He paused for a second, then grinned. "Do you think we'll be singing, *People Will Say We're in Love?*"

Struck speechless, her cheeks turned bright crimson, which embarrassed her even more than his words.

"Oh, how sweet," he laughed, "to see a woman blush."

Mercifully the waiter appeared, saving her from having to answer. Cathleen sipped her martini, grateful for the wonderful feeling of comfort it gave her.

"You're a long way from home, Ryle." What a dolt you are, Cathleen, she berated herself. Your conversation is nothing less than brilliant. She wished she could think of something exciting to say, perhaps tell a funny story like Peggy, or flirt with him as all her sisters could. But the only thing which came out was, "Aren't you homesick?"

He shook his head. "Home is where you hang your hat. And for the past two years I've been hanging it in Venezuela."

"Are you going back?"

"If you come with me." When he saw her blush he started to laugh, slapping his boots. "Hot damn, I sure like the way you get all flustered." Then sensing her discomfort, he stopped laughing and went on. "Yeah, I'm goin' back. The money's better than in the States, and if a person can stick it out and don't mind roughing it for a few years, there's a whole better chance of getting ahead than up here in the States."

Cathleen glanced at her watch. She was going to miss class. Unlike her sisters, who would skip school whenever there was a good show at the Paramount or Roxy, especially Frank Sinatra, she'd never cut a class in her life. Well, it was too late now. In for a penny, as her Aunt Jenny often said, in for a pound.

"I started out on seismo crew," Ryle continued.

"A what kind of crew?"

"Seismo, that's short for seismograph. That's when we take a shot hole rig and drill a line of shot holes..." He saw the confusion in her face and remarked, "See, a city girl don't know what I'm talking about."

She flinched when he said 'don't'. His English is deplorable, she thought disdainfully.

"A rig has a derrick, Cathleen," he explained. Her heart missed a few beats when he said her name. Despite everything objectionable about him, his clothes and bad grammar, she found herself overlooking them in the excitement he created inside her. It was a feeling she couldn't understand because she hadn't known it before. Certainly not with Danny. She felt as if her whole life up to now had merely been a rehearsal.

"A seismo crew will drill down around two hundred feet," he continued, "to about the base of the weathered layer of the earth's surface, so the force of the explosion isn't absorbed by unconsolidated soil and weathered upper layers. Then they run electric cables with detectors along the ground, in alignment with the surveyed seismic line and on opposite sides of the shot hole. The cables are connected to seismograph records inside the recording truck. After they lower a small charge of dynamite down into the hole and it goes off, the sound waves are recorded on the seismograph. And from studying the graphs which look something like a cardiogram, the geologist, that's me, can determine the existence of a potential petroleum trap."

She was grateful the conversation had turned to something technical for it distracted her stirred up emotions.

"Are you still on a seismo crew?"

"Naw, I ain't working seismo no more. Some guys spend years on a crew, but not this one. I had to make up for the three years I lost in the war."

She sensed his restlessness, the drive to get ahead and she admired it. Why, he was no different from her or Danny going to college at night. Danny, who graduated from high school a year before she and didn't go off to war because he was too young. He seemed like such a boy next to Ryle and she found herself wishing she could have seen Ryle in uniform.

"I didn't volunteer for the Army, they got me in the draft," he said almost defensively. "Doesn't sound very patriotic, huh? Yeah well, it was because getting through college was such a grind and I'd finally gotten a good job. I did my duty though. For over a year I sat around the States, griping because I had to teach a bunch of recruits. Finally made it over for the Normandy invasion. Then I was wishing I was back in the States, especially when I got caught in the Bulge." He paused to take a drag on his cigarette.

"It was bedlam, everyone runnin' and not knowin' where they were going. One guy I came across was standing by a jeep bawlin' his eyes out. Come to find out he was a city kid from Brooklyn who didn't know how to drive 'cause he always rode the subways. Well I drove us out of there in a hurry. Then we found a squad of Limey soldiers, which turned out to be my most frightening experience in the whole war."

Cathleen, mesmerized by his voice and the raw masculinity of his personality, leaned across the table, waiting impatiently for him to continue his story.

"It wasn't the Germans or getting separated from my outfit that was so bad. Or even wondering if I was going to make it out of there alive. It was that week with the Limeys. On account of their rations. Never got a cup of coffee the whole week. I was drinkin' tea until it came out my ears. And that's when I knew I was goin' to make it." He paused, aware she was hanging on his every word. "I figured if I could survive a week of that Limey tea, nothin' could harm me. And nothin' did! Sailed all the way from Malmedy clear through to Berlin."

Ryle had a way of telling stories. It wasn't so much what he said, but he had a sense of exaggeration, knowing when to pause or emphasize certain words. She found herself laughing, and the more she laughed, the more stories he told her. Danny, sweet good Danny, seemed a lackluster boy in comparison.

He leaned back in his chair, staring intently, his eyes boring into her. "Where were you during the war, Cathleen?"

"Why . . . ." When he looked at her that way she felt the butterflies returning. "Why, I was in high school."

"Figured as much," he nodded. "Well, you were worth fighting for."

She felt the blush creeping up her throat, reaching her ears, flooding her face.

"There you go again." His face broke out in a huge grin. "I forgot that girls blushed. Or maybe the ones I came across never did. Anyway, it's sweet, Cathleen, so damn sweet."

Again that rush of happiness whenever he said her name.

"You know what I want to do? Somethin' I've never done before." He pointed to the skaters. "You're probably an expert, so you can teach me. Let's do it, Cathleen. There's so much living we're gonna do together."

She found herself liking the intimation there was a future for them. She wasn't the least bit athletic, she hated gym. But growing up watching Sonja Henie movies always made her want to get on the ice at the first cold snap. She was a good skater, and it gave her confidence to be better at something than Ryle. For she was in awe of all the living experiences he had known. Even the things which repelled her, his boots and string tie, his habit of saying *don't* and *ain't*, all this was forgotten because of the yearning he'd stirred in her.

"Cathleen, take off your gloves. I want to feel your hands in mine. Don't worry, I'll keep them warm." The insides of his hands, callused and hard, only enhanced his appeal, making her feel his strength would always be there for her.

She caught their reflection as they skated past the cafe windows. Her tall, willowy body in an emerald green coat with a black Persian Lamb collar looked tiny next to Ryle's lankiness. He wore no coat. Just a gray tweed jacket and black slacks, with a sweater under his jacket. He seemed indifferent to the cold. His long legs moved in rhythm with hers as he followed her lead around the rink while his powerful hands gripped hers, keeping them warmer than the fur-lined gloves she'd removed. After awhile she was no longer the teacher. He guided them around the rink, becoming more of the leader, his strength overpowering her until she was glad to surrender to his lead, content to follow in whatever direction he wanted.

A gentle soft flurry of snow began to fall. Ryle stopped skating, pulling her with him to the edge of the rink. Looking up she noticed the dark hairs of his mustache laced with snow, making them salt and pepperish. This is the way he'll look when he's older, she thought, and I want to be with him then. Snow fell on her face. She opened her mouth, sliding her tongue out to taste it, as she did when she was a child, marvelling at the snowflake's clean, new taste. His hands moved slowly around her neck until they reached her chignon, where he loosened the pins, following the strands of hair with his fingers as they cascaded down over her shoulders. He had a gentle touch, which surprised her for she was positive someone with such powerful hands would crush anything he touched. As his mouth approached hers, all the emotions she'd experienced since meeting him erupted. The quirky way her pulses raced, the tingling foreign sensations in her body. When their lips met she was again surprised by his gentleness. His mouth brushed back and forth across hers in a tentative exploration. But his arms held her in a powerful grip, so tight she felt like crying out. Then the gentleness of his lips was gone, replaced by an urgency so insistent Cathleen felt faint. As if her emotions were on a roller coaster ride and she had no control. Her lips blended into his, parting as his tongue entered her mouth, frightened a little by this invasion and then joyously reaching out for it.

"I don't want to stop," he groaned, "but I'd better or I'll make love to you right here in front of God and everyone." He pulled away reluctantly.

"God and everyone?" she mocked him. Oh, she was so sure of herself now. She wanted to burrow into his body, if possible slip right under his skin because she felt so safe in his arms. Yes, that was the word, safe. As if she'd been searching a long time for a secure port and had finally found it. They came from such different worlds, but it didn't matter to her. Not now, not with the strong feeling she had that fate had brought them together on a snowy night in December of 1947.

He embraced her again, his lips brushing back and forth across hers in that slow way which made her feel her clothes were slipping off, one piece at a time. "You look so young and untarnished," he whispered, the words coming out in wonder, as if he couldn't quite believe his good fortune in meeting her.

"And your long hair is so beautiful. Don't ever cut it." He looked at her so imploringly, she found herself nodding quickly in acquiescence.

They walked down Fifth Avenue in the snow, holding hands like lovestruck teenagers. The city was theirs, Cathleen felt, it had been created just for them. Stopping to admire the store windows with their holiday tableaux, he told her to pick out whatever she wanted, the sky was the limit. She smiled to herself, thinking that she'd already received her gift. Christmas had come a little early this year, no need to wish for anything else.

Cathleen didn't want the night to end. When they walked by the Biltmore Hotel, she ran impulsively towards the revolving door, pulling Ryle with her. Like children they went around and around, finally exiting to meet the disapproving eyes of the doorman. But his stern face couldn't dampen her happiness. When Ryle insisted they have a nightcap she didn't resist. Sitting at the bar in the Biltmore, she stirred her glass of hot, buttered rum with a cinnamon stick and wished time would stand still. Having had very little experience with men (her courtship by Danny was still at a very chaste stage), Cathleen didn't realize Ryle was making love to her. Not in the physical sense, but with his eyes. When he turned away to pick up his drink or light a cigarette, she looked at him shyly, wanting to memorize every feature on his face. She felt as if she'd finally found her special niche in the world. Small talk which had never been easy for her, spilled effortlessly from her lips.

They walked next door to Grand Central Terminal, lingering on the lower level outside the gate leading to her train. Cathleen hated to leave the warmth of Ryle's arms. Waiting until the conductor moved to close the gate, she reluctantly descended the concrete ramp into the bowels of the station, half hoping she'd missed her train. Reaching the smoking car, she realized it was the same train she would have taken if she'd gone to class. The thought had a sobering effect on her.

What would Ma think, she asked herself in dismay, if she knew what happened tonight? Why, she'd have my hide. Necking in Rockefeller Plaza, kissing him like I did back there in the station. Suppose someone saw me. She looked around to see if she recognized anyone. Can you imagine what the family would think if they ever saw him! Jesus, Mary and Joseph, straight off the range with those boots and string tie. I mustn't think of him, she told herself. I have Danny, sweet, solid Danny. But it was like talking to the wind. Cathleen felt close to tears because she wondered if she could ever be satisfied with Danny O'Hara.

She put her head back on the seat, closing her eyes. It was too much for her to absorb. Feeling restless, she opened her eyes and reaching for a cigarette, looked around the car. It sparkled as it never did before. Try as she might to put a damper on the evening, to rationalize things, she couldn't shake off her happiness. Even the windows with their film of soot now seemed to sparkle with the reflection of the ceiling lights. The hard, green leather seats felt like velvet. And instead of making her sick as it sometimes did, the swaying of the train felt like a cradle lulling her to sleep. Only she was too excited to sleep. She was coming home from the Palace Ball in her carriage, and as the train emerged from the tunnel into the snowy night, the six white mice sped up Park Avenue.

Then she felt a sudden surge of sadness, a premonition that S. J. Rylander would bring her great unhappiness. But the feeling only lasted seconds, and then it was gone. So quickly she didn't dwell on it, for her happiness was too great and once again she felt as if magic had touched her.

The conductor calling out, "Harrison, next stop Harrison," jolted her from her reverie. When she got off the train, she felt as if she floated right down to the platform.

Walking the six blocks to her home, she realized she'd lost her English Lit book, as well as all her notes. Did she leave them at Rockefeller Plaza or Grand Central? Her mind was a blank. The only thing she knew was they were gone, along with everything else in her carefully planned and predictable life.

TWO

Chacari, an oil camp in Eastern Venezuela, 1947

Maguire ran his tongue over the bruised lip he acquired in last night's fight. He hated himself when he lost his temper. But when his wife was insulted he couldn't stand by and ignore it. Sugar Dalhart probably resurrected the old stories, he thought angrily. Why doesn't she leave Sarita alone? Sarita harms no one, and has more class in her little finger than that two bits piece of trash could ever hope to have. *Mrs.* Dalhart, that's a crock, he sneered. She has no more idea what marriage means than a bitch in heat.

He wished they could leave camp, go someplace where no one knew about Sarita. Where she would be loved for her many graces and not condemned for her past. The isolation of the oilfields, sometimes stifling, felt more oppressive than ever today. Got to stick it out though, he reminded himself, until the end of my contract. Then it'll be *adiós* Palm Oil Co. We'll go live in Puerto La Cruz where I'll have my own business and we'll become pillars of society. The idea amused him. Not because he gave a damn about such things for he'd been a loner all his life, but he wanted to give the world to his wife. Ah, how marriage changes a man, he thought. It brings out the poet in us, make us more ambitious, even curbs our vices. Well, almost. His quick Irish temper, which had played havoc with him all his life, still erupted despite Sarita's angelic influence.

It almost got him court-martialed during the war when he hit an officer. He'd been sitting in a San Diego bar when this obnoxious ensign came up and started pestering the girl sitting beside him. She wasn't his date; he barely knew the girl. Yet he felt he had to protect her when the ensign wouldn't leave her alone. Now despite all the promises he'd made to Sarita, he'd gone and decked someone last night. It was to defend her

15

though, something he seemed to be doing ever since their marriage.

Ah, to hell with all those bastards in camp. Throwing his head back he started to sing. His voice, the pride of Pittsburgh's saloons, filled the cab of his Ford pickup.

Adiós Maraquita Linda
Farewell my lovely Mary
I'm leaving for a distant land

His blue eyes sparkled with the joy he felt being alive, so the two hour trip from Chacari to Puerto La Cruz slipped by quickly. He let his tongue roll over the words, savoring them as if they were the finest old brandy. The song had been his favorite since his arrival in Venezuela. He was camp boss then, the most menial job paying $250 a month, plus living allowance, requiring none of the tool and die making skills he'd used at the steel mills. But after the war he was too restless to resume his former occupation, especially when his love life turned to shambles.

Being camp boss though had its humorous aspects. Like the time he instructed the native workers in the use of toilet paper. They didn't know they were supposed to flush it down the toilet or sit on the seat. Which explained the piles of soiled paper on the floor and the scratches from their boots on the seats. Pulling down his khaki pants, he did a fair imitation of taking care of business, receiving thunderous applause from the natives for his performance.

He loved his life in Venezuela and didn't care if he ever saw the States again, or another white Christmas. His butt had frozen too many winters to miss the change of seasons. What he would miss were the tropical sunsets where the sky looked like a box of crayons left out in the summer heat — aqua, pink and purple blending into golden streaks of the setting sun. In Pittsburgh he never saw the stars because of the city lights. But out here in the remoteness of the Venezuelan interior he could look up at the heavens and marvel at their brilliance against the black velvet sky, shining more magnificently than any whore's rhinestone necklace.

He saw a small *cantina* and pulled over for lunch. Digging into the rice and beans accompanying his steak, he realized he'd really gone native. He thought of people back in the States eating ham and Swiss on rye, running for commuter trains in pin striped suits. His friends still sweating it out in the steel mills. And he pitied them all.

When he first arrived in Venezuela he became known as a maverick, mainly because he didn't run around with the other bachelors in camp. The only time he socialized with the Americans was when the married couples needed a fourth for bridge. He preferred to mingle with the Venezuelans because he wanted to learn Spanish and everything he could about the country. Maguire's strongest friendships were with Padre Lopez Machado, the town priest who never lectured him for missing Mass and Pedro Garcia, the police chief with whom he drank and caroused at the local whorehouses.

The company sent all new employees to Spanish school in Caracas. But since something always came up to prevent Maguire from going, he picked up as much as he could by himself. Riding alone in his pickup he repeated phrases and words until they sounded right. Even when he went to whorehouses he did a lot of talking before going off with a girl, which always amused the police chief.

He could do no wrong in the chief's eyes, even when he borrowed his motorcycle and invited one of the ladies of the evening to accompany him. He drove out to the pipeline and managed to get the bike on it, riding for several miles. It created quite a sensation, the whore clad in the flimsiest attire, hanging on to Maguire tightly while screaming her lungs out in a mixture of fright and exuberance. Afterwards the Venezuelans started to think of him as one of their own, calling him *un palo de hombre*, a man's man.

The company quickly spotted Maguire's potential. Despite being a ninth grade dropout, he was extremely efficient and intelligent. That, along with his fluency in Spanish, got him quickly promoted to warehouseman. He wasn't a company man though, aiming to work his way through the ranks to the top, for he didn't plan to stay with Palm Oil. He needed money, a lot more than the oil companies could pay him, and the only way to get it was to start his own business.

Maguire met Sarita when he was stationed near Maracaibo. The city which he first saw from the ferry was little more than a hot, humid backwater. It wasn't until the mid-50s that it started to boom with the appearance of the *Hotel del Lago*, it's nightclub featuring an ice skating act from the States and the Hotel Detroit with entertainers imported from Cuba. Or the Shamrock Hotel which offered none of these amenities, but was a popular place for the Americans to hang out. Even so, to the *petroleros* in the late 40s Maracaibo was the big city. Booze cost more, but there were a few restaurants and the whores more sophisticated than the ones who worked the fringes of the oilfields across the lake.

When the ferry pulled in, Maguire instantly felt the cool breeze off the lake turn into humid, almost suffocating heat. A mass of humanity threw themselves at him, vendors hawking live chickens, beggars pleading for attention and taxi drivers clamoring for fares. Around him the air was thick with the smell of sweating bodies and excrement from the dogs roaming the streets, skeletal bodies attesting to their never ending quest for food. When he finally cleared the harbor area, leaving the din of high pitched voices behind him, his shirt clung to his body like a second skin.

That night he visited two whorehouses before he discovered Hortensia's. The first, *El Pompei*, offered women of every nationality. But he left after one drink because of the stiff prices. The second, Mariela's, featuring a live band, resembled a nightclub more than a brothel. He struck up a conversation with the musicians when they went on break and discovered that the lead trumpet player also taught at the Music Conservatory. Maguire liked talking with people from all walks of life. What he didn't like at Mariela's were the whores, who were so obvious in their hustling. Slipping into the booth with him, they ran their hands up and down his thighs, trying to unzip his fly so they could fondle him.

The whores in Hortensia's were more to his liking because they didn't rush him. And he was amused by the colored lights strung across the building's exterior. Seeing a whorehouse ablaze with Christmas lights like homes in the States appealed to his droll sense of humor. The jukebox playing a soft tango appealed to him even more. He wasn't in the mood to lead a conga line, nor invite anyone for a bike ride on the pipeline, for his Irish roguery was dormant that night. Indicating he just wanted to sit at the bar for awhile, the whores left him alone.

Sipping his third *Santa Teresa*, Maguire noticed one whore who seemed so out of place his curiosity was aroused. The cleft in her chin initially drew his attention, but what intrigued him was the aura of serenity and innocence which lit up her face. He decided that maybe he'd put away too much rum when he started to see whores resembling church statues. He felt eerie, especially when he noticed she wasn't wearing a ton of jewelry as the others did, just a gold cross on a chain. He knew from past encounters that a lot of the whores had religious statues in their rooms. It didn't spook him. But now seeing a whore who resembled a novice ready to profess her vows in a nunnery shook him into sobriety. Unable to stop staring, he slipped off the bar stool and approached her.

"Does your mother know you're out tonight?" he asked in English.

"¿*Perdón*?" Brown eyes looked up and the first thing he noticed was the glow in them, something the other jaded whores lacked. Her skin was dark, not black but a soft shade of cinnamon.

"It's a joke, honey. Asking if your mother knows you're out tonight," he explained. "Almost a cliché, the same as if I'd said, 'What's a nice girl like you doing in a place like this'?" Then seeing the confusion in her face, he switched to Spanish. "Just thinking out loud," he assured her. "Enough of this *gringo* talk. ¿*Cómo se llama*?"

"My name is Sarita," she replied, in a voice so delightfully soft and feminine he became even more interested. Something about her absolutely bowled him over. He didn't know if he was experiencing a virgin/whore fantasy or if it was her incredible serenity. He was more inclined to think it was the latter. Being with her made Maguire feel that all was right in the universe. And what the other whores had failed to achieve by furtively exploring his body, this woman with the saint-like face and peaceful manner did. She aroused him as he hadn't been for longer than he cared to remember.

He asked her to dance. He knew he could have just given her money and gone to her room. But he wanted all the preliminaries. He especially wanted to know her better. At one point he asked, "And from what convent did you escape?"

She didn't giggle inanely as the other whores would have done, only smiled softly. It wasn't the first time a man had been drawn to her virginal looks. Hortensia, the madam, liked to boast she had a virgin for any customer so inclined.

"How much for this girl?" he asked Hortensia. "I'd like to take her to my hotel for a night or two."

Hortensia's eyes lit up with visions of great wealth, yet she was hesitant, and she knew Sarita was, too. There had been another request for her to leave which hadn't turned out well. Sarita's look of innocence triggered the customer's twisted inclinations and he beat her up. When she got back to Hortensia's she wasn't a pretty sight. So black and blue she wasn't able to work for weeks. Very bad for business, Hortensia remembered, very bad for Sarita. She decided to quote Maguire a rather high price.

"*¡Caray!*" he pulled back. "I just want to rent her services, not do any serious buying." He was being stiffed because he was an American, he told Hortensia hotly. Surprised at his fluency in Spanish she relented a little. Shaking his head he started to walk away.

"Okay, okay, *gringo petrolero*," Hortensia cried out. "Have it your way. But you are robbing me blind." And she quoted him what she said was her rock bottom price. "This girl is worth much more."

"Of course she is," he replied, handing her the *Bolivares*, called *Bs* by the English speaking foreigners.

"*Ven conmigo*, Sarita," he said, taking her arm.

"*Mira, mira,*" the other girls chirped like birds. "The blond *petrolero* is taking you for a little honeymoon, *chica*. But don't forget us, little Sara, don't forget to bring back some presents when you return." They all started to laugh, Hortensia joining in. What a terrific deal, she gloated. If only she could make as much money with the rest of the *muchachas*.

....

Maguire woke up with a horrible hangover. He'd been putting away the rum steadily since he landed in Maracaibo, especially at Hortensia's. He remembered he brought one of the whores back to his hotel. Turning over in bed, he saw she was gone. Of course, she'd probably rolled him and taken off. What a sucker he was. Taken in by that innocent face. It was all an act. He got out of bed and walked gingerly to the bureau, surprised to find his wallet still there. And even more surprised to discover it hadn't been emptied. Reaching for a crumpled pack of Camels, he slipped back into bed, thinking about the girl. The damndest thing was he couldn't remember if he'd had sex with her. He kept going over the night before in his mind and he remembered everything until they got back to the hotel. Then he went blank. Reaching for another cigarette he heard the key turn in the door.

"*Buenas tardes*." It was Sarita carrying a covered dish and cup. "Are you hungry?"

"Well I'll be dammed," he cried out in English, "you didn't run out on me."

"It's going to get cold," she said, removing the covers from the plate and cup. "Especially the coffee."

Seeing the ham and eggs, with rice and beans, he felt ravenous. Amazingly everything was still hot, including the coffee.

After he finished, Sarita turned on the shower and called out to him, "*Ya está listo.*" Shedding his boxer shorts, he stepped into the shower. Standing there with the water running down his chest, he shook his head in disbelief.

"You sweet little thing." She'd joined him and he felt her hands washing his back. Damned if I didn't get the best whore in Venezuela, he decided happily. Then his thoughts turned to last night and not remembering if they'd done anything. After they toweled down and were back in bed, he asked her.

"*Nada,*" she replied.

"Nothing?" Looking at her, he found it difficult to believe. Her breasts with their chocolate nipples were so pillow-like he wanted to bury his face in them, while her stomach had just enough roundness he couldn't wait to run his hands over her velvet skin. How could he have not wanted her?

Responding to the puzzled look on his face, she offered, "Maybe too much *aguardiente*?"

It didn't happen often, but once in awhile when he put away too much liquor, he couldn't do a damn thing. Now thinking about it, he got embarrassed. Why, he couldn't figure out. She was just a whore. He paid for her, to do as he damned well pleased. Feeling he had lost time to make up, he mounted her, roughly spreading her legs apart. Her soft, brown body looked so inviting he quickly plunged inside her, pumping her to get the most satisfaction for himself. And then he stopped, unable to go on. Angry with himself. What the hell was the matter with him? It wasn't her fault he couldn't get it up last night. He pulled out, almost wanting to apologize. He really wanted it nice and easy. But most of all he wanted to make it good for her. She was just a whore, he kept reminding himself. But when he looked into Sarita's face he forgot he paid for her. All he could think about was giving her pleasure.

Afterwards he asked himself, when was the last time he'd really made love to a woman? Not since Sally, he realized. His enchanting Sally, with the quicksilver personality. Sally, who was lost to him forever.

....

Maguire made another discovery when they went out to dinner that evening. Sarita peered intently at the menu, but she was holding it upside down. He reached across the table and turned it right side up.

"It doesn't matter," she sighed. "I can't read."

"Well, now it looks like you do," he smiled.

"I'm embarrassing you," she apologized.

"No you're not." He didn't care what other people thought, but he found himself wanting her to shine in other people's eyes.

She didn't know what to say; she felt so completely out of her element. She wasn't ashamed of her profession, but she wondered why this *petrolero* brought her to such a fancy restaurant. She and the girls from Hortensia's sometimes went out to eat, but not to a place like this. She glanced at the couple sitting at the next table, observing how the woman held her fork and raised it to her mouth. She realized this was the correct way to eat.

"I asked you last night how long you've been at Hortensia's and you told me a short time," Maguire said, unable to take his eyes off her. "How long is a short time?"

"One, maybe two years." She shrugged her shoulders. "I'm not sure."

"And before that?" Noticing her hesitation, he blurted out, "It's okay, you don't have to answer. I'm just a curious sort of guy, probably too damned inquisitive for my own good. I guess I was just wondering why someone like you worked in a place like Hortensia's."

"And who would take care of the men who seek women if there was no one like me?"

"*Touché!*" he grinned, loving her quick intelligence.

"What I mean," he continued, "is that you don't look like the average ...." He felt like a stammering teenager asking for his first date. "You just don't look like .... oh hell!" The more he tried to talk, the worse it got. "What I mean is, you look like a sweet *señorita* who should be married with a couple of kids."

"People of my class don't marry," she explained. "They live with a man until he leaves them with a bunch of children." A look of fleeting sadness crossed her otherwise serene features. "Marriage is for the upper class," she continued. "Anyway, I never had a choice. God decided I should be a prostitute and so I am." She said this with an air of serenity.

The waiter arrived with the food. She picked up her fork holding it just as she'd seen the woman at the next table do. Because she'd grown up never having enough to eat, she always wolfed down her meals. But she noticed how Maguire ate and she paced herself to follow him.

Sarita always observed other people, for she found out at an early age how important it was to survive. Abandoned by a mother with too many children, never knowing her father, she was one of the legions of children who lived on the streets. Sleeping in alleyways, stealing or begging food, until she was taken in by a family, the head of which had a good racket going. All the children were sent out to beg, and if they returned home without money, they were beaten and not given anything to eat. So she learned early she had to get money. She never wanted to go back to the streets again with a hungry belly. When she found out there was another method of getting money, more than she could get begging, she accepted this without reservation. She certainly saw enough of the mating ritual in the crowded hovels she shared with a succession of families to know this was how it was between a man and a woman. This blond American who was buying her dinner would never be able to understand that world, no matter how many questions he asked.

The whorehouse was the only true home she'd ever known, the only place where any measure of kindness was shown her. She arrived in sheer terror. One night, living with her third or fourth family, she woke up feeling someone had tapped her on the shoulder. Looking around she saw it wasn't any of the other children, for they were sprawled around her sleeping soundly on the dirt floor. Then she heard Mama Yolanda talking in the living room with her husband of the moment. The house where they lived, a shack with walls made of packing cases and a flattened tin can roof, was incredibly tiny, almost too small to partition off into rooms. Yet Mama Yolanda had done it, for she set great store in having a *sala*, a living room. Since the room partitions were also made of packing cases, everyone could always hear what was said in the next room. And what Sarita heard terrified her.

Mama Yolanda had decided to keep Sarita, she told her husband. She was a good girl who knew how to bring home the money. It was probably that innocence of hers, the husband remarked. Exactly, Mama Yolanda agreed. People saw that saint-like face and couldn't resist when she threw out her hands begging for a few *centavos*, or a 12 ½ cent *locha*. Just think how much more money she could get if Sarita were crippled, Mama Yolanda said excitedly. Then who could resist that face of an angel? There was a 'doctor' who did these little operations, and tomorrow she would take Sarita to see him. In a short time, Mama Yolanda cried out, we'll be *riquísimo*, wealthy people!

Overcome with fright, Sarita soiled her pants. After Mama Yolanda and her husband went to bed, she slipped out of the house and ran. The dirt streets of the shantytown clinging precariously to the Caracas mountainside, and home to its impoverished, were a maze. But Sarita knew her way through them, darting in and out, feeling the devil himself in pursuit. She fled from slums where running water was unknown and the smell of human and animal waste hung in the air. Gasping for breath she made her way to a paved street. The houses were dark, but the streets were illuminated. She kept running, fear pushing her. Eventually she wound up in the whorehouse district, at that time of night the only place with lights on in the houses and people awake.

Finally she could run no more. Collapsing to the ground in exhaustion, she crawled up to a house. Its exterior was hard and unyielding, yet she clung to it for comfort for she heard laughter and music. There was happiness inside this house, she could feel it coming through the walls, promising her safety. Panting, her breath still coming out in sharp gasps, she watched as a man was shown out, the woman bidding him good night smiling warmly. Such warmth Sarita had rarely seen before. It beckoned her as a light did to a crazed moth. As her heart stopped racing and her breathing became more normal, she realized the house was very big, *más grande* than anything in the shantytown. Her eyes peered at the entrance where she saw the front door was not quite closed. In an instant Sarita slipped in the house. To the right of her were the lights and warmth, the music and laughter. But instinctively she knew she mustn't reveal her presence. Moving like a cat she made her way to the darkened back patio. Finding a corner, she curled up and fell into a deep sleep until she was discovered the following day.

It was a rude awakening. One minute Sarita was fast asleep and the next minute Esperanza, the cook, was screaming at her, chasing her around with a broom. By then some of the whores were up having breakfast. One prostitute, a French girl named Simone, went to see what the commotion was about and found Esperanza trying to push a filthy child back into the streets. Sarita, dressed in rags, smelling absolutely rank, pleaded with them, crying out, "*Zopo, zopo,*" the word for cripple, begging Simone to let her stay. She offered to work, she promised she wouldn't eat much or bother anyone, if only they wouldn't put her out on the street.

Simone's heart went out to the waif. She knew the only way to stop her hysteria was to reassure her she could stay. Simone told Esperanza to bring one of her blouses and a bar of soap. Then she stripped Sarita of her filthy clothes, hosing her down with the *manguera*, the hose used to water the patio garden. Sarita, intimidated by the soap, cried out in fear until Simone's soothing voice calmed her. When Esperanza and Simone saw what was underneath the filth and stench, they didn't have the heart to turn her out. At least Simone didn't. To Esperanza she was just another nuisance.

Simone dressed Sarita in her blouse, combed the snarls out of her hair. And that is how Sarita at the age of ten came to live with the whores where she found the closest thing to home life. She helped Esperanza in the kitchen, assisted Magdalena the inside girl strip the beds for Maria the laundress. She took care of the garden. No chore was too much for Sarita. She was so grateful to be inside the house, where she felt safe, she always did more than expected so they would keep her. It was years before she would venture outside for she was absolutely terrified of running into Mama Yolanda. It didn't matter if she worked from the time she got up in the morning until late at night, or if she slept on the kitchen floor. For the first time in her life she wasn't hungry. And she was safe. She was never paid, nor did she think to ask.

But Sarita learned to use the bathroom and not do *caca* in the dirt of the patio where Esperanza found her and beat her again. She learned to take a shower. She was given the whores' castoff clothes and was grateful to receive them. Gradually, as she grew up, she aspired to be a whore. They were her mothers, sisters, aunts. From the smart ones she learned to take care of herself so she wouldn't get pregnant. She didn't want any child to suffer the horrors she'd known. To her that was the most important lesson, and keeping clean so she didn't come down with any sickness as the careless whores did.

This took place in the capital, Caracas. Sarita moved to the *Occidente*, the western part of Venezuela, when some of the girls found out how much money there was to be made from the foreign *petroleros* in Maracaibo. Eventually they wound up with Hortensia. It was much too long a story to tell this man who had only hired her for a few days. And she doubted he would be interested, despite his curiosity and the decent way he treated her.

After dinner Maguire took her to the movies. When he parked the pickup, they were immediately surrounded by small boys, all asking to guard it. Throwing them a few coins, he escorted her to the theater. It was a new experience for him; it didn't have a roof, but was completely open to the sky. Sitting there under the stars, laughing at the foibles of the Mexican comic, Cantinflas, long before he enchanted audiences in *Around the World in Eighty Days*, delighting in his double entendres, John Maguire felt incredibly happy being with Sarita. And it wasn't because he'd missed too many boats or was lonely.

That night when they returned to the hotel and made love, he discovered something else. He'd been with more than a few women in his life, he was in his late 20's, but that night he found himself thinking of sex with Sarita as different. He kept searching for the right word, and finally as he was drifting off to sleep, it came to him. Wholesome. Yes, he told himself, that's what she is, a wholesome whore. And then his reverie snapped and he sat up, shaking. He didn't ever want to think of her as a whore. Maguire took Sarita in his arms. She's just wholesome, that's all. He pulled her closer to him, inhaling the sweet scent of her skin.

The next morning he decided to go swimming. Maguire knew he should check with the customhouse. He made no effort to do so though, because once the material he came to pick up was cleared, he would have to head back to camp. And he couldn't bear the thought of leaving Sarita. Since Sears & Roebuck hadn't entered the Venezuelan economy yet, nor any of the smart boutiques which later proliferated Maracaibo, he took Sarita to a general store which sold clothing, automotive parts, kitchen utensils, as well as fine silver and china. The Lebanese owner, or *Turco*, as the Venezuelans called any dark skinned foreigner, brought out a white bathing suit for Sarita. There were no dressing rooms, but Maguire found a corner surrounded by stacks of truck tires where she could change. Since there were no mirrors, she had to take his word the suit fit. What he didn't say because he was afraid to voice his emotions, was how magnificent she looked, the white fabric showing off her beautiful brown skin.

When they walked out the store urchins surrounded them, pleading for money. The store owner came running out. "Damn beggars, they're very bad for business," he shouted shooing them away.

"But they're not hurting anyone," Sarita protested, opening her purse and giving a coin to each of them.

"You're encouraging them to stand in front of my store," the Lebanese shouted angrily. "Now they'll never go away."

"Don't worry," Sarita replied. "I'll tell them to go somewhere else," and her few words sent them flying.

"Such a rich man, *ese Turco*, with that store of his," she cried out, her eyes blazing. "But he has no charity in him."

Maguire realized this wasn't the only time she'd reached into her purse for beggars. Leaving the restaurant last night, the same scene occurred. She had coins for every child.

"You're very generous, Sarita."

"It's because I know how it is. I was once like them, roaming the streets, hungry, without a family."

"Oh God, I kept asking you all those stupid questions," he tried to apologize. He'd seen the poverty in Venezuela, knew it was prevalent throughout Latin America. But ever since he met her, she fascinated him so much he couldn't think straight.

"How were you to know?" she replied softly. "This isn't your *país*, your country."

"It's because you're so different from the . . . ." and once more he found himself at a loss for words.

"Than the rest of the *putas*?" She didn't find it difficult calling herself a whore. "I don't know if I'm all that different. And if I am, who knows the reason." She shrugged her shoulders. "Perhaps my father was educated, even rich. I'll never know. Nor do I remember my mother, for she abandoned me at such an early age."

By now they were out of the city, driving north toward the beaches.

Along the dusty highway *Guajira* Indians walked, their faces painted like multi-colored masks which they believed warded off the heat. The women wore long, tent-like dresses reaching to their ankles, with colorfully embroidered sandals on their feet.

"Look," he pointed, "we're coming to the water." They drove through a grove of *Chaguaramo* trees to a deserted beach on the Gulf of Venezuela. The sad mood which hung over Sarita like a shroud when she talked about her past disappeared with the sight of the beach. Slipping off her shoes and dress to the white bathing suit underneath, she ran down to the water's edge. It was the first time she'd seen the *mar*, the sea as she called it. She gazed in awe at the incoming waves while the breeze lifted the bangs of her straight, black hair.

" *Ven*, come." Maguire, noticing her hesitation, took her hand. "There's nothing to be afraid of. Look, it's low tide. We can walk out for a long way, all the way to China, and the water will only be up to our knees." He slipped down into the water, floating on his back. She looked down at him, still not sure she believed him. "I'll show you how to swim," he said gently. "See there's nothing to it." He made a cradle for her with his arms and hands, showing her how to kick her legs and move her arms.

"¡*Qué maravilla!*" she cried out.

Afterwards when he went out by himself for a swim, she sat in the shallow water following him with her eyes. He looked so strong to her, his arms slicing into the water while his legs propelled him, she found herself thinking of him as her *catire*, her blond man. Then sadly she reminded herself he was just a *gringo* who'd hired her for a few days. She felt like she wanted to sit there forever and let the water wash away the sadness which had engulfed her when she told Maguire about her past. Sometimes memories invaded her usually placid nature and she experienced great loneliness. When she listened to *novelas*, the soap operas on the radio, she yearned to know love. Yet she was afraid of it for she didn't want to give her heart to a man who would go off and leave her with a big belly. She kept reminding herself she was too smart for that. And she had accomplished so much with her life. From begging on the streets to sleeping on the kitchen floor of the whorehouse to getting her own *chinchorro*. And from the hammock to sleeping in a bed in her own room.

Oh, how the madam had laughed when she told her she wanted to be a whore, she the skinny *muchachita* who stripped the beds and made the patio garden blossom as it never grew before. But when her body began to fill out and the first signs of womanhood appeared in her face, the madam hadn't laughed anymore.

Maguire was swimming back to her, riding the waves. When he got to the low tide area, he stood up, walking towards her. His floral print bathing suit clung to his slim body, accentuating his male organs. She had seen so many nude male bodies she was completely indifferent to them. Yet, seeing him walk towards her stirred a feeling of such intense desire that it frightened her. Even the sight of his bowed legs which detracted from the symmetry of his body failed to suppress this desire. She realized, looking at him, he wasn't especially handsome. His high forehead showed signs of a receding hairline and his nose was too large. Yet in her eyes he was perfection. She wondered if she was falling in love. She didn't welcome the feeling because she knew it would only bring her heartache.

Then he opened up another world to her. They sat with their backs against a palm tree, seeking shade from the intense sun while Sarita made little swirls in the sand with her hands, sculpturing tiny sand castles.

"*Mira*, look," he said slicing through the sand with his finger, writing the letter 'A'. "This is how you learn how to read. 'A' as in *agua*." Then he wrote the word for water, deciding it was the best word since they were surrounded by it. He took her hand, guiding it in the sand, helping her trace the letters while she repeated their sounds over and over.

"The letter 'A' is like two *palitos*, two little sticks meeting at the top with a smaller stick connecting them," she cried out in wonder. "*Ya entiendo*, now I understand," she laughed. He had such a logical way of explaining things, she told him, it was easy to learn anything. Maguire however, thought there was another reason; she had the most marvelous concentration he'd ever seen.

"¡*Ay! Juan*," she burst out calling him by name for the first time, "you have taught me something so wonderful."

"It takes more than one word." His voice was tinged with regret. If only he had enough time, he could really teach her.

Returning to the hotel that afternoon they both felt shy with each other. For some reason he was hesitant to touch her and she was equally reticent. They went out to eat, then came back to the hotel where he showed her how he made smoke rings. Turning off the light he remained on one side of the bed and she the other, both trying to fathom what had changed between them. Eventually she dozed off and when she woke up, he was holding her in his arms, kissing her.

Just for one night, Sarita reminded herself, then tomorrow we go our separate ways. She slipped out of her professional role, responding to him because it was the most natural thing to do. She kissed him back, savoring the taste of his mouth and exalting in the strength of his arms around her. When he entered her, all the emotions she'd never known before in her mean little life overpowered her in their intensity. She felt like the flowers she used to tend in the whorehouse garden, bursting into life from the warmth of Maguire's gentle love.

The next morning they knew it was time to go. When they arrived at Hortensia's, she turned to him. *"Gracias, Juan,"* her words came out sweet and delicate as she kissed him softly on his lips. Then she extended her hand, shaking his very formally in a typical Latin American manner.

"Vaya con Dios," she said before she walked into Hortensia's.

"Adiós, Sarita Linda," he replied reluctantly, then turned and walked back to his pickup.

His business with customs took surprisingly little time and Maguire was able to arrange for the material to clear and be shipped to camp the following day. Then he headed to the harbor, watching the ferry chug across the lake towards Maracaibo, chainsmoking, which he did whenever he had something on his mind. His favorite song, *Adiós, Maraquita Linda* kept echoing through his head. Today though, the ballad gave him no joy, only making him exceedingly sad.

The ferry docked, discharging its cargo and he reluctantly turned the key in his ignition when the deckhand signalled him to start boarding. Putting the pickup in first, he inched slowly up the ferry ramp and was about to drive on deck when he pushed his foot down on the brake and stopped.

The driver behind him banged on the side of his car, calling him names. But Maguire ignored him, slipping the pickup into reverse. Leaning out the window he called out, *"Emergencia, emergencia,"* backing off the ferry. As soon as he got on the dock, he gunned the motor and headed up *Avenida Bella Vista*. Impatient with the traffic, he turned left at the first side street and wove his way through the city until he reached 5 *de Julio Boulevard*.

He didn't know what he was going to do. He had no idea how to make the impossible become possible. All he knew was he couldn't leave Maracaibo without Sarita. He couldn't say good-bye, just walk away and forget they'd ever met.

THREE

Cathleen threw confetti and rolls of serpentine to her family on the dock. Her mother blew them a kiss and Aunt Jenny called out *Bon Voyage*. But from her father, nothing. No words, not even a gesture. "Just be grateful he came," her mother whispered as the family left the ship. Oh Pa, she wanted to reassure him, I know what I'm doing. Trust me, I've made the right decision.

Her father wasn't the only who disapproved of her marriage to S. J. Rylander. Her boss, Barry, had done everything he could to discourage her. "Never in a million years did I figure you would jump into something like this," he burst out. "Miss Cool, Calm and Collected who always knows what she's doing."

"I do know what I'm doing," she replied firmly.

"Really? It's not like you see in the movies, with everything in glorious technicolor and Carmen Miranda dancing around with a bunch of fruit on her head." He struggled with the shock of her news. "Venezuela's a beautiful country, but you're not going to Caracas, the capital. You're headed straight for the oilfields which are out in the boondocks."

"I know it's primitive down there," she insisted, "and I'm not going to have all the things I do here. But I can adjust."

"Cathleen, it'll take more than adjustment," he insisted. "You're used to city streets, theaters, big department stores. Those oilcamps are in the middle of nowhere with only a commissary to shop in, and that's only for food. When you leave the camp there's miles of emptiness stretching to the horizon." He picked up a pencil and absently drummed on the desk. "It's rough down there for a woman. A man has his job and even that's not enough at times. But at least he has that to keep him busy six days a week. But for a women it's a whole different ball game."

"If the other women can take it, so can I," she replied.

"It's the monotony," he explained, "the damn monotony of camp life that drives everyone crazy. That and the isolation. You just can't turn on a radio and expect to catch Jack Benny or Charley McCarthy." His fingers stopped drumming and he looked intently at her. "That's what gets to the women and why some of them turn to the bottle."

"Well, that certainly won't happen to me," she replied disdainfully. "You should know me better, Barry."

"But that's what the place does to you," he cried out almost pleading with her. "You go down there your own sweet self, and after being in the oilfields you change. Oh boy, do you change."

Cathleen flipped her steno pad open, hoping he would get the hint and start dictating. And leave her personal life alone. She appreciated his interest, but she was a big girl.

"Two months I'll give you," he continued, his words coming out in heated spurts. "Three at the most. And then you'll be back. The heat will get to you, the bugs, the isolation and the boredom. Yeah, most of all the godawful sameness of camp life. Why, I'm so sure you'll be back, I'll make a bet with you. I'll buy you dinner at any restaurant you want."

"Well I won't be back, except for vacations, and then I'll buy you dinner." Her words came out sharply, with a hint of defiance to them. Barry was so sweet to be concerned about her, she sighed to herself, but he just doesn't know what it's like to be madly in love. Which is probably the reason he's still a bachelor.

"How do you know Rylander is really in love with you?" When he saw her shocked struggle to answer him, he continued prodding her. "A lot of guys who are based in Venezuela fall in love real fast, Cathleen. And you know why? They're so far from home it's like living in Never-Never Land, and with ten men to one single woman, a man gets awful lonely. Hell, I can remember when I was there guys swore up and down they wouldn't come back for another contract unless they were married. So how do you know it's not just because you're the first pretty single woman he's seen in two years?"

"He was engaged to a girl from Oklahoma, just as I was engaged to Danny," she replied. "So I don't think we're two lonely people looking for love, Barry." Her smile was brimming with confidence.

"What does your family think?" he persisted.

Ah, that's another story, she thought remembering the stormy scenes which had greeted her announcement. Her father shouting she was marrying someone she hardly knew, and what about Danny? Her mother crying because she was marrying outside her faith. While Aunt Jenny slyly hinted perhaps there was a reason for such a hasty marriage. It had been difficult trying to make everyone understand that life without Ryle would be no life at all. Everything they said was true, things had gone much too fast. It certainly wasn't what she'd planned for her life. Dropping out of college, breaking up with Danny, marrying Ryle and leaving home for Venezuela. It made her dizzy sometimes just thinking about it. But life without Ryle was drab and colorless. When he went to Oklahoma for a few weeks to visit his folks, she missed him with a passion she didn't realize she possessed. Ached for his arms around her, the feeling of security and safety she felt within them. Felt bereft without his mouth brushing her lips in the slow, erotic way which aroused her. And she missed his stories, the way he could take something so utterly commonplace and turn it into a humorous event. She was a captive audience whenever he revealed little things about his past. He was the most fascinating man she'd ever known. Never mind, as her mother pointed out, that she'd known few men to make this comparison.

Cathleen admired Ryle for making something out of a life which began in abject poverty. Leaving home in his early teens to work the oilfields as a roustabout, winding up a driller. Then still not satisfied, despite the good money, because he wanted to be a somebody, not just another oil hand. Her parents didn't know how much there was to respect in someone like Ryle. That he'd worked his way through college, sometimes struggling to stay awake in class because he was so exhausted from the multiple jobs he took, not only to make ends meet but to help his parents financially. Why, in comparison, getting *her* degree was a piece of cake.

Ryle was the essence of everything masculine and no matter what her family thought, Cathleen just couldn't live without him. She *was* exhausted trying to make them understand the strength of her feelings. Sometimes she wished they all lived in another state. Ryle though envied her. "You don't know how lucky you are having all those brothers and sisters."

"Lucky? It's too much! All that bedlam." He was driving her home from work in the Chevy he'd come to New York to buy because of the good deal he got through the company. "You never mention your family. Any brothers or sisters?"

"Just me," he laughed. "I guess they figured someone so perfect couldn't be duplicated, so they'd better rest on their laurels." There was a gallows quality to his laughter.

Then his mood changed and he burst out, "Naw, it's not like that at all. Though it sounds pretty damn good. Truth is my folks split up."

"Oh, I'm so sorry," she said in sympathy, wanting to make up to him for all the things he'd missed in his life.

"Don't be sorry," he said shrugging his shoulders. "They went back together again, so I guess that's what matters. It was the years in between that were rough. Mama and me lived with my grandmother. When they got back together again, they just decided to forget about any more kids. Or maybe it was too late."

He stopped talking as if he were weighing what he would say next. Then he blurted out, "The fact is they don't even sleep together anymore. They each have their own bedroom."

He swerved the car to avoid a patch of ice on the Merritt Parkway. "Anyway, that's all water under the bridge. I don't even know what made me talk about it. But see, that's what you do to me, baby. You make me reveal stuff I haven't told anyone else."

Ryle took his eyes off the road for a brief second, looking at her adoringly. "I guess it's because you're my family now."

And you're my family now, Cathleen thought looking down at her parents on the dock. Especially since mine has practically disowned me. She thought back to her wedding and her father's refusal to give her away.

"I want no part of it, Cathleen Erin," he stormed, calling her by her full name, which he only did when she displeased him. "You can marry that cowboy if that's what you've set your stubborn mind to doing, but it will be without my blessing." Her brother Bubba stepped in and it was on his arm she walked down the aisle. But she walked proudly. Her white, lace *mantilla* veil was draped over a high comb encrusted with rhinestones, while tiny pearls cascaded down her white satin dress. And when she reached Ryle at the altar there were no doubts or second thoughts. She *was* doing the right thing, the rest of the world just didn't know it yet.

The reception held at her Aunt Maureen's home wasn't elaborate, but it was a decided contrast to the tension preceding the wedding. Perhaps it was her family's Irish fondness for a good party, always livelier when whiskey flowed freely, or an unspoken decision that since the deed was done life should go on. Whatever the reason, there was lots of laughter. It amused Cathleen to hear Aunt Jenny tell people that Ryle was the spitting image of Clark Gable. Of course he wasn't, the only similarity was both men had mustaches. She smiled at other snippets of conversation, especially when her cousin Sean commented on her honeymoon. "Imagine," he marvelled, "a cruise ship, six days in the Caribbean. Stopping at all those tropical islands before they get to Venezuela. And it's all paid for. Ryle told me the company pays their transportation every two years, either by air or ship. Whatever a person wants. Well now, maybe Cathleen didn't do so bad for herself," he pronounced.

Cathleen thought she'd done quite well for herself. Spending the first night of their honeymoon, prior to boarding ship the next day, at the Waldorf Astoria. How many times had she walked by the hotel and dreamt of drinking champagne and dancing in the Empire Room. When the dream became reality she knew she'd caught the brass ring on the carousel. But then, she'd felt that way ever since Ryle kissed her in the snow six weeks ago.

Several times in their desire for each other, they had almost crossed the line into intimacy. Yet something held them back. She because of her religious upbringing; Ryle because he had her on a pedestal. Or in a glass case, to be admired but not touched until the proper time. All the women in his past — the easy ones he'd made out with in the back of his pickup, the married ones he'd taken to sleazy motels, Thelma King in Tulsa who took her pants off wherever and however he wanted her, whom he planned to marry before he met Cathleen because he was tired of the single life and weary of the Venezuelan whorehouses — all these women now seemed cheap and common. He felt he was wiping the slate clean by marrying Cathleen. For she had that certain something he hadn't known before, but recognized immediately, class.

Which made him determined not to screw up things. They were going to have a proper wedding night. He couldn't ever remember wanting a woman as much as Cathleen, and it took every bit of self-control not to rush. While at the same time he anticipated the exploration of her body and discovering all those places which would arouse her and in this arousal, make him want her even more.

On their wedding night he wanted to undress her, peel off each piece of her clothing, one at a time, but Cathleen would have no part of this. She entered the bathroom and shut the door firmly. When she emerged in a filmy, white peignoir edged in lace covering an opaque white nightgown with thin lace straps cut just low enough to reveal the top of her milk-white breasts, for a moment he hesitated. She looked so innocent yet so sensual, he was fearful when he touched her he would be too rough.

Grateful for the champagne he'd ordered, he willed his emotions to a standstill so when he turned around with it, he was back in control of himself. He wouldn't rush a thing, he vowed. Ryle who knew just about every variation of the sexual act, who'd experienced so many women (too many he feared) wanted desperately to act like a considerate bridegroom. He tried to remember what it was like for him the first time, but that was so long ago and there was certainly no love involved. He was a big strapping boy in the eighth grade ordered as punishment to stand in the cloakroom. When he got there he discovered two girls who'd been sent there by another teacher. For forty-five minutes the three of them were together in the semi-darkness and within five minutes he had persuaded one of the girls to play doctor with him. Afterward he didn't have to persuade the other girl. She pulled her panties down and begged him to do the same thing to her.

Now as Ryle sipped champagne and admired his bride, he wanted her initial taste of sex to be something she wouldn't forget, a first class act. Then a remark Barry made about Cathleen ran through his mind. She was known in the office as the Frigid Digit. What would he do if she disliked sex? There were women like that, although he'd never run into them. Just what the hell would he do? He couldn't go without sex for any great length of time, which is why the whores had a steady customer in him. For a brief moment a crazy thought swirled around in his brain. As much as he wanted and loved Cathleen, maybe he should have married Thelma, whose appetite matched his. He knew what he would get with her, while Cathleen was an unknown quality.

He put down his champagne glass, hoping they wouldn't disappoint each other. Reaching over he brushed his lips against hers, watched her put down her glass and come into his arms. Then all his apprehension disappeared. She's no Frigid Digit. Underneath that cool exterior he could sense a passion just waiting to explode into life. All she needs is the right initiation. His lips moved across hers, teasing them in a way he knew would excite her.

Cathleen responded eagerly. They could go much further than kissing tonight she realized. He drove her crazy brushing his lips across hers, then when he stopped and their lips met in a full kiss she melted and went slack with surrender when his tongue slowly parted her lips. She wondered if she would have to confess this French kissing they were doing. Then she pushed aside her feelings of guilt. She was a married woman now and whatever they did was allowed. Or so she hoped. When Ryle's hand slid into her nightgown searching out her breasts, she momentarily stiffened in surprise before giving into the warm feeling of pleasure it brought her. She looked down in shock when he took her nipple in his mouth. She didn't feel right letting him do this, yet she did nothing to stop him. The sensation of enjoyment spread from her breasts and ran down her body until it settled between her legs where it started to throb like the pulses of her wrists did when she became excited.

And then he stopped. Just when she reached a point where she felt she would explode, he stopped. Scooping her up in his arms, Ryle carried her across the large, sumptuously decorated salon and into the bedroom. The thin straps of her lace nightgown slipped down her arms, exposing her breasts. Embarrassed she tried pulling up the straps. When her husband slipped the peignoir off she closed her eyes, giving into the excitement of being undressed.

Mother of God, she was so confused. She really loved all the things he was doing to her, but she felt embarrassed. She asked Ryle to turn out the lights, and in the darkness what they did somehow didn't seem quite so scandalous. When his hands traveled over her body, caressing her in ways which excited her beyond anything in her experience, her self-consciousness abated. And then it flew out the window when he parted her legs and his finger caressed her. She gave into the elation of responding to his touch, reveling in his words of endearment, her body fluttering and shaking when his finger slid inside her, until she lost all control and suddenly she felt she was riding a lightning bolt. Afterwards she collapsed in his arms, reaching out to him, embarrassed and a little shocked at the way she had cried out in that final moment of ecstasy.

"Oh, baby," Ryle laughed softly, "we're gonna be so great together." He hugged her reassuringly, rocking her in his arms, his mouth reaching out for her, the hairs of his mustache feeling like silk. And when he entered her, his movements slow and gentle, she arched up to meet his body for by now she was half crazy with longing for him. Oh, how lucky she was. She had really caught the brass ring. She started to rock in rhythm with him as he moved around inside her. She loved this sensation, their bodies swaying in unison. She could feel him moving deeper inside her and then once again she was riding a lightning bolt.

"We're going to last forever, baby," Ryle whispered as he stroked her hair. And to Cathleen his words sounded like poetry. The poetry she had grown up reading, the fairy tales she read as a child. She would always find love and security in Ryle's arms. Their love, now in its infancy, would grow. And this new found sexual excitement would only get better.

He was still inside her and when she felt him growing large again, she sighed contentedly. Then the excitement started all over again. More than when he fondled her into a climax with foreplay. She moved her body in unison with his and when he asked her to wrap her legs around him, she discovered a new sensation, holding him deep inside her.

Now standing on the ship's deck, Cathleen remembered the happiness of her wedding night. It softened the sadness of leaving her family. Even her father's last words didn't hurt anymore. "Now that you've made your bed, Mrs. Rylander, you'd better lie in it. If it doesn't work out, don't coming running home with your tail between your legs." As if she ever would, she thought looking down to the dock.

"We're going to last forever, Pa," she cried out to him across the ever-widening gulf as the ship pulled away from the dock. But he never heard her. Not with the horns blowing and people calling out last minute farewells. She continued to look down at him expectantly, hoping at the last minute he'd have a change of heart. With a gesture or a wave he'd give a blessing of sorts to her future.

But it was her sister, Beebe, who did that. Beebe who'd hugged her good-bye and told her to be happy. Beebe who now stood behind her father, her fingers split in a victory sign, waving her hands back and forth. Cathleen threw another roll of serpentine to Beebe, clinging to her end of the streamer. When it tore in the wind, she felt the final link with her past had been severed. Clutching the torn crepe paper in her hand, she folded it into a tiny square and placed it in her purse. She would keep it just as she'd kept the first corsage Danny O'Hara gave her, pressed between the pages of a poetry book.

Standing beside her Ryle waved to her family. "In two years we'll be back on vacation, baby," he assured her, straining to make himself heard over the din of the ship's whistle. He took her arm and together they walked to the front of the Santa Maria.

With the wind off the Hudson River blowing her long, blond hair back, Cathleen's profile resembled a carved figurehead on an old sailing vessel. As the tugboats moved the ship down the river and the New York skyline grew smaller she experienced mixed emotions. While she was sad to be leaving her family, a stronger emotion dominated her feelings — eagerness. She sailed to Venezuela wide eyed and full of confidence. She couldn't wait to embrace her new life. There wasn't a thing she feared. There was so much adventure waiting for her and Ryle. Despite Barry's warning and her father's stern disapproval, she was going to come out the winner. After waving a last farewell to the Statue of Liberty, she didn't need any coaxing from Ryle to go to their cabin. She clung to his hand, feeling the strength from his fingers, shivering in anticipation of their lovemaking.

When she returned two years later she had buried her heart in foreign soil.

FOUR

Caracas, Venezuela

Maruja had been enchanting men from the day of her birth, and she seduced them even further at her *quinceañera*, the traditional coming out *fiesta* for *señoritas* reaching their fifteenth birthday. They swarmed about her like bees, bewitched by *Maruja la Bruja*. The nickname had been hers since childhood. How she acquired it no one remembered. Probably her siblings discovering that her name, Maruja, rhymed with the word for witch, *bruja*, couldn't resist teasing her, chanting in a singsong manner, "*Maruja la Bruja*". After awhile the name became part of her and was even used with a degree of affection. For no one could deny Maruja had that certain something which never failed to enchant people. It was more than her beauty, blue black hair framing a heartshaped face. It was mainly her eyes, sparkling with enormous vitality, promising, teasing and throwing men into a frenzy. While her voice, throaty and sensual, had a catch which hypnotized everyone who heard it.

She received many marriage proposals. Yet five years had gone by since her *quinceañera* and she was still single. By Caracas standards almost a *solterona*, an old maid. Her mother, Misia Isabel, worried, while her father laughed it off. Maruja without a man, *imposible*! There would always be a flock of them following her. But her mother persisted in worrying. She's much too fussy, Misia Isabel thought. Why, practically every eligible man in Caracas wanted to marry her and she had turned them all down. If she kept this up, there would be no one left. All the good mangos would be picked off the tree.

"*Mami*, there will always be another crop of mangos," Maruja assured her airily. "Besides, I would never think of marrying a Venezuelan. Only when I find the right *Inglés*, the perfect Englishman, will I consider marriage."

41

Not for her a Venezuelan, the waiting at home while he ran around on her. It might be an age old custom for married Latin American men to have several mistresses, proof of their masculinity, their *machismo*, but she was not going to travel the route her mother, sisters and cousins had. No, she would only marry when she found the right Englishman. Not an American (whom she considered boors) or a Frenchman (who were just as bad as the Venezuelans with their mistresses), but only an *Inglés*. For truly the English were so refined and such gentlemen. And most of all they took marriage seriously.

A *musiu*! Her mother threw up her hands in horror. The word, a corruption of the French word *monsieur*, was used with derision to label any foreigner. Her daughter with a *musiu*! But then Misia Isabel had never been able to do anything with Maruja. Ever since she was a baby she'd asserted herself, throwing her bottle through the slats of her cradle, tiny feet kicking away any toy which didn't interest her. And the older she grew, the stronger her will became. By the time Maruja celebrated her eighteenth birthday, Misia Isabel's aversion to her marrying a foreigner had weakened. She just wanted her daughter to be settled down and married.

Yet Maruja remained indifferent. The Venezuelans pursued her relentlessly, and she allowed them to do so because she considered them fantastic dancers. Occasionally she graced an American party, but not very often as they all seemed so crude to her. She became the darling of the international set, especially the English Embassy. However, despite this constant social life, none of the men she met touched her emotions or evoked love.

Bueno, she told herself, it looks like I just might wind up an old maid. She laughed at the idea, an old lady still going to dances, still flirting. Sometimes though, alone with her thoughts, fear would creep into her heart. It was the only time she admitted to herself she was frightened. Perhaps she would never know what love was, maybe she would never meet her *Príncipe Azul*, her Prince Charming. Then she would shrug off her mood, tell herself it was better to remain alone than marry a man who bored her. Not for her, a half loaf of bread. If she couldn't have what she wanted, then she would accept no substitute.

Then she met him in the most unlikely place. No orchestra played a wild *guaracha*, nor were their bodies swaying in a bold tango. She wasn't dressed in one of her glamorous evening gowns, all French design for the Venezuelan women preferred French fashion. None of this, only the organ winding up the one o'clock Sunday Mass at the Cathedral. As she walked to the back of the church she struggled to stifle a yawn. Her sunglasses had remained on during the entire service so she could catnap and no one would be the wiser. She had arrived home at two in the morning, having attended a reception at the French Embassy, with a stopover for onion soup at the Paris Restaurant. Misia Isabel had been waiting up for her as usual, something which irritated Maruja no end. She'd been out with her married cousins, Pilar and Paco Calcaño, and therefore properly chaperoned. But Maruja knew what her mother was thinking. She had certainly told her enough times that women in her day were courted at the front parlor window, separated from the men by the security of the wrought iron bars, with the chaperon sitting in the back of the parlor. Not like today with all these parties and dances, staying out till the wee hours. Sometimes Maruja wondered if *Mami* wasn't talking about her great-grandmother when she referred to the old ways of courting. It certainly sounded to her like something from colonial days.

When she reached the back of the Cathedral, Maruja put her hand in the holy water font. *¡Ay Dios!* She was so tired. She thought longingly of the *siesta* she would take when she got home. As she pulled her hand out of the font, preparing to make the Sign of the Cross, she felt another hand. It jolted her. Her eyes glanced down at the hand, then travelled upward to its owner. *¡Que curioso!* Imagine this happening in church. The humor of it all caused the corners of her mouth to twitch and she had difficulty suppressing her laughter.

"*Perdón*," he murmured.

"*De Nada*," she replied.

His eyes, such a deep blue it was like looking at the sky, showed surprise. While his fair complexion, which even a tan didn't hide, along with his sandy hair, cried out he was a *musiu*. Here he was, her Englishman! One look at his clothes reassured her for they had that unmistakable English style. She flashed a brilliant smile, the smile which had melted all the male hearts in Caracas. There was something extra though in her smile. While it teased and taunted, it also contained a hint of something lacking before — surrender. She felt as if she were dancing on air. How *ridículo* to meet in church, hands colliding in the holy water font. Hardly a romantic tale to tell our children, she thought. But *no importa*, for we will make plenty of romance. And we can always say that from the beginning we had God's blessing.

"Why are you hugging the holy water font?" her maiden aunt *Tía* Nellie asked, tugging at her elbow.

Maruja and the stranger moved aside while the elderly woman reached in, dipped her fingers, then blessed herself in an elaborate Sign of the Cross. Maruja guided *Tía* Nellie out of the Cathedral. From the corners of her eyes she saw the *musiu* standing by the door. Looking up flirtatiously she heard him say, "*Hasta luego.*"

She crossed the street to the Plaza Bolivar, the main plaza in Caracas, with her sister Maria Elena, whom everyone called Malena, both escorting *Tía* Nellie. Glancing back she saw the Englishman follow them. She tried walking leisurely, but her sister kept urging her to hurry.

"*Tortuga,*" Malena chided, calling her a turtle.

Didn't Malena know she had just met her Englishman? She started to explain, then decided against it. It was so new, so exciting she still hadn't gotten used to it herself. Plenty of time to tell Malena. Plenty of time to let the whole world know.

....

Guilt, not faith, brought Frederick Hardesty IV to the Cathedral that fateful morning. Guilt from not going to church on the anniversary of his mother's death. Guilt because he'd missed Mass so many times. Since his arrival in Venezuela he'd become very lax about Sunday Mass because he was based in Chacari, an oil camp far removed from a church. But now that he was attending Spanish school in Caracas, he told himself there was no excuse. Despite his hangover, he vowed he would make Mass.

When the service ended Fred couldn't wait to get back to the hotel, grab a cold beer, then settle down for some ZZs time. Making his way to the back of the Cathedral, he felt so groggy he didn't look where he was going. But he woke up in a hurry when his hand collided with the gorgeous *señorita*. Geez, imagine meeting a girl in church. Talk about being struck by a thunderbolt! He couldn't take his eyes off Maruja and quickly followed her.

He got the chills thinking how he almost hadn't made it to Mass. Not only had he gone drinking the night before with his buddies from the Hotel Waldorf, but they'd visited one of the local establishments run by the *Mujeres de la Vida Alegre*, the Women of the Happy Life, as prostitutes were sometimes called in Venezuela. Someone had spilled a bottle of rum on his suit, the only one he had; his other clothes were in the cleaners. He'd been able to borrow a jacket and pants from an English buddy, no easy feat since he was so tall. Otherwise he would have missed Mass and the chance meeting with this knockout of a beauty.

He saw the girl glance back, then another girl he supposed was a sister tug at her to hurry. By now they had arrived at the far side of the Plaza Bolivar, preparing to cross the street. Following, he saw them walk down one block, up another, turn the corner and enter a house. He wrote down the number of the house, as well as the name of the street because from the outside all the houses looked alike to him. Then when he arrived at the corner he noticed it had another name. He was thoroughly confused, as anyone unfamiliar with the address system in the colonial downtown sector of Caracas would be. There was no rhyme or reason; each corner had a different name, either that of a favorite saint, a family name or the name of a national institution. If one lived between the corners of San Francisco, where the outdoor stock exchange was located, and the *Biblioteca Nacional*, that would be your address, between the corners of San Francisco and the National Library. Fred decided to ignore the names and concentrate on keeping the sequence of blocks straight in his mind.

And then what, he asked himself. He'd just met a beauty and he didn't know what his next move would be. Finding his way back to the Plaza Bolivar, he noticed an empty bench and sat down. Suddenly he felt very foolish. And his hangover, which dissipated in the thrill of pursuit, had returned in force. He really wanted to get back to the hotel and catch up on his shuteye, but he sat there absently watching the procession of people stream by. The Sunday promenade through the Plaza Bolivar, almost a ritual in Caracas, unfolded before him. The young women walking in one direction, the men in the other, giving both sexes the opportunity to look each other over with chaperons always nearby. Children played noisily. Old men thrust their canes out in front of them as they strolled leisurely in the Sunday sunshine, most of them dressed in *Liquiliquis*, the traditional white linen suit with its high collar jacket, gold cuff links and the loose, well tailored trousers. And, of course, there were the lovers who strolled together, caressing each other with their eyes, their chaperons right behind them.

But Fred saw none of this, only the girl with the shiny black hair and teasing, challenging smile. When a blind man selling lottery tickets cried out, "*Mira Chico*" — an expression meaning "Hey, Kid," which applied to young and old alike — and the elderly flower vendor caught his attention, he stopped daydreaming.

"*Mira Chico*," the lottery vendor assured him, "the winning number is right here."

"*Flores para su novia*," the toothless flower vendor persisted pushing the flowers into his hands. "For your sweetheart."

"Buy this ticket," the lottery vendor said, "and you'll be a millionaire."

Fred shook his head, then noticing the lottery vendor was sightless, he bought an entire sheet of tickets. As for the flower vendor, he began to bargain. No one ever paid the full amount. It was a game with the price deliberately inflated. At first he shook his head in mock dismay, then tiring of the theatrics he handed her five *Bolivares*. He knew he was paying too much, but he wanted to get rid of her. Standing up he stretched, then started walking toward the girl's house.

By the time he arrived Fred had rehearsed the little Spanish he knew, combing his brain for all the phrases he learned in Spanish School. He raised his hand to knock and the portal opened very slowly before him. Geez, just like the Inner Sanctum, he thought as he walked down the short vestibule to another door. This one, though, remained closed. He felt almost foolish when his knocking brought no response. Finally the grill at the top of the door opened and dark eyes peered out.

"*Buenos Dias*," he said smiling. Or should he say '*Buenas Tardes*' he wondered. His smile became wider as he held up the bouquet of flowers. The grill snapped shut. He was left standing in the vestibule. He hesitated about staying, but reasoned he might as well stand his ground. Someone had seen him. The Cathedral clock chimed the quarter hour. Again the grill slid open and another pair of eyes inspected him, then the door opened and a slim, short man stepped out into the vestibule. He looked at Fred, then at the bouquet of white roses and back again to Fred. The faintest suggestion of a smile appeared in the corners of his mouth, but his eyes remained neutral.

"How can I serve you?" he asked, bowing ever so slightly.

Fred told him he wished to present the flowers to the *señorita*. When asked which *señorita*, he described her. Not in the best of Spanish, but he knew he made himself understood.

"I have three sisters, all fitting your description."

"Well," Fred drawled, "I'll know which one she is when I see her."

"Oh, no," the man shook his head firmly. "It's not permitted today." Shrugging his shoulders he added, "*Quizás mañana.*"

"Maybe tomorrow?" Fred repeated incredulously.

"*Sí, mañana,*" he nodded. Taking the roses he bowed and walked back into the house, shutting the door. Once inside he went to the center of the front patio and called out, "Who claims these white roses from a *musiu?*"

Maruja knew who brought the flowers, for when the maid announced a *musiu* was standing in the vestibule, she ran upstairs to her parents' bedroom. Looking down from their balcony she saw Fred walk out. Feeling pleased because he had come calling, she was about to step back into the room when he looked up and waved to her.

"*Hola,*" the Englishman cried out, a large smile spreading across his friendly face. "*¿Cómo se llama Ud?*"

"My name is Maruja," she replied. *Ay,* if *Mami* knew she was talking to a stranger she would have a fit. She just hoped her sister, Maria de Lourdes, the family tattletale, wasn't lurking nearby. But then, what did she care? What difference would it make? Her Englishman had finally come into her life!

"And what is your name?" she called down in English, feeling somewhat like Juliet speaking to Romeo from the balcony. When he replied that his name was Fred Hardesty, her first thought was how very English it sounded. Continuing the conversation she asked him what part of England he called home. Oh, she so hoped it was London and not some provincial city.

"England?" he replied shaking his head. "Why m'am, I'm from Texas and proud of it!"

"*¿Tejas?*" She was so shocked by his words she reverted to Spanish. "*¿Un Americano?*"

"Sure am," he grinned. "I work for Palm Oil Co., a petroleum engineer." He saw the confusion in her face. "I'm a *petrolero*. Isn't that what you call us oilmen, *petroleros*?" he repeated, hoping to make her understand.

She couldn't believe it. Her Englishman was an American! *¡Ay Dios!* She stepped back into the bedroom gazing down from the shadows. Not only an American, but a Texas cowboy. And even worse, a *petrolero*, one of those crude, loudmouthed, heavy drinking oilmen. *¡Que desastre!*

FIVE

"I guess it's time to get up, Mrs. Rylander." Ryle was reluctant to release Cathleen from his arms and she was equally unwilling. Venezuela lay outside their stateroom porthole, the pilot boat having arrived in the wee hours of the morning to bring the ship into port. Slipping out of bed, Cathleen ran to the round window, taking everything in.

"Isn't it gorgeous?" The panorama of emerald mountains rising from the ocean, disappearing into the clouds had her senses dancing. Their majestic sweep up and down the coast, melting into the horizon, made her think of castles guarding a fabled land.

Ryle joined her, admiring the view. "First time I've seen it from a ship. I don't know what's more impressive," he remarked. "Looking down from a plane and seeing it all spread out under you, or coming in close like this. Either way it's a beautiful place." He playfully patted her bottom. "Well, woman, since you went and left my bed, I'd better get cracking. Have to get our passports to the immigration officials."

When he returned, he looked her over with approval. "It's a gorgeous outfit, but you're going to melt in those clothes."

"It's a summer suit," she replied, straightening the seams of her stockings, tightening the straps of her slingback blue and white spectator pumps. "Just what I'd wear in New York on a July day." She stuck a pearl hatpin in the crown of her large, wide brimmed white hat.

"This is the tropics, baby," Ryle smiled indulgently. "Not at all like summer back home. Why don't you put on that yellow cotton dress you wore in Curacao yesterday? And take off your stockings."

"Everything is packed. I'll be okay." But as the day wore on first the gloves came off, then the jacket and ultimately her hosiery, which clung to her legs like adhesive tape.

Leaving the customs building, Cathleen's senses were assaulted.

49

Street vendors, smelling strongly of sweat and grime, implored them in a babble of voices to buy their merchandise. Cheap little mirrors, clothing in the most garish colors and sleaziest materials, were thrust into their faces, along with fruit and *raspados*, snow cones made from blocks of dirty ice by men with even dirtier hands. Beggars, hands outstretched, pleaded for money. She'd never seen such a miserable collection of humanity. A tiny creature, a child she thought at first, before she realized he was a dwarf, tugged at her skirt. A blind woman held out her hands. Not only were their pleas sad to hear, but she thought she would pass out from the odor of rotting garbage, unwashed bodies and breath sucking humidity. Within minutes her white gloves became black and sweaty.

"*Hola, patrón.*" A brown, barefoot boy tugged at Ryle's sleeve. "Hey, boss, shoe shine?"

"Too much for you, Cathleen?" Ryle inquired, guiding her to their car which cleared customs quickly through the power of the company name.

"I've never seen anything like it. I felt so sorry for them, yet in a way they sort of frightened me." She struggled to find the right words, all the while dabbing her face with a lace handkerchief in an effort to blot up the beads of moisture. "Such terrible poverty."

"Yeah," Ryle nodded. "You see lots of it here, even though Venezuela is one of the richest countries in South America. Besides the oil, there's gold and diamonds, iron ore. For the most part though there's just two classes, the rich and the poor. About the only exception are those working for the oil companies. Yet there's always some foreign magazine or newspaper article about the oil companies exploiting the natives. But if anyone can get with an oil outfit, they'll jump at the chance. Oil camps have free schools, medical facilities and inexpensive housing."

The trip to Caracas, 'climbing the hill' as it was sometimes called, was a frightening experience. The road was never straight, just a narrow, winding ribbon clinging to the mountains. At times the road had a guardrail, other times nothing. At one point they saw the dented, rusting hulk of a car perched on the edge of the highway. Silent testimony to a fatal journey. Legend said it belonged to a honeymoon couple who couldn't wait to exchange kisses. Looking down, Cathleen saw deep ravines. Even when they reached Caracas, it was more uphill driving, for the city was in a valley three thousand feet above sea level surrounded by hills and more mountains.

Years later Caracas would become a sprawling metropolis growing helter-skelter in all directions, the houses perched on mountainsides, the *autopistas* heavy with traffic and smog. But in 1948 the air was clean; factories and cars hadn't mushroomed to pollute the atmosphere. WWII refugees — Lithuanians, Estonians, Yugoslavians, Polish, Hungarians, Rumanians, as well as Spanish, Italian and German immigrants — were still in the throes of getting settled in their newly adopted country. They hadn't yet given Venezuela its first middle class. Subways and skyscrapers weren't built. Or the *teleférico*, the cable cars climbing to the crest of the mountain which separated the city from the Caribbean. Nor any of the showcase architecture encouraged by the dictator president, Perez Jiminez. Caracas was still a little gem of a city where offices and stores closed at noon for a two hour *siesta* and people took time to enjoy life.

Sometimes scenes went by too quickly for Cathleen to absorb. People banged car doors because horn blowing was prohibited. There were no traffic lights, only stop signs most motorists ignored, so driving became a form of Russian roulette. In the evening students from Caracas University propped folding chairs under street lights. While education was free, some had no electricity at home.

When they left Caracas the next morning the sun was just breaking over the mountains. Cathleen turned for one last look, wishing she could bottle the crisp mountain air. She had fallen in love with the city and could understand why the natives called it the Land of Eternal Spring. Flowers were everywhere, days were warm and sunny, while nights turned cool enough to use a sweater, a welcome change from the intense heat into which they were returning as the mountains became hills and they entered the Venezuelan interior. The heat and motion of the car made her drowsy. Added to which she had a hangover, for they closed the bar of the Hotel Avila just a few hours before and she was now paying the price. She didn't know what was worse, her throbbing head or her terrible thirst. Icy cold water was all she could think about.

"Well, baby, you can't have it," Ryle said. "At least not now. You don't drink the water down here until you're some place where you know it's been boiled and filtered to get rid of the amoebas. How 'bout a Coca-Cola or Orange Crush?"

She made a face. She wanted water. The blacktop had given way to a dirt road. They were fine as long as no other cars appeared on the road.

As soon as one drove by a film of dust rose, swirling upward, making it impossible to see. They had to roll up the windows, which made the car stifling, and crawl along at a snail's pace.

Cathleen gave in to her dry throat and drank a soda, which never really quenched her thirst. Whenever they passed a river where women were washing clothes, pounding them with stones, the water, though muddy, looked so inviting she longed to jump in and cool off. Besides her thirst, which made her feel she was slowly going mad, there were no service stations with rest rooms. Ryle would pull off the road and take a walk to relieve himself, but she was afraid of snakes and felt embarrassed at the thought of lifting her skirt and pulling down her panties.

The rainy season had ended two months before. Trees were leafless and it was difficult to visualize the flat landscape as cattle country for there wasn't a blade of grass in sight. Much too hot to eat, they pushed on. She overcame her squeamishness and took a rest stop. She didn't care anymore if someone saw her, but she was still afraid of snakes and sent Ryle ahead to scout the area.

"Good thing we have the car," Ryle declared at one point. "This trip would be murder on you in a pickup."

She hated to think what that would be like since she found it rough enough in the car. Whenever they stopped for sodas, she pulled out her compact and groaned at what she saw. A face streaked with sweat and lips dry and parched. When she brought out her lipstick and stick cologne, she discovered they'd turned soft and runny from the heat. At times the dirt road became a rutted washboard, rocking the car back and forth so whenever they stopped she felt as if she had grown sealegs.

"Some day I'll take you to western Venezuela where the mountains are so high some have snow," Ryle said. The thought of snow, cold and clean, was tantalizing. It seemed like another world, almost impossible to realize, yet only a week had passed since they'd left winter in New York. Ryle parked the car under a clump of leafless trees to give them a breather from the constant pounding of the rutted roads. He pulled her towards him and despite feeling wiped out from the heat and humidity she went eagerly into his arms.

"Hmm, you smell good," he said, nuzzling her neck which she recently rubbed with Blue Grass cologne. "Oh, Cathleen, you're so beautiful." His words came out in a soft groan and she experienced the sensations he was so good at arousing. An almost hunger-like need for his mouth. The throbbing which only abated when he was inside her.

"On board ship we made love morning, noon and night. You spoiled me," he sighed.

His words spoken in that soft drawl which always turned her insides into jelly, made her want to throw all caution aside. I have no modesty left, she decided, no shame whatsoever because if he wanted to make love right here and now, I would do so without a moment's hesitation.

He kissed her, then reluctantly pushed her away. "You're such a temptation. I want you so much. But I'll be damned if we'll put on a show."

"But there's no one around."

"That's what you think," he replied turning the key in the ignition. "It's almost spooky the way it looks deserted out here in the bush. I've pulled over so many times for a rest stop positive I was alone, and then out of nowhere someone popped up." When they drove off she looked back and was startled to see a man step out from the trees, his hand clasping a *machete*.

"He wouldn't hurt us," Ryle reassured her. "They all carry *machetes*. But you see what I mean about feeling you have the place to yourself."

He reached for her hand, squeezing it affectionately, "As soon as we get to camp, the minute we step inside our house, I'm taking you to bed," he promised.

"Oh, yes," she replied, wanting this interminable trip to end. The heat and humidity which had been forgotten in their desire now seemed harsher than ever. Her dress stuck to the seat and she asked him to stop the car so she could change into shorts.

"Can't do that, Cathleen. People down here don't go around in shorts, especially out here. It's just not the custom. Why, in Caracas one of the company engineers was washing his car in his driveway and because he had on shorts, a policeman issued him a warning and made him go inside and change to long pants." He nodded at her look of disbelief. "As soon as we get to camp, you can wear all the shorts you want."

First he told her she couldn't drink the water, Cathleen thought crankily as the heat became more oppressive. Now she couldn't change into something cooler. And her hangover was not getting any better. The day dragged on, then in late afternoon she saw what she thought was a huge fire on the horizon.

"We're in the eastern Venezuelan oilfields now," Ryle said pointing to flares burning off gas from the wells.

"Why do they let the gas burn off — to prevent the wells from exploding?"

"No," he explained. "Gas is flared from a well only because the cost of constructing a gas line to a distant market is not economically justified. Maybe later on they'll pump gas back into the ground in an attempt to maintain high reservoir pressure. At least that's what I've been reading. But right now it's only in the thinking stage."

"That's an oil well?" she asked in amazement. "Where's the derrick, I mean the rig?"

"Oh, that's long gone. A rig is only used for drilling. As soon as a well starts producing, they pull off the rig and install a christmas tree with control valves and pressure gauges if the well initially produces by natural pressure. If the well won't flow naturally at the time of completion, then a pump is installed."

"And when does it gush up in the air? Oh, I can hardly wait to see that." Her impatience with the heat and the long drive was forgotten in the excitement of finally arriving in the oilfields.

"Well you won't see them gushing," Ryle smiled indulgently. "That's only in the movies. It's not like that anymore. See, when they had them gushers it was because they didn't know how to control a well. When they hit oil it just gushed up, and it was normal to let it do so until the pressure was spent." He pulled the car over to the side of the road.

"Sometimes in the early days of the oil industry," he went on, "they used to drop a can of nitroglycerine down the hole to fracture the subsurface rock formation and help the oil flow more easily. It was pretty dangerous and that's why those guys who drove the nitro trucks made such big bucks. They never knew if they would live to spend it. They just might blow up with the nitro before they even got to the wellsite. Anyway, that was a long, long time ago. Only trouble is Hollywood don't know it," he laughed. "Now it's very scientific. They drill down 'til they hit oil, if they hit it, remove the rig, and allow the well to flow using a choke valve to get maximum ultimate recovery." He turned the key in the ignition. "I'll take you out to a wellsite one day and you'll understand it a lot better. Let's make tracks, in an hour we'll be home." As they drove off, she asked him why he became a geologist and not a petroleum engineer.

"Why did I become a rock hound? That's what they call us geologists, y' know. Because everyone said it was a snap course in college." Laughing a little he continued. "Naw, it really wasn't that. I just found geology a lot more interesting."

By now the car had stopped jumping around and through the dusty car window she saw a paved road.

"*El Tigre*," he pointed out. "We're back in civilization for the time being. This blacktop was built by Gulf Oil and goes all the way to Puerto La Cruz. They even put in a telephone line. One of the few places that has one."

"No phones?"

"I told you this was way out in the boonies, didn't I?" Ryle was amused by the expression on Cathleen's face.

"How do people talk to each other?"

"Every oil company has a radio system. We talk to the home office in Caracas every day, as well as the other oil camps by radio. See, city gal, it's not as isolated as you think."

Driving on the blacktop was a pleasure. The sun started to set, making the air cooler. She took out a comb and made an attempt to repair her hair, which she'd put up in a chignon, but now was slipping from the heat and humidity.

"Somehow I thought it would be a jungle out here, with lots of lush trees and vegetation," Cathleen commented, looking at the flat, arid land.

"Like something out of a Tarzan movie?" Ryle laughed. "No, this part of the country is sort of like the southwest back in the States. Vast and desolate. But see, that's the fascination of Venezuela. All different kinds of scenery. Oh, there's jungle all right and some of the oil camps are smack in the middle of it. But not where we're based."

Dusk turned into darkness and the only illumination came from the red flares burning brightly against the night sky. She began to feel human again, the slight breeze blowing tendrils of hair away from her face. When she saw the fence with the familiar Palm Oil logo, it took away some of the strangeness of being in a foreign country. Ryle slowed the Chevy down when he turned into camp and drove over the cattle guard. A uniformed guard dozing in a chair snapped to attention, then waved them through.

"Welcome to Chacari," Ryle said, pointing to a building with huge screen windows. "That's the mess hall. Sure ain't gonna miss that food." Across from the mess hall was the bachelor quarters. Then further down the dirt road the administration building where a few lights shone.

"Someone burnin' the midnight oil," Ryle remarked. "I'm just going to stop and get our house key. Do you want to come in and meet some of the crew?"

The thought of meeting strangers, looking grubby as she did, horrified her fastidious nature. Shaking her head, she watched him walk away, long legs taking easy strides, arms moving along with his legs. She loved to watch him walk and found herself blushing with memories of his naked body. His maleness hanging between his strong legs. How it would swell up when he became aroused, which seemed to be most of the time. She continued her reverie of their honeymoon on board ship. She was embarrassed spending so much time in their stateroom, positive everyone knew they were newlyweds. About the only time she could get Ryle out was for meals, especially the evening one where they dressed in evening clothes and danced after dinner. Cathleen loved their nights on board ship. Ryle wasn't a great dancer, but she didn't mind sitting out the fast ones. Slow dancing to the romantic ballads the band played, *That's My Desire*, *Blue Moon*, and especially *It Had to Be You*, made her feel the songs had been written just for them. She was still reminiscing when Ryle got back in the car.

"Listen, Cathleen," Ryle cautioned hesitantly as he drove into the carport. "Don't get too discouraged when you see the place. It's not much to brag on. But you'll be able to fix it up. You'll see how some of the other gals doll up their houses." A yellow light, meant to discourage bugs, burned outside the kitchen door, but insects still buzzed against the bulb.

Cathleen wasn't expecting much, and she had deliberately conditioned herself to expect a primitive setting, but even so, the house was a shock. Entering through the kitchen door she quickly noticed the concrete floor, painted dull red, feeling hard and unyielding to her feet.

"Water, all the water you want," Ryle said opening the refrigerator. "My boss's wife, Nadine, stocked the fridge with a few things. Chicken, potato salad, even some cornbread."

But Cathleen wasn't interested in food, only water, gulping it down greedily. She couldn't ever remember water tasting so good, icy perfection reminding her of clean snow, so refreshing to her parched mouth she felt like a fat cat lapping up cream. After her thirst was satisfied, she looked around the kitchen, finding it terribly depressing. A single light bulb dangling from a chord hung over a white wooden table and two chairs. She followed Ryle into the dining/living room where she noticed the dining room furniture didn't have one matching piece. Several panes of glass were missing in the china cabinet. The living room furniture did match though, a rattan couch and two chairs with faded brown and white cushions. The coffee and end tables had scratches on them.

"Let's get some air in this place." Ryle walked over to the windows, opening the screened wooden jalousies which were painted an anemic green to match the walls. A short hall led to the bathroom and two bedrooms. The double bed in the master bedroom sagged in the middle, its headboard a dull gray metal. Two gray metal chests stood side by side against one wall and next to the bed was a single nightstand.

What an ugly, little box of a house, Cathleen thought despondently, remembering longingly the room she'd shared with Peggy and Beebe. The frilly white bedspreads, the kidney-shaped dressing table with its matching gathered skirt and the mahogany chest of drawers. The nightstands next to their beds with the brass lamps spreading a warm glow over the room. That's what's wrong with this room, she tried to console herself. It just needs sprucing up. I'm only feeling this way because it's been such a long day. In the morning everything will look better after a good night's sleep.

But she didn't have that luxury. All the water she consumed woke her up. Looking at the small alarm she saw it was three in the morning. Making her way to the bathroom, she lifted her nightgown and sat down. She hadn't finished urinating when she heard a strange noise below her. Jumping off the toilet seat she peered down into the bowl where two beady eyes set in a brown, warty face stared up at her. She screamed. Ryle came running. Pointing to the toilet bowl she fled from the bathroom.

"Why, baby, it's nothin' but a frog. I thought you were being attacked by wild lions or something," he said flushing the toilet several times. The frog didn't budge. Reaching in the toilet he picked it up and going to the door threw the frog into the inky night.

Despite Ryle's soothing touch, Cathleen found it difficult to fall asleep. She wondered what other animals could get in the house, and when she finally dozed off, her dreams were filled with snakes.

SIX

Maruja felt restless and out of sorts. Four days had passed and not a word from Fred Hardesty. Of course she could care less since he hadn't turned out to be the Englishman of her dreams, but an American *petrolero*, which should have made her lose interest immediately. Except there was something different about this *musiu*. She'd known handsome men before, but none of them made her feel this way. Giddy one moment, pensive the next. Irritable and impatient with the way time was dragging its feet. Her days and nights had turned into utter boredom.

Feeling fidgety and thirsty, she decided to cajole the cook into making her favorite drink, guava juice and barley water. Her mother would have a fit if she knew she was visiting the servants' quarters. It was something she did as a child, but now that she was grown up, Misia Isabel didn't think it was proper. Which made Maruja all the more determined. How she loved doing things which were forbidden.

On her way to the back patio she passed one of the maids who was pouring boiled water into the *filtro*. The filter, about the size of a refrigerator, had a latticed door and sides. A huge ceramic urn caught the water dripping down from the large stone filter. The maid, standing on a small stool, struggled with the huge pot of water and Maruja wondered for a moment who would come out the winner, the maid or the pot. Then making a bored face, she continued toward the kitchen. But when she got to the back patio, she decided to sun herself on the *embostadero*, a round cement platform where the laundry had been spread out to dry.

"Be careful, *señorita*." The laundress's sharp and irritated voice broke into her thoughts. "Don't you dare get my laundry dirty with your shoes."

"Don't worry, Anselma," Maruja assured her airily, "I've never soiled anything yet." She stepped carefully between the clothes on the *embostadero.* Then finding a place to stretch out, she looked across the courtyard at Anselma. Here was someone who could divert her. Stooped over the tub, the strong black arms of the laundress went up and down the washboard, keeping time to the song she was singing, the ever present cigarette dangling from her mouth. Whenever the cigarette became too heavy with ashes, she flipped it inside her mouth with her tongue and continued smoking. How she managed to flip the lit cigarette in and out of her mouth and make the ashes disappear, and also continue smoking, never ceased to amaze Maruja. Ever since she was a child she'd been fascinated with Anselma's smoking. It was better than watching the jugglers in the circus. She started to sing along with the laundress.

> *Dígame que siempre recordarás*
> *El día*
> *Que nos conocimos*

Would Fred Hardesty, as the song promised, always remember the day they met? Or had he forgotten her? He certainly wasn't pursuing her as Venezuelan men did, with flowers and strolling musicians playing love songs. For the past four days, *nada, absolutamente* nothing. This *gringo petrolero* was driving her crazy! A man ignoring her — why, this had never happened before in her entire life.

She wished she brought her bathing suit; she could sunbathe. If only her mother would move to the suburbs, they could have a house with a swimming pool. But no, Misia Isabel insisted on staying downtown in this house which the first de los Reyes family had built who knows how many hundreds of years ago. If they had a house in the suburbs she could be sunbathing on a chaise lounge now instead of sitting dreamily in the servants quarters on the *embostadero.* Or would she? It was just another way of defying convention.

What made her so different from the rest of her sisters and brothers puzzled even her. *Mami* often said she was like *Papi's* aunt who ran off with the *llanero*, the cowboy. Or perhaps she didn't even belong in this family, but was the result of *Papi's* escapades, the daughter of a mistress brought home to be raised. It happened, 'cousins' brought up with the other children. It took a very understanding wife to allow another woman's child into her house. She would never permit it.

"Ah ha, I knew you were here," a voice cried out excitedly, interrupting Maruja's daydreams. It was her sister, Maria de Lourdes, the family tattletale. "*Ay*, if *Mami* finds out you're here in the servants' patio," Lourdes continued in her singsong voice which irritated Maruja no end, "you're going to be in a lot of trouble."

Maruja shrugged her shoulders indifferently. Marriage and a child had not improved Lourdes' personality one iota. She was still the same busybody who couldn't stand it if she wasn't stirring up trouble. "Well, she won't know," Maruja said, yawning in Lourdes' face, "unless you blabber to her. Besides, I don't care. So hike up that ugly dress you're wearing, big mouth, and go run and tell her."

"Well, I think you might care to know something else," Lourdes replied, determined to goad Maruja. Maruja knew her sister couldn't keep that tongue of hers from wagging and in a matter of seconds she would burst out with whatever was running through that silly, empty head of hers. Which she did. "The florist just delivered some flowers for you."

Jumping off the *embostadero* Maruja ran towards the front of the house.

"*Oye, hey Maruja la Bruja*," Lourdes called after her in malicious glee, "I don't think your *musiu* sent them."

Which he hadn't. Disappointed Maruja tore up the card. Just Dr. Emilio Maldonado, who'd been sending her flowers for months now. That idiot never gives up, she thought irritably. He's the biggest bore of them all.

"Isn't it wonderful?" Misia Isabel cooed. She loved the flowers Maruja received from her admirers; they made lovely centerpieces for the dining room table. Sometimes they had different arrangements every day. Emilio Maldonado was such a catch, Misia Isabel sighed to herself. Only Maruja didn't think so. But then, what man had she ever considered good enough? Lourdes had been talking about a new admirer who brought her white roses last Sunday. Perhaps he might be the one. She recited five Hail Marys, praying fervently that God would send a man who would entice her capricious daughter into settling down and getting married.

···

Fred wanted to go back to Maruja's house the next day. Her brother didn't scare him at all. Now that he knew her name and where she lived nothing stood in his way, except he was having second thoughts. From what he heard, asking a Venezuelan girl for a date was no easy matter. The family was very strict and there was this chaperon business. He didn't want to ask her out if it meant taking another member of her family along. He'd fantasized about heavy necking sessions, how could he do that with a third party around? Worst of all, he heard if you started going out with a Venezuelan *señorita* the family thought you were serious and wanted to get married. Gawdalmighty! They'd have him hog-tied before he even got out of the corral.

Every day he talked himself out of returning to Maruja's house. Then Sunday morning came and he knew he couldn't stay away from her any longer. He dressed hastily to make one o'clock Mass at the Cathedral. The priest was reading the gospel when he arrived. Standing in the back Fred noticed the congregation consisted mainly of women, the same as last Sunday. Evidently attending Mass wasn't a Venezuelan male priority, even though it was a predominantly Catholic country. From the advantage of his height he scanned the church for Maruja.

....

She purposely sat at the end of the pew. It took maneuvering; her sister Malena insisted she move in and *Tía* Nellie fussed at her for being so obstinate. But Maruja knew what she wanted and that was to sit at the end of the pew. After Mass started she slowly inched inward so there was now room for another person. When they rose to recite the Apostles Creed she turned and looked around the Cathedral. He was here, she just knew he was here. When their eyes locked, she felt dizzy with desire. He in turn, confronted with the perfection of her heartshaped face framed by a pink hat, forgot all his intentions not to get involved and bolted down the aisle, slipping in beside her. She put aside her pique because he hadn't showered her with attention this past week and her disappointment he wasn't English. All was forgiven when he sat down beside her. It was written in God's book when we were born, she decided. It was meant to be, the two of us. Why else would we have met in church? Her smile, the practiced smile she'd been flashing ever since she discovered the opposite sex, melted in even further surrender.

Maruja's proximity made Fred forget all his reasons for staying away. He loved her perfume, a delicate rose fragrance which hovered over her like a gossamer veil. He admired her tiny hands, the nails painted a pale pink. Then he noticed the ring on the third finger of her left hand, a square cut emerald surrounded by diamonds. She's taken, he thought, she must be engaged. But he didn't dwell on this possible obstacle. That wouldn't stop him.

His eyes left her ring and travelled down to the hem of her pink dress, under which the lace of her slip could be faintly seen. He started thinking about her slip, wondering what the rest of it looked like, especially where it curved under the swell of her bosom. The thought of her breasts, their shape, size and texture a total mystery, excited him so much he had to kneel down immediately, even though the congregation was still sitting. Geez! How embarrassing. He was grateful when the altar boy rang the bell and everyone knelt.

....

Maruja didn't know if her father would be home that afternoon; ordinarily he liked to go to the Sunday horse races in El Paraíso. She rushed Malena and *Tía* Nellie home after Mass, hoping to catch him before he left.

"*Papi, Mami,*" she called out dashing through the house. Her father was in the dining room finishing up a late breakfast, studying the horses he would play in the *Cinco y Seis*, the main race of the week which paid big money if one picked five or six winning horses in one race.

"The man I'm going to marry is coming this afternoon," Maruja announced.

Don Eugenio put aside his newspaper, shock showing in his face. Misia Isabel came running from the library and studied her daughter carefully. Could it be that her prayers were finally answered? "*¿De veras?*" Misia Isabel gasped. "Really?"

"And who is this lucky man?" her father asked.

"He's *un ingeniero*, a petroleum engineer," she replied.

"Ah . . . . a *petrolero?*" Her mother's eyebrows shot up first in skepticism, then resignation. "So you finally met your Englishman?"

"*Bueno*, not exactly," Maruja hesitated. "He looks like an Englishman, he dresses like one. At least he did the first time I met him, but it appears . . . . he's an American."

"*¿Un Americano?*" both her parents burst out. "But you never liked Americans."

"But this one is so *guapo*, so handsome," Malena piped up as she joined them in the dining room, "I could fall in love with him myself."

"He's the one who brought the white roses last Sunday." This last bit from Lourdes, who, afraid she might miss something, had come dashing in without her house slippers.

"I met him when he brought the flowers," Lucho the oldest son added. The dining room was quickly filling up with people.

"How is it everyone in this family has met this *musiu* except me?" her father asked irritably.

"But, *Papi*, you're going to meet him this afternoon," Maruja replied in her most persuasive manner for she knew how difficult her father could be at times. "He's coming to talk to you, *Papi*."

"And where did you meet him?" Don Eugenio persisted. "That Malena and Lourdes and Lucho know him and I don't?"

"In the Cathedral," she replied triumphantly. "Can you imagine, last Sunday our hands collided in the holy water font! It was the will of God we should meet in His house."

"Don't be impertinent, *señorita*," Don Eugenio snapped as he struggled to gain control of the situation. It was a futile gesture though, because Maruja always wound up getting whatever she wanted.

"And he came and sat down next to her at Mass this morning," *Tía* Nellie added walking slowly into the room. "But I kept an eye on him and he acted with proper decorum." Knowing *Tía* Nellie was practically blind, Don Eugenio threw her a quizzical look.

"No horse races today, Eugenio," Misia Isabel informed her husband.

"Of course not, *mi amor*," he agreed.

The house was spotless. It always was with the army of servants Misia Isabel had at her disposal to keep the floors waxed, the furniture polished, the garden blooming and the bird cages clean. Nevertheless with only an hour to go, she pushed the servants to make the already impeccable house even more shining.

"So, it's come to this, Eugenio," Misia Isabel moaned. "One of our children marrying a *musiu*, and a *petrolero* at that. What will the neighbors think? Can you imagine the field day the gossips will have with this one?" Despite everything Maruja had said about marrying an Englishman, Misia Isabel never thought she would actually marry a foreigner.

"She's not marrying anyone until I give my permission." Don Eugenio admonished his wife. "Don't get yourself in an uproar."

His words had no calming effect on his wife. In fact the whole house was in turmoil. When the Cathedral clock struck four o'clock however, and Fred knocked on the front door, everything and everyone was in place.

This time he didn't have to wait an eternity for the door to open. He entered the vestibule through the intricately carved mahogany doors which again opened to his touch, after making sure he had the right house, since from the outside so many of them looked alike. But he remembered Maruja's house, which had two stories, took up an entire city block and the entrance door was flanked by two white columns, with a delicately carved frieze overhead. Wooden shutters behind wrought iron grilles remained closed, except for the central panels which had been left open to let in the afternoon breeze.

When the servant ushered him inside, the beauty of the house, so completely different from the harsh exterior, took him by surprise. Sunlight spilled into the large patio where flowers and plants grew in oversized planters placed between white pillars reaching to the second floor. Against the far wall a bougainvillea could be seen, its branches heavy with purple flowers looking very much like a still life painting. Interspersed with the planters he saw bird cages, from which came the sweet songs of canaries. A lone parrot sensing he had a new audience shouted a raucous greeting to him. What claimed his attention, though, was the fountain in a framework of colorful, Spanish tiles with seats encircling the base. When he sat down in a white wicker chair, the fountain continued to fascinate him, the continuous cascade of its water lending a soothing rhythm to the scene.

As he looked around, he noticed an open gallery adjacent to the planters, behind which were windows and doors. One of these doors opened and he heard footsteps coming towards him. An older version of the man who took the white roses from him last Sunday appeared. He wore a *Liquilique*, the same white linen suit Fred had seen in the Plaza Bolivar. Fred jumped out of his chair, towering over Don Eugenio. Motioning Fred to sit down, Maruja's father studied him and then the two men began talking. At first Fred's words came out easily, he'd been going to Spanish school for two weeks now, but once he got past the basics he started to flounder. Shrugging, Fred's face broke into a huge grin. He smiled even more when Don Eugenio told him to speak English, explaining that while he couldn't speak it, he did understand it. Maruja's father responded to Fred's friendly personality. Responded even more when Fred gave him what he said was a foolproof method of picking out winners at the races, something Fred's grandfather had taught him. Remarking on the beauty of the mansion, Fred learned that the architecture was a carryover from the Spanish/Moorish influence, a design to insure privacy as well as protection for the family. Subtly Don Eugenio elicited the information he wanted from Fred. Within a short time he knew quite a bit about him.

Again Fred heard footsteps in the gallery. Misia Isabel appeared, followed by a servant carrying a tray. Her button eyes looking at him through rimless glasses hid her reservations. She was the soul of graciousness, offering him *Ponche Crema*, an eggnog type drink, followed by little cups of black coffee, strong and thick, into which *papelón*, unrefined brown sugar had been stirred. Misia Isabel's eyes communicated her uneasiness to her husband. 'What do we know about this man?' they asked. 'Aside from the fact he's twenty-two years old, just out of college, and his father is also a *petrolero* in Texas. His mother died a few years ago and he has three sisters and no brothers. And, for a *musiu*, he appears to have good manners. But other than that we know nothing.' Don Eugenio ignored his wife's agitation, and frustrated, she excused herself.

In the short time she was out of the room, the word marriage came up. Seeing the startled look in Fred's eyes, Don Eugenio quickly changed the subject. So this young man isn't thinking of marriage, he thought laughing quietly to himself. In spite of just meeting this *musiu*, Don Eugenio liked him immensely. Even though right now he has no serious intentions towards Maruja, knowing her they will get married. Lord help him, Don Eugenio mused, she will lead him a merry chase. And because he is so smitten with her, he will wind up doing whatever she wants, all the time so entranced, so bewitched he will follow her around like a little puppy. More like a St. Bernard, Don Eugenio decided, noting Fred's large physique. So be it, when this *musiu* asks for Maruja's hand, I will give my permission. It will be like keeping it in the family, he later informed Misia Isabel. All the land they owned in the interior which was leased to the oil companies, why, now they would get back their investment through their son-in-law who would bring in the *petróleo*.

Fred wondered if the person he really wanted to see would ever appear. A steady succession of Maruja's family entered the patio, her brothers and sisters, *Tía* Nellie, all of them wanting to meet him. When she finally appeared the babble of voices ceased for a moment. *Sí*, they all agreed, their voices returning excitedly, the two of them are without a doubt *comiendo caramelos*, eating caramels, a Venezuelan slang expression for being in love. All of them liked Fred. Even Maruja's second eldest brother, Alejo, who was violently anti-American and who wished all the *musius* would leave Venezuela to the Venezuelans. Alejo, who had grown up ashamed of his family's great wealth, had a secret life which would have caused Misia Isabel far greater concern than Maruja's willfulness. He was a member of the outlawed Communist party.

Maruja's appearance made all the hoopla Fred went through seem insignificant. Burn my clothes, he cried out to himself, I'm in Heaven. If she isn't the cutest little doll. Why, none of the girls he dated in the past could hold a candle to her. His mind started working overtime, figuring out how he could slip her away from the chaperonage of her married brother, Jorge and his wife, Carolina, who would accompany them on their date. Looking at her dainty white gloves he wondered how long it would take before he could slip them off to hold hands with her. And from there to kissing her. His eyes drank in her light green organdy dress with its puffed sleeves and Empire waist, the dark green velvet sash cinched just below her breasts.

He had to restrain himself from hugging her as they walked to the movies, cutting through the Plaza Bolivar to the Avila Theater. He was very much aware of their chaperons. Only when they were in the darkened theater did he dare think of touching her. And even then he felt Jorge's eyes on him. Neither of them had any idea what was taking place on the screen. Fortunately Jorge and Carolina quickly became engrossed in the Errol Flynn opus, and when Fred reached for her hand, no one noticed. He could feel Maruja's rapidly beating pulse when their hands locked. Slowly he slid his arm around her. The lights coming on at the end of the movie took them by surprise. Jorge glared at them and Maruja looked back defiantly.

It was after seven in the evening when they went next door to the *Confectionaria Avila*, but to *Caraqueño* society it was tea time. It was what people did after attending a Saturday or Sunday matinee, go to the confectionery shop to be seen and to see who was there. People waved to each other, *holas* were exchanged, some showing off their newest conquests, others making mental notes so within an hour the telephones would be buzzing with the latest gossip.

Maruja loved to create a stir. She frequently acted out little scenes so they would be reported in great detail. This time was different. Now she didn't have to stage a performance for she was with her *novio*, her sweetheart. And while he wasn't English, she had forgiven him for being a Texan because she had finally fallen in love.

Around them people drank tea, hot chocolate and black coffee, biting delicately into pastries, popping *Ping Pongs*, chocolate covered peanuts, into their mouth. Maruja sipped her tea daintily, taking an occasional bite of pastry, for she was much too excited to eat. Her words were animated. Skillfully she led the conversation, making sure Fred and her brother and sister-in-law all interacted. Although Jorge and Carolina spoke very little English, and Fred only a beginner's Spanish, it didn't stop Maruja from weaving their little circle into behaving as she wanted them to. In the future she and Fred wouldn't have to worry about Jorge guarding them like a hawk.

Fred was also much too excited to eat. He took sips of black coffee and, because he felt it was expected, he nibbled on a few pastries. What he really longed for was a cool beer, a car and Maruja beside him in some lovers lane. Was there a lovers lane in Caracas, he wondered, where he could escape with her, away from the family, just the two of them? He was tempted to ask her, but the whole Venezuelan dating scene had him baffled.

He did find a lovers lane a week later. They had gone on a picnic with the ever present brothers and sisters to *El Pinar*, a pine studded park in one of the older suburbs, *El Paraíso*. Slipping away from the group they walked up the curving mountainside, their feet crunching the pine needles underfoot, the air getting cooler as they ascended. They managed to veer away from the footpath and wound up deep in the forest, surrounded only by the silent trees.

"I don't believe it," Fred declared, lifting Maruja off the ground in a passionate embrace. "The first time we've been alone since I met you."

"Baby doll, you're driving me crazy," he groaned when her breasts pressed against his chest. He wanted to slip his hands inside her blouse and touch them. Maruja felt ripples of excitement run through her body. The way he held her, their bodies almost blended as one, was so thrilling she thought she would die from the excitement.

"Oh, no," she heard Fred groan.

"¿*Qué fue*? What is it?" she gasped breathlessly.

"Someone's coming," he said in frustration, putting her back down on the ground. Some sixth sense made him look up. It was the days spent trying furtively to hold hands with her in movies, putting his arms around her when he thought no one was watching, which made him always look over his shoulder.

"Geez," he sputtered, "this is the most frustrating romance I've ever tried to have."

"So, you've had a lot of romances, eh?" she shot back.

"Who said that?" he asked warily. Every once in awhile they got into an argument. He never knew how it started, but she was very jealous of his past, wanting to know how many girls he had gone out with, how serious he'd been with them.

"Well, you said it's the most frustrating romance you've ever had," she persisted. "Meaning you've had a lot of them."

"Ah, *muñequita*." By now he was calling her 'little doll' in Spanish. "You just don't understand me. It must be the language barrier. I never said I had a lot of love affairs."

"*Ay*, but I know you've had."

"And you haven't?" he prodded, for he was just as jealous of her. "Haven't all the men in Caracas been wild about you? That's the story I got from your family."

"But, *mi amor*," she purred, "they meant nothing to me. While you on the other hand, how many times have you been in love?"

The truth was Fred had been in love with just about every girl he took out. Not heavy in love, but each one had something special in his eyes.

None of them, though, made him feel the way this Venezuelan doll did, all tied up in knots. And frustrated, Gawdalmighty, was he frustrated. He didn't know if this was due to the restrictions imposed on them by her family and the Venezuelan culture, or if he'd fallen for her.

"Well," his eyes screwed up like a little boy trying to find the right words, "none of them were like you, that's for sure. You got me crazier than a fox after an armadillo. Oh *muñequita,* why'd ya have to be Venezuelan? It would have been so much easier if you were American and we could go out on normal dates so I wouldn't have to be always looking over my shoulder. Ah nuts," he cried out, "you just don't understand what I'm trying to say."

When she looked up at him from her teasing eyes he pulled her toward him in a tight embrace. "I guess the truth is I'm crazy about you. You're the cutest little doll I've ever known." Then out of habit, looking around first, he kissed her quickly. Nobody's coming, he thought, nobody's looking. A guy has to be swift with these Venezuelan girls. You have to snatch whatever bit of lovin' you can, because just as sure as God made little green apples, the family doesn't leave you alone.

By the time Christmas arrived they had become quite adept at sneaking secluded moments. For no matter who went along as their chaperon, they all wound up liking Fred. His easy-going, friendly personality and hearty laugh endeared him to everyone. When Fred was invited to dine with the family, he rhapsodized over the Venezuelan cuisine. Starting with the *bocas,* the hors d'oeuvres. *Tequeños,* little cheese fingers fried to a succulent crispiness with the cheese oozing inside, *bollitos,* little *tamales* wrapped in banana leaves. Or *tostones,* green bananas fried like potato chips. And to see him eat *plátanos* — plantains which are first cousins to bananas but must be cooked before eaten, either baked in brown sugar or fried in sweet fresh butter — why, one would think he'd been born a Venezuelan. *Chayote,* a vegetable so bland that to be called one meant a person with no personality, even this vegetable which had to be served in a cheese sauce to be palatable, he liked. The *guasacaca,* a spicy hot relish, reminded him of Tex-Mex cooking. No matter what was put in front of him, he invariably came out with the same words of appreciation, "*¡Qué magnífico!*"

By Christmas Eve, he'd become so much a part of the family he'd been invited to skate with them to Midnight Mass. The first time he learned of this Venezuelan custom was at four o'clock one morning. The noise of steel wheels hitting the pavement, sounding like an army thundering through the streets, woke him from a fitful sleep and he jumped out of bed. Looking down to the street he saw it was filled with people roller skating. He was relieved to find out this only occurred from the middle of December to Christmas Eve, because every morning in the wee hours before dawn the skaters woke him up on their way to the *Aguinaldos* Mass. Ordinarily he was a sound sleeper, but in the weeks since he met Maruja he found himself tossing and turning, never sleeping the whole night through.

After Mass he and Maruja joined the other skaters on the hilly Caracas streets, Then in the early hours of the morning they returned to the house for champagne and *hallacas*, large *tamale*-like squares filled with chicken and pork. It was the strangest Christmas Fred had ever spent because there was no Christmas tree. Only a *Nacimiento*, a Nativity tableau with figures so large and striking it took up an entire wall of the living room. No gifts were exchanged on Christmas Eve or even the following day, but rather on January sixth, the Epiphany, when the arrival of the Three Kings was celebrated. And it wasn't until this day the statues of the Three Kings were placed in the *Nacimiento*. The following day the *Nacimiento* was taken down and the Christmas season ended. It also marked the end of Fred's stay in Caracas.

"*Muñequita*, I'm sure going to miss you," he told Maruja. "Are you going to write to me? Or will you be so busy with your social life you'll forget all about this ole Texas boy?"

"I'll be as busy as you will be," she replied evasively, already jealous of the unknown women he would be seeing.

"Well, then your social life will be a big, fat zero because there's nothing to do in the oilfields except work, and there sure aren't any single women."

"None at all?" she asked coyly.

"Well, maybe an occasional school teacher or nurse, but not in Chacari where I'm based. You got to get around the big camps like Creole's Caripito or Sinclair's Santa Barbara. And so far, baby doll, I've been out in the boonies."

The news pleased her. She knew he adored her and when they got married, he would be faithful to her. But that was the problem. He hadn't proposed! In the five weeks since they'd met, not a word from him. In fact he hadn't even told her he loved her. Unheard of in a Venezuelan who would have declared his undying love long before this. Here she had informed her family he was the man she was going to marry, and he hadn't asked for her hand. Her pride was wounded, but she would never let him know. Instead she assumed an attitude of indifference.

"So, what will you be doin' after I leave?" he persisted.

"Oh, the same things that I did before I met you," she replied nonchalantly. "Probably getting ready for Carnival, which is no small feat since it's even better than Christmas and New Year's put together."

"What'd ya mean, even better?" he asked suspiciously.

"It's the last fling before Lent. Parties, dances, dressing up in costumes," she explained. "It's a wild time, even with the chaperons." She paused, eyeing him in a flirtatious manner she knew drove him mad. "It's also a very romantic time," she continued, "when many people fall in love." What she didn't mention because she didn't think it proper, was the population usually increased nine months after Carnival.

The thought of his little baby doll being with other men, flirting and dancing, gave him conniptions. Just suppose, he worried, she met someone after he returned to the oilfields. He knew she could have her pick of anyone she wanted. Then he might lose her.

"I used to think you were engaged the first time I saw that emerald ring on your left hand," he blurted out. "But I don't guess you are or else you wouldn't be going out with me."

"No, engagement rings are worn on the right hand in Venezuela because it is the hand which goes over the heart." She crossed her right hand over to her heart.

Suddenly he'd steered the conversation to engagements. Whatever made him do that? And what he said next surprised him even more. "We couldn't get married right away, y'know."

"Oh," she said laughing to herself, but so softly it came out in an enchanting smile. He was leading up to marriage, she knew that now. All she had to do was sit back and let him do the talking. She hadn't lost her charm, she was still *Maruja la Bruja* who could bewitch any man into doing whatever she wanted.

"What I mean is, when I give a girl an engagement ring, I'd want to give her my mother's. When she died Daddy put it away for me," he explained. "In the bank back home in Texas," he continued, hoping this explanation would delay his neck winding up in the noose.

"I'm just an oil hand, *muñequita*," he cried out. "What do you call us? *Petroleros*. And *petroleros* don't make the kind of money you're used to. Oh sure, we make a lot more than we could in the States, but it's peanuts compared to the kind of moolah you've grown up with. And I'm just starting out, nothing more than a Junior P. E. And if I stay in Venezuela, I'll be working in the interior for years and years before I get promoted to Caracas." He was presenting a good argument, he thought. The initial panic which he felt when the conversation turned to marriage had subsided.

"I can't see you in the oilfields, especially in one of those company houses. Why, the whole house is no larger than your living room. Just little boxes, all of them exactly alike. You're used to livin' high on the hog." He started to pace up and down. "Why, even back home in Texas you'd be out of my league. Not that my family's poor, there was always money for college and things like that; Daddy gave me a new car when I hit sixteen. It's just I'm not a *Pan Grande*." He used the Venezuelan slang expression, a large loaf of bread, meaning a big shot.

Maruja didn't say a word. She just looked at him, her eyes teasing and her mouth inviting in a half open smile which made his insides quiver. He knew then, looking at her, that his fooling around days were over. Goodbye to all the women he would never know. *Adiós* to the tall ones, the short ones, the quiet ones, the vivacious ones, the sweet virgins, the horny ones who loved sex as much as he did. Goodbye to them all. He let out a sigh.

"I don't want anyone else bird doggin' you when I'm not around, because the truth of the matter is . . . . I'm in love with you." Well, now he'd gone and said it! "But you gotta think on this real hard." He took a deep breath, feeling somewhat like a diver about to make the plunge off a steep cliff into unknown waters.

"I'm askin' you to marry me, but before you say anything, remember all I got to offer is me. If you're willing to tough it out in the oilfields with me, if you'll live on what I make. See, what bothers me is you're so rich. I got my pride, I just won't ever take any of your money. So, if knowing all this, if you'll take a trip out to the oilfields to see what it's really like out there . . . . well, if you want me, doll, I'm askin' you to marry me."

Fred never imagined he would make such a long speech. Despite being able to talk a good line, 'shoot the shit' as his father described Fred's loquaciousness, he was truly amazed by what he'd said. He honestly hadn't thought about marriage. Somewhere down the road he thought it might catch up with him, but it was a long way off. He was still young, one year out of college. Having missed out on WWII because he was too young, he signed up to work in Venezuela just for the adventure. He didn't even know if he'd return when his two years were up. Not that he found the oilfields as lonely as most men did. Even though there was a scarcity of single American women, there were still all the Ladies of the Night he hadn't sampled. So it wasn't the loneliness of the oilfields which prompted him to propose. No, it was simply because Maruja had mowed him down. Just looking at her he felt an erection coming on and he turned away, hoping desperately it would subside before she noticed it.

Maruja saw him turn away. As passionate and eager for love as she was, she was still innocent of the facts of life. She never realized what had happened to him. How strange these Americans are, she thought, why doesn't he take me in his arms after his declaration of love?

I don't care if the oilfields are *rústico*, she told herself, I don't care how primitive life is out there. I will follow him to the ends of the earth. For he was the only man who ever made her want to get married. *Por fin*! At last there was a mango on the tree she wanted. She would be like that aunt of *Papi's* who eloped with the cowboy. She would find her *destino* on the plains of her country. Only this time, instead of a cowboy, she would find happiness with a *musiu petrolero*. Strains of *Alma Llanera*, *The Soul of the Plains*, a folk song considered the country's second national anthem, ran through her head and she hummed a few lines.

> *I love, I cry, I sing, I dream*
> *with carnations of passion*

When Fred turned back to her, the brilliance of her smile bedazzled him. And then she gave him her answer. "I will think about it."

Think about it? Is that the best she could come up with after he'd cut away his last vestige of freedom? If that ain't the berries! He asked her to marry him and all she could say was, she'd think about it! Funny thing was now he wanted her more than ever. She just had to say yes. Gawdalmighty, now he was the one who could hardly wait to get hitched.

SEVEN

As Cathleen and Ryle walked toward the camp superintendent's house, her stomach churned. Everyone will be looking me over, she agonized. Mother of God, it will be like jumping into an ice cold lake. She tugged at Ryle's hand, wishing somehow they could skip the party.

"Everyone's dying to meet you," he murmured bending down to plant a brief kiss in her hair, unaware of her uneasiness. "Wait 'til they see you. Baby, you'll knock their socks off." He looked approvingly at her yellow paisley halter dress and the matching cotton stole draped casually over her shoulders. Because of the heat she'd combed her hair in an upsweep.

"I'm not good meeting strangers," she murmured, wishing the palpitations in her chest would subside. What if they didn't like her, or she said the wrong thing? Sometimes her shyness caused her to clam up, making her appear distant and remote, hesitant to open her mouth for fear she would make a fool of herself.

Ryle threw a puzzled though indulgent look at his wife. Her sophisticated manner and cool confidence were the qualities which attracted him. Though they'd never discussed his ambitions in detail, so wrapped up were they in their love for each other, he assumed she realized his aspirations to become president of Palm Oil and that he counted on her being a social asset to him.

I should have had a drink before we left home, Cathleen decided as her panic became more acute. She couldn't remember being so terrified of meeting strangers. She needed a quick shot of instant courage so she could sail in as if she'd been going to parties all her life. An ice cold martini would chase away the butterflies nesting in her stomach. She could almost taste its stinging dryness, feel the warmth and confidence it always gave her.

But she couldn't have a martini. That was one of the things Ryle informed her before they left for the party. People came to the oilfields to make and save money. Since imported liquor was very expensive, people drank the native rum, Santa Teresa. They tried to live on their $225 monthly living allowance without touching their salary. With the house rent $30 a month, including utilities, that left $195 for food, help and entertainment. Since there was no place to go except back and forth to each other's homes or the clubhouse where movies shown twice a week cost a *Bolivar*, equivalent to thirty-three cents, and a dance every Saturday night with rum going for the same amount, most people were able to get by on their living allowance.

I can't let this throw me, Cathleen decided with determination, I must get control of myself. Taking a deep breath she entered the Dalharts' house aware that eyes followed her every step. Her dress, which she had thought so stunning, she'd bought it in the cruise section of Altman's, now felt dowdy. Its longer length, so much in style in New York, seemed out of place here next to the knee-length cocktail dresses of the other women. She noticed some of the men wore khaki pants and shirts, which made her think they looked like they were in the Army, minus their stripes.

"Sip this nice and slow, Cathleen," said Ryle handing her a tall glass of rum punch splashed over chopped ice. "Don't be deceived by the lemonade taste. They're pretty potent. See Jim Cheney over there." He pointed to a burly man whose stomach hung over his khaki pants. "One minute he was drinking rum punch and the next minute he passed out. Didn't wake up until the next morning, still sitting in the same chair 'cause no one could move him." What Ryle didn't explain was the reason for the drink's potency. Because the rum hadn't fermented properly, it was like drinking bathtub gin. Venezuelan rum, in later years a smooth liquor exported to discerning palates, was then a raw drink known for its knock-you-on-your-keister quality.

It does taste like lemonade, Cathleen decided. And because she wasn't crazy about sweet drinks, she started out sipping it slowly. But her uneasiness surrounded by so many strangers and the object of their inspection made her soon regard the rum punch as her only friend. She took larger sips.

Some of the women had called on her that morning, bringing baked goods and casseroles. She felt flattered they had taken the time to welcome her, not realizing that time was something they had in abundance. And as soon as another woman moved into camp, there would be a rush to meet her. She was fascinated by their speech. "I swan if this ain't the hottest day of them all," saying 'hey' for hello. Some of the women's names — Johnny Mae, Jimmy Lee — intrigued her. It was these little things which helped push aside her shyness; the fascination she felt meeting so many characters in the flesh rather than entering their world through a printed page.

Nadine Fickett, whose husband was district geologist and Ryle's boss, welcomed her with a self-confident warmth Cathleen longed to possess. She listened while Nadine gave her a few pointers about housekeeping in the tropics.

"You got to boil the water, then pour it through the ceramic filter. Of course it's heavy work, but that's what a maid is for. Fresh milk isn't available," Nadine continued in her friendly, breezy manner, "so you use the powdered stuff. It's not bad once you get used to it. Why, my youngest boy prefers it to real milk and I have a heck of a time getting him to switch when we go home on vacation."

"And the fresh vegetables, whenever you can get lettuce and cabbage for salad, you got to wash it in boiled, filtered water and even that's not enough. You drop two Halazone tablets into the water to kill the amoeba." She reached into a voluminous purse and took out a bottle containing tablets which resembled aspirin. "I stopped by this morning to drop these off, but you were still sleeping. Poor baby, driving over those killer roads. Ain't they a gas?"

She leaned over to whisper in Cathleen's ear. "Even brushing your teeth or douching," she warned, "you have to use the boiled water. Why, Gal," she chortled, "you could get amoeba in your twat."

Cathleen quickly raised the rum punch to her lips and took a huge swallow. She had visions of little bugs swimming around inside her. For a brief moment she wanted to bolt out of the house and run all the way back to New York. Mother of God, what had she gotten herself into?

"The Commissary has canned and frozen goods, so it's not like we're completely cut off from civilization out here. But the meat! Lord knows what they do to it because it's cut like you never saw it cut back in the

States." Nadine shook her head in disbelief, her combed waves quickly losing their vitality in the heat. "Just forget Porterhouse, don't even dream of Sirloin, honey. About the only recognizable cut they got down here is *Lomito*, Filet Mignon and that's delicious. But the rest, believe me gal, is a challenge to your cooking creativity."

She never mentioned Leg of Lamb, Cathleen realized. Her mouth watered remembering the Sunday roasts her mother prepared. She was about to ask Nadine if lamb was available in Venezuela when Nadine steered Cathleen toward the kitchen, continuing her non-stop monologue.

"You have to keep the spices separate from your other things. See here," and she opened the door of the end cabinet. "It has a light bulb in it to keep them dry. Otherwise the dampness will ruin them. Store sugar and flour in the refrigerator so the ants and bugs can't get to them. Put them in old mayonnaise jars. Forget the pretty canisters you got as a shower gift."

Ants? Bugs? Remembering her encounter with the frog last night, Cathleen started to feel queasy. My God, she was going to have a regular menagerie in her house. She took another healthy swig of rum punch.

"And after you've done all this," Nadine said sipping her rum punch slowly, "if things have bugs in them, don't pay them no never mind. You're going to swallow a lot more bugs than that before you leave this place. Besides which," she laughed, "if they're dead, what difference does it make? They can't eat much!"

That's a consolation. Oh Ma, you'd never believe what I'm hearing. Then Cathleen remembered her father's last words. She looked around at the other women. *If they can hack it, so can I.*

"Oh, you're gonna do just fine, honey," Nadine said looking approvingly at her. "Ryle is one lucky fellow to have found you. I could tell the moment I laid eyes on you there's no dust under your feet." Her smile grew wider. "And I just love the way you dress. My stars, you make the rest of us look like Zazu Pitts." The warmth of Nadines's words gave her a rush of confidence.

"Cathleen, where have you been? I want you to meet my former roommate." A mock grimace broke out on Ryle's face. "I'm sure glad I don't have to bunk with this character no more. Not only are you prettier, but you don't snore like him."

Standing next to Ryle, Murray Bluestein looked like the other half of Mutt and Jeff. His short, wiry body swept low in an elaborate bow. "*Enchanté*, Madam," he murmured in an unmistakable Bronx accent as he kissed her hand. Hearing a voice from home gave her even more confidence, making her feel she had a pal in this sea of southern drawls and western twangs. She immediately liked his cocky, brash manner.

"I gotta hand it to you, Ryle," Murray's mouth slanted into a crooked grin. "For once in your life you showed some taste. What she sees in you though, I don't know." He turned to Cathleen. "What's the story, Toots, didya feel sorry for him?"

Cathleen laughed, liking Murray even more and accepted his invitation to dance. "Stick with me, Toots, I'm a better hoofer than Ryle will ever be." It wasn't an idle boast. Not only was he a smooth dancer, but he sang along with the music coming out of the record player. Cathleen hearing the lyrics of *They Say That Falling in Love is Wonderful* thought how wonderful, indeed, it was.

"How long were you two roommates?" Cathleen asked him when the music stopped.

"Too long!" Murray shot back in mock horror. In a way, though there was a grain of truth to his statement. He thought back to his arrival in Chacari. In the beginning, he and Ryle hadn't hit it off. At first he wondered if Ryle was anti-Semitic. But as time went by, he realized that wasn't the problem. Ryle was a man of many moods.

"Why do you have to sing every morning?" Ryle would snarl. "Who needs an alarm clock? Every day I wake up hearing you chirping away like some fucking bluejay."

"Why not?" Murray replied, nonplused by Ryle's irritability. "Life has enough gritty moments without making it worse."

Whether it was because Murray learned to live with Ryle's moods or the contagiousness of his disposition softened Ryle, they wound up liking each other. They had little in common, yet this only enhanced their friendship. Murray, to relieve the boredom of camp life, looked on Ryle's moodiness as a challenge. In a short time his wisecracks had softened Ryle's disposition to the point where Ryle developed an admiration and affection for him. Murray was the one who could make him laugh at himself.

But like Ryle, Murray had grown up with the taste of poverty in his mouth. And in the East Bronx he learned early he had to stand up to trouble. Because he was the smallest kid on the block the bigger ones thought he was easy pickings until he showed them otherwise. He was such a scrapper his Uncle Moshe used to joke that if Murray had been around when the family fled from the Cossacks, they might have ridden out of Russia on horses instead of running.

Education was a sacred thing in his family and he promised his parents he would graduate from City College. Yet the Monday after Pearl Harbor, he took the subway to Times Square and enlisted in the Marines. His mother pleaded with him to finish out the year and get his degree in Accounting. It was a promise he would have to put on hold, he explained firmly. If he didn't do his part, there might not be a country left for any of them. He hadn't lost a fight yet, he assured them cockily, he would come through the war alive. Then he would finish college.

Like a lot of servicemen who passed through California on their way to the Pacific, he fell in love with the state and vowed he would return after the war. But his father's death a month after his discharge put a halt to that dream. He was at loose ends trying to keep the family afloat until he saw Palm Oil's ad in the New York Times for accounting trainees. Then everything fell into place. He'd go to Venezuela, send money home to his family and salt away the rest. After two contracts he'd have enough to head to California, finish up his degree and start his own accounting firm.

Because he'd fought on one isolated island after another in the Pacific, the remoteness of the oilfields wasn't intolerable. There weren't any Jap bullets to dodge and the only real problems were the boredom and loneliness. He coped with them as the other bachelors in camp did, he frequented *La Luna de Oro*, the local whorehouse, otherwise known as the Looney Door. A name coined by Buck Henderson, a driller whose attempt to speak Spanish was never quite successful. Declaring the name was a mouthful of shit, he promptly christened it the Looney Door.

Looking at Cathleen, he told himself Ryle was one lucky guy. Holding her in his arms as they danced was pure bliss. They were the same height for Cathleen had on flat sandals and the sight of her lips just a few inches away had him dreaming. Why, her mouth is right out of Esquire magazine, he decided, she's a regular Petty Girl. Soft and sensual like a rose bud. Except he couldn't imagine her posing in a provocative way.

She was too elegant for that.

He was twirling her around, doing his great dip which always guaranteed a few laughs when he noticed Ryle dancing with Sugar Dalhart, the camp superintendent's wife. The words of *Fools Rush In Where Angels Fear to Tread* coming out of the record player jolted him into looking at Ryle and Sugar more closely. It also turned him from a neutral observer of oil camp society into one of its principal players. He knew too well Ryle's sex drive was always in high gear. You'd better not run around on Cathleen, he thought. And you'd better keep your pecker away from Sugar Dalhart. It was no secret the camp super's wife adored flirting with the bachelors and he'd always had a hunch that Ryle was Sugar's favorite. And that somehow in the goldfish bowl life of Chacari, where gossip was everyone's hobby, Sugar had let Ryle get into her pants without the rest of the camp finding out.

But he also saw that despite Ryle's marriage, Sugar had no intention of staying away from him. Her arms were wound tightly around Ryle's neck as they danced, her thin almost boyish body so close to his, Murray thought disapprovingly, not even a piece of tissue paper could be inserted between them. Her laughter, Ryle bending down to catch the words she whispered, her every gesture displayed such intimacy Murray felt embarrassed for Cathleen. Shit on a stick, what the hell was the matter with Ryle? It was one thing to respond to Sugar's flirtations when he was single. But now with his bride of less than two weeks on full display for the whole camp, Ryle was setting her up to be the target of nasty gossip. Murray's eyes darted around the room, catching Wilma Wilcox following Sugar and Ryle's every move. That old biddy, he fretted, she's one of the biggest gossips in camp.

He had to break up that hot *tamale* situation, right now. Steering Cathleen towards them, Murray tapped Ryle on the shoulder. "I'm reluctantly returning your wife to you." Then he deftly pulled Sugar into his arms.

"You've been avoiding me, you little Magnolia Blossom you,' he said flirtatiously to Sugar. The strains of *Siboney* floated through the smoke filled living room. "Let's show them how a rhumba should be danced," he whispered in her ear, knowing how she loved to be the center of attention.

Sugar glared at him. "If I wanted to dance with you, Murray," her

South Carolina accent almost hissed the words, "I'd have let you know."

"Swivel your hips more, Sugar," he instructed, ignoring her anger. "Don't move your shoulders so much. That's the difference between amateurs and smooth dancers." His lead was so strong she couldn't break away from him gracefully.

"Are you telling me how to dance the *rhumba*?" she asked him scornfully. "I'm not some Latin from Manhattan. Remember, honey, I was born in this country."

Murray shrugged his shoulders, grinning idiotically. "So I'm not in training for the diplomatic corps." He leaned forward, whispering in her ear. "You're going to give every guy in this room heart failure."

"D'ya think so?" she replied, the pleasure shining out of her overly large hazel eyes.

"I know so," he purred, relieved her vanity and short attention span had won her over. "Every guy in camp is crazy about you, especially yours truly."

"Why, Murray," she laughed, drawling her words. "I declare, I never knew you felt this way." Her eyes ran shrewdly over his lithe body, admiring his black, curly hair and olive complexion. "Those eyes of yours are somethin' else," she giggled.

Now, he thought wearily, this two-bits cracker is going to tell me I have bedroom eyes. When she did, he responded with a lazy smile. Careful, he told himself, don't let this get out of hand. He couldn't believe what he was doing, leading the super's wife on so she would forget about Rylander. He looked around the room, searching out her husband. Emmett Dalhart, the salt of the earth, the perfect gentleman who had the distinction of being the only person in camp no one ever badmouthed. And who also was the only person unaware of his wife's roving eye. To him she was just having a good time, laughing and joking and making everyone's life a little brighter, the way she did his.

By this time Cathleen was feeling no pain. Being with Murray was so effortless, not only because he carried the conversational ball but she didn't have to pretend to be someone she wasn't. She was happy though to be back in Ryle's arms as Harry James' rendition of *It Had to be You* floated through the room. Ecstatic was more the word. She snuggled closer to him, his embrace making her feel loved and secure.

But she wasn't in his arms for very long. Just as the women had rushed over this morning with their offering of baked goods, now the men, married and single, made a run to dance with her. Not only for the obvious reasons, but they welcomed her presence as a diversion from the hunting stories they'd been swapping. For Venezuela was a hunter's paradise. Rich territory for bird shooting (doves and ducks) as well as jaguars and tigers. In the western Andes deer roamed freely while trout jumped in the cool, mountain streams. The Caribbean which washed ashore in the northern part of the country was home to *pargo*, red snapper and grouper. And for the more adventuresome there were sharks, sailfish and tarpon to land. This was something the men could escape to whenever the oilfields began to feel too confining. Ironically, their isolation was the reason game was in such abundance, the lack of cities and roads in the country's interior, the wide open spaces which stretched endlessly to the horizon.

And when they weren't swapping hunting and fishing tales or talking about women, the bachelors were always bemoaning the absence of single, American women; hence their dependence on the brothels not only for their sexual but also their social needs. Then their conversation turned to the one thing from which they could never escape — their work. To relieve the monotony they traded jokes, those most recently returning from the States or Caracas having an edge on the others. If they ran out of new ones, old stories were resurrected, it being an unwritten rule that no matter how often a joke was told, it was always greeted as a new one.

So Cathleen's entry into their lives was like a breath of fresh air. They all agreed Rylander had landed a beauty. Even those who didn't especially like him (he wasn't the most popular guy in camp for his blatant ambition rankled more than a few), admired his bride. Later, when Cathleen's shyness, which didn't melt until she had a few drinks, manifested itself in an aloofness the other women resented, the men still maintained their loyalty and admiration, as if they had a model or movie star in their midst.

Those were Fred Hardesty's thoughts when he asked her to dance. Though counting the days until he could return to Maruja next month, he was smitten with Cathleen's cool, blond beauty. She, floating on a rum punch cloud, found Fred to be the best dancer she'd ever come across, outshining even Murray. She had no trouble following him in steps which up to now had only been names to her. When she complimented him on his expertise in the *rhumba, guaracha, tango* and *mambo*, he just grinned, blessing all the Ladies of the Happy Life for teaching him the intricacies of Latin American dancing. When the music changed to a lindy, a dance she didn't know very well, Fred made it easy, as if she'd been doing it all her life. The fast beat of Al Dexter's *Pistol Packing Mama*, the Merry Macs' *Mairzy Doats* and Glenn Miller's smooth trombone leading *A String of Pearls* and *Little Brown Jug* filled the room. Conversation faded as everyone's attention gravitated to the center of Sugar Dalhart's living room to watch Fred and Rylander's new bride cut a rug. He's so smooth, Cathleen thought gratefully, barely feeling Fred's arms behind her back, his hand pushing her firmly but gently out, then pulling her effortlessly back into the circle of his arms. Her feet never missed a beat, and as she ducked her head under his arms for a spin she felt like she was gliding on ice skates.

Then the Andrews Sisters heated things up with *Hold Tight*. Lost in the music, Cathleen didn't realize what happened until she heard people clapping, saw Ryle staring in amazement and then pride. Caught up in the heat of the action, following her partner's lead, she didn't notice Fred pick her up, lift her over his shoulders, throw her down through his legs and pull her out again, where her feet picked up the beat. As if they'd been dance partners from the year one. When the music ended, the whole party erupted into applause.

"Let's try that again," Fred cried out exuberantly, his high pitched laughter filling the room.

Cathleen backed away. "Let's not and say we did," she laughed. He's adorable, she thought, so cute and friendly she knew they would wind up the best of friends. Still, no matter how much Fred cajoled, and he was almost irresistible in his youthful zest, she held firm. The thought of flying over his shoulders again made her dizzy. Most of all, though, she was embarrassed to be the center of so much attention. She longed for a quiet corner where she could fade into a group, be shielded from everyone's admiring eyes. She wasn't comfortable with the spotlight thrust so suddenly on her.

Across the living room, standing near the makeshift bar set up on the dining room buffet, Sugar Dalhart looked Cathleen up and down. In spite of being the hostess, Sugar had barely bothered with her. She'd greeted Cathleen in an overfriendly manner when they arrived, then completely ignored her, making no attempt to make her feel welcome as the other women did, nor take her under her wing as Nadine had done. Now seeing her the object of everyone's admiration, which heretofore had been her domain, she meant to rectify things.

"Cathleen," she drawled innocently, "how come your dress is so long?" She laughed when she said it, but there was an undertone to her words, almost as if she had said, 'How come your underwear is so dirty?' People looked around nervously, women patted their hair, men bit their lips. They all stood still as if frozen in a movie which had been stopped. No one talked or moved. They were all plainly embarrassed.

"Why . . . ." Sugar's voice hit her like a bucket of ice water. "Because," she replied, knowing instinctively something was not quite right, "that's the fashion now."

What had she done wrong? Ryle told her Sugar was friendly and full of fun, and how important it was to become friends with her since she was the super's wife. But, for some reason, she had antagonized her because there was no mistaking the malice in Sugar's voice. Cathleen continued, somewhat confused, as she struggled with an explanation, "It's called the New Look."

"Well, shoot," Sugar smiled innocently, thoroughly enjoying the discovery of Cathleen's vulnerability, "what's wrong with the old look? Men like to look at legs. Don't they, Ryle?" And she kicked her leg out, circling it in front of her teasingly.

Murray groaned inwardly. Now he knew how Sugar would react to Ryle's marriage. She's so jealous of Cathleen, she's gonna puke green. Not only because Ryle had deserted the bachelor ranks for Cathleen, but she's such a classy dame, something Sugar could never be. He saw Ryle hesitate. The son of a bitch, Murray fumed, the asshole is afraid of antagonizing the super's wife. Helplessly he watched the bewilderment on Cathleen's face. Go get her, Toots, he urged her silently, go get that cracker bitch and show her she doesn't know what messing with a New Yorker is. But Cathleen hadn't grown up in the jungle of the city streets. She stood there feeling as if her clothes had been stripped away and she was on display in Macy's windows.

"Isn't that right, Ryle? Men like to look at legs." Sugar persistently egged him on, continuing to kick her leg out, daring him to answer, which so far he hadn't. He still hesitated and in those moments of indecision,

Cathleen saw her knight in shining armor slip a little from the saddle of his white horse.

"A lady never shows her wares," a strong voice boomed out. It belonged to the camp character, Pet Ford, who didn't care how she spoke to anyone, much less the super's wife. "That is," Pet continued pointedly, "if she *is* a real lady."

Sugar, ignoring Pet's remarks, continued to taunt Ryle. Then he found his voice. "Of course when a lady has legs as pretty as yours Sugar, they're hard to ignore," he said smoothly. Sugar's leg slid to the floor, a smile of victory on her face. Cigarettes were lit, drinks raised to sweating lips and conversation returned as the women swapped maid stories and men talked shop.

Murray, standing near the kitchen door, struggled with his anger. There were a million ways you could have answered her, he wanted to shout at Ryle. If you had any balls, you would have put that bitch in her place. But, no, you're so consumed with ambition, you'll kiss ass any time it's shoved in your face. Seeing the hurt on Cathleen's puzzled face, he longed to put his arms around her and soothe away her distress. But Ryle was there, his face bent down to hers.

"Hey, pardner," Ryle whispered lovingly, "I like the New Look, the Cathleen Look, or whatever you call it. That's 'cause you're such a classy lady."

"She made me feel awful the way she singled me out," Cathleen cried out in bewilderment, "as if she deliberately wanted to make fun of me."

"Naw," he insisted. "That's just Sugar. She likes to joke around."

"She didn't act like she was joking," she insisted.

"Forget it, baby," he urged her. "Listen, sometimes you got to swallow a little bit of pride if you want to get ahead. And don't let people see you all tore up like this. Smile, be the lady I fell in love with."

Cathleen's cool and sophisticated mask slipped over her face. Dancing in Ryle's arms to the slow strains of Dick Haynes crooning *Those Little White Lies* made her feel the lyrics had been written just for this occasion. As soon as the song came to an end, she fled to the bathroom, still stung by Sugar's baiting. The friendliness shown her by the other women and Nadine's warmth in orientating her to life in the oilfields had been forgotten. What confused her most was Ryle's fawning over Sugar.

There was a stool in the bathroom belonging to Sugar's two year old son, Drew, and she sank down on it, grateful to be alone and away from the crowd outside. She lit a cigarette hoping it would relax her, help her figure out why Sugar didn't like her, and ease the nagging little notion that maybe she didn't really know the man who acted so differently tonight from the Ryle she'd fallen in love with. She dreaded returning to the din of the party and lit another cigarette, finding the stool, despite her long legs, more and more of a comfort. She half wished she could hide in the bathroom for the remainder of the evening. But with one bathroom and a house full of rum-filled bladders, she soon discovered it was impossible.

When she walked into the living room, Pet Ford of the booming voice came up to her. "Don't pay attention to that one," she said nodding towards Sugar. "She ain't nothin' but a spoiled brat who thinks she's the Queen Bee." She put her hand in Cathleen's and Cathleen noticed it was hard and calloused.

"Come on over to this friendly circle of people," Pet urged her. "There are a few of us around, y'know. I was just telling Emmajean that mebbe she shouldn't worry so much about putting on weight. God didn't cut us out of no cookie mold. Like I can't help it that I'm big and fat anymore than Murray here can help it that he's so little and weak and puny." She reached over and tweaked Murray's nose affectionately. "Ain't that right, kid?"

Murray laughed. Pet was one of his favorite people, mainly because she wasn't a social climber or a malicious gossip.

"Anyway, size don't have nothin' to do with being a man, a real man," Pet continued. "Look at my Pete over there, that sweet old fart, ain't nobody like him." Her eyes became soft and warm. "I remember when he proposed and Mama sez to me, 'ain't he too short for you?' And you know what I told her?"

She snorted disdainfully. "I told her it don't matter none how short he was, as long as he wasn't short where it matters the most." Her snort changed to laughter causing her large stomach and breasts to shake. "Which I can tell you, he ain't."

Everyone laughed. Cathleen's face turned crimson and Murray seeing the blush, whispered in her ear. "Did she embarrass you?"

"She told us something so intimate about her husband," Cathleen whispered back.

"But she was giving him a compliment," he grinned. "Look at it that way."

Pet marched over to her husband, who was with a group of men having a contest to see which one could tell the dirtiest joke.

"Come on, darlin', let's do a little dancing." Pet smiled coquettishly down at her husband. "What a bunch of old ladies we got here. A party ain't a party unless everyone dances and has themselves a right good time."

She pulled the protesting Pete into her arms and deftly tucked him under her sprawling breasts. Grinning he followed her to the middle of the room and then surprisingly led her. For a large woman she was very light on her feet and she followed him as if she were a feather of a woman dancing with a bear of a man.

Pet claimed to be part Cherokee. Looking at her one was more inclined to think of a warrior than a squaw, for her arms were powerful, her shoulders wide, and when she walked her long legs took strides rather than steps. Her husband, short and skinny, didn't claim to be anyone other than an Okie who didn't know and didn't give a damn who his ancestors were. They'd worked the Oklahoma oilfields together, she beside him driving their truck while he secured the orders. When they made deliveries — for that was their business, supplying small parts for the rigs — she would carry them off the truck to the well site. Now looking for security in their approaching retirement years (they'd made and lost their money a few times over), they'd come to Venezuela for the big money.

There was a true affection between them, although she had an odd way of showing it. Mainly because she called him 'that old fart', causing him to smile and grin back at her adoringly as if she had whispered the sweetest endearment in his ears.

In his way he was just as colorful. He never learned Spanish, speaking only in English to his native helpers in the warehouse. Surprisingly enough, they understood every word he said. When people asked him when was he going to learn Spanish, his stock reply was, "I've been here three years and them sumbitches ain't learnt English yet."

Cathleen laughed along with the others at the antics of the Fords. "They're better than a floor show," she told Murray, momentarily forgetting Sugar.

"How's my girl?" Ryle said, slipping his arms around her. "Watch out for Romeo here," he said nodding at Murray. "He thinks he's God's gift to women."

"Listen, jughead," Murray snapped back, "for once you did the right thing in picking out Cathleen. She's a very special lady. Though what she sees in you, I'll never understand. You lucked out this time. Don't blow it." He spoke in the bantering tone they always used with each other, but there was an undercurrent, almost a warning, in his words.

"Having a good time?" Ryle asked her.

"I never laughed so hard in my life. That Pet is a real character."

"Yeah well, that she is. But I don't want you socializing with her. You gotta mix, baby, with those people who count. We should make the rounds and join Sugar and Emmett. Then over to the Fickets, Nadine and George. He's the head man in the geology department out here. No big guns from Caracas tonight, so we got to concentrate on the local fish. And then afterwards, I want you to go and talk to everyone, especially those sitting by themselves. Make them feel that you care about each and every one of them. Just because some of the ladies are cliquish, I don't want you to be that way."

Murray, listening to Ryle, empathized with the bewilderment he saw on Cathleen's face.

"I don't want you spending too much time with those who don't count, like Pet for instance," Ryle continued. "You can be friendly, but don't waste time on them. Just enough so they'll like you. I want you to wind up being the most popular woman in camp. Because word of it will filter through to Caracas, which will make them even more aware of me. And that will help my career."

Now he's telling Cathleen she has to make like some damn socialite, Murray thought irritably. She's not that type at all, doesn't he see that?

"You also got to figure out who might be helpful later on," Ryle explained. "Take Fred Hardesty, for instance. You know the guy who did that Lindy with you. Right now he's a nobody, just another engineer. But the rumor is he's got a girl in Caracas whose wealthy Venezuelan family owns *beaucoup* property; just about half of eastern Venezuela, I hear. He might marry her. People like that we've got to cultivate 'cause you never know when they'll come in handy.

"Wow, heavy artillery," Murray commented, hoping to dispel the concern he saw in Cathleen's face. "Tote dat barge, Toots, bale dat cotton." Then looking at Ryle he remarked, "You're not serious, are you?"

"Sure I am," Ryle replied. "If you were staying with the company, you'd be just as ambitious."

"I don't think so," Murray shook his head. "Oh, I'd be ambitious, but I wouldn't go about it the way you are. I certainly wouldn't expect my wife to carry me. I'd have enough confidence to do it on my own."

"Speaking of wives, I was trying to have a private conversation with mine," Ryle glared at him. "So knock it off."

It wasn't the first time Ryle had snarled at him. And Murray with his unflappable mellow disposition could always turn things around. With a joke or some nonsensical remark he could ease the tension between them. Now, though, he wanted to smash Ryle's face in, make him eat dirt for the crap he was shoving at Cathleen. Telling her how to behave, practically making a list of the people she could or couldn't associate with. And then seeing the look of dismay on her face, he realized he had to lighten up things. Shrugging nonchalantly he danced a little on the balls of his feet, but for the first time in his life he was nonplused. The wisecracks which were always on the tip of his tongue had deserted him. A few moments passed, they felt like hours, then a lopsided grin broke out on his face as he tried to get the juices going inside him again.

"Masked Man," Murray grunted. He'd nicknamed Ryle the Lone Ranger when he found out he was from Oklahoma. "No need to get on Silver's high horse. We smokum peace pipe, Kemosabay."

Ryle looked warily at him, then a smile crept across his face. It was impossible to stay angry with Murray.

Standing between them Cathleen felt a little uneasy. The whole night had been so crazy she was beginning to feel a little punch drunk and it wasn't from the rum. The strain of meeting so many people, Sugar's taunts, Ryle's pointing out the people she had to cultivate, and now this hint of an argument between two men who were the best of friends. The best of friends, she wondered, until she came into the picture? She felt the tension between them and it disturbed her, as if something had started over which she had no control.

She watched Murray walk towards another group of people. She and Ryle made the rounds, making small talk. Then when Murray left, she felt like a sleepwalker going through the motions, at a loss without his friendly presence. Later when they got home and Ryle reached out for her in bed, she hesitated for a few seconds, wondering if some of the magic was gone from their marriage. But she quickly pushed aside her qualms. His words of endearment were too sweet, his voice which always thrilled her, still had its hypnotic power. And his touch had so much hunger she loved him back more passionately than ever, hoping it would wipe away all the uncertainties which the evening had created. That with this act of union she could keep them at bay. She had to hold on to the magic, she whispered to herself, if she kept it alive, no harm could come to their marriage.

When Murray walked in the Looney Door he pushed away the whores. He wanted one and yet he didn't. He almost left, but the thought of returning to the abysmal loneliness of the bachelor quarters kept him there. Then he saw one they called *La Rubia*, the blond one. He remembered her as a loud mouthed, talkative German, whose raucous voice always grated on his nerves. One he never gave his money to. But he changed his mind tonight. His only stipulation was she couldn't talk. If she opened her mouth, he warned her, the deal was off. He gave her money to play every slow piece in the jukebox. They danced until she thought her feet would fall off. And then when he had so much rum in him he thought the pain was gone, he took her to bed, where he swept the lamp off the nightstand, heard it crash on the floor, and in the darkness tried to pretend she was anyone but an oil patch whore.

EIGHT

The sight of cockroaches running across the floors sickened Cathleen, but no more than the smell of Flit which had to be sprayed daily. Because of the humidity it clung to the air long after the maid sprayed, while the musty smell of mildew rose from the mattress and pillows. Once a week the DDT truck went through camp, leaving a film on everything and the odor made her gag even more. She learned to sift flour before using it so the dead bugs could be thrown out. Preparation was required not only in the kitchen, but also in dressing. Ryle shook out his boots and shoes each morning, for scorpions and tarantulas loved to nest in their dark recesses. She also discovered tropical living required constant vigilance and nerves which didn't fray easily.

She found this out just a week after her arrival. She had returned some *Look* magazines to Nadine, and coming home she lingered outside because a delightful breeze rustled the night air. She heard something clicking, but thinking it was just another night noise, she walked leisurely up to the house. Then sensing that someone was following her, she quickened her pace. The clicking sound had become more persistent. After she closed the screen door, she called to Ryle.

"What's that noise?" she asked pointing outside. Then she saw it. A rattlesnake, its back arched ready to strike. She stifled an urge to scream.

Ryle went quickly for his gun and opening the door he shot the snake's head off. Cathleen brushed aside her fear of what might have happened if she'd stayed too long outside. She concentrated instead on the thought that now she had something to talk about at the next coffee. She wouldn't have to comb her brain wondering what tidbit she could contribute to the conversation.

Something she didn't have to worry about on Wednesday and Sunday nights when the camp went to the movies. With no radio programs to amuse them, the movies were their window to the outside world. Folding bridge chairs were placed in pickups, covered with old sheets to protect them from the dust, and brought into the clubhouse. When Cathleen first saw the building she understood the need for chairs, for the few pieces of furniture were outcasts from the houses. Compared to the Creole Petroleum clubhouse in Jusepin which looked like it belonged in a posh country club (she and Ryle had gone to a square dance there her first weekend in Chacari) the one in Chacari resembled something thrown together for a poverty stricken relative. There were no walls, just wooden posts supporting a tin roof, with screening wrapped around to keep out the bugs. The bar, which had no stools, was a plank over a few empty oil drums.

When Laurence Olivier's *Hamlet* was shown, Cathleen was surprised at the rapt attention it received. She thought since it was Shakespeare, a subject most kids squirmed through in high school, people would be bored. But they sat, fascinated. Afterwards she realized why. In the oilfields people took movies seriously, no matter what was playing. They plunked down their money with the same fervor and enthusiasm the early movie goers did with silent flicks. For a few hours they escaped to another world. When the lights came back on, they returned to reality. The bar became crowded, some men playing Liars Dice. At the tables people talked about the latest party. There was always someone who got smashed, or did something funny and invariably suffered a terrible hangover the next day, vowing never to drink again. Various cures were discussed, anything from a Prairie Dog to beer mixed with ginger ale. Others vowed if they took B-12 pills they never woke up with a hangover, while one claimed if he drank rum with milk he never suffered. Tonight, though, there was a lot of talk about the lindy she and Fred had danced. Fred throwing her over his shoulder had the camp buzzing for weeks.

Cathleen was deluged with invitations to morning coffees, cocktail parties, dinners and afternoon bridge games, even though she didn't play the game. Making conversation was still an excruciating effort, and becoming more difficult as time went by. She found that seeing the same people every day she quickly ran out of things to say. The only exceptions were the parties where a drink always helped her over the hurdles.

The parties started out with the men on one side of the room talking shop, the women on the other side comparing maids or talking about their children. As the evening progressed and people loosened up with rum punches, their tight little world expanded. Taking a drink not only quenched their thirst, it brought a feeling of instant camaraderie. Some claimed it was the only way to survive in the tropics, that if one drank enough it killed all kinds of amoeba and prevented dysentery. Whether that was true was a moot point. But it brought a lot of fun into their isolated way of life.

Cathleen realized this and because she wanted to be accepted, she looked on a drink as her passport. And if part of the game to get Ryle out of the oilfields and into Caracas was becoming a social asset to him at parties, she didn't want to be left off the team.

The women had an unspoken contest to outdo each other when they entertained, for time hung heavy on their hands. It gave a little juice to their lives. They poured over their cookbooks, looking for the one recipe that would be different from what they'd eaten at the last party.

Everyone looked forward to the weekends. Starting work at seven in the morning to avoid the heat made for early bedtime hours during the week. But as soon as the whistle blew at noon on Saturday, the adults, except those working on rigs, were ready to party. A few men went home first for lunch. Most headed for the club. The cups and dice came out for Liars Dice. Or just craps. It was mainly petty ante. But occasionally on a Saturday someone would go for broke. And if they lost a bundle in a poker game, it became the main topic of conversation that week.

After dinner the Saturday night party commenced. If there wasn't a house party somewhere in camp, then people went back to the clubhouse. Records were brought from home. Women got dressed up in evening dresses and men in jackets and ties. They might be living in the middle of nowhere with no place to go, but people refused to let it affect their morale, they dressed as if they were members of the most elite country club.

By the end of the first week Cathleen had been in just about every house in camp. Since they were all alike, most of the women tried to put their stamp of individuality on their homes. The ones who had survived the first two years and returned after stateside leave brought back pictures, throw rugs to cover the ugly red cement floors and pillows to hide the faded rattan cushions. The more enterprising ones made slipcovers, while others cut out large squares of material and then pinned them to the bottoms and backs of the cushions. This way, when they were transferred to another camp, it was a simple matter of unpinning the material and taking it with them. Some women put up curtains, others didn't bother for they felt the wooden jalousie louvers were enough. One woman just returned from the States put up the latest rage, paper curtains. The ones whose husbands had worked the oilfields in Peru, Ecuador, Argentina and Mexico had beautiful wall hangings and *llama* rugs, along with silver tea and coffee sets, for silver was plentiful and inexpensive in Latin America.

Coming home from a coffee one morning Cathleen passed a house she hadn't been in, although it was directly behind hers. The yard stood out from the others because of its garden. Whoever lived there had a definite green thumb. Pink hibiscus bushes bordered the house and a red bougainvillea was being trained to form an archway over the front door. The hedge surrounding the lot wasn't scraggly as some of the others in camp, but thick and lush looking. As she walked past, a woman looked up from the orange hibiscus flowers she was snipping. Cathleen stopped, fascinated by the woman's Madonna-like face. Large brown eyes crinkled with warmth, while the cleft in her chin gave a distinctive air to her face. Cathleen's first thought was she must do a lot of sunbathing for her cinnamon-hued skin contrasted sharply with her lemon colored sundress.

"Would you like some flowers?" the women called out. "By nightfall they close up and die, but I can always give you more." She spoke with a definite accent.

"How sweet of you," Cathleen replied taking the flowers. "I hate to admit this, but I can't remember where I met you. I've met so many people since I arrived in camp. You're. . . ."

"Sarita Maguire," the woman replied.

The maid came around the side of the house and a torrent of Spanish was exchanged.

"Oh, you speak such beautiful Spanish," Cathleen remarked, absolutely fascinated by Sarita. "I'm waiting for our personal effects to arrive. I have the Berlitz Spanish course on records." She found it difficult to take her eyes off Sarita's striking features, still trying to remember where she'd met her. "Do you play cards? Perhaps that's where I met you, at one of the bridges or maybe one of the morning coffees?"

"No, I don't think so," Sarita replied shaking her head. "I rarely go out, there's too much to do here." She pointed to the garden. "And inside the house. I'm always trying to make it a little prettier."

"Well, if it's anything like the outside," Cathleen said looking in admiration at the garden, "it must be gorgeous."

Sensing Cathleen's curiosity, Sarita invited her inside. Following her into the house, Cathleen had the feeling she entered a bit of paradise. It was the same basic furniture everyone had, but the rattan living room pieces had been varnished with shellac and the cushions covered in a green Chinese print. The dining room set was painted Chinese red. Small rugs were scattered over the cement floors. A print scarf of an Oriental teahouse, which had been stretched and framed, hung over the sofa; while other "pictures" had been created with bits of colored fabric — a still life of fruit, a beach at sunset, a smiling puppy.

"I have no talent as a painter," Sarita explained, "so I create pictures with cloth."

"I've never seen anything like them," Cathleen shook her head in amazement. "It takes real talent to create something like that." She was enchanted with Sarita's house. "How clever of you," she exclaimed walking over to the windows to examine the cafe curtains. "They give you privacy, yet let in the light as well as the air."

But the best part was the master bedroom. The ugly, steel gray furniture had been painted a soft yellow, so soft it had an ivory tinge to it. The bedspread was a riot of flowers, with the cafe curtains picking up its dominant color.

"It looks just like a garden in here," Cathleen's hands flew out enthusiastically. "I'd love to show my husband. Could I bring him over?"

"*Mi casa es su casa,*" Sarita replied graciously.

"*Mi casa* is what?"

"It means my house is your house," Sarita explained. "That you are always welcome here."

"Oh, how sweet. How do you say that?" She repeated the phrase a few times. "My first Spanish lesson!"

The second bedroom was a combination workshop and study. A sewing machine sat on a table and newspapers were spread out under a chest of drawers, which was in the process of being painted. In the corner books were spread out on a desk. Because reading was her passion,

Cathleen automatically walked over and examined them.

Sarita smiled shyly. "The Maguire School."

"You're kidding. You're studying English poetry?" She looked at Sarita in admiration. "No wonder you don't have time for all the coffee klatches. You're learning this all by yourself?"

"Oh, no," Sarita replied with pride. "My husband is *mi profesor*."

They both heard the pickup drive into the carport and a voice call out, "Soogie, where are you?"

Walking back to the living room Cathleen met Sarita's husband and she was immediately struck by their great love for each other. John Maguire's eyes sparkled when he looked at Sarita, while she hung on to his every word. Cathleen knew it was time to go home, yet she hated to leave. When they invited her to stay for lunch, an invitation she was sure had been extended because she lingered, she accepted gratefully. Sarita's serene personality continued to intrigue her, while John's Irish face made her feel she was home. Why, she thought happily, he could be anyone in her family, a feeling strengthened by his sense of humor which had a wicked bent to it, somewhat like her uncle, Charley Cavenaugh. Being with them, she decided, was like visiting her favorite relatives. As they waited for the maid to serve lunch, John regaled them with a story about his grandfather.

"The old man was a holy terror, you never knew what was going to come out of his mouth. He was doing some carpentry work at the Cathedral and he came home one night and says to my grandmother, who was a very devout Catholic, 'You know Rosie, today I was working down in the crypt'."

Maguire's eyes sparkled with mischief, Cathleen sensed he was enjoying the punch line before he even got to it. "And my grandmother says to him, 'Glory be to God, working so near the graves of the Monsignor and Father Dougherty, what fine company you was in today, Joe'.

"And then he replied, for he loved to shock her, 'And you know what, Rosie? They stank just as much as you and me will'. Well, one hell of a fight broke out between them. She wouldn't speak to him for days after that."

"Now I know where it comes from," Sarita laughed.

"You mean the way I'm always shooting off my mouth?" he asked.

"I guess you're right. The apple doesn't fall far from the tree."

"Oh," Cathleen's eyes beamed. "I haven't heard that expression in years. My grandmother always used it." More and more she felt as if they had known each other for a long time. Not only was she delighted with their company, but until she met the Maguires, Cathleen hadn't found anyone in Chacari with her passion for reading. Even though Ryle was a college graduate he never read books, only magazines, and it made her aware of the wide gap between them. Though it didn't stop her from loving him, she was lonely sometimes for intellectual companionship.

....

When John left for work, he was pleased Sarita had found an appreciative audience, for he thought there was no one like her. She never ceased to amaze him how quickly she learned to read and write in Spanish and then English. She insisted it was because he was such a good teacher, but he knew it was more than that. She was so bright and possessed an innate concentration, the likes of which he'd rarely seen before. He hated to think how her life would have turned out if they hadn't met.

But he wondered about Cathleen Rylander and how long her interest in Sarita would last. He knew too well how the camp regarded his wife. Because of this he and Sarita kept to themselves, except to play bridge with Pete and Pet Ford. Maybe Cathleen will be different, he hoped, she and Sarita certainly hit it off immediately.

It would be different, he thought angrily, if Sugar Dalhart weren't always planting those sly innuendos about Sarita's past. What right did that sanctimonious bitch have to make judgment on his wife? If only she knew the horrors of Sarita's childhood, maybe she'd show a little more compassion. *Oh yeah, the esteemed Mrs. Dalhart is going to make like some Sister of Charity. Dream on, Maguire!* He angrily reached for a Camel, cracking open his Zippo lighter as if it were the cause of all his pent up frustration. Then inhaling the cigarette deeply he felt the anger slowly slide away. He began to blow smoke rings. Watching the smoke flutter out the pickup window, he remembered another time when he'd used the little smoke ring trick to quiet his mind.

It was the day he brought Sarita back to Hortensia's after their three days together. He frowned as he recalled the empty feeling he experienced sitting on the dock in Maracaibo, waiting for the ferry to come in, hating every minute it got closer. Then his frown changed to a soft smile with the memory of what happened next. The ferry docked, he reluctantly started to drive up the ramp, then impulsively he made a decision. He just couldn't go off without Sarita. No matter what the obstacles were, he was going back for her.

The confusion he caused, the traffic jam which ensued, all this came back to him. Racing up *Avenida Bella Vista*, becoming impatient with the traffic, he switched to 5 *de Julio Boulevard*. And when he finally arrived at Hortensia's, he jumped down from the cab of his pickup, ran up to the front door and frantically rang the bell. It was *siesta* time and the window shutters were semi-closed. No one answered the bell; he started pounding loudly on the door. Eventually it opened and the elderly laundress, her hands wet with soap, showed her face. She shook her head angrily and told him to come back later. These crazy *petroleros*, she muttered angrily, didn't they knew it was *siesta* time? He paid no attention to her protests, demanding to see Sarita. Finally he stormed into the house, calling out her name, going from room to room. By now the whole house was awake, the whores coming out of their rooms to see what was happening, some thinking another revolution had started. The madam's appearance stopped him from going any further.

"I've got to see Sarita," he insisted. She was about to tell him no one ever disrupted her establishment, but she saw something in his eyes which told her she could bend the rules this time. Going upstairs, they found Sarita returning from the shower. "Now keep it quiet, we're all trying to rest," Hortensia snapped, pushing them both into Sarita's room and closing the door.

"*¿Tu quieres venir conmigo?*" When she didn't answer him, he asked her again, "Do you want to come away with me?"

For a moment Sarita couldn't talk because she was so shocked seeing him again. "Go where?" Her voice came out in a whisper.

"To the *Oriente*, to eastern Venezuela where the company is transferring me."

"You want me to go with you?" she replied incredulously. He hired her for a few days and now he returned and wanted her for a longer period of time. Not only that, he wanted to take her clear across the country.

He realized she was confused. He knew what he wanted, and in his impatience he assumed she understood. "Sarita, I want you to be my woman," he explained gently. "That's why I'm asking you to come away with me."

She knew some of the whores retired and went off with a man. But it never lasted and they always came back to the profession. Now this *petrolero* wanted her to go off with him, but one day he would leave her, either to go back to his country or for another woman. It had been difficult enough parting from him after a few days. Imagine, she told herself, how it would hurt after being together a few months. No, she would never go off with him. Then when Maguire started talking again, she found his words even more unbelievable.

"Oh, my *Sarita Linda*, I still haven't told you my feelings. But it's only because I didn't recognize them myself until a short time ago." He caressed her face, his fingers tracing her lips, her high cheekbones, resting finally in the cleft of her chin. "Waiting for the ferry, I couldn't stop thinking of you. And then I realized that I cared too much to ever leave you."

Seeing the fear in her eyes, he took her in his arms, holding her close, running his fingers through her damp hair. With her warm body in his arms, he felt that all was right in the world.

She broke away, shaking her head. "I know what I am. Someone you hired for a few days. Now you think you want me for a longer time. *Gracias* for asking. I will always treasure the memory. But we come from two different worlds. I know it, but I don't think you do."

"Ah, that's one of the things I love about you, *Sarita Linda*," he smiled, "that incredibly intelligent, sensitive mind of yours. It hasn't been educated in the formal sense, but it has so much potential I think you will run far ahead of me one day. I know who you are, and I don't care." He kissed her gently. "I just know I want to spend the rest of my life with you. However long it is, it has to be with you." His words thrilled her, but she knew one day he would leave her. He was unaware of her feelings, though, for he was too keyed up by his decision to return for her. He didn't know what he cared for most, her soft brown body or her sweet disposition. All he knew was since he'd met her, he was at peace with the world. All the anger which erupted from his impatience with life — his quick temper which got him into trouble, the cutting remarks which popped out of his mouth when people annoyed him, and a lot of them did,

for in spite of his surface charm he was not a lover of the human race —
all these were erased when he was with her. He saw the world through
different eyes.

Sarita sat silently on her bed, trying to sort everything out.

"Do you know what I want the most?" he continued. "I want us to
grow old together. *The best is yet to come*," he assured her in Robert
Browning's words, "*grow old along with me*."

His words tugged at her heartstrings, but she knew it would never
work. He would give her a big belly and then abandon her. Just as her
father did to her mother.

"Sarita, I'm asking you to marry me — if you'll have me."

"*¿Matrimonio?*" she gasped.

"*Sí* marriage, *mi querida* Sarita." He pulled her gently back into his
arms, inhaling the sweet scent of her hair, his lips moving towards hers,
so overcome with love he felt he would die if she didn't accept him.

He could be her *hombre catire*, she thought, caught up in his
enthusiasm. The feelings and yearnings for love which she experienced
at the beach yesterday came back to her in a rush. She so wanted to believe
it was possible. But she shook her head.

"You will always be reminded of what I am," she said sadly. "Not that
I am ashamed of it. But in the back of your mind there will always be the
thought that I am a *puta*." She shook her head resignedly. "It would never
work."

He felt the anger stirring inside him and he was afraid of what he
would do. He was furious with the whole circumstances of her rotten,
lousy life. He got up and paced the room, hoping the physical movement
would calm him down. Then he walked resolutely back, and sitting down
on the bed, he took her hands in his.

"Promise me you'll never call yourself a whore again. I know you're
not ashamed of it, and neither am I. If you weren't working at Hortensia's,
I would never have found you." Just the thought felt like a knife piercing
his heart.

"Did you ever stop to think about it? We would never have met each
other. Oh, honey, I don't think of you as anyone other than my *Sarita
Linda*, whom I want to marry and take care of." And looking into Sarita's
sweet eyes, thinking of all the things he wanted to do for her, he pulled
her into his arms, holding her tightly. Reluctant to release her, half afraid

that the only good person to come his way might disappear, and he would be screwed once more by life.

"We all have things in our past," he whispered. "Let's just bury them and forget they ever existed," he urged her. God, how he loved holding her in his arms. "You have my word I will never mention your past."

She nestled her head in his chest, a little frightened, a little joyful. It was difficult for her to know or recognize happiness. The fear which had been with her ever since she could remember, a man abandoning her with child, was too strong.

"I'll never leave you," he promised. "You have my word."

Because he was so insistent, Sarita started to believe him. And then she made her decision. *Sí*, she replied sweetly, she would be honored to become Mrs. John Maguire. She wouldn't ever disappoint him, she told him, vowing to do everything in her power to make him proud of her.

"Lady, you don't have to prove yourself to me," he replied passionately. "You're *oro*, pure gold, and it's me who's the lucky stiff."

And Maguire really believed that. To him she was one of God's better creations. If his conscience troubled him by what he was about to do, he refused to dwell on it. The way he felt was if he didn't seize the moment, they might lose each other. It'll work out, he reassured himself knowing he hadn't been entirely honest with her or himself. I'll straighten it out later, he promised himself. Before long he'd rationalized the whole thing in his mind so he felt no guilt. But then, Maguire had never been one to play by the rulebook.

....

They planned to get married in Maracaibo, but when he discovered she didn't have a *cédula*, her identification booklet, he knew they would be spinning their wheels if they attempted to get anything done in Maracaibo. He didn't know a soul there, but he did know just about every official in the town of San Felipe, especially the chief of police and the priest, Padre Lopez Machado.

He drove to San Felipe, and after he introduced Sarita to the priest and the chief as his *novia*, his fiancée, he asked to see the two of them alone.

"I want to get married tonight," he told them.

"She's a beautiful woman, Juan. I would marry her myself," the chief replied. "That is, if I weren't already married. I didn't know you were going with anyone, much less thinking of marriage."

"Where is she from?" the priest asked suspiciously. "And why is she travelling alone with you, without a chaperon?"

"I met her in Maracaibo," Maguire replied. "And the reason she's travelling alone is because she has no family. She's an orphan."

"*¿Una huérfana?*"

"Yes, an orphan. Now listen, she doesn't have any papers. So I want you to issue her a *cédula*, Pedro," he told the chief.

"Is she a fugitive or something?" The chief looked at him suspiciously. "Why doesn't she have any papers?"

"I just told you she doesn't have any family. Since she doesn't know who her parents were, how could she have a birth certificate?" Maguire fought to stem the impatience building up inside him.

Padre Lopez Machado looked at Chief Garcia and they both nodded their heads in agreement. Another child born on the wrong side of the blanket. While the father hadn't acknowledged her as his legitimate daughter, he could have registered her as his natural child, which obviously he hadn't.

"It's as if she was never born," the chief declared in his most official voice. The priest nodded in agreement.

"Well, I can tell you she was born," Maguire shouted. "Damn it to hell, you can see that she was born." He was beginning to get very irritated. He knew Latin Americans could discuss a subject for hours at a time, and ordinarily he would have been a willing participant in their philosophical discussions, but not now. He had so much to do and so little time. Somehow he had to get the chief to issue Sarita a *cédula*. He was well aware of the Venezuelan fondness for examining all the issues, and the red tape and bureaucracy which invariably slowed things down even further. He had to get things moving without antagonizing them or losing his temper.

"Tell me, Juan," Father Lopez Machado asked holding his chin in thought, "where did you meet this lovely lady? And why didn't you get married in Maracaibo?"

"Because she doesn't have papers," Maguire replied wearily. "The company is transferring me to eastern Venezuela, and I want to get married before I leave. There's so little time." He looked at them pleadingly. "That's why I thought you could help."

"*Ay! Juan*, you didn't tell us that you were leaving. *Claro que sí*, of course we'll help you." The chief stood up. "But you know this will take time. I doubt very much this can be done tonight."

"You can issue the *cédula* yourself," Maguire persisted. "You don't have to get anyone involved."

"You know this is done by the Ministry," the chief replied.

"Well then," Maguire insisted, "get a blank *cédula* wherever you can. Please." By now he was pleading with them. He put his hand in his pocket to get his wallet, but the chief threw out his hands to stop him.

"*Ay hombre*, do not insult our friendship," the chief protested indignantly. "You do not have to pay me."

The four of them went to the Police Station where a *cédula* was issued to Sarita. She didn't know what day she was born nor the year, and when she whispered this to Maguire he picked a date, May 19, 1927, which they wrote in her *cédula*. He figured she was around that age. As for the name of her parents, he made that up also. She was listed as the legitimate daughter of Eduardo and Maria del Carmen Bermudez Ortega, both deceased, the last name being her mother's maiden name. The *cédula* gave a legitimacy to Sarita, as well as an identity. It was stamped and sealed, she was fingerprinted and told to sign it. Maguire, knowing she couldn't, reached for her hand and putting a pen in it, guided it with his hand until her signature was written in the *cédula*. This last bit of business didn't go unnoticed by the priest and the police chief. When Sarita went to the bathroom to wash off the fingerprint ink, they both pleaded with him.

"*Chico*, she's a beautiful girl, but why are you rushing into this?" The chief put his arms around Maguire in a typical Latin American *abrazo*. "*Compadre*, either she's a servant, and I doubt that because she shows great intelligence. But she can't even sign her name! So, that leaves only one other occupation. Set her up as your mistress. Have your fun with her. But marriage? *Carajo*, do you know what you're doing?" His arms shot out in bewilderment while he punctuated his words with rapid gestures. "Of all the crazy *yanqui petroleros* in this country, I never figured you would react this way. You don't have to marry her."

"But I want to," Maguire insisted. He wanted Sarita to have the protection of his name. He knew there would be talk, that the Americans wouldn't welcome her with open arms. But as long as she was his wife, they would have to accept her. He wanted Sarita to feel there was a place for her in the world. He was too much of a loner to care what people thought, but he did want something more for Sarita. And he did want to spend the rest of his life with her. As far as he was concerned, he had found his soulmate.

"*Mira*," the chief continued, "you did a good thing for her. You gave her an identity, made her a legitimate person with those names and dates. Why not let it rest with that?"

Maguire shook his head stubbornly. He refused to budge. He was one step further ahead than he'd been this afternoon. If only he had more time, he would drive back to Maracaibo and get married there since she now had a *cédula*. But he had to get back to camp. As it was, he was long overdue. Now that he had committed himself to Sarita, he didn't want to jeopardize his job. His need to make a lot of money was more urgent than ever.

"Now to get married," he said turning to the priest.

"*Imposible*," the priest protested. "First of all the law says there must be a civil marriage before a religious ceremony can be performed. But even if you get married *al civil*, I wouldn't marry you. Marriage is a solemn sacrament not to be entered into lightly," he said admonishingly as if delivering a sermon. "Especially with someone you have just met and whose background is so dubious, so very dubious."

Maguire walked away from the priest. Memories of his tackling a nun in the second grade when she wrapped him on the knuckles with a ruler, of being kicked out of high school because he'd gotten into a fist fight with one of the Jesuit fathers flashed by his eyes. He felt so frustrated he didn't know if he could control his temper a moment longer. He was sick and tired of the whole rigmarole.

"Okay, okay," he waved his hands. "Forget the church ceremony. We'll go with the civil one." Then he turned to the chief. "Can you marry us?"

The chief shook his head. "A judge, a magistrate could. But there isn't one in this small town."

"Well, then, let's find one," Maguire prodded him.

"At this time of the night?" The chief had never seen his friend in this state. "*Chico*, it's going on eleven o'clock. Even if we found someone, there are papers to be filled out. And all these things take time."

"I don't have time, Pedro," Maguire said looking at the chief with burning eyes. "I've got 350 *Bs* in my wallet. Now let's go find someone who will marry us."

Maguire was so persistent they eventually found a judge from the Andes who was in town visiting his mother.

The next morning when Maguire walked into the camp super's office to explain the reason for his delay and he introduced Sarita as Mrs. John Maguire, the news spread rapidly through camp. After the initial shock, everyone agreed that his actions weren't all that surprising. After all, they declared, he'd always chosen to run around with the natives rather than stick with his own kind. And if he preferred a dark-skinned gal, why, that was also to be expected. The speculations on Sarita ran the gamut from her being a nightclub stripper to a maid. One camp wit declared she wasn't that dark, she just had a healthy suntan from using too much Coppertone. Finally a driller settled it once and for all. He claimed to have been her client at Hortensia's. But Maguire and Sarita were long gone when the truth came out.

They drove across the country in Maguire's pickup. When they got to Barquisimeto, he bought them gold wedding bands. They also went to a photographer where they posed for a picture, she in a blue dress with a white sash and he in a blue, pin striped suit. They never said it was their wedding picture, but people seeing it on the dining room buffet always assumed it was.

Their arrival in Chacari was just as Maguire expected it would be. The story of Sarita's past had preceded her. Maguire didn't care about socializing with the camp. What did bother him was Sugar Dalhart's malicious gossip about Sarita.

Sarita assured him it didn't matter if she didn't have a lot of friends in camp, their life together was enough for her. Besides, she assured him, she had so much to learn. When he left for work in the morning, she took out her exercise book and practiced writing. Then she studied the reading assignment he'd given her, which they went over when he came home for lunch. She wanted to learn English. But since he didn't want her getting confused with the two languages, he promised he would teach her English later. In the afternoons though, after he went back to work, she looked through the American magazines, trying to pick out words, finding it difficult because, while Spanish is pronounced the same as it's written, English is not. But she did pick out recipes. For the longest time she thought one cup of sugar was pronounced one coop of soogar. They laughed about that, and from then on he started calling her *Señora* One Coop Soogar, which in time he shortened to Soogie. He had a variety of names for her. Sarita never knew which one he was going to use when he came in the door, but the one he used the most was Soogie. In time, it became her only name.

After the sugar incident, he showed her his Spanish-English dictionary. From then on, it became her bible. When she discovered she could look up a word and the dictionary would not only give her the pronunciation but the translation as well, she started flipping the pages between the Spanish and English sections at such a fast pace he told her she looked like a blackjack dealer. Which involved more explanation and nothing would do but he had to teach her the game. She had the most amazing luck. Whenever he lost, which was almost always, he told her when they retired they would go to Reno where she could support him in his old age.

Maguire's explanation to Sarita that he'd become so much of a Venezuelan, the Americans forgot he was one of them, didn't fool her. She knew there were other Venezuelans married to American men. No, it was because she once had been a *puta*. And it brought her great sadness. Only because she loved her *hombre catire* so much she didn't want anything to upset him.

NINE

As Cathleen waited for Ryle to come home, she thought about the instant rapport she experienced with the Maguires. A rapport she hoped Ryle would share with her.

She was enchanted with Sarita, and found herself wishing she had a sister like her. Her relationship with Beebe, Peggy and Moira had never been a close one. Because they possessed such vivacious and powerful personalities, she'd grown up living in their shadow. Almost like a timid mouse in a family of fat rats. Their gregariousness and ability to take charge of any social situation had given her a terrible sense of inadequacy. Plus their frequent criticism of each other disturbed her. She longed for a doting and supportive family who didn't carp on each other's shortcomings. Sometimes she wondered if this wasn't wishful thinking, just as the music which poured out of the radio promised there was someone who would love you forever, and as soon as that person came into your life all your problems would be over.

In the Maguires she saw a nurturing couple who accepted each other unconditionally. She felt so much at home with them. If she made no lasting friendships in Chacari other than John and Sarita, she would be content.

When she heard Ryle's pickup in the carport, she ran to the kitchen door to meet him. "I have so much to tell you," she cried out, standing on the toes of her sandaled feet to kiss him. He was hot and sweaty with dust clinging to his clothes, and his heavy beard, which no amount of shaving could conceal, was showing five o'clock shadow. But he still tasted good to her.

"Yeah well, I've got some news for you too," he replied, going to the refrigerator for a Polar. Uncapping the bottle he raised the chilled beer to his lips, almost groaning in pleasure. "The best drink of the day, when

109

you come home from work and have that first cool brew. It was a killer out there today. Felt like it was over a hundred degrees." He made his way to the bathroom, peeling off his clothes as he walked and throwing them in a ball into the hamper.

"Guess who might be our next door neighbor," he called out from the shower. "Your dancin' partner." "Which one?" she called back, wishing he'd hurry up so she could talk to him about their other neighbor. She wanted his undivided attention when she told him about the Maguires. As she waited for Ryle to finish showering, it occurred to her that she'd never heard him mention John Maguire. Of course they worked in different departments, still they must come in contact with each other. John was so intelligent she was positive he'd wind up a big shot in the company. Surely Ryle would consider him worth cultivating. Sometimes she balked at Ryle's wanting to only associate with those people who would be an asset to his career. Although she did want to help him in any way she could.

"Still haven't guessed which one of your dancin' partners might be living next door?" Ryle stepped out of the shower, his wet footsteps making a path to the bedroom.

"I've had so many," she replied thinking of her cousins back in the States who would probably give their eye teeth to have such a large selection of bachelors to choose from.

"But none of them threw you over their shoulder."

"You mean Fred?" She was elated with the news since he was one of her favorite people. His infectious laughter and easy going disposition were impossible to resist. "Then his Venezuelan girl friend must have said yes."

"I don't know if she has," Ryle replied slipping into a pair of shorts. "But you know how it is out here. He put in for a house before someone else gets it."

"Then we'll be surrounded by perfect neighbors," she replied, more elated than ever. And she proceeded to tell him about meeting the Maguires.

"You what?" he bellowed at her. "You went in that whore's house. Are you trying to ruin my career?"

"Ryle, what are you talking about?" She looked at him in confusion.

"I'm saying she's a whore. For chrissake, Cathleen, he picked her up in some crib in Maracaibo. Everyone knows that."

"I've never heard anything like that," she protested.

"Yeah well, maybe no one has said anything because no one in camp bothers with her, except for those who don't matter, like Pet Ford. It's common knowledge."

"Common knowledge? Who made up such a horrible story?" She was so shocked she felt close to tears. "Just because she's on the dark side, everyone automatically thinks she's a prostitute."

"Listen Cathleen, I don't want to get into it with you. A man comes home from a hard day's work and all he wants is a cool drink and some peace and quiet." He walked into the kitchen for another bottle of beer. She followed him.

"What proof does anyone have?"

He brushed past her and headed for the living room where he flopped on the couch.

"Proof?" He reached into the humidor on the coffee table and took out a cigar. "Okay, he goes off to Maracaibo for a few days while he's waiting to get transferred here. When he comes back to camp he has a wife. In three days! Come on, no decent Venezuelan would marry him in three days. Not the way they are in this country about chaperons."

"I still don't see why you assume she was a prostitute," she persisted.

"One of the guys in camp remembered her. He'd been to the whorehouse where she worked. That's the proof. And now Maguire is trying to pass her off as his wife. What a crock."

"Of course they're married," she insisted. "Why, I saw their wedding picture."

"Oh baby," his voice softened, the anger leaving it. "You're so trusting and naive. Anyone can get their picture taken. Just think about it, all the coffees and card parties, the cocktail and dinner parties; have you ever seen them there?"

Cathleen's brain whirled like a carousel as she tried to make sense of Ryle's words. But she continued to look for an explanation.

"I think they don't socialize much because she's so busy with her house and garden. It looks like something out of a magazine."

"Cathleen, they keep to themselves because they know their place. They know she doesn't belong in a camp where decent people live. So now you come along and want to upset the applecart." He picked up a two month old magazine which had come in that day's mail pouch. "Anyway, that's all I want to hear or talk about Maguire and that whore he's passing off as his wife. Just forget about them and stay away from their place. You have to associate with people who count, the ones who can do us good, not harm. Like Sugar. She's the real power here. Besides, she's a pistol, you'll always have a good time when she's around."

Oh yes, I'll have a wonderful time with Sugar, she groaned inwardly, wondering what she'd criticize about her next. She was furious with Ryle. Not only because he was treating her like a child, telling her who her friends could be, but she was horrified by the odious gossip about Sarita. In her limited experience she had no idea what a prostitute was like. To her they were characters in a book, Belle Watling in *Gone with the Wind* or Mildred in Of *Human Bondage*, neither of whom bore any resemblance to Sarita.

There was so much she wanted to tell Ryle about the Maguires, but he had cut her down so quickly she knew it would be futile to discuss them any further. Another time, she told herself, but not now. He'll come around. When the time was right, she would get him to see her viewpoint.

That night as she tossed and turned, she realized they'd had their first quarrel. His ambition which at first impressed her, now took on another color. She had the sinking feeling that Ryle would do anything to get ahead, and the cost be damned.

She would have to cultivate those people who could do them the most good, ignore those who couldn't, even if it meant losing a good friendship, always acting the perfect company wife, going where he wanted, doing what pleased him. The fact that some of this might be distasteful to her didn't seem to occur to him.

....

"Rolls, cases and cases of frozen rolls. That's all that came in the commissary this week. Of all the dumb things." Eula Mae Thompson was always on the warpath, but this time everyone was in agreement. "Why, some of us make our own bread just for something to do in this godforsaken place, so we need rolls like we need a hole in the head. They'd better get some frozen vegetables in next week or there's going to be one angry Texan down at that commissary."

Heads nodded in unison.

"Do you know that Gulf Oil brings in frozen milk from Miami for their commissaries?" Now the battle cry was taken up by Jimmie Lee Jones. "I can't see why this dumb outfit can't do the same thing. My kids may be used to *Leche Klim*, but I can't stand that powdered stuff. *Klim* — hmph! Milk spelt backwards. And brother, it tastes just like it's spelled."

"I heard Seth Barnes lost $3,000 at poker on Saturday night," Wilma Wilcox declared vigorously.

"Two months' salary!" one of the women cried out and everyone looked around trying to identify her. Salary was something which was never discussed, although everyone was always curious to know what their neighbors earned.

"When are the Stillwells retiring?" Dotty MacGregor asked. "She promised I could buy her deep freeze."

"Well, she promised it to me," Wilma said.

"That can't be. Why, I spoke to her about it last year," Dotty cried out angrily. When people talked about leaving or retiring, it paid to get your order in early. Deep freezes, radios, china, linens, cars were always in demand even if they were used, because new ones were so expensive and hard to get.

"I heard Margo Johnson is having an affair with one of the company pilots," Maudie Stillwell said in an effort to put a stop to the war of the deep freezes.

"I think so, too," Janey Carruthers added. "She went out of camp with him the other night after the movies. Just as brazen as could be. Her husband's away in Caracas so I guess she thought she'd better make hay while the sun shines. She said they were going to *El Tejero* for a drink."

"*El Tejero*?" several women cried out in unison. One of them, rolling her eyes, looked around the room in indignation. "Tell me, what decent woman leaves camp to have a drink with a bachelor? Hmph, she's giving away for free what they pay for at the Looney Door."

As Cathleen listened to the women talking, she suddenly felt bored and restless. She thought back to her delightful luncheon with the Maguires. Sarita is so lucky, she thought enviously, she can stay home and do want she wants, she doesn't have a husband who wants her to get out and socialize. Cathleen had the wildest desire to get up and walk out.

The morning coffees were becoming tedious affairs. At least playing bridge was a challenge, Cathleen thought grumpily, every hand was different. And at a cocktail party there was always a drink to liven up things. Suddenly she had the strongest desire for an ice cold martini.

"Cat got your tongue, Cathleen?" Sugar asked, her drawl making several syllables of her name. "You've hardly said a word. Do we bore you?" Again those little barbs which Sugar liked to make, always singling her out.

"Oh no," Cathleen protested. "It's just that I don't have anything exciting to add to the conversation." She smiled hesitantly, wishing desperately she could think of some humorous remark, some funny story to make them like her. Her sister, Beebe would have had them all rolling in the aisles by now. Why had Sugar picked on her again? Cathleen grew uneasy wondering what she'd done to earn her animosity.

Nadine came to her rescue when she turned the conversation around. Within minutes they were all laughing about Barbara Smith who listened to the camp radio all day. When she heard a shipment of Christmas trees being discussed, Barbara went down in a huff to the Superintendent's office and demanded to know why none had been delivered in time for the Christmas holidays. As uproarious laughter filled the room, Cathleen longed to join in. Except she didn't see the humor in the story, which Sugar picked up immediately.

"I declare, Cathleen," Sugar's voice cut through the laughter, "if you're going to be an oil company wife, you don't ever want to show your ignorance. A christmas tree, as everyone knows," she said pointedly, "is what they put on the well when they take away the rig. It has control valves and pressure gauges, honey."

"That's very interesting," Cathleen replied. "And thanks for furthering my education." Her patience with Sugar was beginning to wear thin. I'll never come back to these coffees again, she vowed. No matter what I do, Sugar just delights in taunting me. If only their personal effects would arrive, she'd have a good excuse to stay home and unpack. She realized she'd hardly opened a book since her arrival in Venezuela. It would be preferable to stay home and read, she decided, than being the target of Sugar's tongue. Her thoughts flew homeward; she missed her job and especially the stimulation of college. She'd used her brain then, now she felt it was slowly disintegrating into tiny useless pieces. The realization that she would have to return all these invitations depressed her even further. Sneaking a look at her watch she realized she'd only been there twenty-five minutes. It felt like hours.

When she was finally able to leave, she walked home dejectedly. Passing Sarita's house, she looked for her in the yard, wanting desperately to see her for she knew Sarita's company would turn her from the disgruntled woman she'd become into a human being again. And then the depression which had begun at the coffee deepened as she remembered Ryle's violent objections to her associating with Sarita. She wouldn't go up and knock on Sarita's door, she told herself, but if she was working in her garden, surely he wouldn't object to them exchanging a few words. But Sarita's yard was empty. Listlessly Cathleen walked up to the front door of her own home, only to hear the maid mopping the living room floor, the pail moving gratingly over its rough surface. She turned and walked around the house to the carport door. Sometimes she wished she didn't have a maid. They were constantly under foot, the house was too small and she had no privacy.

What she really wanted to do was go for a walk. Sitting down all morning had made her edgy, but where could she go? A wave of homesickness washed over her as she remembered her daily walks up Fifth Avenue to the office, the fun of window shopping. It grew more acute as the remembrance of cold autumn days filled her head, she could actually smell the crisp November air, see herself walking to the library, or Trotta's Drugstore for a cherry Coca-Cola. And to the movies. For a moment she was back in that old theater which was such a dump everyone in town called it the Ranch House. Oh, she'd give anything if she could be there right now. To escape into the welcoming darkness of its plain ugly walls, sit again in one of its hard seats. Lose herself in a double feature with her girl friends on either side of her, and not have to think about the friends she wanted here, but couldn't have, or the friendships her husband told her she had to make.

She walked slowly into the carport, looking hopelessly at the Chevy parked outside the kitchen door. If she drove, she could escape from camp. Go to Santa Barbara, Jusepin, even Caripito which she'd never seen but heard so much about. It was a couple of hours drive, but it would be worth it just to get away from Chacari. Why, everyone said Caripito was a regular country club with a golf course and a swimming pool.

Imagine, a pool to escape from this infernal heat. Creole Petroleum took good care of its employees. Not like Palm Oil, she grumbled to herself. Why didn't Ryle work for them instead of this cheap outfit?

She continued staring at the blue Chevrolet and realized how futile it was to day dream. Ryle still hadn't taught her to drive. She was stuck here. If they'd put her in jail and thrown away the key, she couldn't have felt more like a prisoner.

She walked into the kitchen and sat down at the table waiting for the maid to finish the floors. Feeling restless, she got up and went over to the window, adjusting the louvers to let in more light. Lines from a Keats poem kept running through her head.

> *Perhaps the same song was heard by Ruth*
> *When sick for home*
> *She stood in tears*
> *Amongst the alien corn*

That's really where she was in Chacari, in the midst of alien corn. She felt so out of place. She knew she would never fit in. She had tried to adapt to camp life, but she realized her heart wasn't in it. As nice as the women were, not all of them were like Sugar she realized, she found it hard to make friends with them. Except for a few like Nadine whose husband was Ryle's boss. And because she held this position, Cathleen hesitated becoming too close to her. The ones she really felt at home with and wanted to be friends with were forbidden to her by Ryle. Sarita and Pet Ford, who was rough around the edges, but such a character and so funny that being with her was like escaping into a good novel. Maybe that was her problem. She was too much of a book worm and not enough a people person. How she wished she were different, someone who could fit in as the other women seemed to do.

She wondered if she really knew Ryle. Sometimes she wondered if she'd made a mistake marrying him so quickly. These feelings of uncertainty though didn't linger long. Not with the great physical hunger they had for each other, the knowledge she couldn't live without him, no matter how confusing it was coming to terms with the many facets of his complex character.

Looking out the window and across the yard she saw the fence. No matter where she looked, the fence was always there. Almost like being in a concentration camp. Oh, how she wanted a drink, even if it was only eleven in the morning. Shaking her head, she reached for a cigarette. She wasn't going to fall into that trap, no matter how positive Barry was that she would. Thank God for Lucky Strikes, the best little friend a girl ever had. She sucked the smoke into her lungs and started coughing. She really had to cut down, back home a pack would last her a few days. Now she was smoking over a pack a day. She ran the cigarette under the faucet before throwing it away. Oh God, she thought desperately, I don't know what I want.

And then she heard the children's laughter, saw them riding their bikes up and down the street. An oil camp is a wonderful place to raise children, she realized. No fear that some reckless driver would run them down. The freedom she longed to have was theirs as it would never be back in the States, no matter how small the town. Away from the houses, in a field near the fence, she saw a baseball game in progress. They could hit a home run and no windows would ever be broken. For the kids it's heaven, she thought.

It's all in the way you look at things, Cathleen my girl. She could hear Ma's voice as clearly as if she were standing next to her. *So look for the plus things and forget the minuses.*

Cathleen nodded her head slowly as if answering her mother. That's what I have to do, she decided. And what am I mooning around this way for? My life is going to be filled with children. If I take after Ma, I'll have a houseful. So I don't have to worry about not fitting in here, for I'll be too busy raising my kids. She looked out the window, no longer frowning in discontent. Those were her little girls riding the bikes, her boys running around the field, sliding into home plate.

TEN

When Ryle arrived at the well site, the last person he expected to see was John Maguire.

"What in the hell is a pencil pusher like you doing here?" he snarled as he got out of his pickup. In the past he'd always managed to avoid Maguire, the two of them exchanging nothing more than a few perfunctory words of greeting. Now seeing Maguire, the recent cause of his quarrel with Cathleen, he resented his presence. "You ought to be back in the warehouse dispatching and receiving material, not goofing off to take a joy ride out here."

Maguire, taken back by Ryle's unexpected hostility, hesitated only a moment before replying. "Got a hair up your ass today?" he snapped, bewildered by Ryle's words but already on the offensive. "And since when are you in charge of personnel? I don't answer to you."

"You do, mister, as far as my wife is concerned," Ryle shot back at him. "I don't want any coffee klatching between your house and mine, understand?" He had half a mind to tell him to keep his whore away, but he knew that would result in a fight. He was too conscious of image to provoke a brawl, for it would look bad on his record.

"So, that's the reason for your friendly greeting," Maguire's lips curled in sarcasm. "The hospitality we extended to your wife. Don't worry," he said bitterly, "we don't expect it to be reciprocated." Then he leaned back in the seat of his pickup, making no effort to get out. Let the bastard make something out of my being here, he thought defiantly.

But Ryle, having told Maguire off, walked quickly towards the rig. As he climbed the steps of the platform, he noticed the men on the rig floor had just finished replacing the drill bit. Not a quick or easy operation, since it involved pulling out the bit which had become dull, and breaking the pipe — the entire drill string consisting of anywhere

118

from several hundred feet to several miles of pipe — and stacking them in ninety foot lengths inside the rig structure. And then after inserting a new drill bit, re-attaching the entire drill string and going back into the hole. He hadn't forgotten how time consuming it was, especially if they were drilling in very hard formations where a bit could lose its sharpness and become dull after only a few feet of drilling.

His eyes scanned the platform to see how the work was progressing. It wasn't his responsibility, the toolpusher was in charge. He was here to collect some cuttings and core samples. But old habits die hard, and he often involved himself mentally in a drilling operation. He watched as the drill bit, which was attached to the drill string and revolved by the rotary table, dug into the rock mass under ground.

As the drill bit went deeper, Ryle noticed the depth to which the last casing string had been set. This casing prevented the hole from caving in and protected it from underground water. Below the casing shoe, the drill pipe continued its downward journey, along with drilling mud pumped down through its hollow interior and then forced back to the surface between the inside walls of the casing and the outside walls of the drill pipe. This mud served a multitude of purposes. It lubricated and cooled the drilling bit, while at the same time it plastered the sides of the well to prevent cave-ins and hold back any gas, oil or water eruptions which might result in a blowout, a blowout which could turn into a fire if the gas and oil ignited.

It also flushed rock cuttings to the surface where they were trapped in a shale shaker for study by geologists. Then the mud started its return journey, travelling from the mud trough into a sump where it was picked up by pump suction for recirculation in the well.

After Ryle collected the rock cuttings from the shale shaker and placed them in glass jars, he went back up on the drilling platform to collect core samples. He'd come out to the well to check the sands, a term oilmen used even though oil isn't usually found in sand, but in the pores of solid rock. Somewhat like a sandwich between a bottom layer of water-filled rock and a top one of gas-filled rock. By studying the cores which are the cylindrical sections cut out of rock with a special bit, a geologist is able to determine the porosity of the oil sand.

"Hey, you ole rock hound you!" Ryle felt a friendly slap on the back and turning around he saw Fred Hardesty. Ryle grinned back. Now here was someone he was glad to see. To Ryle's way of thinking, Fred's contemplated marriage to a Venezuelan wasn't a step down as in Maguire's case, for Fred's choice was a high class Caracas débutante.

Fred kidded Ryle about being a rock hound, but as a petroleum engineer he also studied the cuttings to determine their porosity. While a geologist ascertained the possibility of oil in an area, it was the engineer who analyzed and decided the best method of extracting the oil. By calculating the rock porosity and permeability, reservoir pressure and oil viscosity — those factors which allow oil to migrate through underground rocks — he determines what will give the best ratio of yield.

"Hey *hombre*, did your girl say yes?" Ryle asked.

Fred shook his head. "She's going to give me her answer when I go to Caracas next month for Carnival. But I think she will." His high pitched laugh was drowned by the din of the rig's noises. "Who can resist me?" His cocky words belied his feelings. Fred the ladykiller, who had fallen in and out of love as casually as changing shoes, was sweating out Maruja's answer.

"See you later, alligator," Fred nodded as he made his way down the platform steps and over to his pickup. He turned and waved to Ryle, "If you're at the club after work I'll buy you a drink."

Sitting in his pickup, John Maguire watched Fred drive away and waited impatiently for the shipment of casing to arrive. That was the reason he was out here. The drilling department had been complaining about the sluggish delivery of material, and he had decided to spot check the trucking contractors personally. The trouble with the truckers, he thought irritably, is they don't have enough competition. Too much opportunity in this country and not enough people to seize it. When I have my own trucking company, he told himself, then the oil companies will see what efficiency is. And I'll have my share of the gravy. If he only had enough money, he could go in business tomorrow. If, if — the word sometimes stung him like a persistent wasp. If he had his own business, he could get Sarita out of Chacari and into a town or city where they could live anonymously without her past tormenting her. If he had enough money he could thumb his nose at the likes of Sugar Dalhart and the power she wielded in camp. He had hopes Cathleen Rylander would become Sarita's friend. Fat chance now. He must warn Sarita not to be so trusting and open with people. When he had enough money, life would be a lot sweeter for her.

He scanned the horizon looking for the casing trucks. But he saw nothing. Deciding he would have a better view from the rig platform, he climbed the stairs. As he did so, he wondered to himself what he was doing here. He could be back at the warehouse, going through his paperwork, checking up on shipments with the company radio. But because he was someone who couldn't abide sloppy work, he'd taken it upon himself to personally check out the truckers. He should adopt the same attitude as the deadbeats, put in your time and take the money.

He looked around at the men on the platform, noticing the toolpusher's red, puffy face. A condition not brought on by the sun, he warranted, but too many rum punches. Did everyone drink too much in the oilfields, he wondered. It was so damn hot that a beer always slid down easily. But beside the heat, was the isolation of camp life a contributing factor? Although he never personally experienced it, he knew a lot of the bachelors were lonely with no family around. Even people with families lived with the loneliness of homesickness. The feeling of detachment, of living in someone else's country, with no roots to put down, caused a few to quit and go back to the States. The climate also highlighted their estrangement. The melting sunshine relieved only by the battering rain during the wet season made them long for home with it's change of seasons. But stronger than that was the need to see kin, be a part again of a person's origins. Be with people other than the same faces one saw in camp month after month. Oh yes, that was something he could relate to, Maguire told himself. As much as he loved Venezuela, he could become exceedingly irritated with the sameness of camp life. If a man wasn't strong, it would be easy to look for companionship in a bottle because there was something about the isolation of camp life which could bring out a person's heartaches faster than anywhere else.

Maguire's vigil was rewarded with the sight of the casing trucks on the horizon. Between his run-in with Rylander and his irritation with the truckers, his temper was short. As he strode impatiently across the platform, he rehearsed the choice words he would hurl at the truck drivers. Behind him Ryle was filling narrow three foot wooden boxes with four inch rock cylinders which had been cut from a core barrel. He would then take them to the geology shed where he would analyze them under a microscope before making out his reports to the company and the government.

All of a sudden the rig platform started to shake, stronger than it usually did from the normal drilling operation. Maguire heard a rumbling noise, and as the platform swayed, he wondered if they were experiencing an earthquake. He'd been through a mild one on his one trip to Caracas.

"It looks like it might kick," he heard one of the drillers shout to the toolpusher. "Cut the motor before this sucker turns into a blowout."

Maguire spun around and saw the men race to shut down the drilling. But he didn't linger. He wanted to get the hell off the platform which was vibrating more and more with each second. As he ran towards the platform stairs, he heard one of the drillers cry out "Ah shit, it's a blowout alright. You son of a bitch! You'd better not ignite."

But his voice was drowned out by an ear-splitting roar as the gas erupted from the casing, shooting up into the air at a speed faster than sound. And as the gas ejected, the driller's hopes and pleas went unanswered. For when the gas reached about thirty feet in its upward journey, it burst into flames. Whether the fire was caused by a spark created by one piece of steel hitting another or a hot exhaust pipe on the drilling rig's engines, no one knew nor did they take the time to find out.

Like leaves falling from a tree during a heavy hurricane, sparks from the fire showered over the drilling platform. Ryle screamed when he felt his shirt start to smolder. Hurling the mason jars and wooden boxes over the platform rail, he ran towards the steps, pushing Maguire aside.

Jostled by Ryle, Maguire momentarily lost his footing. Then he stumbled down the stairs, running as fast as his legs could carry him. On the rig platform the crew scrambled to kill the fire with their emergency equipment.

But the fire was breathing as lustily as a newborn baby's cries, growing stronger with each passing moment. Orange red flames, giant tongues of fire, shot up to the sky, while the rig platform crackled as the fire spread across it like ignited prairie grass.

The men ran to abandon the rig, some leaping down the stairs, others jumping off the platform. Maguire looked in horror as a human fireball screaming in agony zigzagged aimlessly, reminding him of a chicken whose head had been severed. Maguire feeling the heat from the flames on his skin, agonized helplessly for a split second, then as the driller whose clothes and body were being consumed with fire ran by him, Maguire's booted feet shot out and tripped him to the ground, rolling him over with his feet because he was afraid to touch him with his hands. He kicked up earth over the driller's body to smother the flames. The smell of charred flesh filled the air, creeping up into his nostrils, making him gag as he struggled against the nausea churning in his stomach.

Then he heard Rylander's cry of fear and grimaced when he saw that his khaki shirt was on fire. Maguire's hands went instinctively to the back of his own shirt. Nothing, no spark had flown through the air to set him on fire. The luck of the Irish, he thought gratefully.

But Rylander wasn't as fortunate, he realized. The idiot, Maguire thought contemptuously, doesn't he see what he has to do? The mud pit was but a few feet away. It was his only chance. For a moment all the bitterness Maguire felt toward Rylander almost overcame his sense of fair play. A moment when he was tempted to let him burn up.

Then realizing what he had to do, he raced toward Rylander and making a flying leap, tackled him. Tackled and pushed him into the mud pit, falling in alongside him. The both of them fought to keep from choking on the thick drilling mud, spitting out the grayish brown fluid, their eyesight becoming blurred. But just as drilling mud can stop a fire in the hole, it extinguished Rylander's shirt.

Something snapped in Ryle though and he started to fight Maguire. He lunged and pushed him under the mucky substance. As Maguire struggled to escape from Rylander's hands, he regretted his good samaritan gesture. Was he going to end his days drowning in a mud pit?

He managed to slip out of Rylander's grip and started crawling out of the mud pit. But each time he tried to escape, he felt himself being dragged back, Rylander's huge hands pushing his head under. This is it, Maguire thought angrily, he was going to choke to death in a cruddy sea of mud. He should have let the bastard burn.

Then he heard a tremendous roar, felt the earth shake underneath him and Rylander's grip loosened. He fought his way to the top of the muddy pool. Pipe and drilling equipment were shooting up into the air, all becoming lethal weapons as they landed helter skelter. He felt as if he were smack in the middle of a huge Fourth of July fireworks display. The fire crackled closer to the mud pit. Fear ran through every muscle of

Maguire's body, and he started to shake, positive he was going to burn to death.

The mud sucked on his legs as he struggled to climb out the pit. Then a miracle happened. Rylander's hands were no longer pushing him under. He felt himself being dragged and pulled as Rylander made his way out of the mud pit.

"Oh God, you saved me from burning up," Ryle's word came out apologetically "I don't know what got into me, maybe crazy from the shock of it all."

Maguire looked at Rylander contemptuously. "Go to hell," he snarled, the mud between his teeth making his face look like a ghoulish Halloween mask.

"I owe you," Ryle grunted. "Thanks."

Maguire didn't answer him, but walked with great effort towards his pickup, wanting to run, but absolutely wiped out from fighting for his life with Ryle. Behind them the flames continued to shoot up, an orange red geyser tinged with blue filling the sky. Debris from the well was scattered around them. Men fled from the blazing rig, some of them burned. The injured ones who weren't able to navigate by themselves were carried, half dragged, away from the inferno of what had once been Well #4821. The smell of burnt flesh permeated the air while the sheet of flames crackled like a huge fireplace.

The sounds, the smells of the mayhem around him brought back memories of the war to Ryle. He relived the horror of Malmedy as he stumbled unsteadily towards his pickup, his back throbbing with pain. His first thought was that he had to get on the radio to Chacari.

But it was Maguire who reported the fire to camp. For Ryle passed out on the seat of his pickup, his right hand reaching for the mike.

All efforts to kill the fire were met with failure. Despite drilling a directional hole at a slant to intersect the bottom of the burning well and pump in drilling mud and cement, the well continued to burn.

Experts were brought in from Houston, the M. M. Kinley Co., predecessors of the famous Red Adair. Founded by "Dad" Kinley, who pioneered the shooting of explosives in the 1913 Signal Hill fire in California, and taken over by his sons, the fire was brought under control with sticks of dynamite, a cylinder of Fuller's earth wrapped in heavy waxed paper and saturated with a selected percentage of nitroglycerine, and then packed into steel drums.

....

If it hadn't been for John Maguire, Cathleen wrote her mother, she would have lost Ryle. The fear of what might have happened haunted her sleep the weeks Ryle was in the Sinclair Hospital in Santa Barbara recovering from his burns. Burns which hadn't been fatal thanks to John's quick thinking and the T-shirt Ryle wore under his khaki shirt. A lot of men didn't wear them, claiming it was too hot. She was grateful he thought otherwise.

But she was saddened by the deaths of two men from Chacari. A toolpusher whose skull was crushed as material rained down from the top of the blazing rig and a driller, whose body was blown to bits.

Like clockwork she woke up every night shaking with fear. If she went to bed early, sleep would desert her at two o'clock. If she went to bed late, she woke up at the same time. Woke up reaching for Ryle and finding nothing but his pillow. I don't know what I'd do if anything ever happened to him, she thought as she got up and started pacing the floor, her fingers trembling as she lit a cigarette. Married just over a month, and I almost became a widow. The silence of the house heightened her uneasiness, a silence broken only by the buzzing of the night insects drawn to the yellow light bulb outside the kitchen door. A light usually turned off unless they were expecting company. But the recurring nightmare of seeing Ryle burn before her eyes and the lack of sleep made her afraid of being alone. Sometime she turned on every light in the house so the darkness wouldn't swallow her.

She reached for her Rosary beads and for a short time, felt safe as she counted off the Hail Marys. Then the fear returned. What I wouldn't give, she thought as she lit another Lucky Strike, if I could just pick up the phone and talk to Ma.

ELEVEN

Like storm clouds, a pall hovered over Chacari after the fire. Its inhabitants became subdued and somewhat withdrawn. And then after the initial shock wore off, instinctively they reached out to each other.

They rushed to offer comfort to the widow and two sons of the dead toolpusher and helped pack their personal effects, for they knew how anxious they were to leave. Since the driller had been in Venezuela only seven weeks - company policy required employees to go through a three months' trial period before their families could join them - his wife and children were still in the States. They never received his remains though. His body, blown into scattered pieces, made identification impossible. Whatever was found was quickly buried.

Cathleen and Nadine passed the toolpusher's house on their way to visit Ryle in the hospital. They saw the heavyset woman get into a neighbor's car, her two young sons clinging to her in fear and bewilderment. As Cathleen watched the car drive away to the airport in Maturín, her nightly nightmares flashed before her.

"That could have been me," she cried out to Nadine.

"That poor soul, it could have been any one of us. But it isn't. And that's what you got to keep telling yourself, gal." Nadine shifted her car into first as she drove over the cattle crossing and out of camp. "Still having those nightmares?" she asked. When Cathleen nodded, Nadine shook her head sympathetically. "Why don't you let me send Julie over to spend the night? You'd probably sleep right through if there was someone in the house with you."

"That's awfully sweet of you." Cathleen's voice was full of gratitude. Nadine wasn't the only one who'd been there for her; other women had brought over food, or asked her to dinner so she wouldn't be alone. It took a crisis like this to make her realize that despite the drawbacks of camp

126

life, people genuinely cared about their neighbors.

"I'd love for Julie to come over," Cathleen said, already feeling release from the tension of her insomniac filled nights.

"You're in for a real treat," Nadine chortled. "She snores just like her daddy. You won't feel alone listening to her saw away."

A Palm Oil pickup passed them and when they automatically waved to each other, Cathleen realized it was John Maguire.

"If it hadn't been for John, I would have lost Ryle." Her hands shook as she reached for a cigarette.

"That was right quick thinking on his part," Nadine agreed.

"I'm so fond of John and Sarita," Cathleen said. She hesitated for a moment, wondering if she should confide in her. As friendly as Nadine was, Cathleen still thought of her as the boss's wife. Then deciding Nadine was someone who didn't take such things seriously, Cathleen decided to go ahead.

"Nadine, the Maguires are such lovely people, yet people ignore them. Why? Because of some odious gossip about Sarita's past? It just bugs me the way people are always gossiping about everyone all the time," she burst out.

"Honey, you got to understand a few things about life in the oil patch," Nadine replied. "People gossip not out of some malicious streak, but just for something to do. Time hangs heavy on our hands out here. Oh, there are a few nasty ones, but on the whole it's harmless talk."

"I don't know if it's so harmless," Cathleen replied hotly. "Look at the horrible things they say about Sarita."

"We're just like any small town back in the States," Nadine explained. "Somebody new comes into town, with talk of their past arriving before they do, people just naturally are suspicious. And Mrs. Maguire is different — y'know, sort of exotic. She just doesn't look like the rest of us, so people don't know how to take her."

"And it could be some of the ladies are a little afraid," she continued. "If they're friendly with her, their hubbys might take a shine to her."

"Oh Nadine, that's ridiculous. She and John are too happily married. And Sarita certainly doesn't flaunt herself as, as . . . . some other people do."

"You mean like Sugar," Nadine chuckled. "She's something else. Sometimes I wonder how ole Emmett can keep up with her."

Nadine and Murray had been taking turns driving her to the hospital because although she had her driver' license, she still didn't feel secure enough to drive by herself.

Ryle had come home one day waving a long piece of ruled paper. "Here's your license, signed, sealed and delivered." She looked in bewilderment at the *papel sellado* covered with multi-colored stamps. "But I don't know how to drive," she protested.

"It doesn't matter," he assured her. "You can start driving around camp and when you can handle the car, I'll take you out on the highway."

Although she'd progressed to driving out of camp, she still wasn't sure of herself, especially when she drove through *El Tejero*. The streets of the old town were narrow, most of them one way. And whenever she went in the wrong direction, it invariably brought everyone out of their houses where pedestrians and drivers alike shouted, "*Flecha, flecha,*" all of them gesturing to the one way arrow. It was bad enough being the center of so much unwelcome attention and enduring everyone's taunts, all shot off in machine gun Spanish, under the best of conditions. Now with her nerves so frayed, it was an experience she could do without.

After weeks which lingered like months, Murray drove her to the hospital to bring Ryle home. "It's over, Toots."

"Until the next fire," she remarked despondently.

"There's not going to be another fire. What happened was a freak accident," he assured her. "Believe me, the oil companies would soon be out of business if their wells were always catching on fire."

"I almost lost him, Murray." She felt her throat choke up as she struggled to control her emotions. But it was no use, all the pent up fear and anguish she'd been living with the past weeks came out in a torrent of tears, accompanied by loud sobs.

Murray pulled the car over to the side of the road, watching helplessly. Then he took her in his arms, whispering words of comfort, caressing the tight knots in her neck, brushing away the strands of hair which the tears had glued to her face. Cathleen clung to him like a drowning sailor.

"Murray, I'm so sorry — slobbering all over you."

"Anytime, Toots, you need a shoulder, I'm your man."

"It's a good solid shoulder," she replied.

"You'll give me a letter of recommendation?" His lopsided grin brought a wan smile to her face.

"Oh yes. I'll type it up today." She looked at him affectionately. "Oh Murray, you have the most wonderful quality of making everything OK."

Wonderful for everyone but myself, he realized ruefully.

....

"It seems like a hundred years," Ryle's words came out in a hoarse whisper, like a man who knew death had almost snatched him. He looked around their little house, drinking in the faded cushions of the old rattan living room set as if they were sparkling new. "I'm so grateful to be home, it looks like the Taj Majal," he murmured as his eyes ran over the chipped dining room buffet.

His body trembled with emotion when he drew Cathleen into his arms. "Oh baby, you'll never know how much I missed you," he murmured brushing his lips against hers, almost fearful that in doing so she might disappear and he'd wake up from the nightmares he had every night in the hospital. Then tasting Cathleen's sweetness, a sigh of exaltation escaped from his throat. This was no dream. He was alive, really alive. He tenderly covered her mouth with his, reveling in the gift of holding his wife once more in his arms.

Cathleen hugged him gratefully, burying her face in his chest. The desire for him which she had been afraid to think about the past weeks came rushing back. A desire which grew when his fingers reached for her lavender blouse, hastily unbuttoning it and moving towards her bra, not taking time to unhook it, but slipping it down quickly so he could take her breasts in his mouth. When he called out her name in a soft sob, Cathleen's legs went weak and rubbery.

They hadn't made it to the bedroom yet, his tongue darting from one breast to another as they stopped in the short hallway. "I love you so, Cathleen — sometimes it scares me," he confessed. "Needing you this much."

Cathleen cried out his name, feeling his hardness against her body. As his hands pushed her violet print skirt and half slip up, they moved across her thighs and pulled her pants down. By now Ryle and Cathleen had progressed to the door leading to the bedroom, and as his fingers caressed her, she moved with their rhythm and then jerked in an orgasm which erupted so quickly it took her by surprise. She threw her arms around his neck then, wanting to kiss him, have his tongue search out hers as it always did before he entered her. And if he wanted her standing against the wall, she didn't care. The past weeks of living with the fear and nightmares of what could have destroyed their lives was finally over.

But Ryle picked her up and carried her into their bedroom. "All the time I was in the hospital," his voice raspy with emotion when he put her down on the bed, "I kept thinking of how I almost died."

"Don't think about it," she urged, her lips moving over his face in hunger. "We're together again and that's all that matters." She snuggled in his arms, aching to have him inside her. But his mouth went down between her legs. She stiffened in embarrassment, thinking she ought to stop him. Her eyes followed the outline of his head moving beneath the material of her skirt. She struggled in her mind what to do, how to get him to stop. She would just push him away, she decided, that's all she had to do. But Cathleen did nothing. She lay there feeling his tongue caress her, torn between embarrassment and excitement. An excitement which grew when his tongue made its way inside her. This time she didn't resist, she stopped struggling in her mind and she gave in. Let herself go, thought of nothing but the pleasure he gave her with his mouth. He'd taken her across another border into intimacy.

Then after a day of intense lovemaking, he woke up anxious to get back to work. "I've lost too much time," he said impatiently, pushing her away. He was going back to work today no matter what the doctor said. "While I'm screwin' around in bed, the company is getting along without me."

"And you'd better get on the stick too," he admonished her. "Our personal effects are arriving today." He rushed off to work, refusing breakfast.

Screwin' around he calls it. The words stung her. Every day she discovered another layer of Ryle. One minute affectionate, charming and humorous. Then in a second, cold and indifferent to her. She threw herself into unpacking, still hurt by the sharpness of his words.

When she found her record player, she placed it on the bookcase and searched for the boxes of records. Finding them was like seeing old friends again, especially those by Frankie Lane. They can keep Sinatra, she thought, I'll take this Frankie any day. When his mellow voice filled the tiny living room with *We'll Be Together Again*, the promise in its lyrics eased her disappointment.

As the records flipped down on the turntable, some of them brought back memories of their honeymoon on board ship. Whenever Ryle turns moody, she decided, that's what I have to do. Remember the good times and eventually they'll come back.

She continued unpacking her wedding gifts - the silver coffee and tea service from her parents, the flatware from Aunt Jenny. The best part was her linens. Now she could return all the company issue, the white towels with the words 'Palm Oil Co.' running down the center blue stripe, the sheets with the name stamped in indelible ink. But she still had to live with the company name plates on the furniture and appliances. One day, she thought longingly, we'll have our own furniture, and I won't feel like another number.

Unpacking the lace tablecloth crocheted by her grandmother brought a lump to her throat. She made a face when she unpacked the Russell Wright chartreuse dishes, too modern for her taste, which had been passed on to her by her cousin Marge from her wedding gifts. She hoped that the maid, who was forever dropping things, would make short work of them. Putting on another stack of records, she sat back and listened to Bing Crosby and Connie Boswell dueting *Between 18th and 19th on Chestnut Street*. It was an old song, not on the Hit Parade, but one of her favorites. Next the wispy voice of Wee Bonnie Baker took over with her rendition of *Oh! Johnny, Oh! Johnny,* a song from the late 30s.

Listening to the song made her think of John Maguire. She wondered if Ryle would thank him personally for saving his life. Maybe at the office today. If he doesn't then he must go to his home, she thought, no matter how strong his aversion is to associating with them. When Ryle was in the hospital, she'd gone over several times with fudge and penuche when she discovered John's sweet tooth, despite Ryle's warning to stay away. She was positive that since John saved Ryle's life, he would have a change of heart.

"Anyone home?" Sarita's voice called out breaking into her thoughts. She opened the front door which oddly enough faced the Maguire's back yard. "Cathleen, I'm returning the plates you brought the candy in, with a little something I made today."

"Sarita! Come on in. I was just thinking about you."

"Good or bad?" Sarita asked, hesitant to enter when she saw the array of boxes and crates.

"Good, always good. Don't you know you two are my favorite people in camp? Don't mind the mess. Our personal effects came today. Now sit down and you'll see why I was thinking about you and John." Cathleen put on *Oh! Johnny, Oh! Johnny*.

Listening to the song, Sarita's eyes grew large with wonder. "I've never called him Johnny. But you know, I like it." And she repeated the name, her accent making it sound like 'Yonnee.' She asked Cathleen to replay the record so she could learn the words.

"I'll get it all for you," Cathleen replied, taking down the words in shorthand. Rummaging through the boxes, she found her little portable Royal and sat down to transcribe the song.

"That's one of the things I want to learn next," Sarita said, pointing to the typewriter.

"I'll teach you," Cathleen smiled, showing her how to press down the keys, "and you can teach me Spanish." As she handed the typewritten words to Sarita, she decided to give her the record. Looking into the sweetness of her face, Cathleen found it difficult to understand why people stayed away from her, despite all of Nadine's explanations. Even if what they said about her past is true, she thought sadly, she's no longer in that life. Why can't people give her another chance?

"I must go home," Sarita said getting up. "Thank you so much for the record." Her eyes were beaming with happiness. "I will treasure it always."

Cathleen walked with her out the door. As Sarita started to take the path to the street, Cathleen pointed to the hedge.

"That's a good neighbor hedge. It's just like back home when two neighbors cross back and forth to visit," and she pointed to the gap in the hedge, remembering the one between her parents' home and the Fennelly's. "There's one there already. You have to use it."

"You miss your home, don't you?" Sarita asked, catching the longing in Cathleen's voice.

"I never thought I would," Cathleen laughed. "I come from such a large, screwball family that I was always anxious to get away from them and have my own home. There was so much confusion and commotion going on all the time. My brothers were always getting into fights with each other, a common enough thing in big families. Especially Irish families! And my sisters were forever borrowing my clothes and jewelry. I'd go to put on something and it was gone. Things like that. But now, I find myself thinking about them all, wishing desperately they were a little closer than three thousand miles." It was the first time Cathleen admitted to herself how much she missed the whole crazy bunch of them.

"And you?" she asked Sarita. "Do you miss your family? Of course, they can't be too far away. At least they're in the same country."

Sarita shook her head. "I have no one, only John."

Again that strange feeling she had when she first met Sarita, that she'd found a sister. She hugged Sarita goodbye and watched her part the hedge. She hated to see her go, feeling the serenity which always emanated from Sarita depart with her. Ryle will just have to come around, she thought with determination, he cannot deny me this wonderful friendship. He'll change his mind, she reassured herself, it's just a question of time. But until then, she had to juggle things a bit. Keep peace with her husband and also continue her friendship with Sarita and John. Not an easy feat in the fishbowl atmosphere of camp life. It's like trying to sneak out and have dates with someone your family disapproves of, she decided.

But Cathleen's hopes for Ryle coming around were dashed by Sugar Dalhart.

"I declare, Ryle, I've really tried to be friendly with your wife," Sugar remarked when she stopped by the office that morning, "but she avoids me like I have the plague or something. It looks like she'd rather be friendly with that little nigger of Maguire's than anyone else. Why, they're thick as thieves. I know you're grateful to Maguire for saving your life, but it doesn't mean you have to get sociable with them, right?" The camp superintendent's wife rolled her eyes in disapproval. "Cathleen is just so new in camp," she continued, "she probably doesn't know about that woman's background. But you do, and you wouldn't want your wife associating with the wrong kind. Now would you, honey?"

"How could you do this to me?" Ryle cried out when he came home from work, his voice filled with anger. "I told you to stay away from that whore's home."

"Her husband saved your life," she protested. "I didn't think you would object to me taking them some candy."

"I don't, it was a nice gesture," he replied. "But why couldn't you stop at that? Why did you have to keep going over there?" By now, his words had a pleading quality to them. "I thought I made it plain the way things are."

He started coming home at odd hours, as if he were checking up on her. A few days later when he found her coloring her hair, his voice was filled with disappointment.

"And I thought it was natural," the tone in his voice intimating she had deliberately deceived him.

"I never claimed it was," Cathleen declared. She'd started highlighting her dirty blond hair the day after she graduated high school. "If I'm such a disappointment to you, Ryle, maybe you ought to get me a ticket out of this place."

He didn't answer. The thought of going home in defeat, admitting to her friends and family her marriage was in trouble, especially her father, who would not welcome her with open arms, wasn't something she wanted to think about. She found herself lighting up cigarettes, and just as quickly stubbing them out. Only a straight shot of Scotch could numb her thoughts.

After a few days he came home with a gift, a Mexican silver charm bracelet, more affectionate than ever. "Please baby," his words coming out in that soft drawl which always turned her insides into jelly, "please do what I ask you to do. We can accomplish anything if we just stick together." The way he said it made her feel she'd been the one at fault. That and the magic of his touch, something she'd been missing. When he started making love to her, wiping away her fears that he was disappointed in her, she resolved to do anything which would keep their lives intact, telling herself she had to conform more and not be so independent. And she was touched by the gift, knowing it was his way of apologizing. Something she was certain he couldn't put into words.

She avoided Sarita, never going out in her yard. When she walked home from an afternoon bridge, she used any street but the one going past the Maguires' house. But she looked for her. Tilting the jalousies in the living room, she could see her working in her garden. That became her only contact with Sarita, the surreptitious glances from the window. The desire to be with her, to nurture their friendship was still strong, but even stronger was her desire to make her marriage work. The feeling of being in the midst of alien corn grew.

....

"Soogie, do you think I'm shooting blanks?"

"*¿Cómo?*" Sarita's eyes mirrored her puzzlement. "What is this word, blanks?" She always insisted John talk to her in English, although they invariably switched back and forth between the two languages. "Maybe you'd better tell me that *en Español.*"

"Well, I don't know how to say it in Spanish," he replied shrugging his shoulders. "What I'm trying to say, honey, is, how come you're not getting pregnant? Is it me, or are you doing something to prevent it?"

She didn't reply. Right away he knew the answer.

"Why, Soogie? Why don't you want to have our children? They would be so good looking, if they took after you." He looked at her lovingly, his fingers tracing the features of her face, coming to rest in the cleft in her chin. "Ah, that's the reason, you're afraid they'll turn out *feo*, ugly like me," he said teasingly.

"No, no," she protested. "They'd be very fortunate if they took after you. And you're not *feo*."

"I'm not?" He laughed. "Well, that's a relief."

When she didn't say anything, Maguire continued to question her. "Then what is it? Are you afraid they'll inherit my awful *genio*? Honey, your sweet disposition will offset my terrible temper."

When she still didn't answer him, his bantering stopped. "I thought you'd gotten over that notion. Because that's all it is, some foolish notion that I'd leave you. Don't you know I could never make it if we weren't together? Why, without you, a part of me would die. You're like my breath going in and out. Without you, it would just stop."

Again his words. Those words which could sway her, make her throw all common sense to the winds. And she would start to believe him, believe that her past wouldn't haunt them. That his love was strong enough. *Puta*, child of a *puta*, that's all their children would be. Isn't that what Ryle had called her? She could still hear him. She'd been working out in the garden last week when he shouted at Cathleen. Hidden by the hedge between their house, no one saw her. But she heard him. It was hard not to what with the houses so close together and the intensity of his rage projecting his voice. Now the wonderful friendship she had with Cathleen would come to an end.

But hearing Ryle's words brought home her situation, stirring up her old childhood fears that her husband would one day leave. And she would wind up like all the women in the *barrio*, pregnant and abandoned.

As much as she wanted to believe him when he told her she was a part of his being, that he couldn't live without her, she was too wise in the ways of life. Of course he meant it when he said these words. But she knew all too well emotions can change, that what one declares fervently one day can change the next. This was the only dissension between them. This desire of John's to start a family and her unwillingness to do so. And she hoped it wouldn't create a rift between them.

"How's Cathleen?" John asked, breaking into her thoughts. "She hasn't been around lately. I was becoming very fond of her terrific candy."

"Oh, *querido*, you know how it is. She's new in camp and everyone is bending over backwards to entertain her." She didn't want him to know the reason for Cathleen's absence. If he had any inkling of Ryle's words, it would provoke a fight. That quick temper of his would erupt and then things would really be sticky.

Maguire didn't pursue the subject with Sarita for he knew he would get no answer. Her Indian blood could throw a mask over her emotions and thoughts. He had hoped after saving Ryle's life, Ryle would forget their words on the rig the day of the fire. But evidently he hadn't. Still the same old crap, he thought wearily. When he returned to the office after lunch, he stopped by Ryle's office.

"You can buy me that drink now," Maguire told him. The first day Ryle went back to work he'd walked around the building to the warehouse looking for Maguire, thanked him for saving his life and offered to buy him a drink. Maguire barely acknowledged his presence. Not only because he was deep in paper work, but he had little desire to go drinking with Rylander.

"Sure, I'll meet you at the clubhouse," Ryle replied warily.

"No," Maguire said. "Not the clubhouse. I'll see you at the *cantina* in El Tejero."

"Suit yourself. It's El Tejero then." Relieved that they wouldn't be meeting in camp, Ryle wondered why Maguire had changed his mind. He felt uneasy about this meeting, but he did owe the guy for saving his life.

Maguire, nursing a rum and water, was waiting when Ryle arrived. "You don't have to drink that native stuff," Ryle remarked. "I'll buy you a real drink. What will it be? Scotch, bourbon or gin?"

How magnanimous of the bastard, Maguire thought. He forced a smile to his lips. "I prefer the native stuff," he replied cheerfully, "but then you already knew that."

Ryle's gray eyes looked suspiciously at Maguire. Taking out his cigarettes he pushed the pack toward Maguire. "Chesterfield?"

Maguire shook his head. "No thanks, I'll stick to Camels." He blew out smoke rings hoping they would still the anger churning inside him. He watched Ryle walk over to the bar to get a bourbon and ginger for himself and a refill of Maguire's rum. When Ryle returned with the drinks, Maguire raised his glass.

"*Schlante!*"

"Haven't heard that one before," Ryle remarked.

"It's an Irish toast, meaning good health," Maguire said. "Now that you're married to an Irish girl, you might want to know things like that."

"She's American, just like you and me," Rylander replied defensively.

"True," Maguire agreed. "But she still has Irish blood in her. And we Irish tend to remember our roots."

Ryle shrugged his shoulders indifferently. He had no desire to dwell on his roots. If anything, he wanted to forget them.

"Do you want the best for Cathleen?"

Maguire's question caught him off guard. "Of course I do. What a dumb question."

"No, not really. You see, I want the best for my wife. And it pains me when she doesn't get it."

Ryle had the feeling he was being pushed into a corner.

"I know you told me you didn't want any coffee klatching between your house and mine," Maguire said, feeling like a beggar with a hat in his hands and hating every minute of it. The memory of Ryle lashing out at him the day of the fire was still sharp in his mind. But for Sarita's sake he had to swallow his pride and try and make Ryle understand.

"But if you saw Cathleen and Sarita together, I think you'd change your mind. They're so fond of each other." Maguire saw Ryle stiffen. He just knew Ryle was going to tell him to go to hell.

"You don't approve of my Sarita," he continued before Ryle could break in, "because she once sold her favors. But let me ask you something. When you were in Caracas, do you remember the kids on the streets? The dirty little boys in ragged pants who begged to shine your shoes, the filthy little girls in smelly, tattered dresses who implored you to throw them a few *centavos*?"

"Well, yeah," Ryle replied uneasily. "But what's that got to do with things?"

"Because that's where Sarita came from, Ryle. Her mother just left her in the street one day and never came back. So there was this kid surviving the only way she knew how, begging. Then something happened, something she won't talk about, all I know is that she ran away from this bad situation and wound up in the middle of the night in one of the high class whorehouses. Where she pleaded with them to let her stay. The servants wanted to kick her back out in the street, but one of the ladies of the house, Sarita said her name was *Simone*, insisted Sarita stay." Maguire's voice shook a little as he reached for a cigarette. "I will be grateful to that French prostitute the rest of my life."

"Sarita did all the dirty work the other servants didn't want to do and never got paid a cent. But she didn't care. Sarita told me she was so grateful to have a house to live in and something to eat every day that it was like living in paradise."

"Paradise, huh?" Ryle remarked shaking his head in sympathy. "You see those kids on the street and you throw them a few coins, but you never think about what it's really like for them."

"Yeah, we never do," Maguire agreed.

"Well, I'm sorry your wife had such a crummy childhood." He didn't know what else to say, although inside he was more than a little shaken by Maguire's story. "But hey, she's got a home now and you."

"Yeah, it's pretty wonderful," Maguire's smile lit up his face. Then he frowned. "I don't give a damn about making the camp social scene. But if my wife wants to be friends with someone, I don't want it denied her."

The sympathy in Ryle's eyes evaporated. "Like I said, I'm sorry she had it so bad. But listen, none of us had it easy. I gotta make it to the top of the ladder, Maguire. And nothin' is gonna jeopardize that."

"And your wife associating with mine would put a squeeze on your plans?" Maguire remarked bitterly.

"Well yeah, it would." Ryle sighed. "I'm sorry your wife had it so tough. But all my sympathy isn't going to change the way things are. I'm not gonna get lost in the shuffle, Maguire."

"You've forgotten something, Rylander." Maguire's eyes frosted over with a hard, cold veneer. "You owe me. When a man saves another man's life, he is indebted to him forever."

Ryle groaned inwardly. *He really has me by the short hairs.*

"I'm not telling you that you have to make the social scene with us. I know that would cramp your style seeing as how you're such a social climber." Maguire's words came out slowly, measured. He was tired of begging. "But I am telling you that I don't want anything interfering with Cathleen's friendship with my wife. It means the world to Sarita. And it means just as much to your wife, in case you don't know it." He struggled to soften his words.

"See, you haven't seen the two of them together, but I have. It's instant friendship. And to forbid Cathleen to see Sarita would be cruel to both of them." But especially to my Sarita, he thought in despair. "Oh, I know you've told Cathleen to stay away. I don't know the particulars, but I can guess." His words became bitter. "Just as I know how this camp has ostracized her because of the unfortunate circumstances of her past."

Ryle, sitting silently across the small table from him, saw moisture in Maguire's eyes. He felt compassion for him. That guy really loves her, he thought, it just sticks out all over him. He's crazy about her. Just like I'm nuts about Cathleen. He picked up his drink, swallowing it hard. But she'll always be a whore in everyone's eyes. He had his career to think about. Image is everything in this game, doing the right thing, associating with the right people. He couldn't let anything spoil his chances of getting ahead.

Ever since he could remember, he'd been on the outside looking in. Something he'd bet Maguire couldn't understand. Maguire who didn't seem to give a damn what anyone thought and thumbed his nose at the whole world, except when it came to his wife. Not like him who had wanted things all his life and never knew what it was to have them until he went out and scrounged for them. Murray knew. Yeah, Bluestein knew. He'd grown up surrounded by the same kind of scratch anywhere poverty. Except he had something I never had, Ryle thought bitterly. Bluestein had family. They may not have had a pot to piss in, but they pulled for each other. He had an old man he was proud of.

Ryle didn't know when he started hating his father. There were times when he thought he was born hating him. It wasn't only the poverty of their lives brought on by his father's inability to make a living because of his fondness for schnapps. Stronger were the memories of his father's know it all attitude, his insistence that his way was the right way. And when he was thwarted, his derisive tongue lashed out at his mother and him. All he could remember from his childhood was growing up ashamed of his father. Ernst Rhinelander, who ran away from Germany so he wouldn't have to serve in the Kaiser's Army in World War I. Who made his way west to Oklahoma where he changed his name to Rylander thinking it would sound more American. But he never lost his funny accent, nor his fondness for the beer and wine which made him the town drunk. When Ryle was shipped to Europe instead of the Pacific, he got a revenge of sorts. Every time he took a shot at a Kraut, he was aiming a bullet at his father. And when the old man came down with his first stroke and lost his speech, he felt no sympathy or compassion. Oh no, just jubilation. And the thought that now the son of a bitch couldn't shoot off his big mouth anymore. He didn't deserve to be taken care of, Ryle thought morosely, I should have let him waste away in some charity ward. But he'd taken care of the medical bills. Just as he'd been helping them out financially ever since he left home in his teens to work in the oilfields. Only because he wanted his mother to have something more out of life than the little she'd gotten with his father.

Maguire doesn't have the hunger in him that I do, Ryle thought looking across the dimly lit *cantina*. He was grateful to him for saving his life, but he just couldn't agree to what he wanted. He'd worked too hard, had planned too carefully to throw it all away. Letting Cathleen become friendly with his wife. The camp would never stop talking about them. It would be taking a step backwards. He got the heebie jeebies just thinking what it would do to his name and his career.

"I can't repay you for saving my life," he told Maguire. "And I'll always be grateful. But what you're asking — it's just not going to work.

You're telling me how to run my life and I can't do it."

"You owe me, Rylander." Maguire's voice became edgy.

"Yeah, well, I'll just have to repay you some other way," Ryle insisted.

"There is no other way as far as I'm concerned." Maguire snapped at him. "Okay, you want to play dirty? I can play dirty with the best of them," Maguire continued, the anger rushing up his throat. "You're just not giving me any other choice."

"And what's that supposed to mean?" Ryle asked.

"I like Emmett. He's one of the best supers this company has. But more than that, he's a gentleman in every sense of the word. Something not too abundant around here," Maguire replied sarcastically. "I wouldn't want to do anything to hurt him, but if you push my back to the wall, I'll do it."

"Do what?" Ryle asked suspiciously.

"Let him find out that you were screwing around with his wife."

"Rumors, just a bunch of idle gossip," Ryle scoffed.

"I don't think so." Maguire shook his head. "In fact, I know it was more than that."

"I don't know what you're talking about," Ryle replied.

"I was coming back from Puerto La Cruz one night". Maguire took out a cigarette and very slowly lit it. "It was very late because I had a hell of a time chasing down one of the customs agents. On the way back I stopped to take a leak in a clump of *Divi Divi* trees. I thought I had the place to myself. Until I spied another clump of trees where a pickup and a car were parked. The pickup I recognized immediately, it had the Palm Oil logo on the doors."

"At first I thought the pickup had broken down. That's why I went over to look at it. And then I saw a car that I would recognize anywhere. Mrs. Dalhart's light blue Pontiac." He saw Rylander's mouth twitch. His gray eyes remained neutral, there was no emotion in them whatsoever. Only his mouth gave away his uneasiness.

"It was so dark in there, the reason I guess you two chose that spot, that I couldn't see too much. But I could hear what was going on inside that light blue Pontiac. Especially when Mrs. Dalhart cried out your name several times in the throes of ecstasy." Maguire's voice snickered over the words. "And it was your pickup for I checked out the number the next day." Oh, he had him now. Right between the balls.

"You could never prove it," Ryle replied defiantly.

"Not only would Emmett be interested in this bit of exciting news," Maguire continued, "but I think your bride would also find it illuminating. Especially since it involves Sugar Dalhart who's been giving her such a hard time ever since she landed in camp."

He would never go that far, that would really be hitting below the belt because Cathleen would be the one to suffer. But until he got what he wanted, he was going to keep hammering away, bluffing Rylander as far as he could.

"Of course this happened before you got married, so Cathleen couldn't accuse you of being unfaithful. But you can imagine how she'd take it."

"You wouldn't dare," Ryle shot back.

"Just try me, old buddy," Maguire assured him. "It's so simple what I'm asking. Just a harmless little friendship between two neighbors. And it's not going to be forever," he said cajolingly "I hear they're going to transfer me to Puerto La Cruz, to be in charge of the K-9 camp."

"When?" Ryle asked suspiciously.

"In a few months, maybe sooner. So you see, we're not talking a lifelong friendship. Just a few months. Then poof! and we're gone."

"You're trying to blackmail me."

"Call it what you want," Maguire replied stubbornly. "I never would have brought it up except you forced me. And what I'm asking is such a little thing, a few months' friendship, and we'll be out of your lives."

He lit another cigarette, struggling to contain his temper, then he burst out angrily. "Why the hell am I begging you? If I hadn't thrown you in that mud pit, you'd be dead. I should have let you fry."

Fry. The word brought it all back to Ryle. The panic he felt when his shirt caught fire. The fear that he would turn into a human fireball and die a horrible death. Never to realize his ambition to become president of the company, or to love Cathleen again. The gratitude he felt when he was given another chance at life. A chance given him by Maguire. He struggled with his emotions. And as he did, his conscience nagged him. He could understand all too well Maguire's desire for his wife to belong; it was no different from his wanting to fit in and be liked by everyone. To be finally invited to the party and no longer looking in from the outside.

Ryle nodded his head in agreement and put out his hand to Maguire. He'd given his word. There was no turning back now. He didn't know if Maguire would say anything to Cathleen, but it was a chance he couldn't afford to take.

It always pays to know where the bodies are buried, Maguire decided as he drove back to Chacari, to have something to hold over people when you're negotiating. And then remembering the skeleton rattling around in *his* closet, he got a little queasy. None of us are immune, he sighed to himself. We all have our secrets.

TWELVE

"Just don't flaunt it around camp," he warned her. Cathleen didn't question the reason for Ryle's change of heart about Sarita. "Oh, you're so understanding." She threw her arms around him. He came around, she thought jubilantly, just like she knew he would. Wanting to be just as conciliatory, she vowed to cultivate the people he thought necessary to further his career.

Sarita, having heard Ryle's tirade, was wary. She didn't know what to make of Cathleen's frequent visits and Cathleen sensed her hesitancy. She probably heard Ryle call her those awful names, Cathleen realized in despair. What's the good of his changing his mind if he spoiled it between us? Then it came to a head when Sarita refused her invitation to lunch.

"But why not?" Cathleen persisted. "Ryle is out of camp and John has gone to Puerto La Cruz."

"I have some things I need to do at home," Sarita replied evasively.

"Oh Sarita, can't they wait? That's one of the things I miss here, going out to eat. Even though there's no restaurant around, it would be such fun fixing something the guys wouldn't touch — like a cheese soufflé."

"You've made other friends in camp." Sarita quickly refilled Cathleen's iced tea glass. "Perhaps they could accept your invitation."

"But you're the one I want, just the two of us." She doesn't want to come, Cathleen realized.

"I don't think it would be wise. You know that your husband doesn't approve of me."

She did hear Ryle, Cathleen realized despondently. Sarita seeing the disappointment in Cathleen's face, took her hands in hers. "It's all right, I understand," she said sweetly. "We'll always be friends in our hearts."

"But things have changed," Cathleen insisted. "He said he didn't

144

want to stop our friendship. I know you heard him say those awful things. It'd be a miracle if you didn't, the houses are so close." The words tumbled out of her mouth she was so anxious to make Sarita understand. "But he's come around, Sarita. Just as I knew he would."

"It's true what he told you," Sarita said gently. "I was once a prostitute. Perhaps it's wise not to associate with me."

"I don't care what you were," Cathleen said passionately. "What difference does it make now?" She felt close to tears, embarrassed because Sarita heard Ryle's nasty words, and angry because it would never be the same between them again. "I'm not staying away," she said stubbornly. "Our friendship means too much to me. Maybe you won't come to my house, but I'm coming here."

"Yes, oh yes," Sarita smiled, hugging her. The two of them laughed and cried in each other's arms, Sarita's skin making a dark splash against the milkwhite tones of Cathleen's. "You must always come here, *es tu casa.*"

....

A month before Fred went to Caracas for Maruja's answer, he met a nurse from the Sinclair Oil Hospital in Santa Barbara. Fran Young was exceedingly tall, just an inch under six feet, and not especially pretty. Her face had an almost horsey look to it, and despite all efforts with makeup, she never lost that plain look.

She wasn't born Fran Young. Because she'd been an avid movie fan who'd grown up adoring Kay Francis and Loretta Young, she took their names when she emigrated from Europe after WWII. Her name, Irina Miracovici, was too foreign sounding and she wanted to lose her old identity. Not only forget her struggle to stay alive during the war, but her former life. Although her husband was reported to be dead, she wanted no association with him or her past.

She was bent on going to the United States, but the fastest way out of the DP camp was Venezuela, where her application was looked upon with favor because of her nursing background. When she arrived in Caracas and discovered the abundance of single American men, she knew she'd found her passport to the States. Since the majority of them worked for the oil companies in the interior, she immediately applied for work there.

She thought she had put her past behind her, but the oilfields brought back a flood of memories. Of the country she had left behind, for Rumania, rich in oil, was ripe pickings for Hitler's war machine. The setting wasn't the same, the flatness of eastern Venezuela different from the Ploesti oilfields at the base of the Transylvanian mountains. But seeing the rigs again brought back the horror of the bombings in '42, first by the Americans in June and then again in September by the Russians.

The Americans came back again in '43 with their three hundred tons of bombs for the refinery. Not even fleeing to Bucharest brought any relief, for the whole country had become a prize to be fought over by the Germans and Russians. In August of '44 when the German bombers dropped their bombs on Bucharest, she knew it was time to leave Rumania. Her mother and father had been killed in the Ploesti raids, her brother Vasile the recipient of a bullet at the Kuban front. As for her husband, who had promised her so much and had given her so little, she erased him from her memories as if he never existed. To be the widow of someone suspected of being a Nazi was asking for trouble. Somehow she managed to flee, how she survived she chose not to remember. When there was nothing left to sell, she sold herself until she found refuge in a displaced persons camp.

She'd come a long way from her past life by the time she met Fred in January of '48. Her accent, which she worked very diligently to eradicate, showed only traces of her background. At first she didn't see Fred's face, she only saw him towering over most of the men at the bar. While she wasn't looking for love, she did want a man who was tall.

When he turned around, though, she felt like a schoolgirl with her first crush. Even the realization he was younger couldn't stop her heart racing back to life. It wasn't his handsome face, but his warm, friendly smile and devil may care attitude which shouted life to her, promising an antidote to all the death she'd known. This is what made the years slip away, blotting out the hardships and despair she'd experienced. She was eighteen years old again, in a rose colored satin dress and white pumps, with her mother's gold locket hanging around her neck, going to her first dance.

"What do you think?" Fred asked Murray when he saw her walking towards the bar.

"OK, if you turn the lights out," Murray replied, "and don't look at her face. She's got a fantastic body though. Legs like a racehorse and some pair of jugs."

"I'll flip you - heads I ask her to dance, tails you do." Fred reached in his pocket for a *Bolivar*.

"Naw, go ahead," Murray replied. "She's too tall for me anyway."

Perfect, Fran thought when Fred whisked her off to the dance floor. He's at least 6'3". Why, she'd even be able to wear high heels. The feelings she had when she first saw Fred intensified, she just had to have this man. It didn't matter that he was younger or that she had promised herself to never fall in love again. This was the man she wanted. And despite her lack of beauty, she had a lot in her favor. He had a year and a half to go on his contract, he was stationed nearby in Chacari, and she knew how lonely men were in the oilfields. She'd make him care for her. She was an expert when it came to making a man feel good. She hadn't survived those years fleeing across Europe on luck alone. She invited Fred to a picnic the next day. And checked off in her mind the other people going. Just one single woman and she had a steady. The rest were married people. Oh yes, there was a lot in her favor. As for the rest, she would just have to make her luck.

Until he met Maruja, Fred was always looking to meet women. Now when he went to a dance, it was just something to pass the time on a Saturday night until he got back to Caracas. He hadn't stopped going to the Looney Door, his hormones were too healthy. But he wasn't, to use Murray's expression, chasing skirts. Still when Fran came along and pursued him as aggressively as she did, he reasoned he wasn't being unfaithful to Maruja by having a last sexual fling. Fran was so eager for a little bit of loving, he assumed she wanted sex for the same reasons he did.

Fran, glowing with Fred's attentiveness (this was the way he acted with every woman) mistook it for love. When he fussed over her and complimented her, she thought he'd fallen just as hard for her as she had for him. Until the night of the Valentine Dance at the Jusepin Club.

"Now don't get too serious over this young buckaroo," one of the drillers from Chacari commented. They were standing at the bar waiting for another round of daiquiris. "He's spoken for."

"Oh? What does he mean, you're spoken for?" Her accent became more pronounced. It always did when she became excited, the w's coming out sounding like v's. "Are you married, Fred?"

"Am I married? Now answer her." Fred poked the driller. "This statuesque goddess thinks I'm married."

No one had ever called her a statuesque goddess before. How like Fred, who was forever coining unique phrases, making her feel she was special. He mustn't be married. Of all the unlucky experiences in her life, this would be the hardest to take. She knew more than a few married men passed themselves off as single while waiting for their wives to arrive.

"No, he ain't married," the driller said. "He's too ugly. But he does have a gal in Caracas."

"And I got one back in Houston, two in San Antone and three in Austin," the words slipped effortlessly from Fred's lips. "How many hearts have you broken, Franny? How many guys did you have on a string back there in Paris?" For some reason he seemed to think she was French.

She loved it when he called her Franny. It made her feel so tiny and petite, and for him to intimate that she'd left a trail of broken hearted lovers made her ego soar even higher. So much so, she momentarily forgot the driller's remark that he had a girl in Caracas. But later after the dance, when they were parked in his pickup far out in the bush under a clump of Acacia trees, she wondered about it again. They had just finished making love and as she relaxed in his arms, the fear he wasn't hers made her question him.

"Yeah, there's a girl in Caracas," he admitted.

"Are you serious about her?" She almost dreaded his reply.

"Yes I am, Franny."

"How could you do this to me?" she cried out, pushing him away from her. She struggled to pull on her dress, a strapless black faille she'd flown to Caracas to buy. Tearing off the homemade corsage of red hibiscus flowers he'd given her, which she had pinned to her evening bag, she threw it out the window.

"Giving me flowers, wining and dining me, making me feel that you cared. Always with the compliments," she cried out.

"And why not? You deserve them, you're a fine lady," Fred replied. While he didn't love her, he had grown to greatly admire her.

"A fine lady, but not good enough for you. Oh no, only the one in

Caracas is good enough for you," she sputtered.

"Now Franny, don't go getting so upset," he said softly, concerned because he'd hurt her. "It's certainly not because you're not good enough for me. Most likely it's the other way around. I like you, oh Franny, I like you a helluva a lot. And I thought you knew the score, that it wasn't anything heavy." Because he didn't want to hurt her feelings, he didn't point out she was the one who had initiated the friendship; that he hadn't pursued her or made any promises.

She pulled her net stole around her shoulders and then took out her compact. Looking at herself in the tiny mirror, she had difficulty holding back the tears. Her brown hair, fine and difficult to manage, which she'd cut short and in bangs to make her look younger seemed to mock her. She had never felt so old, her long nose and thin lips looking more pronounced than ever.

"So now that you've had your fun, it's goodbye Fran Young, right?" Her European pronunciation had slipped back into her carefully cultivated American accent.

"Not if you don't want to," Fred replied. "I hope we'll always be friends, Franny."

"Stop it," she cried out angrily, "don't you ever call me Franny again." And coldly she told him to take her back to the nurses' quarters. Where she spent a sleepless night trying to push him out of her thoughts, but not succeeding. Remembering what a wonderful dancer he was and his laughter which made everything so much fun. And especially his considerate skill as a lover, tender yet bursting with passion. Now she had lost all this to some girl in Caracas she didn't even know existed. She tossed restlessly, wondering if she was an American or English. For some reason it never occurred to her that her rival was a Venezuelan.

And when she found out, for she couldn't stay away from Fred, telling him she wanted to remain friends with him, hoping she could make him change his mind, she wanted to know everything about Maruja. So that after awhile Fred no long experienced the guilt she'd made him feel, and he began to believe Fran when she said she still wanted to be friends. He hated to hurt a woman, he always tried to be straight up with all of them. Sure he made a fuss over any woman he dated. It was his nature, just as he'd grown up always complimenting his three older sisters.

When he went to Caracas for Carnival, she refused to dwell on her disappointment and concentrated on him coming back to her. By now, getting Fred to love her had become an obsession. If she thought constantly about him, poured her energy into visualizing him loving her, it would happen. She had used the same total concentration during her odyssey across Europe, she was positive it was the reason she survived life in the DP camp. Because she hadn't given up.

....

Fred arrived in Caracas at the height of Carnival. Water filled balloons sailed through the air, hitting cars and people, bursting on impact. When he got out of his taxi at the Hotel Waldorf he saw one coming and caught it, throwing it back where it exploded, drenching several people. Letting out a high pitched, rebel yell, he ran into the hotel, dodging more balloons.

An hour later he arrived at Maruja's home where she was waiting for him with a costume her dressmaker had created, the comic strip hero, Batman.

When Maruja's mother, Misia Isabel, found out Maruja was going as Batman's sidekick, Robin the Boy Wonder, she was scandalized. For the past weeks there had been an ongoing battle between them over Carnival. It started with Maruja wanting to dress as a *Negrita Ratoncita*, every woman's favorite costume for it presented all sorts of intriguing possibilities, mainly going out without a chaperon. Dressed completely in black — a sweater, skirt, long gloves, stockings — her face covered by a mask, it was difficult to guess her identity. Especially when it was enhanced by a wig, lots of jewelry and scarves and she disguised her voice by talking in a high pitched squeal like Minnie Mouse, hence the name *Negrita Ratoncita*.

"*Absolutamente no*," Misia Isabel decreed. Both she and her husband, Don Eugenio, agreed that just because Maruja was almost engaged, this didn't mean she could go out during Carnival dressed as a black laundress. Whatever possessed the child to think her parents would allow such libertine behavior, they asked each other.

"It's because of that *musiu* she's fallen for," Misia Isabel remarked disdainfully.

"Nonsense," Don Eugenio replied. "That has nothing to do with it." More and more he was delighted with Maruja's choice of Fred. "No, it's because Maruja is Maruja and who could ever do a thing with her?"

Maruja was furious with her parents. Even though she would be married shortly, they continued to treat her like a child. All her life she had wanted to go out at Carnival disguised as a *Negrita Ratoncita*. Never mind the old wives' tales of the crimes of passion committed during Carnival when a woman donned the costume. She had hopes with such a disguise she and Fred would be able to slip away from their chaperons.

Misia Isabel couldn't understand this passion for wanting to dress up like one of the servants. Whatever happened to elegance, she wondered. Marie Antoinette or Cleopatra, now those were costumes. It was just a sign of the times, she told Don Eugenio, the moral laxity which made these woman of today want to dress up in such a low class outfit, traveling freely from ball to ball, going up to the men and asking them to dance, disguising their voices in that ridiculous high squeal. Which had led to some humorous circumstances. Such as the time Carlos Urdaneta, Caracas' biggest womanizer, took a *Negrita Ratoncita* to his secret love nest, only to discover under the disguise his own wife. Oh, the gossips had a most delicious time with that!

Frustrated, Maruja decided on Batman and Robin. But not without further words from her mother.

"You're going out in pants?" Misia Isabel shrieked.

"*Sí mami*. You wouldn't let me go out as a *Negrita Ratoncita*, so I had to think of something with a little bit of fun to it. This Batman is very big in American comic books, and as for me going out in pants, it's the style now. After all, I'll soon be a married woman. I can't continue to act and look like a teenage *señorita*."

"Oh, so you've decided to marry him?"

"But, of course," Maruja replied, as if there had never been any doubt.

"Well, then we can plan a wedding for next year."

"Next year?" Maruja looked with amusement at her mother. "*Ay* no. Maybe next month."

"Next month," Misia Isabel cried out in exasperation. "What is the matter with you, child? During Lent? What will everyone think? You know how tongues wag in this city. The gossips will have you pregnant."

"To devil with the gossips. They'll see in time that it's not true.

Maybe we'll plan the wedding for two months from now. But I definitely won't wait a year. I don't care what the custom is. I'm marrying an American, and they don't fool around, they get things done *ya*." And she snapped her fingers to show how quickly Americans acted.

Fred was intrigued with their costumes. "If you aren't the smartest *señorita* this side of the *Río Gran*, dreaming up these outfits. Wait 'til I tell the guys back in camp." He doubled over in laughter. "What am I talking about? I'll show up at the Mess hall as Batman and it'll rot their socks!" His blue eyes crinkled with anticipation, and his high pitched laugh filled the dance floor of the Jockey Club. He looked around to see if anyone was looking and then he quickly lifted the half black mask off her face and kissed her. "Since we're dressed as a team, does that mean we're goin' out together at Carnival the rest of our lives, that you're goin' to marry me?"

"*Claro que sí*, but of course," she replied blithely, as if he should have known all along.

"Oh *muñequita*, you little doll you. Well, another good man hits the dust." When he saw her wrinkle her nose which she did whenever she didn't understand his English, he hastened to explain his words. "That's a saying we got back in Texas when a man gets himself lassoed, gets hitched. It means —" He started to say it means a man is dead, but he had a feeling the joke would get lost in the translation. So instead he quickly picked her up and whirled her around the dance floor while the band played a fast *paso doble*. Dancing to the music played at bullfights, their feet simulated the same steps the *torero* used while whirling his cape at the bull before the final kill.

When he got back to the oilfields and told Fran of his impending marriage to Maruja, she was crushed. He's going through with his marriage, she realized with resignation, and I've lost him for good. So much for concentrating on him coming back to her. There are some things a person can't will into happening. For the first time in her life she contemplated suicide, convinced there was no happiness in her future.

Gradually though, the same instinct for survival which had kept her going the past years pulled up her emotions. It will never last, she reassured herself. A wealthy, spoiled Venezuelan who'd grown up in the lap of luxury living in the oilfields? She knew what coddled lives they lived for she'd done private duty in a Venezuelan home before signing up with Sinclair Oil. Whenever they wanted anything, they'd call to the servants to bring them this, do that, and the servants came running all the time. No, this Venezuelan society girl would never make it in the oilfields. As soon as the honeymoon was over she'd tell Fred to go jump in the lake. That and his damned oil camp.

Fred thought he was madly in love with Maruja, but she knew it was merely an infatuation. So many oilfield marriages were the result of the bachelor's loneliness. The oilfields made for hasty marriages, where the women were swept off their feet by men who went back to the States with their pockets full of money and no one to spend it on. These marriages almost had the urgency of wartime. She was convinced this was the reason for Fred's marriage. Maruja had caught him at a time when he was lonely and vulnerable

They parted with Fran praying Fred's marriage would fail and Fred thinking they were good friends. For he did like her. Not only because she was erotic, she aroused him as few other women had, teaching him a lot of sexual games, but he also admired her. Although she kept a lot of her past to herself, bits and pieces came out and he couldn't help but be touched by what she'd gone through. And that part of her which she deplored — being older — was the quality which fascinated him the most.

She started concentrating on Fred's bride leaving him to go back to her charmed life in Caracas. She may have lost this skirmish, Fran consoled herself, but she would be around to win the final battle. Fred was going to be her man. Maybe not now, it might take a year or so, but he would come back to her. That's why it was so important they remain friends.

Never burn your bridges, she remembered, or cut loose your moorings. Life is like a wheel, whatever goes around has to come around again. She hadn't survived the bombings or fled across Europe one step ahead of the bullets to lose out now to some pampered Caracas twit.

THIRTEEN

March seventeenth started out like any other day. But as the hours trickled away, Cathleen grew more and more homesick. For St. Patrick's Day spelled family to her. And hers always celebrated in a big way, the parties rotating from one relative's house to another. This year, her mother wrote, it was being held at the Cavanaughs.

She'd given up cigarettes for Lent, but since St. Paddy's was a day of dispensation from Lenten abstinence, she lit more than a few that morning to ward off the blues. When Lent started she debated whether to give up cocktails, and then decided against it. Having a drink was a way of life in Chacari, and she didn't want to feel left out of things.

Feeling restless, she cut through the hedge and knocked on the back door of the Maguires' house, only to be informed by the maid that Sarita had gone to Puerto La Cruz with John. Good for her, Cathleen thought enviously, at least she got out of camp for a day. But it was really John she wanted to see. She never thought before about her background, growing up in a town with a large Irish-American population. But now far away from family with the pangs of homesickness so strong this day, she longed to see John because he had the same roots. Of all days for them to be away, she thought morosely. The last couple of days she found herself getting cross at the slightest provocation. Her period was late and she wondered if she was pregnant.

Ryle was out of camp, he hadn't even come home for lunch. Nor was there any bridge party going on. What's the matter with everyone? No one thought to have a St. Patrick's Day party because it didn't fall on the weekend? Why, back home that never stopped anyone. As she thought about the party she was missing at her cousin Charley Cavanaugh's house, she burst into tears. She lit a cigarette to calm herself and then overcome with waves of nausea, she barely made it to the bathroom in time.

By Saturday she felt positive she was pregnant, but was determined that no matter how nauseous she felt, she would make the St. Patrick's Day party at the clubhouse. It was bad enough spending the most miserable March seventeenth of her life, she wasn't about to miss out on the only St. Paddy's Day party in this godforsaken piece of the world. She'd grown to love the Saturday night parties, everybody letting their hair down, getting a mellow glow with a few rum punches and dancing the night away. Especially when the Latin American records were played. It was impossible to ignore their infectious invitation to get up and have the time of your life.

As she dressed for the party she sipped ginger ale for it was the only thing which calmed her stomach. Trying to get her hair to stay in place was proving to be an impossible task; finally she wound it in a chignon. And then she slipped into a dress which she bought for just this day. Emerald green in the softest layers of chiffon which billowed out from a tapered waist, the low cut bodice was held up by several strands of spaghetti straps.

"You look gorgeous," Ryle remarked admiringly as he zipped up her dress.

An insistent *mambo* was pouring out of the record player when they arrived at the clubhouse. The music punctuated by the strong trumpet sounds of Perez Prado, with his trademark 'Ugh' grunted from time to time, had everyone dancing. If the music wasn't Irish, the decorations made up for it. Green crepe paper climbed the pillars, while paper shamrocks bobbed from the ceiling. Each table had a green derby filled with noisemakers. All courtesy of one of the members of the Decorating Committee who'd brought them back from her last trip to the States.

There was a rush of bachelors asking Cathleen to dance, but she declined their invitations because of her queasiness. Also, she never knew how Ryle would react. Sometimes he seemed pleased with the line of single men wanting to dance with her, proud that other males found his wife so attractive. Other times he became extremely jealous.

"All these bachelors need someone to dance with, especially a pretty young thing like you," Nadine scolded her affectionately when the Rylanders sat down at their table. Nadine had been a USO hostess during the war, and to her the bachelors in camp were no different than the soldiers in a canteen.

Sugar Dalhart, the camp superintendent's wife sitting at the same table, heard Nadine's remark. Damn Yankee girl should have stayed in New York or wherever the hell she came from, she fussed to herself. She couldn't remember any woman annoying her as much as Cathleen. *It's because she thinks she's so much better than the rest of us.* The way she dresses, like she's some movie star or a model on the cover of a magazine. Sugar took in Cathleen's green cocktail dress, noting enviously how the gold and green shamrock hanging from a gold chain nestled in the cleavage of her breasts. Full, rounded breasts were something Sugar didn't have.

She hadn't as yet admitted to herself the reason she disliked Cathleen. But now looking at her, the resentment swirled to the surface. She missed Ryle dancing attention on her the way he used to. She knew she always got him hot and bothered, but not now. *It's because he's giving it all to that bitch.* The idea of Cathleen being the recipient of Ryle's sexuality filled her with anger and hatred. *I want her out of my camp,* she fumed, *out of my way, out of my life.*

Emmett Dalhart, seeing the anger in his wife's eyes was puzzled. No matter what the reason and he couldn't imagine any, she should know better than to display her feelings so openly. She had a position to maintain, something she'd always been aware of before. Then he heard Sugar laugh, and any doubts he had about her were dispelled. For his wife's laughter had the power to chase away gloom, rub out heartache and lift him into the company of angels.

The first time he heard it he was sitting at the bar of the *Hotel Avila* in Caracas, nursing a lonely drink. The laughter he heard filled him with so much joy he found himself smiling in return. Then, curious as to its source, he got up and followed its sound. What he found was a girl with light brown hair framing a face which held no great beauty, a body so thin it was almost boyish. But when she laughed, he understood what attracted him and why she was surrounded by an admiring group of men.

"I just love the way you laugh," Emmett told her when he got up the nerve to ask her to dance.

"Shoot, I bet you tell that to all the girls." Sugar gave him her best Scarlett O'Hara imitation, batting her eyelashes, whipping out an imaginary fan. "I kinda like something about you, too."

"Me?" His speech became flustered. She was so young, he almost felt embarrassed holding her in his arms, convinced he was behaving like a dirty old man.

"Yeah you," her laughter seemed to bubble up from a bottomless well. "What I like is that hair of yours, it's like silver. You sort of remind me of a fox, a silver fox, all set to raid the henhouse."

"Silver, huh? It's only a lot of grey turning white. Just an old man showing his age." He felt he had to establish he was older than she. As if she didn't know, he snorted to himself. Just one look at this old warhorse and anyone could tell.

"You sure don't dance like an old man." This last remark produced more laughter which he found himself joining. And when he followed her in the *Limbo*, moving his body under the pole each time it was lowered, he forgot he was forty-one years old with a bad back which kept him out of wartime service.

Emmett was almost resigned to being unlucky in love. Moving around from oilfield to oilfield hadn't allowed him to offer much in the way of a stable home life, or so his first wife had informed him. She chafed at the idea of traipsing from one place to another and not being able to put down roots for their two children. His second matrimonial attempt was with someone who didn't mind the travelling. He suspected she was running around on him, but overlooked all the signs until the night he came home from working the second tour and got into bed with her. If he had been a violent man, he might have killed her that night. Instead when he discovered she was still wet and soiled from the previous occupant of their bed, he got up, took the longest shower of his life, packed a bag and left.

He'd come to Venezuela for the same reason most people came, the money. His second wife had cleaned out his bank account and there was still child support for his children from his first marriage. Like most of the bachelors, he visited whichever whorehouse was handy. He hated paying for sex, but consoled himself with the thought that one way or another, a man paid for everything in life.

But all that changed when he met Sugar. She chased away the blues, made him feel alive again.

"I was just thinking of the night we met," he whispered in Sugar's ear when they got up to dance. "Any regrets?"

"Why honey, you know I adore being your wife." Which she did for the simple reason she had found her kingdom. It might be hell's half acre to some people, or 'The Place They Forgot to Remember' as others called Chacari, but not to her. She would gripe along with the other women about the commissary, the lack of conveniences, the monotony of camp life, but she was royalty here and she made sure no one forgot it. Better to rule in hell than serve in heaven.

She felt it was her due for she'd grown up with a lot of attention. Born to a couple who were almost beyond childbearing age, her entrance into their lives was something they'd given up hope would happen. From the beginning, she was a happy baby, laughing and gurgling, responding to their constant love. She's so incredibly sweet, her daddy declared one day, she's just like sugar. She'd been named after her grandmother; her passport read Charlotte Cummings, but everyone called her Sugar. People said her parents spoiled her rotten, giving her too many toys, too little discipline, but their reply was you could never give a person too much love or affection.

This outpouring of attention from her parents, though, wasn't enough. She grew up half ashamed of her father, because in her eyes there was a limit to what he could do for her. Her father, unaware of her feelings, thought he'd done quite well. So did her mother. Hadn't they shaken the dust of the small North Carolina town they hailed from? Brought to Caracas by Alas Cigarette Co., they found a life there they never dreamt existed. A house they could never have afforded back home, membership in the Caracas Country Club where her father played golf three times a week and her mother hosted bridge parties and luncheons. And parties for Sugar in the garden of their Spanish style *quinta*, a house they named '*Quinta* Sugar'. Birthdays with *piñatas* stuffed with candy and small toys, further enhanced with merry-go-rounds or clowns. And as she grew older, dinner dances held in the lantern lit garden. Her life was one perpetual party after another and she saw no reason to change. Why shoot, she told Emmett the night they met, that's what life was all about, having fun.

She was attracted to him because he was so different from the boys she knew in Caracas. His unusual looks, the silver hair and body tanned from all the hours spent outdoors on a rig held a rugged, masculine attraction for her. Their difference in ages, so disturbing to him, was even more appealing to her. The pale blue eyes which looked at her with such longing had seen a lot more of life than she had, and this she found intriguing.

When she finally got him into bed, for he was a reluctant lover, still hurting from his second wife's infidelity, she was unprepared for the intensity of his lovemaking. Having made up his mind to bed her, he let all his emotions which had been bottled up for so long, spill out. No one had ever wanted her this much before. She could feel it in the strength of his arms, the way his lips worked hers so she became weak with desire. Her body experienced such intensities in orgasm she just had to have him for more than a fling. She decided he would be the perfect husband, especially after he was promoted from head toolpusher to superintendent of Chacari. Here was a man who was going places and she meant to go with him.

Ignoring Emmett's warnings about life in the oilfields, she refused to be discouraged. When he still hadn't proposed, despite all the trips he made to Caracas to see her, she arrived unexpectedly one Saturday in Chacari. By the next day they were planning their wedding, prompted by the fact she was pregnant. Sugar honestly didn't know if Emmett was the father, but she felt he would make a good one for the child she was carrying.

If there was any talk of her youth, of the difference in their ages, it was quickly smoothed over by her vivaciousness, the sound of her laughter and her endless energy. She could drink large amounts of rum punch and never have a hangover.

What thrilled her most about the oilfields was the surplus of single men. Even though her marriage would confine her to one bed, there were still all those men to dance attention on her.

But Emmett warned her. "I'm a two time loser, Sugar. I just couldn't take another failure. Don't ever run around on me. If you do, I'll walk away so fast, you won't even see my dust."

In the beginning, she remained faithful, contenting herself with the constant admiration of the bachelors. When their feelings became too intense and she teased them into a state of complete horniness, the Looney Door did a landslide business. She knew what she was doing to them. It made her sex life with Emmett more exciting because she could fantasize there was another man in bed with her. But after the second year of marriage, monogamy became boring.

She was too much in love with her position, though, to jeopardize it. She realized she would have to be very careful. At first it was monthly trips to Caracas to visit her parents, where she left Drew with her mother to tryst with former lovers. Then one of her girl friends from Caracas, now married and living in a neighboring camp, provided the perfect cover. Sugar driving out of camp to visit her didn't arouse any suspicion, even at night when Emmett was away on business. Emmett never doubted her. For she smothered him with attention. Oh, he knew she was a flirt, but to him she was just having a good time, making everyone's life a little brighter as she'd made his. Hadn't she erased the scars from his previous marriages? If he ever questioned whether Sugar's pregnancy had pushed him into a hasty marriage, all he had to do was look at the son she'd given him. Drew Dalhart, who made up for the sons his first wife's new husband wanted to adopt.

In his eyes, she had only one fault, and at times he wasn't even sure it was a fault, as she had a way of turning things to her advantage. There was a quirky side to her when she would come out with a scathing remark, as she did about Cathleen's dress, then in a split second she'd cover it with such a delightful laugh no one knew whether she meant it or not. Her saving grace was she never went over the line.

Cathleen, unaware of the reason for Sugar's resentment, was just as ignorant of Murray's growing interest in her. When she walked into the clubhouse that night, he greedily devoured every detail of her appearance. You put these crackers to shame, he crowed inwardly, noting how the color of her green dress changed the aquamarine of her eyes. He recognized her shyness and admired the way she covered it with a manufactured poise. He also knew having a drink helped her mingle, for he'd seen the look of reticence in her eyes when she first arrived at a party. He worried that life in the oilfields would change her, that taking a drink would become a way of life with her.

"You're a knockout, Toots," he remarked when he asked her to dance. "Wanna run away with me tonight?" Seeing his lopsided grin, Cathleen's face broke out in a smile. Being around Murray was always such a tonic. She was almost tempted to get up and dance with him, except for the fear she would spill her cookies all over him.

Then she felt she could sit still no longer. The *mambo* and *samba* records had been replaced by Irish songs which made her feet tap in time to the music. And inwardly she cringed as she watched people dance. Jesus, Mary and Joseph, would you look at them! Hopping around like a bunch of rabbits, thinking they knew how to dance the Irish Jig. Didn't they realize they were supposed to point their toes? That they should be executing the whirls much quicker and they should be bobbing, not jumping like a bunch of clodhoppers? Ah, if only there were someone here to dance with, she'd show them. She almost had half a mind to get up and dance by herself, for back home at the family parties lacking a partner was never a detriment when the music called out to you. But looking around she knew she couldn't. Stone cold sober with ginger ale, she had been robbed of her courage.

Now the crowd was singing along with the music coming out of the record player. Sitting quietly in her green dress and sliding the shamrock back and forth on the gold chain, Cathleen fought to keep at bay her longing for home. Sometimes she sang along, pretending a rowdiness with everyone when they sang *Who Threw the Overalls in Mrs. Murphy's Chowder*. Experienced goosebumps when Murray's voice soared above the crowd to *My Wild Irish Rose*. But it was *I'll Take You Home Again, Kathleen* which opened the floodgates of her emotions. She would give a year of her life if she could be home now. Even a few hours would be enough. She would throw her arms around her brothers, whose boisterousness sometimes got on her nerves, hug and kiss her sister Beebe whose nonchalant use of her clothes had always irritated her. But most of all she would be so content to be in her mother's kitchen again. She looked around, the longing for home so strong she felt she would go mad. Strangers, all of them complete strangers. A sob escaped from her throat, sounding somewhat like the cry of an animal caught in a trap. Waves of nausea washed over her, and although she bolted to the ladies room, she wasn't quick enough. The contents of her stomach lay all over the bodice of her new, emerald green dress.

Murray sensing her outburst was caused by homesickness, wished he could do something to cheer her up. Ryle bewildered by this sudden shift in his wife's mood looked at her in embarrassment. Sugar lit a cigarette, savoring the scene she just witnessed. She's going to be one of those women who can't take life in the oilfields, Sugar gloated. Any day now she'll be taking a plane out of here. And then I'll have Ryle back. Just as soon as Miss America flies her butt out of here, it'll be like old times again.

....

Ryle was exuberant about Cathleen's pregnancy. He wanted a son so badly, he could taste it. Cathleen was just happy being pregnant, it didn't matter to her what the baby's sex was. It was too much of an effort, for her energy level had slipped into low gear and all she wanted to do was sleep. When she wasn't sleeping, she escaped into books. She started reading *David Copperfield* again, and for the rest of her pregnancy went through her entire Dickens collection. The advantage of being pregnant was now she had a valid excuse to avoid the morning coffees.

But she had to save her energy for the weekend parties. For no matter how blah she felt, Ryle wanted them to get out. She didn't drink or smoke anymore because she felt it would harm the baby. She sipped ginger ale, growing to loathe its taste, feeling like a limp dishrag because she was missing out on the fun which a glass of rum punch in one hand and a cigarette in the other always gave her.

It wasn't easy being pregnant, she discovered, and married to S. J. Rylander. She didn't know whether it was because she had so little energy, or his mood swings had gotten worse. But living with him had become increasingly more difficult. Except when they went to bed at night where his ardor was so strong it was like living with another man. She wanted to talk things over with him, but his cold and distant manner discouraged conversation. She didn't know how to handle his silences. When he ignored her, it cut her up into little emotional pieces.

"It's like walking on eggs living with you," she burst out one day, unable to contain her feelings any longer. "You're either telling me how to act or what people I should associate with. Or you get into one of your moods and act like I don't exist. And then when you decide to be human again, I have to overlook how distant you've been. I'm supposed to spread my legs and be glad to see you."

She saw him stiffen, shocked at her words. Real shanty Irish talk Cathleen, she berated herself. But it's the truth.

It's a plague being pregnant, she decided despondently, battling daily with the nausea. Her oldest sister, Moira had sailed through her pregnancies, declaring that she never felt better in her life. Why couldn't she? When her clothes became too tight she got even more irritable. There was no store she could go to for maternity clothes, not that she wore that many dresses. It was too hot, and most of the time unless she was going to the clubhouse or to a party, she lived in shorts. When she cut the waist from her shorts and wore long blouses over them, Ryle's remarks upset her even more.

"You can't go around like that," he shook his head in dismay. "A pregnant woman should be wearing a dress, not shorts. You're gonna look like some goddammed stork with those thin legs of yours and your stomach getting bigger every day." What he didn't say, but implied, was she was letting herself go. She'd been fastidious about her appearance all her life, and she hated herself for becoming such a slob. If only she had the energy to care.

It was Sarita who made everything better.

"For you, Cathleen," she said softly, handing her a green print dress. "See, it has elastic in the waist and as you expand, so will the dress."

"Oh, Sarita, you are the best friend anyone could ever have," Cathleen cried out, throwing her arms around her. "Where did you get it? I've written to my mother to send me maternity clothes, but who knows how long that will take."

"I bought the material in *El Tejero* and in no time I ran it up on my sewing machine. I'll make you more dresses, but I wanted to see how this fit." She pulled the material in around Cathleen's shoulders, adjusting it with some straight pins, for she could see that she'd made it too large in the bodice.

"You'll want to pick out your own choice of material. Perhaps when you are up to it, we can go shopping."

Sarita's gift did wonders for her morale, as did her offer to make more maternity clothes. The next afternoon, for by mid-day her stomach would settle down somewhat, they drove to *El Tejero*.

"There's nothing like getting new clothes," Cathleen cried out jubilantly as they passed the security guard and headed east. It was the first time she had driven since she became pregnant and it added to her sense of well being, making her feel she was in control of her life again. She and Sarita were so caught up in each other's company she didn't notice Sugar passing them on her way back to Chacari.

Sugar stopped her car, looking at the Chevy in her rear view mirror. Miss America with Maguire's nigger, she sneered to herself. Well, if that don't beat all. She took out a cigarette, thinking about what she'd just seen. The news of Cathleen's pregnancy hadn't set well with her. She'd been so positive Cathleen would leave. Now Miss America will never go, she thought, angrily grinding out her cigarette in the ashtray. She started the car up and headed back into camp, so irritated she almost drove past Ryle who was walking from the administration building towards his pickup. Putting the light blue Pontiac into reverse, she shot the car back.

"Hey there, Ryle," she called out flirtatiously. "Ain't you a sight for sore eyes."

"You're not hard to look at either, Sugar," he replied walking slowly towards her. Watching his slow amble aroused her, reminding her of the leisurely way he made love, never rushing but taking his time to do all the things he was so good at. Now remembering those times long gone, an anger began to swell up inside her.

"I almost died when I passed Cathleen on the road just now," she said breathlessly. "Oh, honey, you know that associating with Maguire's whore isn't the thing to do in this camp."

"She's just being neighborly," he remarked looking guardedly at her. He wasn't too happy about Cathleen accepting the dress from Sarita, but he'd given his word to Maguire and he couldn't go back on it. Now hearing Sugar badger him about Cathleen's friendship with Sarita, and knowing his romp in the hay with her was the reason for it, he burst out, "I didn't have much choice. Maguire knows about us."

"What do you mean, knows about us?"

Recounting his conversation with Maguire, he wondered why he ever became involved with her. Should have gotten my relief at the Looney Door, he swore to himself. Only it was more than relief, he realized. It was the thrill of doing something with a measure of risk to it; cutting things to the edge always excited him. It wasn't the first time he'd screwed the boss's wife.

"Nobody would believe him," she sputtered. "Why, he doesn't have an ounce of proof."

"Yeah well," Ryle replied. "It's a chance I don't feel like taking. You know how people gossip here. He could start a rumor and pretty soon the whole damn camp would be talking."

"Guess you had no other choice, honey." Sugar's smile was the soul of understanding. But underneath she was shaking. Her position as the super's wife would go up in smoke if Emmett ever found out about her little flings. All because of Miss America's friendship with that whore. She has to go, Sugar screamed as she drove home, not caring if anyone heard her. That damn Yankee, who thinks she's some movie star or something, just has to go. She was so positive she wouldn't last, that Cathleen would have run back to the States with homesickness by now. It's because she had to go and get pregnant, Sugar decided, lighting up another cigarette. Now she'll stick to Ryle like glue.

Drew came running to her when she walked into the house, pulling at her skirt, whining for her to play with him. She pushed him away. "Not now, honey chile, Momma's got things on her mind." But when he persisted and started climbing up on her lap, she screamed at the maid to take him for a walk. And Drew who really didn't want to go out started whimpering, only stopping when her hand flew out and smacked him. He was scared to death of his mother when she went into one of her rages. He ran in terror to the maid.

If Cathleen weren't pregnant, that damn Yankee would have been long gone, Sugar brooded. But if she had a miscarriage, that would be another story. What a shame the houses in camp didn't have two stories. Hadn't she seen a movie where Gene Tierney fell down the stairs so she would lose her baby? Well, there's more than one way to skin a cat, she decided. She would just have to come up with something to make Miss America lose that damn baby.

FOURTEEN

Ecstatic about his wedding, Fred got carried away and invited the entire camp. Very few accepted. Going to Caracas for the weekend cost money; it would mean dipping into their salary that month. Cathleen was grateful Ryle didn't feel that way. Or perhaps, she wondered, it was his desire to associate with the 'right people' in Caracas society. Whatever the reason, the chance to trade the heat and humidity of Chacari for the cool mountain air of the capital had her senses dancing. By now her bouts with nausea had receded and she was excited about becoming a mother. And for more than the usual reasons. Because Ryle's moodiness made her feel sometimes he was bored or disappointed with her, she feared their marriage might be foundering. She had hopes a baby would bring them closer.

But sitting in the Cathedral Saturday afternoon waiting for the wedding to begin, she had no such doubts. Ever since their arrival last night at the *Hotel Avila*, where they'd spent the last days of their honeymoon, Ryle had been loving and attentive.

It was such a pleasure being able to wear nylons and gloves again, and especially a hat. Glancing down at the fabric of the coral dress Sarita had made for her, Cathleen was still amazed at Sarita's ability to look at a picture of a dress and copy it. One day, Ryle told her when he complimented her on the wide brimmed hat she wore to the wedding, one day we'll be stationed in Caracas and you'll be able to wear all the hats you want. It can't come fast enough, she thought, dreading their return to the oilfields.

Her eyes darted around the Cathedral lingering on the beautiful paintings by Rubens and the Venezuelan artist, Michelena. Then she noticed the outfits of the Venezuelan women. Especially the hats which made hers look plain in comparison, for Venezuelan women delighted in wearing hats decorated with artificial flowers so exquisitely fashioned they looked real. And the jewelry! She'd never seen such a collection of gold, no one seemed to know what costume jewelry was. But that was another facet of Venezuela's enormous wealth. Besides its oil, there were the gold mines of Guayana. She was especially intrigued by the jewelry -- earrings, pins and bracelets fashioned in a delicately shaped orchid design, either in gold or silver, with pearls from the Island of Margarita adorning the tips of the orchid stigmas. Ryle had given her a gold orchid bracelet that morning, at the same time promising one day he would buy her a larger diamond ring. Despite her protests that she was perfectly content with her one carat ring, he kept insisting he wanted to give her a bigger one. Finally caught up in his enthusiasm, she told him a pear-shaped solitaire wouldn't be hard to take. And an emerald and diamond wedding ring to match, he persisted, throw out the plain gold band. I always want you to look expensive, he told her, so people will know I take good care of you. Just take good emotional care of me, she wanted to tell him, for without that, the jewelry is meaningless and just window dressing. But she kept her thoughts to herself, for she knew it would hurt his pride since he put such store in displays of material possessions.

Whispers grew louder among the Venezuelan women when the best man and groom appeared on the altar. *Que guapo*, they commented, Maruja had certainly snared a handsome *musiu*. Handsome if one liked a man who looked like *pan blanco*, one remarked indifferently, his fair looks reminding her of a large loaf of white bread. She preferred someone more Latin looking, like the best man. Now there was a *hombre* for you. *Epa*! another one sighed, he looks like he could keep a woman dancing all night. *Sinvergüenzas*! *Tía* Nellie hissed, how shameful to be talking like this in God's house.

The cause of these comments was Murray, whom Fred had asked to be his best man. "Nothing to be nervous about, kiddo," Murray reassured him as they waited at the altar.

"Who's nervous?" Fred replied feeling he was about to jump out of his skin. His eyes traveled to the back of the Cathedral looking for Maruja. But all he saw was her sister, Malena, fussing with Maruja's veil. Then the music changed and the bridesmaids made their way up the middle aisle of the Cathedral. He wished they would speed things up, this was the second marriage ceremony he'd gone through in two days. If that don't beat all, he thought, they really make sure you get married in this country. For a church ceremony didn't amount to a hill of beans if you hadn't gone through a civil one. He teased Maruja after the civil ceremony, hinting that now they were legally married they could run off on their honeymoon. Although her laughter showed eagerness, his 'half-laws' as he referred to his future in-laws, hadn't appreciated his sense of humor.

And then Maruja appeared, walking majestically towards the altar on the arm of her father. If she isn't the cutest little doll God ever created, he marvelled. Her princess styled satin dress made her tiny waist appear even daintier. Cascading from a pearl tiara her train was held by four flower girls, while a thin veil covered her face. But he could see her eyes through the lace, they flashed with anticipation.

When Maruja reached the altar, the fragrance of her rose scented perfume filled the air. He made himself concentrate on the ceremony, trying to remember the rehearsal yesterday. She gave him thirteen silver *reales*, about the size of an American dime and equivalent to half a *Bolivar*, pledging with these thirteen coins her dowry to him. He balked at this part of the ceremony, that she would be bringing her wealth to their marriage. For he wanted to think of himself as the breadwinner. But assured by Maruja that it was just a symbol, a Venezuelan tradition, he went along with it. Of course they would live on his salary, she promised him, she wouldn't touch a penny of her dowry.

After he pocketed the *reales*, Fred reached for the ring which Murray handed him. He started to slip it on her left hand, then caught himself when she reached for his right hand. Actually he liked the idea of wearing their rings on the right hand for Maruja had made it sound very romantic. "The right hand is the one you hold over your heart and that's why in Venezuela we wear our wedding rings on this hand." He was so nuts about this little Venezuelan doll if she wanted him to wear the ring in his nose, he would. The ceremony was finally over and when she lifted the veil from her face, he bent down to kiss her. Did you ever see such perfection, he wanted to shout to everyone in the Cathedral. They turned around and walked down the aisle, the music giving him goosebumps. He grinned down at her, squeezing her hand, while she looked up at him with those eyes which had always driven him wild with their promise.

That night the promise in Maruja's eyes was no longer just an invitation. At last she was free to express her love for him. She had waited all her life for *un amor* such as this and embraced it eagerly.

For months Fred had been undressing Maruja in his mind. He couldn't ever remember wanting to take off a woman's clothes as much as he wanted to peel off Maruja's. The pink cloth buttons marching down the front of her pink dress seemed to beckon his fingers. And with each button he undid, Maruja's murmuring "*Que delicioso*," heightened his excitement. When his finger reached the last one and he slipped the dress off her shoulders, the sight of her breasts peeping through the lace of her slip made him dizzy. He literally felt the room spin around him. How many times had just seeing the hem of her slip excited him, making him long to see what that slip covered? Moving his hands inside her slip he cupped each breast, marvelling at the texture of her skin. Then he could stand it no longer. He just had to see what they looked like. He pulled the straps of her slip down and gazed in awe at her tiny, but full breasts.

"Oh *muñequita*," he groaned, "they're prettier than I dreamt they would be." His mouth brushed over them, tasting the sweetness of her skin. As his hands pushed her slip down to the floor, her body responded to his touch. She wriggled her hips rhythmically, as if performing some ritual dance. Yearning to see how she looked with just a garter belt and stockings, he slowly pulled down her panties. And then he had to stop. He closed his eyes because if he didn't get control of himself, he was going to have an orgasm.

When he opened them, he intended to pull her stockings off one by one and then remove the last garment, her garter belt. But as his hand rolled the pink tinged stocking down the thigh of her right leg, he gave up. He just couldn't stand it any longer and his lips burrowed into the inviting ripeness of her body. Little moans escaped from Maruja, each new thing he did to her was more delicious than the last. She cried out to him, impatient to know what it was like to have him inside her. Forgetting all his intentions of entering her slowly so that her virginity wouldn't be bruised, Fred responded to her urging. "*Ay! Que fantástico*," Maruja murmured each time they came together, never wanting them to stop. When they did, both fell asleep exhausted, their bodies clinging together. Not for long though, within a short time Maruja was wide awake urging Fred to do all those marvelous things to her again. When they got up the next morning to receive room service, her garter belt was still wrapped around her waist.

It was the shortest of honeymoons, for he wasn't due to get his local leave until the end of the year. On Monday morning they took the Avensa flight to Maturín. Although deliriously happy with his bride, Fred was a little uneasy as to how she would react to the oilfields. He tried to explain just how different it would be from what she was used to in Caracas. He even asked her to come out before the wedding and look around, but she insisted it wasn't necessary.

Of all the women who arrived in Chacari, Maruja was the least prepared. When she saw their little box of a house with its concrete floors and the rattan furniture with the faded cushions, it jolted her. She'd grown up in a mansion surrounded by servants. Like all wealthy Venezuelan households, hers had servants who each knew their own bailiwick. The cook reigned in the kitchen and would never lift a finger to do anything related to the laundry. This was the laundress's domain, who in turn would never enter the house and do any dusting and cleaning which was done by the 'inside maids'. The shopping for the household was never done by Maruja's mother, for the cook was the one who went to the market or purchased chickens and turkeys from street vendors, which she had to slaughter before cooking. Even the smallest details of gardening, watering the plants and flowers which grew in the patio, were taken care of by the servants' children, who also had to clean the bird cages.

But unlike some of the American women, she didn't break down and cry, or refuse to speak to her husband for weeks after her arrival, or take the next plane out. It was a rude awakening for her. But if being with Fred meant living in the bush as he called it, so be it. She proceeded to look for help and the first lesson she learned was that the servants were a different breed than those in Caracas. Aside from mopping the floors, they had no idea how to take care of a house. And neither did she. It never occurred to her she would have to cook, for no one in her family had ever been in the kitchen. The culinary skills of the servants in the oilfields consisted of preparing black beans, rice, plantains and tough meat. Even Fred's easy going disposition began to wear thin after a steady diet of the maid's cooking. What saved her was her irrepressible charm and the invitations she received as the newest arrival in camp. She found herself looking forward to the morning coffees, the afternoon teas and card parties, the cocktail and dinner invitations because it was the only time she and Fred had anything decent to eat.

The women who'd heard rumors of Maruja's wealth were smitten with her. Her clothes and the solid gold jewelry she wore made them feel they were in the presence of royalty. But most of all her charming personality seduced them, just as it had enchanted people all her life.

"Pat," she cried out one morning at a coffee, her eyes sparkling with animation, her rings flashing as her tiny hands make extravagant gestures in the air. There was an immediate silence in the room, the women stopped chattering and all eyes were on her. She knew how to exhibit some theatrics and could turn any event into instant drama. "Pat," she cried out again, "you must save my marriage!"

Pat Davis, the hostess, set her coffee cup down and looked skeptically at Maruja. Pat's body was usually draped in a tent-like dress, and with her beady eyes and heavily rouged fat cheeks she resembled an aging chipmunk, a name some of the women called her behind her back.

"What's the matter with your marriage?" Pat barked in a voice made husky by years of hoisting rum punches. "Hell, you're still on your honeymoon."

"*¿Quién sabe?*" Maruja shrugged her shoulders. "Who knows if we are still on our honeymoon!" Her words had a ring to them which immediately intrigued the women. "I think Fred might send me back to Caracas. You've got to help me, Pat."

By now the whole room's attention was focused on Maruja. Her startling revelation was made with such sincerity, she looked so tiny and defenseless sitting there, they all wanted to help her.

"What's the matter, Maruja?"

"Oh, you poor baby."

She waited until everyone had stopped talking and there was complete silence. Then she spoke.

"The truth of the matter is that Fred can't go on eating the horrible meals our maid cooks."

The room filled with laughter, coupled with a few sighs of disappointment. Nothing juicy or scandalous, just maid problems, something they all went through at one time or another.

"Not being prepared for this marriage business to an American *petrolero*," Maruja continued, "I don't know a thing about cooking or what to tell the maid to do. But you, Pat, you are such an accomplished cook and your house always looks so lovely, won't you please help me? Could you teach me how to cook? And take care of a house? For if you do, you will save my marriage!"

Within a few minutes she had every woman lined up to give her cooking and housekeeping lessons. When she became a good cook and her chili and corn bread became famous in the region, the camp was more in awe of her than ever. In their eyes it was like seeing the Queen of England get down and scrub floors.

Like most people in camp, Maruja lived for the weekends. Although she kept busy going to the coffees and card parties, she missed Caracas. Sometimes the silence of the camp depressed her. She was used to the noises of Caracas, all of them attesting to life being lived. The vendors crying out their offerings, the cab drivers insulting each other in verbal bouts while banging on the sides of their taxis, the Cathedral clock chiming every fifteen minutes. And she missed her big house on the corner with the constant traffic of relatives who visited back and forth. In camp there were no diplomatic balls or embassy receptions to attend. She longed for the places she and Fred used to frequent - *El Paris* Restaurant which served her favorite meal, Champagne Steak and where she always wore one of her extravagant hats. Dancing at the *Hotel Avila*, or dining at the *Cremaillaire* Restaurant with its delectable assortment of French pastries wheeled to the table on a two tiered cart. And the nightclub, *Mi Vaca y Yo,* located high above Caracas in the quaint, little mountain town of Baruta, which featured a floor show with a dancing cow where everyone got in a festive mood by singing of this wondrous cow which gave not only evaporated milk but condensed as well. Or Montmartre, the nightclub with its signs for the ladies' and mens' rooms both leading to the same place. She missed them all, but she knew she wouldn't exchange any of them for the happiness she had with Fred.

Someone had bought Spike Jones' records on their last trip to the States. The whole camp knew *Chloe* by heart and when it was played, people stopped whatever they were doing and started singing along with the record, acting out its antic lyrics. Maruja watching all this take place thought that these *petroleros* were indeed a crazy bunch.

She received her initiation as the wife of a Texan the first party she attended. She and Fred had just sat down after dancing a fiery *paso doble* when he got up again and stood at attention, along with a lot of other people. Looking at them standing ramrod straight, Maruja had the impression they were listening to their national anthem, and she halfway expected someone to run in with a flag.

"Stand up darlin', you're one of us now," Fred called down to her. Getting up she listened to verse after verse of *Deep in the Heart of Texas* and *The Eyes of Texas. Ay Dios!*, she wondered, am I really one of these *loco petroleros* now?

"Isn't she the cutest little thing?" Cathleen remarked to Ryle as they watched Maruja trying to absorb everything.

"She sure is," he agreed, hoping now that Maruja lived next door Cathleen would forget about their other Venezuelan neighbor. "I can tell you one thing, she's not about to become buddy buddy with the Maguire woman. This one comes from an entirely different class."

But he didn't know Maruja. When news of Sarita's background filtered back to her, she was absolutely intrigued with the idea that a former 'woman of the happy life' lived in camp. And more than curious to meet her. *Ay!* If her sister Lourdes knew she'd have a fit, she thought with relish. Why, the whole family would be scandalized. Oh, this was too delicious for words.

"You must introduce me to this Sarita," Maruja declared fervently one morning when she discovered Cathleen knew her. "What is she like?"

"She's an angel," Cathleen smiled, leading her out her front door to the gap in the hedge.

"We'll be like the three *mosqueteras*," Maruja declared after meeting Sarita. She blithely ignored Sugar's condemnation of her and invited Sarita to every morning coffee, afternoon bridge and party she hosted. Cathleen, seeing the fuss she made over Sarita, suspected it was Maruja's curiosity which prompted her desire to meet Sarita. She wondered if Maruja's delight in defying convention made her continue this friendship. But as time went by, her doubts receded. Maruja, with her inimitable charm, succeeded in achieving what John Maguire wanted more than anything else for his wife. Acceptance and appreciation. The rumors of Sarita's former life were slowly laid to rest. With the exception of the one person who wasn't about to forget, Sugar Dalhart.

As Maruja, Sarita and Cathleen grew closer, Cathleen's homesickness became less acute and the loneliness of the oil patch no longer threatened to strangle her. This is what happens to people overseas, she realized, friends turn into family. Very strong family.

FIFTEEN

The rainy season, lasting from May to November, came early. Within a few days the parched countryside, which resembled a lunar landscape, burst into life. Red blossoms grew heavy on the limbs of the *Bucares* while the *Apamate* trees threw a pink canopy over the *llanos*. The dull brown plains changed to a green so brilliant they became an emerald sea. Purple pods encasing fragile buds appeared on the banana trees. And the leafless *Araguaney* trees, always naked and forlorn without their golden blooms, turned into giant yellow umbrellas. Everywhere one looked life renewed itself as the grasses of the plains grew high and lush.

But Cathleen couldn't appreciate any of this splendor. For lakes had formed between the houses and at night the frog population, which always increased in the wet season, started up their chorus. Their voices, harsh and repetitive, kept her awake and made her edgy. Despite the light bulbs in the closets the shoes acquired a film of mildew, and the raw rice in the shakers failed to keep the salt from becoming soggy and damp. Little grayish blobs of mildew formed in the catsup and maple syrup. What bothered her most, though, was the musty smell which made the house oppressive. No matter what she did to dispel it, squirting cologne into the air or boiling cinnamon in water, the mustiness prevailed.

The only good thing about the weather was it kept most people at home. She didn't have to suffer through women dropping in at all hours, smiling and pretending to be gracious as she listened to the same tired gossip. For she was finding everything an effort. Although her daily bouts with nausea were gone, the lassitude remained. Almost as if the baby she was carrying had drained all life from her. Frequent naps were the only thing which kept her going. And as much as she missed Ryle, she consoled herself with the thought that perhaps it was a blessing in disguise he was out of camp, for she wasn't up to much of anything.

175

Although she hadn't felt that way at first.

"Do you have to go?" She was stunned by the news he was leaving her in Chacari to accept a temporary assignment in another camp.

"If I don't, it's sure not going to look good on my record that I refused." Seeing Cathleen's disappointment, he tried to make her understand how important this assignment was. "If I do a good job filling in for the assistant chief geologist while he's on vacation, Caracas will see I have management potential." He was right, of course. Their separation would just take some adjusting on her part. It was probably her condition, she seemed to get upset at the slightest little thing these days. But she dreaded being alone again. Memories of the long nights he was in the hospital came back to haunt her.

"I'm only a radio call away in case of an emergency," he reassured her. "There are other women in camp whose husbands are away."

"That's true," she agreed, pretending a confidence she didn't feel. She buried her head in his chest, already missing the safety she always felt in his arms.

"It's only for a few months, baby," he said when he left. "And I'll try to make it back every ten days or so for a night." But it was a month before he returned. A month when she felt he'd dropped off the end of the earth, for she rarely heard from him. She wrote every day, dispatching letters sometimes with John Maguire, for he looked for ways to send them with the truckers. Remembering his letters and phone calls when he went home to Oklahoma before their wedding, she found his silence a terrible burden.

"It's because I'm so bogged down with work," he explained the first time he came home. There were decisions to be made he didn't have when he was working in Chacari and a lot more responsibility. He just had to do a good job and make the Caracas office remember him.

It's not another woman I have to compete with, she realized. It's his career and the way he pushes everything else out of his life because of it. I just have to learn that sometimes I'm in second place. So she read and slept and dreamt of the time when Ryle would come home. Apart from trips to the commissary and visits with Sarita and Maruja, she rarely went out. About the only exception was movie night. No matter how blah she felt she wasn't about to miss out on that.

When she saw Murray was back in camp she bombarded him with

questions, for she knew he'd seen Ryle. Murray had become an auditor now and travelled from camp to camp, coming back to Chacari only sporadically.

"You look swell, Toots," were his first words. "Pregnancy sure agrees with you." She hadn't realized how much she missed him, for he never failed to compliment her and his sunny disposition always gave her a lift. But she brushed aside his words for she was hungry for news of Ryle.

"He's fine," Murray said. "Yeah, he's working hard."

"Didn't he send a letter with you?" she asked eagerly. Oh surely he'd think to send something with Murray.

Looking at the anticipation in her eyes, Murray wished there was a letter he could give her. But Ryle had given him nothing. Nor would he expect him to. Not after what happened.

"No news is good news," he replied glibly. "Maybe he's got writer's cramp from all those reports he has to submit." He and Ryle had dinner together at the mess hall, he told her. And about the only exciting event was when the cook, who'd lost his glasses, served what he thought was canned okra, only to have the entire mess hall jump out of their seats when they bit into *jalapeño* peppers. He elaborated on the story and then the movie began.

Shit, how he wished nothing else happened that night. Murray watched the Movietone Newsreel and then a Pete Smith Short, but his mind was miles away. After dinner he and Ryle had gone their separate ways; Ryle saying he had some reports to get out while Murray drove to Rosita's, the local whorehouse.

He was walking down a corridor when he passed a room where the prostitute had gone to get her customer a drink, leaving the door ajar. He stopped, then backtracked, hoping his eyesight had played tricks on him. Then pushing the door completely open he cried out angrily.

"What the hell are you doing here?"

"Same thing you are," was the nonchalant answer.

Ryle being in a whorehouse didn't really surprise him, but seeing his mouth and T-shirt smeared with lipstick upset him.

"You shithead," Murray's words came out in a raspy snarl. "After dipping your wick in one of these *putas*, you have the nerve to go home and touch Cathleen?"

"What the hell are you getting so self-righteous about?" Ryle responded, taken aback by Murray's vehemence. "I'm using a rubber. Think I want to come down with the clap? I'm always careful."

"Well, give the Boy Scout another medal," Murray burst out.

"Since when is my private life any of your business?" Ryle shot back. "You're out of line, Murray."

Ryle was right, it wasn't any of his business, but he found it impossible to remain detached. "Cathleen's back in Chacari, carrying your child, pining away for you. And you can't do without one of these tricks?"

"I don't see you giving it up for Lent," Ryle remarked.

"I don't have a pregnant wife," Murray shot back.

"You know what you are, Murray? An old fashioned romantic." Ryle shook his head. "Like some knight charging around on a white horse. Stop making a big deal out of things."

Murray stood there, trying to sort out his feelings. It was seeing the whore's lipstick all over Ryle which set him off. For some reason he couldn't understand, this upset him.

Ryle stared at him, then reaching over to his shirt he extracted a cigar, biting off the end before lighting it up. "Maybe you're in love with my wife."

"Isn't just about the whole male population of Chacari?" Murray replied.

"I'm not talking about some high school crush, Murray."

Murray's eyes became remote and neutral. "I like her a lot. Period. Nothing else." He paused. "And I respect her, something I don't see you doing."

Ryle jumped off the bed, his eyes blazing as he lunged for Murray. But Murray was quicker. Pinning Ryle's hands behind his back he threw him down on the bed. "Are you crazy? Getting into a fight in a whorehouse? You know how the bush telegraph is out here. Cathleen would find out so fast you were here, and then you'd really hurt her."

That's what Murray thought about when the movie started. The run-in he had with Ryle at Rosita's. And having to dodge Cathleen's questions, seeing the anticipation in her eyes because she thought he had a letter for her.

Sitting beside Nadine and George, Cathleen hoped the power didn't go off. She'd been looking forward all week to seeing Jane Wyman in *Johnny Belinda*. Sometimes during a heavy rain the lights went out. And it had been coming down heavily all day. She'd awakened that morning to the sound of it beating down on the roof, missing Ryle. Wanting to slip into the strength of his arms and realizing she had another day to get through without him. Wishing it weren't Easter. The holidays were always the hardest for that's when she missed her family the most.

The mail had been slow; it was over ten days since she heard from home. Sometimes weeks passed with no mail, when she read old letters over and over again, digesting every little scrap of information. A simple sentence — that her mother had gone into town — and she was home again seeing the houses set back from the streets with the huge oak trees lining the sidewalks, hearing the snow crunch under her feet and smelling the sawdust on the floor of the butcher shop. She found herself missing little things; reading the comics, wondering what kind of mischief the Katzenjammer Kids had gotten into, and if Tess Truehart had made any progress with Dick Tracy. She would love to turn on the radio, be able to hear Fred Allen, Eddie Cantor and his sidekick Parkyerkarkus, Edgar Bergen and Charlie McCarthy, and especially Jack Benny.

She'd wanted to go to Mass but the rain discouraged her from driving to Maturin. It discouraged a lot of people and she spent another Sunday without going to church, thinking about home. Wondering how the Easter egg hunt would go, almost tasting the meal her mother would be making, roast leg of lamb with mint jelly, tiny peas and roast potatoes, salad and apple pie. Oh, what she wouldn't give to eat some lamb, a meat unheard of in Venezuela.

Finally, when the longing for home became so strong she didn't think she could stand it a minute longer, she got out of bed and decided to color some eggs. She grumbled to herself because she had to prime the kerosene stove. She still couldn't understand why surrounded as they were by oil wells, with the gas flares burning away day and night, she couldn't cook on a gas stove. After she hard boiled the eggs, she experimented with the food coloring until she got the right shades. By the end of the morning she had some beautifully colored eggs, soft purple ones reminding her of spring lilacs, bright yellow ones looking as if cuddly Easter chicks would pop out any moment, even a dazzling turquoise one resembling a giant aquamarine stone. She placed them in a soup dish which she lined with one of her lace handkerchiefs, making a centerpiece for the dining room table.

And then it hit her that no one was here to share her creation. I hate it, she screamed to the silent house, I hate this being alone, especially on the holidays. She looked out the kitchen door toward Fred and Maruja's house, debating whether to bring them some colored eggs, then decided against it. They're probably in bed, she thought wistfully, doing what Ryle and I would be doing if he were home. Walking to the living room window she looked over the hedge towards the Maguires' house. They're in bed too, sleeping late. Then she saw the shutters of the spare bedroom being opened, a sign Sarita was sewing. Thankful that Sarita was up, she dashed out in the rain with the eggs and was even more grateful when Sarita invited her to Sunday dinner. I got through Easter, Cathleen congratulated herself as she watched the newsreel come to an end. And without any tears, she realized with a measure of some pride. Ever since she became pregnant they seemed to spring out at the least provocation. Now all she wanted was to sit back and enjoy the movie. The rain beat down on the tin roof of the clubhouse so loudly she wondered if they would be able to hear the dialogue. Wind swept the rain in through the open spaces of the screen walls, making people huddle closer.

At one point when the sound track was almost non-existent she heard Sugar, who was sitting behind her, call out, "I'll give you five minutes to take your hands off my thigh — whoever you are." A remark which brought instant laughter.

"Oh that Sugar, ain't she something?" Cathleen heard someone remark. "She's more fun than a barrel of monkeys."

She's something alright if you don't rub her the wrong way, Cathleen grumbled to herself, irritated because she could hardly hear the movie, annoyed with Sugar for spoiling things with her need to be in the spotlight. Then her irritation turned to disappointment when the lights gave out and the movie sputtered to an abrupt end.

"Everyone come to our house," Sugar called out, "and we'll have ourselves a party."

"Might as well." Nadine turned to Cathleen. "Sometimes these impromptu things turn out to be a lot of fun."

Because she didn't want to return to a dark, empty house, Cathleen reluctantly accompanied the Ficketts. The candles and kerosene lamps came out and since they couldn't dance, people did what they always did at a party, drank and swapped stories. But tonight the stories veered away from work, the maids and camp gossip and rain stories were exchanged. And since no one had heard them before, just about any story told was guaranteed a captive audience. Cathleen was having a good time, some of the anecdotes were better than reading a book. But after awhile the smoke which hung heavy in the living room made her queasy. She got up and headed towards the kitchen, hoping it wasn't full of people with cigarettes.

"Hey Toots," Murray called out to her as he reached in a tin tub for an iced beer. "Will you join me?"

Shaking her head she sighed. "I thought the air might be fresher out here. Ever since I got pregnant, I can't stand the smell of smoke."

"Well, I can't stand it either and I'm not pregnant, so that makes two of us," he said offering her his arm. "Let me take you away from all this, my dear. We can run away to Oz."

"Up the yellow brick road?" she laughed, responding to his grin.

"Absolutely, I'll take you all the way to Emerald City."

"Oh, Murray," she giggled. It's funny, she thought, the way I can play the fool when I'm around him. Why can't I be this uninhibited all the time? "But will the Wicked Witch of the West allow it?"

"There's not a thing she can do about it." He flexed his muscles. "Not with me here to protect you, Dorothy."

Oh, he's so much fun to be around, she smiled. "And who will you be? The Tin Man?"

"Me, the Tin Man?" he shook his head in mock horror. "The Tin Man doesn't have a heart, and I'm all heart. Don't you know that?"

"Of course I do," she laughed. "And you're certainly not the Cowardly Lion."

"Not me. I ain't afraid of nothin', Toots."

Cathleen, responding to his self-confidence, felt very protected in his presence. Just the way, she realized ruefully, she used to feel with Ryle.

"Then that leaves the Scarecrow," she continued, not wanting to dwell on anything heavy, eager to resume the repartee they'd been exchanging. "But I don't think you're him either, you're too smart."

"Oh Toots, but I am the Scarecrow because I don't have a brain in my head," he said, all the lightness gone from his voice. "Cause if I did,

I wouldn't go chasing over the rainbow for someone I can't have."

She was about to ask him who that someone was, but something made her hesitate. Cathleen's eyes swept over his face, searching for his usual grin. She sucked in her breath, almost choking when she realized he was talking about her.

"Hell of a situation, huh?" He shrugged his shoulders and smiled. But it wasn't the usual Murray grin. It had a look of such sorrow Cathleen felt as if someone punched her.

"Well, kiddo, I didn't go out looking for you," he went on softly, "that's for sure. It just happened."

"Oh, Murray, it's this place." He was her pal, the one who made her laugh. And he was Ryle's best friend.

"Being here does strange things to people," she said gently. "It can make you so lonely, your imagination works overtime."

"Nope," he shook his head. "This place has nothing to do with it. I would have picked you out of a crowd in Grand Central Station, or walking up Fifth Avenue. I'd have seen you and known right off the bat you were the one for me."

She was terribly confused, finding it impossible to accept his words. "It isn't right," she murmured.

"Damn right it isn't." He laughed, but again it was a laugh devoid of his usual good humor. "Hey, I'm not trying to make time with you or jump in the sack with you, if that's what you're thinking. Not that I wouldn't find it very nice. But I have too much respect for you to ever tarnish it with some cheap little affair."

"What are you going to do?" Her confusion was growing.

"Nothing," he replied. "There's not a damn thing I can do. Unless you want to run off with me. If you ever decide to leave Ryle, I'll be here for you." The intensity of his feelings made his voice tremble; gone was his usual wisecracking, self-confident manner.

"But in the meantime, she asks, what am I going to do?" He shrugged his shoulders. "Love you," he sighed, "think about you, wish the best for you, my blond Irish Rose." Wish the best for you, he thought sadly, and get blue balls thinking about you. Get so frustrated I think I'll go off my rocker because I can't have you.

Cathleen started to laugh.

"What's so funny?" He started dancing around on his feet like a boxer ready to return to the ring. "Here I declare my undying love, and she laughs."

"Think about it and tell me it isn't this place. Look at me," and she pointed to her stomach. "Who would fall for a pregnant woman?"

"I already have, Cathleen, so don't try and talk me out of it. I only wish it were my child you were carrying."

And for a few brief moments Cathleen wished it were. For she knew with Murray she wouldn't have to accept second place because he was obsessed with getting ahead.

"Is this a private party?" Sugar sailed into the kitchen, blowing smoke into the air. "Or can anyone join?"

"As a matter of fact it is," Murray replied. "It happens to be the non-smoking section of the theater. The smoke was a little too much for this mother-to-be."

"Well, pardon me," Sugar waved her cigarette. "Never bothered me when I was carrying Drew."

Sugar looked at Murray, then Cathleen, puzzled by the way Murray seemed to be pushing her out of her own kitchen. Then a knowing smile slid across her lips. "Oh, Cathleen, aren't you the sly one? While the cat's away, the little mouse wants to play." Her throaty laugh filled the tiny kitchen. "Not so little," she commented, patting Cathleen's stomach.

Cathleen flinched when Sugar touched her. And watched warily as she danced out of the kitchen.

"I don't trust that laugh of hers," she groaned.

"Neither do I," Murray agreed. "But don't worry, I'll take care of her. One of us ought to get back in the living room before Sugar starts the tongues wagging." He walked towards the door, then stopped. "Hey, I'm glad I told you. I didn't intend to, it just slipped out." He looked adoringly at her and Cathleen felt her knees grow weak. "But it's nice to be able to share my feelings with you. Isn't that what love is all about, sharing?"

He was right, she thought as she watched him disappear into the living room, love is sharing. Something she and Ryle didn't have much of, unless you counted sex. She pulled a ginger ale bottle out of the ice-filled tub and poured it into a glass. Had she done anything to encourage Murray, she wondered? He kidded her and she responded. She wasn't in love with him. At least she didn't think she was. Could a woman be in love with two men at the same time? All she knew was that every time she was near him, he made her feel good, something Ryle hadn't been doing much of lately. Sipping the ginger ale, loathing its taste, she returned to the living room seeking out Nadine. She really wanted to go home, but she didn't want to spoil Nadine's evening if she and George were having a good time. And then the door opened and she had her second surprise of the night when Ryle walked in.

Murray seeing Ryle bend down to kiss Cathleen could think of only one thing, the whore's lipstick all over his face and shirt. And in that moment the bonds of his friendship with Ryle began to unravel. Whatever they had before, the easy camaraderie, the mock insults they traded, the trust they shared, it all vanished. It started at Rosita's, but it took the sight of Ryle's lips on Cathleen's to cement it once and for all. When Ryle acknowledged Murray's presence, there was a chill in his manner, as if he defied him to reveal what he knew.

That night Murray didn't go to the Looney Door as he usually did whenever he got lonely. Despite Ryle's return and the anger he felt, in some ways he was strangely at peace. He refused a ride home to the bachelor quarters, preferring to walk in the rain which had slackened to a soft drizzle. He knew as he was walking, Ryle was home now making love to Cathleen. The knowledge didn't bother him though. Having revealed his feelings to Cathleen had brought him a kind of release. Nothing had changed, she was still married to Ryle. But she knew now that he loved her. It was a sentiment he didn't have to keep locked up inside him any longer. And for some reason he felt hope.

A ditty from his street days in the Bronx ran through his head.

Oh, she may be sweet
But she ain't Kosher meat

Kosher is not the problem, he told the frogs who were singing to each other. For openers, she's married. And pregnant. Not exactly your Andy Hardy and Polly Benedict kind of love story. As he walked by the motor pool, he heard voices. A woman's laugh and the sound of two people in the throes of passion. So that's where they go to screw in this place. Why not, he asked himself? The all American pastime, making out in the back of a car, and what better place in this fishbowl than the motor pool? He stopped and walked over to the side of the garage, curious to see who they were. A sort of sneaky thing to do, he knew, but there's so little to do in this place, it would break the monotony to find out who's screwing around. Then he stopped. A Peeping Tom he wasn't about to become, no matter how boring camp life was. Enjoy, he told them silently, I should be so lucky. But he really didn't want it that way with Cathleen. Not in the back seat of a car, sneaking a quick lay.

What had Ryle called him, an old fashioned romantic? Murray didn't know what he was, all he knew was this wasn't going to be a simple boy meets girl and they lived happily ever after kind of story.

SIXTEEN

"Soogie," John Maguire cried out in elation as he walked into the spare bedroom. "The transfer came through."

"*Bueno, mi amor,*" Sarita smiled, turning off the sewing machine, "tell me all about it." She linked her arm in his as they walked into their bedroom. Whenever they had something important to discuss, somehow they always wound up there.

"God, it's so good to lie down," he said pulling off his boots. His back bothered him whenever he sat at a desk for any length of time, and he'd spent the entire morning writing monthly reports for the Caracas office. "You're going to be a very rich *señora.*"

"Oh, and how is this going to happen?" She slipped her shoes off and flopped on the bed with him, inwardly a little amused. Didn't he know that compared to her childhood, she considered herself already wealthy?

"We're getting closer and closer to my going into business. I still don't have quite enough money. So our transfer to Puerto La Cruz will give me a chance to rustle up some more capital. Then we're going to form a company and you're going to be the President. *Señora Presidente,* how do you like that? I don't know if Venezuela will nationalize the oil industry like Mexico did in '38, but we'll be staying ahead of the game by having a Venezuelan as head of the company." He looked at her serene face, still marvelling at his luck in finding her. "And we're going to name the company after you, *La India,* my beautiful Indian maiden."

"*¿De veras?*" she asked softly. "You would do that?"

"And why not?" he replied pulling her close to him. "I wouldn't be anything without you, Soogie. If I didn't have you to come home to, I'd really flip out. I keep telling you that, but because of that silly notion you have—that I'm going to leave you high and dry—you still won't believe we're going to grow old together."

186

She didn't reply, for then he would start asking her again to have a child. Instead she remarked, "I think it will be good for you to have your own business, I don't think you'll be so bored." For he really did get bored easily. Once he learned something, he was eager, almost impatient to go on to something else. Would he get bored with her, she wondered? Would she no longer be a challenge to him once he finished educating her?

"But until I get the business going, I've got this transfer to Puerto La Cruz to think about." He would be in charge of K-9, the central shipping depot for all the camps in the states of Anzoategui, Monagas and Guarico. It was quite a promotion for him. Although he had no intention of staying with Palm Oil, the challenge of the new job excited him. There was nothing he liked better than going into a thoroughly messed up situation and organizing it into a smoothly running operation.

The company didn't have a camp in the port, K-9 was merely a work depot. They would be living in Los Gatos, located on the main highway between Barcelona, the state capital of Anzoategui, and Puerto La Cruz. A former oil camp, its houses were now leased out privately to various oil contracting companies, Halliburton, Schlumberger and others, so in essence it would be moving into an anonymous town. And Puerto La Cruz, while still small, would feel like a big city after the remoteness of Chacari. There was even a restaurant owned by Mexican Mary, who made tortillas by hand, where the *Molé* was so hot it brought tears to the eyes.

Cathleen was devastated by the news of the Maguires' transfer. While she loved Maruja's company, their friendship lacked the strong bonds she had with Sarita. For like a bee gathering and dispensing honey, Maruja flitted all over camp, never becoming close to anyone, yet enchanting everyone she met. But Sarita and John had become family to her. And now with Ryle away and her pregnancy continuing to drain her, she needed all the nurturing she could get.

"Oh, how I'll miss you two," Cathleen cried out. "But you're so lucky to get away from this place. It'll be like getting out of jail."

"*Bueno*, I haven't minded it that much," Sarita shrugged her shoulders. Maruja, with her talent for getting people together, had managed to change some people's opinion of Sarita. There were even *despedidas*, farewell parties, given in their honor. "But then, we've always kept to ourselves so we've never been involved in the camp intrigues."

"Intrigues! That's a good name for it," Cathleen sneered. "More like a snake pit." Ever since the movie *The Snake Pit* had played at the clubhouse, she thought it was a good description of Chacari.

"Oh, it's like a small town," Sarita said gently. "People always gossip about their neighbors in a small town. And here in an oilcamp, it's magnified even more because we're all shut off from the outside world. It's not too bad if you keep the proper perspective."

"Oh, how charitable you are, Sarita. If you only knew . . . ." She stopped, embarrassed at what almost popped out of her mouth.

"If I only knew what some people have said about me?" Sarita finished the sentence for her. "But I do."

"Oh, I'm so sorry," Cathleen gasped. She certainly hadn't meant to turn the conversation in this direction.

"There's nothing to be sorry about," Sarita replied firmly. "If some women in camp condemned me because I was once a prostitute, I can't let it upset me. I have too much to be grateful for."

"It doesn't bother you, the way some of them treated you?"

"No," Sarita shook her head. "I know it bothered John. That's why he got into those fights. Although lately, thank goodness, he's calmed down." Sarita poured them another cup of tea. She loved fussing over Cathleen and would miss her terribly when they moved. She paused, covering the pot with the tea cozy. "Your husband will probably be happy that we're leaving camp. I know he doesn't approve of our friendship."

"It's not that he doesn't approve," Cathleen replied, carefully choosing her words. "It's only because he has this ambition to get to the top and he thinks one of the ways he can do it is by associating with the 'right people'. You know how much I like Pet Ford because she's such a character, but she's not the 'right people' either." It was times like this when she wished she had a cigarette, it always seemed to get her through a rough situation. "But of course you can see how wrong he is. Look at John, he got this terrific promotion and it was based on his work and not because you two made the social scene."

Sarita laughed. "Yes, you could say that he got ahead in spite of his wife."

"Don't say that," Cathleen burst out, angry because Sarita considered herself a liability. "He's crazy about you. I just wish that Ryle needed me half as much as John needs you."

"Oh Cathleen, who knows how long he will feel that way?" Sarita sighed. "Nothing good lasts forever." Her eyes had a look of bittersweet resignation to them. "Well, not even the bad times last either, which is a consolation."

"Enough of this *triste* talk," Sarita said reaching out for Cathleen's hands. "You and I will always be friends. This I feel inside me. We'll see each other soon. You'll come to Puerto La Cruz to visit us and we'll go swimming at La Lechería."

When word got around camp of the Maguires' transfer, a lot of people wanted their house for they'd heard how beautiful Sarita had made the interior. In the end, though, it didn't matter who had seniority, or put their request in first. Sugar as the camp superintendents's wife, got the house. She'll never keep it the way Sarita did, Cathleen agonized, devastated because the Dalharts would be her new neighbors. She was equally positive the garden with its carefully tended shrubs and flowers would turn into weeds, for she couldn't see Sugar messing her hands with yard work. But Sugar found an *obrero*, a laborer in the native camp, whose green thumb made the shrubs and flowers thrive. And while she was glad to see this, Cathleen resented Sugar inheriting the fruits of Sarita's creativity.

Sugar started dropping in as if they were old friends, which struck Cathleen as odd for she knew Sugar didn't like her. She had the feeling she was being studied, somewhat like a bug under a microscope. Even when Ryle came home she dropped in, something the other women didn't do for everyone knew how little time they had together. Ryle, aware of Sugar's position, did nothing to discourage these visits. When Sugar invited Cathleen to go to the beach in Puerto La Cruz, he accepted for her.

"Why then, it's all settled," Sugar smiled. "We have to take advantage of this lull in the rainy weather. This sunshine isn't going to last forever. We'll leave around eight in the morning, get down there at ten and flop on the beach all day. I'll make the sandwiches and you can bring the drinks."

"Don't ever do that to me again," Cathleen burst out angrily after Sugar left. "Make decisions for me."

He brushed aside her objections. "Baby, an invitation from the super's wife is one you can't turn down. And I'll be leaving tomorrow. I only accepted for you because I know how much you love the beach."

Cathleen did love the beach. There was something about being near the water which always relaxed her. Even back home, Rye Beach, though not on the ocean, felt enough like it to induce the same feeling of contentment. When they drove out of camp and started toward the port, she grudgingly forgave Ryle. She always felt let down whenever he left, so perhaps this trip would take her mind off his departure.

They'd been driving less than a half hour when Sugar cut off the main road to a dirt one. "Lookit, Drew honey," she called out to her son who was jumping up and down on the back seat. "See those big pipes, they carry the oil that Daddy's men drill." The pipeline road was nothing more than a maintenance trail, and the car bounced up and down its rutty surface. Drew loved it. He cried out excitedly that it was like being on a bucking bronco. And the more he screamed with delight, the more Sugar played the car like it was a horse. She zigzagged all over the dirt road, and when they all flew up in the air and landed on the seats with a hard thud, she screamed and laughed along with Drew.

Cathleen, fearful of what all this jarring would do to the baby she was carrying, asked Sugar to get back on the highway. But Sugar ignored her. Mother of God, Cathleen panicked, she just had to get out of this damn car. Realizing Sugar was indifferent to her pleas, her hands went for the door handle.

"I declare, Cathleen! You've got to stop babying yourself the way you do," Sugar laughed as she slowed the car down to a steady pace. "Imagine a little biddy ride on the pipeline road making you so hysterical." She rolled her eyes and turned around to Drew in the back seat. "You want to go back on the regular road, Sugar Plum? I don't think Cathleen likes our fun."

The boy shook his head, continuing to bounce up and down on the back seat. "Horse, ride a wild horse," he lisped.

"This sure is fun, Sugar, " Cathleen remarked dryly. "I'll bet you did it all the time you were pregnant. A little joy ride like this could cause me to miscarry."

"No, it won't," Sugar snapped. "What are you made of, chocolate?" Her foot pressed down on the accelerator and she and Drew laughed and screamed each time they bounced up and down on the seat. Cathleen braced herself as best she could, putting her hands up to the ceiling of the car to keep herself wedged in the seat. Finally losing her patience completely, she reached for the door handle again.

"Oh, you wet blanket you," Sugar cried out irritably, slowing the car down and heading back towards the highway. Drew began to howl because his game had been interrupted.

"See what you made him do," Sugar lashed out. Then turning to Drew, her voice became soft and cajoling. "That's all right, darlin', we'll come back another time to ride the wild stallion. Now give Cathleen a kiss because she's such a scaredy cat." Drew started pummeling Cathleen furiously. Startled, she dodged his flying fists, then grabbed his arms until he quieted down. He's spoiled rotten by a mother who should never have had him, she thought, and by a father who overindulges him. The rest of the ride was made in silence, a silence broken only when Sugar turned on the radio to loud music.

Cathleen struggled to regain her composure, wishing there were some way she could get home. Then the road curved and before her she saw the panoramic splendor of Puerto La Cruz, its crescent shaped bay looking like a picture post card. To the left El Morro peninsula jutted out of the aquamarine water. They passed K-9 camp which John ran and turned left at the gas station for the road leading to La Lechería Beach.

"See those houses," Sugar pointed to Los Gatos. "Do you know who lives there?"

Of course she did, she started to reply. She and Pet Ford had spent a delightful day visiting Sarita just last week.

But Sugar's words stopped her. "That's where Maguire lives with his nigger whore."

Cathleen looked at Sugar in disbelief, not quite sure she'd heard her right. Then seeing the smugness on Sugar's face she sighed to herself. Why should she be surprised at anything this woman did or said?

"Anyone with any intelligence," Cathleen remarked frostily, "can tell that Sarita's Indian blood is the reason for the color of her skin."

"My, aren't we courageous this morning?" Sugar slowed the car down. "You seem to forget who you're talking to."

"No, I haven't," Cathleen replied firmly. "But I think you have. Someone in your position should know better than to make such stupid remarks. After all, you're supposed to set an example for the rest of us peons, Sugar." She paused, then looked Sugar squarely in the eye. "Sarita is nicer than a lot of perfectly 'respectable' women I know."

Sugar's foot hit the brake. "Get out of my car." Her words came out sounding like a hiss.

Cathleen looked across the salt flats leading to the beach. Vultures hovered in the distance as they waited for an animal to die. Then she looked back towards Los Gatos, which she figured was about a mile's walk. Sarita would be there, and if she weren't, the maid would let her in. Her hand went for the door handle. She had no idea how she would get back to Chacari; right now all she wanted was to get away from Sugar. But as she started to open the door, Sugar shot the car forward.

"You don't belong here," Sugar screamed. "Why don't you go back to New York?"

Good question. She'd been invited to the beach and had to endure a jarring ride over a rutted road so Drew could pretend he was on a wild stallion. Now she'd almost been dumped in the middle of nowhere. She had a husband whom she suspected was more in love with his career than with her, and she absolutely despised overseas life. Why didn't she go home?

And then Cathleen felt the first stirrings of life in her stomach. A tiny pulse fluttering inside her, but unmistakable evidence of the life she was carrying. I mustn't let anything hurt my baby, she vowed, panic flooding her insides. She clutched her stomach to reassure the tiny life inside her that no harm would come to it. Calmly, trying to display courage she didn't feel, she turned to Sugar and said, "I'm not leaving because I'm married to Ryle and where he goes, I go. Just like Ruth in the Bible. For better or for worse, til . . . ." Her words trailed off. Oh God, she didn't want to think of living here year after year. "You have a little boy back there," she gestured towards the back seat. "And he's dying to go to the beach."

The mention of her son brought a semblance of saneness to Sugar. But just barely. The tires screamed as the car flew down the highway. When they got to the beach, Drew begged his mother to go in the water with him. Cathleen, relieved she had an opportunity to get away from Sugar, walked along the white sand, taking deep breaths trying to calm down. The low hills circling the bay were so green they reminded her of a huge jade necklace. It was all the rain she supposed, though they'd had a respite from it the past ten days or so. Putting her toes in the water and feeling its warmth, she sank into the soft waves breaking against the shore. The continuity of the water washing over her was like a steady heartbeat, making her feel everything was all right. She looked lovingly at the skirt of the green maternity bathing suit Sarita had made for her. How she missed her. When Drew called her to join them for lunch, she reluctantly got up.

Watching Cathleen walk towards her, seeing her growing stomach, Sugar swore to herself. She'd been so sure Cathleen would leave and go home. She knew all the signs, having seen them in other wives who packed up and left. Sugar didn't ever remember wanting a man as much as she did Ryle. There were even times she contemplated leaving Emmett and all that his position afforded to run off with Ryle. Not that he asked her, but she just knew with a little bit of encouragement, he would have.

He wouldn't have married Miss America, that's for sure. The men are so vulnerable when they go home on vacation, they marry the first one they set eyes on because they're so starved for female companionship. And that's what happened with Ryle, no one could tell her differently. She just had to get him back. Remembering their times together made her determined Cathleen had to go.

If only Emmett weren't so straightlaced, she wouldn't be so restless. And if only they lived in a more free spirited camp. She'd heard about some of the other camps where they had key parties, everyone throwing their house keys on the floor and going home with whoever picked them up. Now, that would be exciting. She smiled to herself thinking about another party rumored to take place every Saturday night in a camp on Lake Maracaibo. The men standing behind a blanket which was strung across the room, and the women choosing the men by what was poking through the holes. Drew jumping up and down in the sand broke into her daydreams. Now what's the matter with that girl, she thought crankily, the least Miss America could do is take care of Drew for a spell. Fine mother she'll make. And then Sugar's irritation dissipated as she remembered the reason she invited Cathleen to the beach. Maybe she'll never get to be a mother, she whispered to herself, the thought bringing a smile to her lips.

....

Going home Sugar cut across the highway to the pipeline road. Again the car bounced up and down the rutty dirt road and Drew started jumping up and down. She ignored Cathleen's pleas, turning a deaf ear when Cathleen burst into tears. Until Cathleen reached for the wheel and her foot stamped down on the brake. The blue Pontiac flew out of control as the two women wrestled for control of the car and only came to a stop when it hit an embankment on the dirt road.

"I was just trying to have a little fun with my baby," Sugar laughed.

"What about my baby?" Cathleen cried out trembling.

"I really don't give a damn about your baby," Sugar snapped, hatred spilling out of her eyes. "In fact, there's nothin' I'd like better than for you to lose that package you're carrying."

"You did this deliberately," Cathleen flinched in shock. The knowledge that Sugar wanted her to miscarry terrified her, but she knew she couldn't show her fear. "You're going to have a lot of explaining to do."

"What explaining?" Sugar's laugh was low and throaty. "Who are you going to tell? And if you did, why shoot, I'd just deny it. I'd say you were exaggerating." She glared defiantly at Cathleen. "No one would believe you 'cause everyone thinks you're so stuck up. But everyone likes me. I may not be Miss America like you think you are, but I've got more personality than you'll ever have," she said smugly. "But then, anyone has."

"Ever since I arrived in Chacari, Sugar, you've been out to get me. Why?"

"Shoot, there you go again, Cathleen, exaggerating all over the place. I declare, you've got a persecution complex." She took out her compact and began to powder her nose. Cathleen eyed her warily, then opening the car door she got out and started walking towards the main highway. She just had to get back to Chacari. Her stomach started to cramp up and a couple of times she doubled over in pain. I'm going to lose this baby, she panicked. I'm going to be like some poor native woman and give birth right here on the highway. Behind her she heard Sugar calling out to her.

"You'd better get in the car," Sugar snapped.

Cathleen ignored her, struggling to hide her pain. Then waves of dizziness washed over and she slumped by the side of the highway.

"You bitch," Sugar screamed at her, jumping out of the car. "Of all times for you to pull a fainting act. Drew, get your butt out of the car and help me. Open the goddamn front door." She half dragged Cathleen to her feet. "If you think I'm goin' leave you here so you can get everyone's sympathy, you're out of your cotton pickin' mind."

Cathleen overcome with pain was too weak to struggle anymore, and she allowed Sugar to help her back to the car. She's scared now, she reassured herself, Sugar is scared she's bitten off more than she can chew. And that's the only reason it'll be safe to get in the car. Cathleen collapsed on the seat. The rest of the trip was a blur. The only thing she remembered was her determination that the pains in her stomach would subside. It's just nerves, she kept telling herself, nothing more than nerves. I'm not going to lose my baby, no matter what this crazy woman tried to do to me. I'm going to go full term.

....

For two days Cathleen stayed in bed, two days in which she looked for signs of bleeding. She thought about going to the doctor, but convinced herself if she rested and got her mind in a calm state, then her body would follow suit. And she wasn't up to seeing anyone. The shock of discovering Sugar's reason for inviting her to the beach was something she had to come to terms with by herself. If Sarita were here she could talk to her, but there was no one else she felt she could confide in. So many times, out of habit, she went to the living room window looking for Sarita, only to realize she was gone. She missed Ryle, longed to be in the security of his arms. And then she realized she couldn't even tell him what Sugar had pulled. For she knew he wouldn't believe her. No one would, she thought despairingly, only Sarita. And Murray, who was even further away than Sarita. By the third day she felt well enough to get out of bed. She just had to talk to someone, with Ryle gone the house felt emptier than ever. She went next door to see Maruja. She knew she couldn't tell her what happened with Sugar, but Maruja was always so full of fun it would distract her. But when Maruja came to the door, she wasn't her usual vivacious self. She had found out she was pregnant and wasn't at all thrilled by the prospect.

"It's because you're so nauseous," Cathleen said encouragingly. "Once it passes you'll be so excited."

"Oh, who wants this dumb baby?" Maruja wailed. "I don't." Shocked by Maruja's words, Cathleen didn't linger. She just couldn't imagine any woman not being thrilled with the prospect of motherhood. She remembered how excited she was when she found out she and Ryle would become parents. Still mulling over Maruja's behavior, she walked down the street to Pet Ford's house. She knew she could let her hair down there.

"I hate this place, Pet," she burst out.

"My sentiments exactly." Pet nodded her head in agreement. "Hell, you ain't the only one not crazy about it."

"But you're used to the oilfields."

"The oilfields back home ain't nothing like here," Pet declared fervently. "I can tell you that. I ain't used to this coffee klatching, either. I've worked all my life. In fact, I know more about drilling parts than some of them clowns they got working at the warehouse." She lowered her large body down on the rattan couch. "I tell you honey, if there's anything more boring than a bunch of idle women, I don't know what it is."

"But you fit right in," Cathleen insisted.

"Naw, not really." Pet reached in the top of her dress for a handkerchief which she used to wipe away the beads of perspiration on her forehead. "But see, I don't give a shit. Me and Pete are here for one reason only, to salt away as much money as possible. But you're young and your husband's got that hungry look about him, like he wants to go places. So you gotta stick it out."

"Oh God, I don't know if I can," Cathleen cried out telling her about her day with Sugar. "Right from the beginning, Sugar has been out to get me. And it keeps getting worse. And I don't understand why. What have I done to her?" Her nerves were so taut that she burst into tears, hating herself because she couldn't control her emotions.

"She did it deliberately, she invited me to the beach just so she could drive me on that horrible pipeline road. She wants me to lose my baby." She looked pleadingly at Pet. " Do you think I'm crazy? As I sit here, telling you what happened, I still can't believe that it actually took place."

"That Sugar," Pet snorted. "She ain't so sweet. I believe you."

"But why?" Cathleen asked, relieved she had finally unburdened herself and Pet believed her.

"Because you're a threat to her. You're one more young woman to whittle down her edge with the men."

"But she's married."

"Oh, honey, you're so naive. Of course she's married," Pet chortled, shaking her head. "I look around this place and sometimes it's more fun than goin' to the picture show. Why, this camp has got one of them Bette Davis movies beat by a mile." A broad grin broke out in her wrinkled face. "See to Sugar and a few others, living in this place makes them kind of greedy on account of all these bachelors. But it's hard to fool around, what with everyone knowing what everyone else is doing. Though I know of a few who have screwed around and how they done it. But see, Sugar has to be careful, she's got her position to think of. She just loves being the super's wife, always the center of attention. But that ain't enough. Shit, she'd pull her britches down so fast if she thought she could get away with it."

"But I'm no competition to her," Cathleen protested.

"The hell you ain't," Pet laughed. "God, how refreshing you are, Cathleen. A real beauty who doesn't even realize just how gorgeous she is. Half the men in camp are nuts about you." Seeing the blush spread across Cathleen's face, she patted her arm affectionately. "It irks her when she sees the guys all over you asking you to dance. Why hell, they even come up and ask me. And I'm an old fart! But I suspect it's something deeper."

"What do you mean?"

"I think she's got the hots for your husband," Pet explained. "And now that he's gone and got married, she can't stand it. Which is why she's made it so bad for you."

"Enough to try and make me lose my baby?"

"Yep," Pet nodded her head. "That's exactly the way it is. This ain't no tea party you landed in, Cathleen. She's after your hide."

"Oh God, what am I going to do?" Cathleen felt the fear nesting in her stomach again.

"Kill her with kindness in public," Pet advised. "And at the right time, let her know you're on to her game. Soon as you do that, she'll back off. She may talk a good piece, but underneath she's a brainless brat who's got horsefeathers for guts."

The fence around camp seemed to be closing in on her even more. The knowledge that someone meant her deliberate harm added to her homesickness. And helplessness as she tried to quell the anxiety inside her. All the people she cared for were gone. Sarita and John two hours away in Puerto La Cruz, Murray out on the road, and most of all Ryle working and living in another state. Her mother and the rest of her family 3,000 miles away. She didn't ever remember feeling so alone. The longing for a drink or cigarette became stronger each day, she was positive it would steady her shaky nerves. Yet when she tried to find release in them, she threw up her insides.

Sugar continued to drop in unexpected and uninvited, adding to her anxiety. She knew she had to confront her but she kept putting it off. And then one morning she gathered her courage and spoke up.

"I declare, Cathleen, I think you've flipped your wig but good this time." Sugar's laughter filled the tiny living room. "Accusing me of all those nasty things!"

"I may not have your vivacious personality Sugar, as you're so fond of reminding me," Cathleen replied evenly. "But I'm not an idiot lacking in backbone. In my church, we get married for life," she continued. "And I'm sticking. So don't ever think you can scare me off." She felt the baby lurch around inside her, kicking strongly against the walls of her stomach. "And please don't pop in uninvited anymore. When I want to see you in my home, I'll let you know." She walked to the front door. "I'm sure you have to get ready for Wilma's bridge luncheon, just as I do."

After Sugar stormed out of the house, she collapsed on the couch. God, how she hated scenes. The feistiness so much a part of her brothers' nature was nowhere to be found in her. She took no pleasure, as they did, in a good fight. I have to hang on, she thought, not only for myself but for my baby. She longed for the baby's arrival, consoling herself that once he was born she would no longer be alone.

Then on Friday, November 8th, her fortune changed. The day started out like any other, but when she sat down to play bridge that afternoon all the beautiful cards she'd held ever since she became pregnant disappeared. Nadine said it meant the baby was on its way. But Cathleen shook her head. She still had two weeks to go. And Ryle had promised he would be back in time for the baby's birth. No, she told Nadine, this wasn't the day. But when she got home and saw Ryle's pickup in the carport, she flew into the house. Maybe the baby really was on his way.

"Hey, Momma Hoss." He tried to put his arms around her, but in the weeks he'd been gone she had expanded so much it was awkward embracing each other.

"I didn't expect you until the 18th." Oh, how she'd missed him. No matter how moody and unpredictable he was, she hated being apart from him. But today he wasn't moody and distant, today he was the Ryle she'd fallen in love with. Attentive and tender, adoration in his eyes.

"The guy I was replacing returned early, so I came back as fast as I could," he said bending down to kiss her, making a game out of getting around her huge stomach.

"Does this mean you're home now for good?" As awkward as it was, she tried to burrow into his arms.

"Yeah, baby, I'm home for good now." His lips were everywhere, her face, her neck, her hair. It was over, the lonely nights of reaching out for him only to find his pillow, the waking up every morning to the realization that she had another day to get through without him. She felt like a long cruel winter had come to an end and now she could shed all her heavy clothes. "You ready to spring that colt?" he murmured patting her stomach.

"Not for a couple of weeks, but now that you're home. . . ." Her voice trailed off as she remembered the change in her cards. Now that Ryle was here, it could mean that the baby was coming. She patted her stomach. "Okay Junior, we're ready."

And the baby heard her. That night she and Ryle never did sleep. They snuggled in each other's arms and talked until dawn. At two o'clock she experienced little ripples in her stomach which felt like soft feathers tickling her. When they timed them five minutes apart, she wondered if they ought to go to the hospital. But she wasn't uncomfortable and five minutes later when the ripples returned, she pressed his hand to her stomach, the act making her feel very close to him. When her water broke at 6 A.M., Ryle drove her to the Sinclair Hospital in Santa Barbara.

By 9 o'clock she was in fierce pain and was grateful for the injection of Twilight Sleep, where in her dreams she played hand after hand of bridge, always getting 150 Honors in Spades. Her baby was born at a quarter of 11. It was a fast delivery and when she woke up at one o'clock that afternoon, the nurse told her she had a beautiful daughter.

Cathleen had been so sure it would be a boy, she couldn't imagine anything else. That's what they both wanted, especially Ryle. To him, having a boy the first time was proof of his masculinity. They hadn't even thought of a girl's name. But the first time Cathleen held her daughter in her arms, she quickly forgot her disappointment. She was the prettiest baby she'd ever seen. Not a wrinkle, skin smooth as a peach, with black hair and gray eyes, every inch her father's image. She rocked her in her arms and sang a soft lullaby.

Ryle didn't share her happiness and he made no attempt to mask his disappointment. He'll come around, she reassured herself. She hoped if she named their daughter after him, gave her a name which corresponded to his initials, it would please him. "I don't want any girl named after me," he told her coldly.

"But she's your daughter. Why, she's an exact duplicate of you, without the mustache of course." She hoped this last bit might bring a smile to his lips, but the only thing he said was, "An exact duplicate of me would have been a boy."

"Ryle, it didn't turn out that way," she replied trying not to lose her patience. "Sometimes what you want and what you get are two different things. Let's be happy that she's healthy." The closeness they experienced the night before had evaporated, and again she had the feeling she was walking on eggs, never knowing what mood he would be in. He said he didn't care what she named the baby. Two weeks after her birth, Sheila Jane Rylander was baptized. If Ryle noticed that his daughter had the same initials as his, he chose to ignore it. She asked Fred and Maruja to stand in at the christening for her sister, Beebe and her brother Bubba, who would be godparents. Cathleen was too happy to dwell on the indifference in Maruja's face when she held Sheila. When she has her own baby she'll feel differently, she thought. And then she quickly forgot the look of boredom in Maruja's eyes. As any excuse for a party was a way of life in camp, people flocked to their little house for the christening party. The dining room table was heavy with food, a cake Nadine made in the center, the words "Welcome Sheila Jane" written in pink icing. Cathleen loved the inscription, she hoped Ryle did too. Sometimes she felt he was coming around, especially at the party for there was a great deal of back slapping and congratulations offered him. Everyone marvelled at how good Sheila was. She never cried, staying quietly in her cradle taking everything in. She's like her daddy, Cathleen smiled to herself, she just loves to be at a party.

"You look beautiful, Toots, motherhood becomes you," Murray told her softly. He was back in camp for a week. Planting a kiss on her cheeks he whispered in her ear, "And I'm more in love with you than ever." He gave her a tissue wrapped package containing a pink dress embroidered with white bunnies which he'd bought in Valle de la Pascua for Sheila.

Cathleen wouldn't allow herself to dwell on his words of love. She was married to Ryle for better or for worse. Right now, while it definitely wasn't the best, she had hopes it would get better. There were times when Murray was so tempting. How easy it would be to find consolation in his arms, she thought. He would always be there when she needed him, always be the same with none of Ryle's dark moods to plague her.

Sheila's birth helped her cope with Ryle's moodiness. To make up for his indifference, Cathleen smothered her daughter with love. She knew Ryle felt left out because she paid so much attention to Sheila, but she didn't care. Serves him right, she decided. Then she would feel sorry for him because he was unable to accept Sheila, and she tried to bring him into the circle of love she had with her daughter. Sometimes she felt torn between her love for Sheila, a passion almost, and wanting to understand him, longing to recapture what they had in the beginning.

"Look at her hands," Cathleen remarked one Sunday morning as she came out of the bedroom where she'd been nursing Sheila. Ryle didn't like seeing the baby at her breasts, so she'd learned to nurse her in private. "Isn't it amazing how tiny babies are?" she continued. "Why, her hand is no larger than my pinky." She went over to the couch where Ryle was deep in the latest issue of *Look* magazine and sat down next to him, placing the baby across her knees, stroking her dark hair. Sheila grabbed her finger.

"Isn't she strong?" she remarked. Ryle continued reading, ignoring her.

"Ryle, you've got to love her," she burst out. "If her own father won't acknowledge her existence, what's going to happen to her?"

"Cathleen, don't nag me." And he buried his face further in the magazine. Eventually she gave up and returned to the bedroom, putting Sheila down in her crib where she fell asleep immediately. She looked at her watch wondering if she could make the 12 o'clock Mass in Maturin. It was a good hour's drive away, but if she left now, she might make it. For a moment she hesitated, wondering if she could leave Sheila with Ryle, he'd never been alone with her before. Then reassuring herself the worst that could happen would be Sheila would have a soggy bottom, she got dressed. Sheila was still sleeping peacefully. The top of her fine mesh tropical crib had been closed, no flies or bugs could bother her. She blew a kiss to her daughter and then walked out to the living room.

"You've got to make your peace with her, Ryle. This can't go on, it's just not fair to her. She didn't ask to be your child." She clipped on her earrings and then continued talking. "If you don't start paying some attention to her, I don't see much use in my hanging around."

"And what's that supposed to mean?" he asked suspiciously.

"It means that I'll leave you. I'll take Sheila and go back to the States." And she walked out towards the carport.

"Don't threaten me, Cathleen," he called out to her.

"Oh, honey." she pleaded returning to the living room. "This time last year we met and fell in love. Don't let it all go down the drain."

I'd never leave him, she told herself. I'd never go back to the States and admit that I made a mistake, especially to Pa. Just thinking of her father's parting warning made her determined to make her marriage a success. But she had to do something to shake him up. More and more Murray was invading her thoughts. But he's not in love with me, she rationalized, he just thinks he is. It's this place. Life is so unreal here, it's Never Never Land. And besides, she could never divorce Ryle to marry Murray and remain a Catholic. But lately, remaining a Catholic didn't seem the big priority it had been in the States. That's why I must get to Mass, she reminded herself as she drove out the gate and headed toward Maturin. I just can't lose that.

When she returned from Mass, Sheila was in the living room flat on her back in the playpen, playing happily with the jungle gym strung across its top. Ryle had actually picked up his daughter, she realized, the joy of it almost bringing tears to her eyes. He hadn't changed her diaper, she was wet and messy. He would probably never change a diaper. But it didn't matter. He had finally touched his daughter, taken her in his arms and acknowledged her presence in their lives.

SEVENTEEN

Whenever there were revolutions in Venezuela, the foreigners remained neutral. A great many were isolated in the oilfields. Those in Caracas lived in the suburbs, far removed from the danger prevalent in the older, downtown sector of the city. It was an era before revolutions became sophisticated affairs when embassies were invaded, or it was discovered how politically lucrative kidnapping military attachés and business executives could be. Sometimes the revolutions were bloodless coups, merely a matter of the opposing forces taking over the military barracks and radio stations. In twenty-four hours or less the "out" faction fled into exile, returning when their party came back into power. Other times it was more passionate. When the military dictator, Perez Jimenez, was ousted in the late 50s, the crackle of firearms echoed through the streets; mobs stormed homes of the higher echelons and people gave their lives in the name of liberty. This was the beginning of democracy in Venezuela. Presidents elected for a six year term remained in office. Before this political stability was achieved though, on Wednesday November 24, 1948, the elected government of President Romulo Gallegos, Venezuela's most prolific novelist, was toppled after having served a little over nine months and power was seized by the military. Ordinarily the political upheavals of the Venezuelans didn't affect the foreigners. However the coup of '48 was relevant to their lives. For in the previous three years the Revolutionary Junta headed by Romulo Betancourt, enacted legislation resulting in *Utilidades*. This meant that any company making a profit had to share it with their employees. In the case of the oil companies' employees, it was equivalent to two months' salary and given out as a Christmas bonus. It added more money to their paychecks, making life in Venezuela even sweeter.

The coup of '48 brought to a head Murray's feelings for Cathleen. His cousin Bernie was attached to the U.S. Air Force Mission in Maracay instructing the Venezuelan Air Force. Since Murray was doing an audit in the neighboring state of Guarico, they arranged to meet for Thanksgiving. Although the American companies only recognized Venezuelan holidays, he managed to get a few days off. He was looking forward to lazing around the pool at the Hotel Jardin where the U.S. Mission was based and working on his tan. Something the men who worked outdoors on the rigs couldn't understand. His compulsion to sprawl out on his blanket behind the bachelor quarters and grease himself with coconut oil and bake. With his curly black hair and tan he started to look like a Venezuelan. He wasn't aware of this; he thought he had the Miami Beach look.

It was a long, hot drive from Tucupido to Maracay and by the time he entered the outskirts of the city, all he could think of was diving into the hotel pool. He headed for the main plaza where the Hotel Jardin was located. In its heyday it had been a showcase hotel built by the infamous dictator Gomez for his private playground. It was said that Gomez, noted for his cruel streak, had deflowered all the females in the countryside, but not before ascertaining their virginity by breaking their hymens with his fingernail. The hotel was still majestic but showing signs of age and neglect, somewhat like a fading queen. It covered several city blocks with the front entrance facing the main plaza, across from which stood the *Guardia Nacional* barracks, very strategically placed by Gomez so he could control his troops at all times. The first impression one had of the hotel was its openness. Spacious courtyards were landscaped with flowers and fountains, so anyone sitting in the bar or restaurant which overlooked them felt like they were in a park.

Murray first heard the sound of gunfire as he drove around the plaza to the hotel. Seeing a group of men storming the barracks he floorboarded the pickup, making it to the front of the hotel in seconds. Snipers squatting behind benches and shrubs in front of the hotel had joined the battle in progress as he ran into the hotel.

"Holy mackerel, Andy," he greeted Bernie and his wife, Judy. "There's a war going on out there."

"Naw," Bernie replied, "just those Army guys on maneuvers."

"Those were real bullets, Bernie. Believe me, I know the difference,"

Murray insisted. "It was like being back in the Pacific, the only difference was I didn't have my Browning."

Bernie still thought it wasn't anything serious and they went into the bar for a drink. Afterwards when they walked to the front desk to pick up Murray's room key, they noticed the heavy wooden entrance doors had been closed and the front desk clerks looked around nervously. Murray went to his room and stripped; he decided to take a quick shower before going swimming. He didn't know what was going on, but he felt the excitement. Keyed up, he started to sing in the shower.

Oh, she jumped into bed and covered up her head
And said I couldn't find her
But I knew damn well that she lied like hell
So I jumped right in behind her

He was starting into the second verse when he felt something whistle by his ears. A bullet struck below the showerhead, shattering the tile into small pieces. He dropped to the floor, cutting himself on the tile. Having survived one Pacific island invasion after another during WWII, he hated to think he might be a casualty in a Venezuelan coup. All he could think was it would be an inglorious way to end his life. Bare assed on a shower floor, instead of bare assed and in the saddle. The water continued to spray out over him, but outside the guns had stopped chattering. Getting up he dried himself, then dressed quickly and went looking for Judy and Bernie, finding them in the bar with the rest of the Americans. Bernie informed him, sure enough, there was another revolution going on. Dinner was a sporadic affair; most people stayed in the bar, too keyed up to eat. They never did sleep in their rooms, everyone having decided it was safer to pull their mattresses down to the central courtyard and spend the night there. Murray, dead to the world, curled up on his mattress and dropped off into a deep slumber until he felt someone shaking him.

"¡Arriba, levántese!" Looking up he saw the muzzle of a rifle pointed at him.

"Take it easy," his cousin counseled him. He knew what a scrapper Murray was. "They've got the upper hand."

The soldier pointing the rifle motioned to another soldier who grabbed Murray around the neck, pulling him up on his feet.

"Hey Bernie, did you tell them I'm Gary Cooper in disguise?" His mouth formed into a lopsided grin. "Besides I'm too young to die."

The soldiers pushed him out of the courtyard and Judy started to scream. Then Mary McCormick, the petite wife of the head of the American Military Mission, went up to the soldiers and started talking in rapid Spanish.

"It seems," she told Murray, "that some of the soldiers went AWOL from the barracks and they think you're one of them."

"Soldier?" Murray scoffed. "United States Marine!" He tried to turn around and face his captors, but they had a firm grip on him. "Hey *amigo*, this is a former *Gyrene* you got here."

Mary McCormick continued talking, "I suppose with your khaki shirt and pants and your dark hair and heavy tan, they think you're a Venezuelan. Show them your *cédula*."

When he reached for the I.D. in his wallet, his arms were pinned behind his back. Then Mary McCormick let loose a verbal assault on the two soldiers. Listening to her Murray decided she would have made a great drill sergeant. Within a few moments the soldiers released their grip and Mary reached into Murray's pocket, extracting the *cédula* from his wallet, showing it to the soldiers. They looked at it, shrugged their shoulders, said a few words and took off.

"How do you like that?" Judy sputtered. "No questions, just guns pointed at you. If you ask me, I don't think they could read. Why, they hardly looked at the *cédula*.," She turned to Mary. "What did they tell you?"

"Oh, they were going to take him outside and shoot him," she replied.

"Bernie, I think maybe next Thanksgiving you better come and visit me," Murray remarked casually. But his offhand tone of voice gave lie to the fear shaking his insides. "Life in an oil camp may be a drag at times, but brother, at least it's safe." He turned to Judy, who by now was close to tears and put his arms around her. "Hey kiddo, you don't think I would have let them get away with anything, do you?" Then he gave Mary McCormick a sharp salute. "Thanks for saving my skin."

On the drive back to Tucupido he kept thinking what a great story it would make at the next party. The camp would be buzzing for weeks. Then he grew a little more somber as he realized how fragile life was. He'd almost met death, almost lost any chance to make Cathleen his. No more holding back, he vowed. All's fair in love and war. He was past the stage of trying to act honorably. Ryle wearing a whore's lipstick had canceled that. He didn't deserve Cathleen. And maybe, he reasoned, she was no longer walking around in blue heaven. Having roomed with Ryle, he knew how difficult it was to live with his moody disposition and caustic tongue. By now Cathleen might be fed up with Ryle's mood swings, she could be having second thoughts about a man who put his career ahead of her. And if she wasn't, then he would just have to change her mind. He was going to court her openly. Well, as openly as a single man could court a married women in the oil patch.

....

When Maruja met Fred's family who had flown to Caracas from Houston for their wedding, her first thought was how different they were from him. *Ay Dios*, she certainly hoped if they had children none of them took after his sisters or father. For his sandy hair and handsome features inherited from his mother were nowhere to be seen in his sisters, especially his older sister Rita who had bright red hair and a multitude of freckles.

The thought of having children was not a welcome one. Unlike her sister, Lourdes, who was the proud mother of a two year old daughter, she experienced no maternal yearnings. All she wanted was to live happily ever after with Fred, and how could she do this with a baby around? And she didn't look to their coming child as a possible way of salvaging a troubled marriage, as Cathleen had, for theirs was perfection. She didn't want any intruders interrupting this bliss. Nor did Fred. He thought he had years of bachelorhood in front of him. Having met and married Maruja in just a few months still had him wondering what happened. Now with fatherhood on the horizon, he felt even more bewildered.

As he watched Maruja's body swell up and lose the curves which excited him from the first, his ardor didn't cool. Tiny and curvaceous or swollen and misshaped, she was still desirable. And aside from a few weeks of nauseousness, Maruja suffered none of the discomforts or lassitude which Cathleen had. She was still as vivacious as ever and made no concession to her new condition, thinking that if she didn't acknowledge it, perhaps it might go away. The only admission on her part was when she started wearing maternity clothes. Which she looked on as something unpleasant to be endured, but as soon as her stomach became flat again, she would go on with her life as if nothing had happened to disrupt it.

When Cathleen asked her and Fred to stand in as godparents for Sheila, it brought their impending parenthood closer. Except Maruja, holding Sheila in her arms at the baptismal font, didn't experience any anticipation of holding her own child in her arms. In fact, she was bored by the prospect.

She didn't plan to give birth in Caracas, although her mother had insisted that she wanted her grandchild born at the *Centro Médico* where she knew the medical facilities were first rate. No, Maruja decided she would have her baby at the Santa Barbara Hospital just as the other wives of the *petroleros* did, for she couldn't stand the thought of being separated from Fred. But three weeks before the baby was due, they went to Caracas to attend a family wedding. And Maruja went into labor right in the middle of the church ceremony. No one was aware of it though, for she was determined that nothing was going to interfere with her and Fred having a good time at her cousin's reception. They never danced though beyond the first *paso doble*, for by then the pains were so strong she collapsed in a chair and almost had the baby at the *El Paraíso* Country Club.

When the nurse brought her daughter to her she protested she was much too tired to hold anything, much less a baby. Undaunted, the nurse placed the baby next to Maruja, who promptly rolled over on her other side, turning her back to her daughter.

While Fred hadn't given much thought to their coming baby, as soon as he held her in his arms he was awash with paternal feelings. She was the spitting image of his sister, Rita and he fell madly in love. "If she isn't the cutest little thing this side of the *Río Gran*," he exclaimed to Maruja, exalting in the baby's curly red hair and green eyes. "Oh, *muñequita*, you and I have created one sensational kid." He was aware of Maruja's indifference to their daughter, but he attributed this to her being tired and groggy from the anesthesia.

But as the days went by he became disturbed by her lack of interest in their new baby. Maruja sensed his disappointment. She knew she wasn't acting naturally and it troubled her, but she honestly didn't know what to do about it. Why didn't everyone just leave her alone? She had done her part, going through nine months of watching her body inflate until it resembled a balloon about to burst. And having to endure that horrible birth process. Thank God they'd knocked her out before it got too bad. Twilight Sleep they called it, and it was so *delicioso*. She felt like she was floating effortlessly on some featherweight cloud, with Fred beside her, holding her close as he always did when they were in bed. All she wanted was to be with her husband. She didn't want or need anyone else, and couldn't understand all this fuss about wanting children. Wet, wailing little bundles of bother, who would grow up to be even more demanding. She wasn't interested in holding her baby in her arms and she certainly had no intention of nursing her. Imagine someone tugging at her breasts to be fed! Why, the whole idea revolted her.

Fred wasn't the only one upset by Maruja's lack of maternal feelings. His mother-in-law, Misia Isabel, was thoroughly scandalized. And then she realized it shouldn't be such a surprise. For after all, hadn't Maruja been a maverick all her life, defying convention at every turn? She had longed for Maruja to get married and settle down and now that she was, she was behaving as if she didn't want her baby. Surely this was a temporary thing. But no, Maruja wanted to leave the baby with her.

"You see *Mami*," she told Misia Isabel, "it's so primitive out there. I told you about the trouble I had getting good help 'til finally I wound up doing the cooking myself. Can you imagine trusting a baby to one of those *rústicas*?" Maruja threw an imploring look at her mother. "It's best for her to be with you here in civilization. When she gets a little bit older, only then would I feel right about bringing her out there." Maybe for a little while, Misia Isabel agreed.

But her son-in-law had different ideas. "There's no way I'm gonna leave our daughter here," Fred declared. "A baby belongs with her parents, especially her mother, so she's going back to Chacari with us."

Maruja, seeing the determination in his eyes, knew better than to challenge him. She realized that as far as the baby was concerned, she couldn't wind Fred around her finger.

Nor could she get her way when it came to the baby's name. They'd all agreed on calling her Gabriela Maria. Gabriela after an artist Maruja greatly admired and Maria in memory of Fred's mother, Mary. But as soon as Fred heard the nursemaid call the baby *nena*, the Spanish word for baby, he thought it sounded cute and started calling her Nena. It was a common enough nickname in Spanish speaking countries and the family was in agreement, except for Maruja who had an aversion to the name. For it reminded her of another Nena — a maiden aunt who was a fat old woman with a wart on the tip of her nose, whose lack of charm was exceeded only by her vacuousness. But her protests fell on deaf ears.

Since Fred was so determined not to leave Nena in Caracas, Maruja brought a succession of *niñeras*, nursemaids to Chacari. But none of them could adjust to the silence of the *llanos* and the isolation of an oil camp. They cried to Maruja, homesick for the gaiety and throbbing life of Caracas. Not even the promise of extra money could induce them to stay.

Fred, for his part was glad to see the *niñeras* leave. The house was too small for another adult. He especially felt the lack of privacy whenever he and Maruja wanted to make love, which was just about every day. No matter how disappointed he was by her lack of maternal feeling, he was still madly in love with her. He doubted she would ever cease to fascinate him. He made excuses to himself for her lack of interest in Nena — her pregnancy had come too soon in their marriage; because of her background it was too much to expect her to adapt to life in the oilfields, a new marriage and baby in such a short time. So it was Fred who got up in the middle of the night to give Nena her bottle, who when he came home and found her in a soiled diaper, washed her bottom and put on a fresh one.

Next door Cathleen had such strong maternal feelings she felt she would burst with happiness. They helped her contend with Ryle's moods and his lack of interest in Sheila. Every once in a while he demonstrated a spark of emotion and she became ecstatic that at last he'd grown to love his daughter. Then the next day it would be gone. He'll come around, she tried to reassure herself. Hadn't he acted the same way about Sarita? And then did a complete turnaround?

But there were days when she despaired of this ever happening. Days when her mood swings were just as erratic as Ryle's. Is this what happens when you live with someone, she wondered, you start picking up their foibles? It must be wonderful married to someone like Fred, she thought enviously, nothing seemed to bother him. Because the houses were so close she came to listen for his laughter, so full of the sheer joy in life. Whenever she was having problems with Ryle, Fred's laughter got her through difficult days.

Maruja enchanted her, just as she bewitched the whole camp. "Oh Cathleen," she exclaimed when they first moved in, "here you are a bride just like me and already you know everything about this good housekeeping business. How clever you are!" Maruja made her feel, as she did everyone she met, that she was extra special. But as delighted as Cathleen was with Maruja, she could never get close to her. Perhaps because in her eyes Maruja and Fred were golden people who would live enchanted lives forever, and she didn't want them to know hers was not as charmed.

Their pregnancy though was something they had in common, Nena arriving three months after Sheila. But so taken was Cathleen with Sheila, she didn't notice Maruja's indifference to her baby. She didn't know Fred was the one who gave Nena the attention she didn't receive from Maruja. It never occurred to Cathleen that the Hardestys, with their passion and joy in each other, also had problems; a mother who had no interest in her baby, and the sorrow Fred felt because of this.

Cathleen was just as unaware of Murray's love. She continued to believe it was the loneliness and isolation of the oilfields which prompted his declaration that rainy Easter night, until he came back to Chacari after his near brush with death in Maracay. News of his being mistaken for a Venezuelan soldier and almost getting shot spread quickly through the oilfields. He acquired a fame of sorts, so when new people met him, he was always greeted with a touch of awe. The ones who already knew him insisted on buying him a drink so they could hear the whole story. Especially Ryle, who acted as if they'd never had a falling out in Rosita's. But Murray still remembered and continued to feel he had cheapened Cathleen.

When he was taken off the audit team and reassigned to Chacari, it seemed to him that everything was working in his favor. He could see Cathleen every day and he wasted no time in looking for the first opportunity to declare his intentions. *El 5 de julio*, July 5th, Venezuelan Independence Day, turned out to be his chance. Since it was a national holiday, the camp celebrated with a picnic and its annual baseball game between The Pencil Pushers — the accountants and warehousemen — and the Field Hands — the drillers, engineers, geologists and toolpushers. The Field Hands were favored to win, there was a lot of kidding about the men who worked in the office being out of shape. But led by Murray, who made two home runs and a stunning triple play, the Pencil Pushers were so far ahead the second string team was put in.

"You're a terrific athlete, Murray," Cathleen complimented him when he came off the field.

"Hey Toots, I'm Jack Armstrong, the all American Boy," he grinned at her. "That's 'cause I ate my Wheaties. Isn't that right, Sheila?" He looked down at the baby who was sleeping peacefully in her travelling crib. Cathleen took her everywhere she went, carrying the basket by its two handles and setting up the portable wheels when necessary. Today they were retracted and the crib lay on the wooden bleachers next to her.

Ryle had gone in the game at the seventh inning. But his baseball skills didn't match Murray's. He was put out running from second to third on Fred's bunt, and now with him covering second, a Pencil Pusher stole the base.

"It's those boots," Murray remarked shaking his head in disbelief. "How can he run in them?"

"I think he'd feel naked without them," Cathleen replied. "Oh, Murray," she cried out, "I'm so glad you're back in camp safe and sound, that nothing happened to you during the revolution."

"That makes two of us," he replied. "When it was all over my first thought was what a great story it would make at the next party. You know how we all go crazy looking for something new to talk about." Cathleen nodded her head in agreement. "But as I was driving back to Tucupido, it hit me. How uncertain life is. I could be here today and gone tomorrow. There's no guarantee any of us are going to be around to collect our Social Security." Remembering the fire which almost claimed Ryle, Cathleen felt a shudder of recognition.

"And I'd never see you again." His words came out in a low whisper. He was conscious of how little privacy there was, but in looking around he saw they were alone. The game was so one sided most people had left. "Oh, Cathleen, never to have the chance to try and make you mine. Now, that would be a waste."

She bit her lip, trying to think of the right reply, but no words came out.

"Are you happy with Ryle?" She didn't answer him, but a frown spread across her forehead. "I don't think you are. Look," he said gently, "I'm not the type to go around busting up a good marriage. But I've seen the hurt and loneliness in your eyes. You've been married just over a year, you have a beautiful baby, you should be walking on air. But you're not. And I can guess the reason. It's rough living with Ryle. Those moods of his can be killers. I know. Remember, I used to room with him."

Cathleen's shoulders slumped. She'd been putting up a front for so long, pretending to the world and herself that things would get better, that Ryle would come around. And now confronted with the truth, it was almost a relief not to have to pretend anymore. Before she realized what was happening, words tumbled out of her mouth. The feeling that maybe Ryle didn't need her, his bitter disappointment in Sheila not being a boy, the warning from her father not to come home with her tail between her legs.

"You don't have to go back to New York," he assured her. "I'll take you to Reno, in six weeks you'll be free. Then we'll go to California and I'll show you what happiness really is."

Sheila cried out in her sleep until her thumb made its way to her mouth. "And I'll love Sheila like she was my own," he assured Cathleen, looking lovingly at the baby.

Divorce Ryle? Jesus, Mary and Joseph, there'd never been a divorce in her family. She could imagine what an uproar that would create. She'd never be able to show her face at home again. Her father would disown her, and her mother would have to bear the brunt of her father's temper. And not only would she devastate her family, but she'd be excommunicated from the church if she married Murray.

"No, I don't even want to think of it," she said firmly.

"I love you, my blond Irish Rose." He looked intently into her aquamarine eyes and then quietly continued, "I've never said that to any woman before. Sometimes I used to think I never would."

"It's this place," she insisted. "You'd never feel this way if we were back in the States." She reached for Sheila who was sleeping peacefully and took her in her arms, feeling the need to hold her as she struggled with the emotions unleashed by Murray's words.

"The hell I wouldn't," Murray cried out. "Oh, Cathleen Erin, what do I have to do to convince you that I really mean it?"

"How do you know my middle name?" She hadn't been called by her full name since her father's warning, and now hearing it again brought back all her fears of admitting her marriage was in trouble.

"I made it my business to find out. Learning everything about you has sort of become my hobby." The lopsided grin which was so much a part of his personality spread across his face.

Cathleen's pulses started beating rapidly and she had the same feeling she used to have when she read poetry — that someone had touched her soul. She shivered a little in fear and then her eyes travelled to the ballfield, seeking out Ryle. Watching his tall, lanky body behind second base, seeing him shift from one foot to another she felt a surge of sadness. He doesn't really need me, she thought despondently. I've disappointed him in some way I don't understand. Maybe by not being the woman he thought I was. Sometimes he makes me feel so inadequate, that I'm not smart enough, or not the person he wants socially. He's even disappointed because I gave him a daughter instead of a son. She wondered if she had the courage to leave him, just pack up and go off with Murray? And forget her family, her religion and all the things she'd known all her life.

"Oh Murray, you make everything sound so simple. But it's not. At least, not for me."

"I know, Toots, it's a big step. But just think about it, that's all I ask. Hey, we're not going to run off today, not even tomorrow." He grinned at her. "Maybe the day after."

"Oh, we're gonna have so much fun together," Murray burst out enthusiastically. "You'll love California. You can do anything out there, skiing up in the mountains or lounging at the beach. It's all there, just waiting for us. Take a chance, Toots. You only pass this way once, so why not live it the right way with the right man?"

Why not? Why should she stick with Ryle, waiting for the crumbs he throws when the mood suits him? Her parents didn't have to live with his obsessive ambition, nor did the Church have to put up with his moods. She owed them no allegiance. What was it her Aunt Jenny always said? Suit yourself and you suit everyone else. Be happy and everyone around you will be happy too. And she would be consistently happy with Murray. There would be no uncertainty with him. As for the passion she and Ryle once shared, a passion she knew she'd never have with Murray, well maybe she didn't want to love anyone that intensely. For it hurt too much when it lost its luster.

But that passion, however much it flickered, still had sparks of life. No matter how estranged she and Ryle had become or how much she grieved over his lack of love for Sheila, he still reached out for her in bed. And she reached back. She had come to learn that their periods of closeness were sporadic, nothing was ever steady. She had just about given up understanding him. Once in awhile, the tenderness he'd shown her in the early days of their marriage returned and she felt alive again.

She questioned whether she was still in love with him, wondering if there was such a thing as constant love. If maybe it was just a physical thing which nature had created so the reproductive system would continue the human race. And thus their marriage continued, close in bed but worlds apart away from that island sanctuary. Until the day he found her baking diapers.

After Sheila was born, the rainy season became a challenge. The maid washed the diapers and hung them in the carport along with the rest of the wash which eventually dried. But Cathleen couldn't wait for the diapers to dry, so she came up with the idea of baking them. She spread the half dried diapers on cookie sheets and in pyrex baking dishes and into the kerosene oven they went. She experimented until she found the right temperature, and she learned to turn them frequently with a large carving fork until they came out with most of the moisture removed. Then they only needed a quick touch-up with an iron.

When Ryle came home that afternoon her cheeks were flushed and her blond hair curled into soft wisps from the heat.

"Hey beautiful," he called out when he opened the kitchen door. Whenever he called her that she knew it would be a good day. She slipped into his arms. He was wet and smelled of sweat, but she didn't care, for the solidness of his arms around her was such a comfort.

"I sure like these homecomings," he murmured. "Maybe I ought to go out and come back in."

"Oh, yes," she laughed playfully pushing him towards the door. When he was in a good mood, she responded instantly. Then she smelled cloth burning and running to the stove, opened the door. Reaching in with the carving fork she turned the diapers. But she saw it was too late for one of them, it had brown charred marks and smoke curled up from its edges.

"What the devil?" He stomped over to the stove, his boots making tracks across the red cement floor.

"I'm just like a pioneer out west," she laughed. "Necessity is the mother of invention my daddy always said. So I'm just using a little of my Yankee ingenuity."

"Pretty smart," he remarked noticing the diapers in the oven and the ones hanging over the backs of the kitchen chairs. "I knew I married you for some reason. Just didn't figure out 'til now what it was."

"You married me because I've got class," she replied folding some of the drier diapers. "Isn't that what you're always telling me?"

"Yeah, you sure do." He sat down on the one kitchen chair free of diapers and started pulling off his boots. "You're what every man wants, a lady in public and a mistress in bed."

Another compliment. She could see this was really going to be her day. She placed a Polar beer on the table for him.

"Finish your diaper drying while I take a shower," Ryle said drinking the beer. But he didn't move. When their eyes met, she had the feeling he was undressing her with his eyes. He reached over, pulling her onto his lap. His lips brushed back and forth across her mouth. "Oh baby, you taste so good." She felt him getting hard under the flimsiness of her yellow cotton shift.

"You think the kid will wake up soon?" Ryle's right hand travelled down towards her breasts.

"She just fell asleep," she whispered, hoping Sheila would stay that way.

"If we keep sitting here, I'm liable to get you up on that table". By now his left hand was travelling up her thighs, his long fingers slipping into her panties.

"Hmm, that might be fun." She loved it when they made love in unlikely places.

"Where's the maid?" His finger moved slowly, caressing her.

"It's Thursday, her day off," she replied, barely able to get the words out.

"I really meant it about doing it on the table." While his finger moved slowly and erotically inside her, his mouth teased. She felt his tongue searching out hers and when he made contact, she had an orgasm. Afterwards he moved her towards the table. It was times like this when she felt they had discovered sex, that no one else knew it existed. She had progressed a long way from their honeymoon on board ship when she would only make love in the dark and in bed. They were so wrapped up in each other's presence that they didn't notice the burning smell.

"The diapers," she cried, hating to move away from him. She ran over to the oven door, turning off the stove and taking out a cookie sheet of slightly overdone cloth.

"Baby, I stink. I'm goin' to get you all dirty, " he murmured when she sat down in his lap again.

"Then we'll just have to take a shower together." She was back in his arms. They started on the kitchen table, but it was too wobbly. She slid to the edge and wrapped her legs around Ryle while he stood, his hands propped up on the table. There were times when she liked a lot of foreplay, but today she was ready for him the minute he called her beautiful. Or maybe she was ready that morning. He'd left around three in the morning so when she woke up he was gone. Woke up missing him, dreaming that she could actually feel him inside her. Now it was no dream. The sensation of his climax inside her stirred feelings she couldn't define. I do this to him, she told herself and pushed away the thought that sex was sex. She wanted desperately to believe him when he told her it had never been like this with anyone else, that she did things to him no other woman had.

Reluctant to part, they went into the shower, where they soaped each other, letting the water run down their bodies while they caressed, stopping from time to time to kiss gently, shyly, like lovers discovering one another for the first time. Everything seemed to encourage these moments of tender lovemaking. The rain came down steadily keeping out all intruders. Sheila slept peacefully in her crib. After showering they tiptoed into the bedroom and looked down at their baby. She lay on her stomach, right thumb in her mouth, her breathing a soft beat.

"She's a cute little thing," Ryle whispered.

Cathleen's heart skipped a few beats hearing the first compliment he'd paid their daughter.

"Of course she is," she replied, her voice trembling. "She looks just like you."

"Sometimes I can be a real shit," he said in a matter of fact manner.

For a moment Cathleen didn't reply. She guessed in his own way he was apologizing. In his admittance of giving her a hard time, he was asking her forgiveness.

"If only you wouldn't put that wall between us," she said softly. "Honestly Ryle, sometimes you act as if I'm not here, that I don't even exist. I'm beginning to wonder if you still love me."

"You think that, after what we've just done?" He looked at her in astonishment.

Isn't that typical of a man's reasoning, she thought. "No, now it's fine, now we're close," she persisted. "It's just that I never know how long it's going to last, Ryle."

"It's goin' to last for a long, long time, baby. We'll be together for the rest of our lives." He pulled her into his arms and they slipped down on to the bed, snuggling together until Sheila woke up. Then he got up and followed her to the kitchen while she prepared Sheila's supper. Cathleen thought he would be tired, she knew he'd gotten up early that morning to drive to a wellsite way out in the boonies. And that it had been a long trip back to camp with his pickup slipping in the mud and getting stuck from time to time, as vehicles frequently did in the rainy season. But he seemed reluctant to leave her and the baby.

"It's so good to be home with you two," he sighed. "I sure hope none of the ladies come over for a coffee klatch."

"They won't, the rain keeps them away. Besides, they see your pickup." She laughed. "You know how it is here, they all know you left early this morning. Everyone knows everything about everyone."

"Well, yeah," he agreed. "But that's the price we gotta pay, right now anyway. But we're not goin' to be here forever. I showed Caracas I could run a geology department when I filled in over there in Tucupido. And from Tucupido we could get sent to Maracaibo. Then from Maracaibo it's just a step to the Big Time — Caracas." Cathleen felt the restlessness creep into his voice. The afternoon had been so perfect she didn't want anything to spoil it now. Their times of closeness, of the barriers being down between them were so few.

"I don't ever want to be poor again, baby." The intensity of his words startled her.

"But we're not poor," she protested. "You're making good money and our savings account is growing."

"What we got is peanuts!" he said derisively. "There's just two things that are important in life, money and power. When you got them, baby, you've got everything."

"Everything?" The intensity in his voice frightened her. "What about love? What about family?"

"A man needs that, but like I told you, if you want respect, you got to buy it. And the only way you can is with power and moolah. Maybe you just weren't poor enough the way I was. Hell, I know you weren't." His lips curled up in a sneer. "You'd die if you saw my folks' place. I hate it anytime I have to go there. That's why I just had to get out. I thought I had it made when I started working the oilfields. First time in my life I had some good money in my jeans. And then I thought I was on my way when I got into college, but in some ways it was worse there." He stared moodily into space.

"How was it worse?" she asked him gently, not wanting to lose the closeness they'd developed.

"Seeing all those guys who didn't have to worry about the next buck." Cathleen knew he sent money to his mother every month. "Envying the ones who went out for sports which I couldn't because I was working at any odd job I could to keep ahead. Seeing all those jokers go to football games and dances."

"So, that's why you like to go out all the time," she teased him.

"I don't ever want to be left out of things no more." He said this so fiercely she felt a great wave of tenderness for him, understanding for the first time why he was so obsessed with success and all its trappings.

"That's why I keep pushing you to socialize. Entertain, become known as the best hostess, make everyone like you no matter what. Smile 'til you feel your ears will fall off. If you have to kiss ass, do it! Anything that will help us get ahead." His gray eyes became glazed. "The important thing is to get ahead, it don't matter how you go about it."

"Oh, Ryle, I don't know if I want anything that badly." The knowledge that he really believed it didn't matter what he did to become successful upset her.

"If you're married to me, you do. It's as simple as that." His gray eyes had a wild look in them. "You either agree with me or you don't. Well, do you?" he demanded.

She was beginning to feel uneasy. All sorts of things ran through her mind. That maybe he only needed her for a bed partner, or a social partner, that he didn't love her, but only needed her to take care of his needs. That they had some kind of business, a private little corporation going between them and once he'd gotten what he wanted from her, he'd discard her. The fear of his losing interest haunted her.

"Cathleen, I asked you a question." He grabbed her wrists and held them tightly.

A loud cry from Sheila, exuberant and full of life as she banged her rattle on the playpen slats, broke the tension. Ryle looked at the baby, then down to Cathleen's wrists which he had in a tight grip. Seeing the red marks on them, he quickly raised her hands to his lips.

"Oh baby, I'm sorry. You know I wouldn't do anything to hurt you. Sometimes I get tied up in knots wanting things so badly."

"Sometimes, Ryle, you can want something too much," she declared. "If you would just relax and not get so tense, things will come a lot easier to you." She almost felt sorry for him. Maybe once he gets a little more ahead, with more money and prestige, he can relax. He can be a good man, she thought, a very tender and caring person. It's because so many things had been lacking in his life, and she suspected it wasn't only money, but also love, that he had this terrible yearning for power. There was nothing wrong with wanting to get ahead. She'd had the same desire, that's why she'd gone to college at night. But she knew she didn't share his obsession with power and money.

Ryle wanted biscuits for dinner. When she saw the flour was full of bugs, she sifted it several times. It used to bother her when bugs got into the flour and ants into the sugar. Now she'd adopted Nadine's philosophy that they didn't eat much. She checked the sugar and saw that a few ants had managed to get in the jar. Not too bad, she decided. If there was a swarm of them, she would have the maid put kerosene in small cans and place them under each leg of the table.

They ate dinner, the baby in her lap while she fed her a bottle of juice. Cathleen thought Sheila looked like the baby on the jar label and sometimes called her 'my Gerber baby'. After feeding Sheila she hated to put her down. It was the most wonderful feeling in the world holding her in her arms. But after dinner she placed her in the playpen where she banged a spoon and then at times slipped it into her mouth to suck.

Cathleen went back to baking diapers and Ryle helped. She was surprised because he wasn't one to do things around the house. But he seemed content to sit there drinking beer and helping her fold the diapers. From time to time he went over to the playpen, picking Sheila up as if he wanted to make up for all the time he'd ignored her. At one point he poured a few drops of beer on his fingers and let Sheila suck them.

"You're going to get her drunk," Cathleen admonished him.

"A few drops? It's good for her," he replied. "She'll sleep like a log."

The rain continued it's steady beat. "It's like winter back home," Cathleen said contentedly. "And we're snowbound, all cozy and snug. Does it snow it Oklahoma? Are we going there on our big leave so I can meet your family?" They had skipped taking their local leave because of Sheila's birth and would let it accumulate for their long vacation.

"Yeah," he sighed. "I guess we'll have to go by for a quickie visit. Not much to see. Like I told you, I hate going there, but still they'll want to meet you. Just don't expect too much."

Sheila's eyes were closing. They picked her up and put her in her crib. Then they turned out the lights and went to bed. Cathleen felt drowsy, beer always did this to her. Ryle reached out and held her in his arms as they drifted off to sleep. Just before she lost consciousness she thought of Murray. Whatever doubts she'd had were gone. How could she leave Ryle? Everything was perfect between them now. He really cared for Sheila, he'd shown that today. And she had gotten to know him better. If she could get him to open up the way he had today, she could cope with his moods. Why, he might even stop going off into those deep funks. Besides, what was that expression Murray used about someone making your motor race? No one made her's race except Ryle. She couldn't imagine living without him. And hadn't he assured her they would be together for a long time, the rest of their lives?

....

"Cathleen, it's your deal," Wilma nudged her. She blinked her eyes. Talk about woolgathering. She'd been daydreaming about the day Ryle came home and found her baking diapers. Maybe it was everyone wishing for rain, or the need to do something with her mind since she was finding it difficult to concentrate on the cards. She'd started playing bridge in the afternoons again only because Ryle had been nagging her to get out more. Things were so much better between them, they were finally a family, that she begrudged any time away from home.

Ryle was beginning to love his daughter. Cathleen would catch him looking at her when she slept. She'd see his eyes light up when Sheila smiled at him from her playpen. Sometimes Cathleen brought Sheila into bed with them on a weekend, making sure the baby was wearing rubber pants for nothing upset Ryle more than having a soggy baby around. Unlike Fred, he had no patience with the everyday mechanics of taking care of an infant. Sheila lay between them, shaking her rattle, at times rolling over and crawling. Then Cathleen would pick her up and place her on Ryle's chest. The first time she did this, Sheila broke out in a big smile.

"See, she knows you're her daddy," Cathleen beamed. "Give her a ride."

Ryle looked at her blankly.

"Honestly, Ryle, sometimes I wonder if you were ever a child, if you just weren't born a grownup." And then she wanted to bite her tongue for she remembered what a lonely childhood he had, no brothers or sisters and he never spoke about cousins. She reached over and placed Sheila on her knee, rocking her back and forth.

"Sheila Mageila," she crooned softly, calling her by her favorite nickname. "This baby just loves to play. And she loves to go out, just like her daddy." They hadn't missed one weekend party thanks to the folding crib Nadine gave them. When they went to a camp dance, they left her in the back seat of the Chevrolet with netting over the crib and the window cracked to let in air, taking turns going out to check on her. At a house party everyone peeked in on Sheila when she slept in the hostess' bedroom. Sometimes when she was awake, Cathleen brought her into the living room to join the party. She never cried or fussed, unlike the Hardesty baby, Nena, who cried a lot because she had colic.

Cathleen tried to concentrate on her cards. Bridge was one of the few things in Chacari which held her interest. It was a challenge because no two hands were ever alike. Lately though her cards had been very dull, she hardly ever had a responding hand, much less one with which to open. She felt guilty leaving Sheila because she'd been sleeping fitfully during her naps. Between the heat which was becoming unbearable and her starting to teethe, she had become a restless baby. Cathleen rubbed her gums with paregoric and then gave her a cool bath with baking soda to alleviate the rash she had gotten from the heat. If only Ryle would stop pushing her to go out and socialize, she could be home now with her baby instead of at this boring bridge game.

She picked up her hand and saw she had nothing more than six points. Now that she'd become a better player, she just wasn't getting the cards.

"You'll just have to get pregnant again, Acey Deucy," Nadine kidded her. Cathleen smiled, remembering the unbelievable streak of high cards she had when she was carrying Sheila. She would love to have another baby. The memories of her difficult pregnancy had been quickly forgotten in the delight of Sheila's company. She saw Maruja roll her eyes at the mention of getting pregnant again. The camp buzzed with the gossip of Maruja's difficulty in keeping a nursemaid. But because she had charmed everyone, her lack of maternal feelings was hardly mentioned. Everyone attributed it to her being a wealthy Venezuelan who was used to an army of servants.

"You should have played the diamond, not the spade," Sugar chided her. "They never should have made that hand."

Wilma fanned her face furiously. "If only it would rain, this damned heat is driving me crazy." When it rained, everyone complained, when it didn't, everyone still griped. Cathleen gritted her teeth. What she really wanted was to be home with her baby. Tomorrow Sheila would be six months old. What a difference the baby had made in their lives. Whenever Ryle got into one of his moods, it didn't bother her the way it used to. Or if she felt homesick and out of place, that panicky feeling didn't threaten to smother her as it did in the past. She had only to look at Sheila and the feeling of being alone disappeared. She glanced at her watch. A quarter to four. Just 15 minutes more and she could go home. Tomorrow she would bake a cake for Sheila's six month birthday. She was thinking about what kind of cake she would make when she picked up her cards and saw her hand had 25 points and 150 Honors in Spades. Finally some interesting cards. She and Sugar went to Seven Spades. Wilma doubled and Cathleen redoubled.

"Lucky in cards, unlucky in love," Sugar laughed with that funny laugh of hers which made it impossible to know whether she was laughing or sneering.

Cathleen was gathering up the last trick, making the Grand Slam she bid, when she heard her maid's voice. She looked up in surprise and saw Maria run into the living room with Sheila in her arms. Cathleen smiled and opened her arms to receive her daughter. And then the smile changed to a scream.

"*Señora*," Maria cried out. "I left her for one little second, one little moment. She was crying so much that I decided to give her a little bath with the baking soda like I saw you do."

Cathleen stiffened. She never allowed the maid to touch the baby. "And then," Maria continued in rapid Spanish, "the kerosene delivery man came to the door."

Her baby was dead. Oh Mother of God, please no, she cried out. It's a bad dream, just like those nightmares I used to have about Ryle after the fire. The cards slid to the floor as Cathleen pushed the table away from her. A wet and still Sheila, her gray eyes staring blankly up at her, was delivered into her arms. Cathleen held her close, putting her tiny head on her shoulder, telling herself Sheila just needed to burp. If she gave a good burp, the water would come spilling out of her lungs and she would be alive again. She clung fiercely to Sheila, refusing to let go of her when Marge Gullett who was a nurse wanted to give her artificial respiration.

The rest of the afternoon and evening was a blur. Nadine went running for the camp doctor. Since they didn't have adequate facilities in Chacari, they rushed Sheila to the Sinclair Hospital in Santa Barbara.

The next morning, on her six month birthday, Sheila Jane Rylander, who had drowned in a bathinette of water, was buried in the cemetery in Maturín. Cathleen looked blankly at the large group of people. Almost the entire camp had come to the funeral. This time yesterday morning her baby was alive. This time yesterday she was playing with her, talking to her, holding her sweet smelling little body close to her, telling her what a wonderful birthday she was going to have. A lone tear slid down Cathleen's left cheek. It wasn't fair to take this innocent baby, she wanted to scream out.

She wondered if there really was a Hereafter. She so wanted to believe that her daughter was safe and happy in Heaven, but her faith which had always been a strong part of her life had deserted her. She didn't know what she believed anymore. Her only thought was how cold her baby must be in that little white coffin. She wanted to reach in and pluck her out, hold her close in her arms, warm up her still, little body.

Her thoughts went back to that dreary day in December when Ryle had walked into her life and snatched her away from everything safe and secure. Memories of the premonition of sadness she felt on the train haunted her. It was a warning of the sorrow she was now experiencing. If I hadn't married Ryle, she kept thinking, this wouldn't have happened. I'd never have left my baby home with a maid because if I were still in the States, I wouldn't have a maid. This wouldn't have happened if Sheila were Danny O'Hara's child.

In that moment Cathleen began to despise Ryle, hating him for the way he continuously pushed her to get out and socialize. He reached for her hand and she pulled abruptly away from him. She couldn't stand for him to touch her.

The priest intoned words which made no sense to her. She stared at him, saw the stains on his dusty cassock, the stubble of his beard, the dirt on his cracked boots. He didn't even look like a priest to her. His words meant absolutely nothing. Her baby was being buried and she didn't understand a word of the service. I want Father Bellini, she screamed to herself, I want to hear him talking in that brusque Brooklyn accent that I've grown up hearing. She looked down at the tiny white coffin and wanted to tear the lid off and take her daughter in her arms before she was lowered into the ground. If she could just hold her one more time. The knowledge that she would never again hold Sheila filled her with despair. A despair which felt like it would stay with her the rest of her life.

The service came to an end. Ryle took the hastily picked flowers out of her hand, flaming hibiscus and bougainvillea, and placed them on top of the little coffin. Nadine picked up a clump of dirt and threw it over the flowers on the coffin. Cathleen wanted to fling herself on top of the coffin and lurched toward it, but Ryle caught her. She pushed him away, pummeling him with her fists, a cry of rage filling her throat. But nothing came out. She tried to scream, to tell him just how much she blamed him. And then she went limp like a marionette whose strings had been cut. Ryle caught her in his arms.

She didn't see Sarita and John, didn't recognize them when they reached out to comfort her. She stared at Maruja and Fred as if they were strangers. She looked right through Murray who helped Ryle place her in the back seat of the Chevrolet. But she didn't resist Ryle when he held her in his arms while Murray drove their car. For she was back in the cemetery with her daughter, holding her close so the darkness of her coffin wouldn't frighten her.

EIGHTEEN

Fran Young was on duty when Sheila Jane Rylander was brought to the Santa Barbara camp hospital. Afterwards, when she slipped into the nurses' lounge for a cigarette, her hands were shaking. She had witnessed her share of death during the war, had seen babies tinier than Sheila die from lack of food. But no matter how hardened she'd trained herself to become, this tragedy affected her. She wondered if it was also due to her yearning to have a child of her own, or because the Rylanders were with Palm Oil in Chacari. Chacari, which spelled Fred Hardesty to her.

She took out her compact, peering anxiously into the small mirror. Just thinking about Fred made her conscious of her appearance. The long, horsey face looking back at her had been perfectly made up when she came on duty, but now the oily pores of her complexion were seeping through the pancake makeup and she needed fresh lipstick. After she ran the powder puff over her face, she fluffed her thin hair which she'd colored ash blond. Perhaps a shade or two lighter, she wondered. Face it, she told herself morosely, you never were a raving beauty and a person can just do so much and no more. She still had a great body though, almost as if fate having denied her one thing, had decided to compensate her with full breasts and slim hips. A body which never failed to attract men. It had certainly fascinated Fred. How ironical, she mused, that here in the oilfields, with ten men to one woman she had to fall for a guy who was in love with someone else. It won't matter in the long run though, she reassured herself. Despite Fred and Maruja's recent parenthood, one day he would be her's. She had to be very patient and never give up. Eventually Fred's marriage to that Venezuelan would come to an end.

There were times though when she wondered if it would ever happen. The first time she met Maruja she felt so dejected she was sure she had completely lost her mind. Who could compete with the likes of that

226

Venezuelan beauty, she thought bleakly? So vivacious, so utterly enchanting that everyone who met her fell under her spell. And why is it, she wondered bitterly, that little women always attract tall men? She looks like an ant next to Fred, Fran decided maliciously, a little black ant.

It was inevitable she would run into Fred, for Santa Barbara and Chacari weren't that far apart. She'd gone to a barbecue given by a Creole Petroleum seismo crew stationed near Maturín. Going to one of their shindigs was always a guarantee of a good time because the seismo guys were a little wild and crazy. Maybe it was all the squinting they did studying those graphs for hours on end which made them want to kick up their heels, or perhaps it was their nomadic life, moving as they did from location to location searching for future oil sites. Whatever the reason, if people in the oilfields liked to party, a seismo crew made it an art form. When Fran arrived, they boasted they had 32 cases of Polar Beer. From the looks of things, half were dead soldiers.

A record player was blasting from one of the trailers and a woman danced barefoot in the center of the dance floor, which in this case was nothing more than a dirt clearing in the center of the trailers. The dancer was without a partner, her husband had gone for further liquid fortification, but it didn't seem to bother her. The music was wild and loud and she never missed a beat. She was a seismo wife who only saw her husband every six weeks when he came to Caracas, and this night was a definite departure from the usual Saturday nights she spent in Caracas going to the movies with the other seismo grass widows. Her husband's friendship with an oil camp couple, who'd extended the hospitality of their guestroom, had made her trip to the interior possible.

When a couple joined her on the dance floor, Fran's heart started racing madly. It was Fred — there was no mistaking his sandy haired good looks or tall, muscular body. And with him a tiny, perfectly proportioned brunette with a heart shaped face. The famous Maruja, she thought bitterly. She watched as they danced the *joropo*, a Venezuelan folk waltz. Unlike the Viennese waltzes which were created to be danced in glittering surroundings attended by royalty, the *joropo* belonged to the *llanos*, the plains of Venezuela and the common people. Fred with his hat set at a rakish angle and his feet stomping the dirt was the personification of a *llanero*, a cowboy. People clapped their hands and tapped their feet in time to the music as they made a circle around the couple. Everyone always did that when he danced, Fran remembered nostalgically. When the song ended, there were calls for an encore and the record player was cranked up again.

"Now you are one of us," Maruja cried out to Fred, looking flirtatiously up at him. Fred remembering he'd said the same words to her when *The Eyes of Texas Are Upon Us* was played, roared with laughter. He was nuts about this little doll. Not only was she a spitfire in bed, but she had a sharp sense of humor. She was full of piss and vinegar and never stopped intriguing him. If he had to bite the dust, he couldn't think of anyone more delightful to bite it for. He danced around her, his hands behind his back, his toes digging into the dirt as he followed the strains of *Alma Llanera*.

Under the shadow of the Acacias trees, bare of their blossoms for the rainy season hadn't started, Fran devoured Fred with her eyes. She told herself she should leave, she was just tormenting herself, but she couldn't stop looking at him. That was how it used to be when they danced together, she thought forlornly. And now she couldn't dance with him anymore, all because of that Venezuelan. Fran stared at Maruja malevolently. When the music stopped Fran continued to follow her with her eyes, not seeing anyone else.

But Fred saw her and called out, "There she is, that statuesque goddess from Paris, France. Miss Fran Young herself." He still thought she was French, probably because she never corrected him.

"Baby doll," Fred said enthusiastically to Maruja. "I want you to meet a good friend of mine."

Fran came out of the trance-like state she'd fallen into and watched him coming towards her. She certainly didn't want to talk to him or meet his wife. She turned around and started to walk away. "Franny, have you forgotten me?" he called out to her. And then she felt his hand on her arm. There was no escaping him. He was so genuinely pleased to see her, as if he had met up with an old school chum. Nothing in his manner hinting that they'd once been lovers.

"Franny is an *enfermera*," he informed Maruja, "so if you ever need a nurse, she's the one to see."

Maruja extended her hand and shook Fran's murmuring, "*Mucho gusto.*" For a moment she wondered if there had been anything between

Fred and this tall, plain woman, for she sensed something. Not from Fred, he was his usual open self. Nor from Fran whose hooded eyes betrayed no emotion. But she felt jealousy in the air, as if unfriendly spirits were hovering over her and an evil eye had been cast upon her. *Que ridícula*, she thought pushing aside her feelings of uneasiness. She had never been superstitious and she wasn't about to start now. She proceeded to charm Fran, taking special care to make her feel she was the most interesting person she'd met that evening. Still her feelings of uneasiness persisted.

Fran, disturbed by Maruja's charm, drank a lot more beer than she usually did, and wound up spending the night with two geologists, hoping that in the arms of two men she could forget seeing Fred and meeting the woman who'd taken him away from her.

....

All his life Murray had been in control of situations and called the shots. Even falling in love with Cathleen had given him options. He could go back to the States and try to forget her. Or he could hang around, hoping she would become disenchanted with Ryle. But now, after Sheila's death, he felt helpless and he didn't know how to handle it. He knew Cathleen was suffering and there wasn't a damn thing he could do to help her. He was aching to see her and soothe away her grief, but he knew she was secluded in her home. What upset him most, though, were the stories circulating around camp, rumors about her which he suspected might be true.

Murray had never been a religious man. All the time he went to Hebrew School for his Bar Mitzvah, and then to temple to please his parents, he always felt the whole thing was a lot of mumbo jumbo. He went to placate his mother, but he never felt a damn thing. Even when island hopping in the Pacific, where foxholes were said to be conducive to conversions, he hadn't prayed. But now he acknowledged a higher being and made fervent pleas on Cathleen's behalf. A month after Sheila's death, Cathleen came out of seclusion for a Wednesday night movie. She had on the lavender dress he loved so much, the one which made her aquamarine eyes take on a violet hue. But now it hung loosely on her because of her weight loss. Her fair complexion was muddied and pale, while her eyes had a listless quality. After the movie he hung around drinking a beer he didn't want just to keep an eye on her. Which is when he noticed two things. She and Ryle never said a word to each other, and she was drunk, very drunk.

After Ryle fired the maid, Cathleen knew that she had to get another one, but she kept putting it off. Making any kind of a decision tended to upset her. Ryle thought maybe she'd want to go back to the States to see her family. But when he suggested this, she shook her head, replying she couldn't leave. He asked her if she would like her mother to come down; he would cable the money to New York. When she didn't answer him, he went ahead and sent a cable and then received a reply that because Cathleen's grandmother was sick, his mother-in-law couldn't get away. Cathleen didn't care one way or another.

After a week or so she started to shake off the stupor she'd been in and made herself get out of bed every morning. She didn't want a maid underfoot, but her feeble attempts at housekeeping made her realize keeping house in the tropics was a different story than in the States. The dirty clothes piled up, and not having brought a washing machine since help was so cheap, she was forced to get a laundress. Mopping the concrete floors with kerosene and then polishing them with wax sapped her strength. She found that she couldn't keep the water supply going. Boiling the water before running it through the filter became an endless job. Roaches and ants invaded the house, and the smell of Flit continued to irritate her lungs. She thought all the physical activity would keep her mind off Sheila, but in a short time she didn't care whether the house was clean or dirty. Ryle hated seeing her do housework. The sight of her mopping the floors annoyed him. Since servants were so cheap, he didn't see any reason for either of them to be concerned with domestic chores. It was only when Nadine found them a maid who came in every morning, that the house took on any semblance of its former state.

Ryle hoped now they had a maid, Cathleen would start to take more interest in herself. Not that he knew what she thought, for she'd pushed him out of her life, acting as if he weren't in the same house. She slept as far away from him as possible, and if he tried to get near her, she got up and slept in the other bedroom. At mealtimes she put the food on the table and then propped up a book and read while they ate in silence. He sensed that she blamed him. Without her putting anything into words, he could feel the anger directed towards him.

"How much longer is this goin' to continue?" he asked one night.

Cathleen ignored him, continuing to read, turning the pages slowly. He pushed aside his plate and his huge hands swept the book off the table. When she reached down to the floor to retrieve it, he grabbed her wrists.

"I'm tired of those damn books. Talk to me, Cathleen. Pay some attention to me."

She looked blankly at him, then down at her imprisoned hands which he quickly released.

"Somewhere in this house there's a piece of paper that says we're man and wife. But it's hard to believe we're married." His voice was hoarse with emotion, taking on an almost pleading quality. "You won't let me near you, you act as if I'm not here."

Cathleen shrugged her shoulders. As she did, the straps of her sundress slipped down from her frail shoulders. Listlessly she pulled them up. "I just don't feel anything for you anymore."

"Ever since Sheila died, you don't feel anything?"

It was the first time since the funeral they'd spoken her name. Cathleen's heart pounded at a furious pace and she reached for a cigarette. "You never wanted her," she cried out bitterly, "so her death is no big loss to you." The sides of her mouth turned down in anger.

"Oh, Cathleen, that's not true." He reached across the dining room table for her hand which she abruptly pushed aside. "Sure I was disappointed at first. Every man wants a boy the first time around, at least this one did. But I grew to love her. I mourn her death just as deeply as you do. Don't you know that?" His gray eyes had a haunted look to them. "What happened should have brought us closer, not pushed us apart like two strangers."

"What happened," and her words came out slowly because it was a terrible effort for her to speak, "should never have happened. I'd never have left a six month old baby with a maid, never in a million years." She paused, trying to catch her breath for she felt as if all the life had been sucked out of her. "But you kept hounding me, pushing me to get out. So I did." And then her voice became stronger as the anger and bitterness gave impetus to her words. "But then ever since we got married, you've been telling me what to do." Her voice broke momentarily as she fought to keep back the tears. "I tried to do what you wanted, no matter how much I disliked it. I went out and made like a social butterfly to help your damned career. And look what happened!"

"Cathleen, it was a freak accident." His words came out in that soft drawl which had fascinated her the day she met him. Now she hated the sound of his voice. "It's time to pick up the pieces and go on living."

"I'd like to, Ryle. God knows I'd like to, but I just don't know how."

"For starters, you could let me near you again. We could start acting like husband and wife again."

"I couldn't stand for you to touch me," she shuddered. "Don't you understand? Whatever we had has gone down the drain. As far as I'm concerned, you're the reason our baby is dead."

"You used to like it when we made love, now you're cutting me off because you blame me for Sheila's death."

"Cutting you off?" Her voice turned hysterical. "Is that all you care about? It doesn't touch you that Sheila is gone. All you're worried about is getting me into bed with you."

"And why not?" he replied defensively. "I'm normal. So were you at one time."

"You keep talking about us being husband and wife." She lit another cigarette. "Brother, I've got news for you. It's a lot more than sex. It's sharing things, talking things over, trusting each other." As she spoke she found herself thinking of Murray and she was filled with a desire to lose herself in his arms. "I don't think I even like you as a person anymore. The first time you held me in your arms, I felt so secure, like I had made it into safe port." She sneered. "Not any more. There's nothing safe about you, you're pure heartache." She got up from the table and went into the spare bedroom, closing the door.

Ryle sat there stunned. Inside he was crying out to her, but he didn't know how to tell her, except reach out for her sexually. She blamed him for Sheila's death. He had the feeling he'd lost her and he didn't know how to get her back.

He'd never thought before about needing people, never admitted to himself just what his emotional needs were. Because all his life he had to scrounge for money, he never had time to think of anything but getting ahead. His career was the most important thing to him, but he did love Cathleen, loved her passionately, even if he didn't share his feelings with her. If something was bothering him, he kept it to himself. To talk things over with anyone was so foreign to his nature he wouldn't know how to begin. He had told her of his ambitions, to his way of thinking that should have been enough.

A lot of things bothered him. Despite his congeniality around people, he was even more insecure than Cathleen. He worried that he wasn't getting ahead fast enough; his biggest fear was he might get lost in the shuffle, be just another geologist in a company filled with better educated and smarter geologists.

When Cathleen accused him of not caring that Sheila was dead, she didn't know how he cried inside for his daughter, carrying his own burden of guilt for his indifference after her birth. If only Cathleen would let him make love to her, he was positive she'd know all these things. It was the only way he knew to make up for their terrible loss, to express his need for her.

But now to be told she didn't like him as a person, that there was nothing but heartache with him was the cruelest blow. So he retreated even deeper inside himself. And because his pride was wounded, there was an undeclared war in their house. Anytime he could avoid going home, he did. He spent more and more time in the field and in the office. At the end of the day he went by the club and stayed until dinner time. Because he knew how quickly gossip spread, he made sure people knew Cathleen was still so grief stricken she needed time to herself. He went to great lengths to preserve the façade of their marriage.

Cathleen crawled further into her shell. When people dropped by, she was so listless they soon left. People felt eventually she would come out of her depression. Perhaps it was best to leave her alone for now. Nothing held her interest. Music, which had always been her escape, tended to make her sad, and she spent the day turning the record player on and off. When she tried to read a book, she found herself reading the same page over and over again, or mindlessly flipping magazines. Nor could she write letters, she tore up more pages than she wrote. The only time she left the house was to drive to the cemetery in Maturín. Her mind told her Sheila was in Heaven, but her heart felt otherwise. While she primarily blamed Ryle for Sheila's death, she carried her own feelings of guilt because she'd left her with the maid. Visiting Sheila's grave was her act of atonement. That and the conviction she couldn't leave her alone. She just knew her baby daughter was frightened and alone in a cold, dark bed. She woke up in the middle of the night trembling from her nightmares about Sheila.

When she got home from the cemetery, the maid had finished cleaning the house. She knew she shouldn't leave her alone in the house every day, that she might steal them blind, but Cathleen was past caring. As soon as the maid left, she made herself a drink. In the beginning it was something to parch her thirst from the heat of the drive to the cemetery. Then because it gave her a lift, she made a second one. She found the more she drank, the more her restlessness and depression subsided. It wasn't that she got giddy or high. It was more of a calm and peaceful feeling which made her feel she could cope. By the time Ryle came home at night she was tranquil enough to cook and put dinner on the table. And concentrate on reading a book. After dinner she sipped another drink continuously and then she was able to sleep. Unless it was a bad night when she woke up seeing Sheila in her grave. Mornings were the hardest because her first thought on waking was regret she was still alive. She longed to go to sleep and never wake up again.

Sarita and John Maguire were worried about her, but living in Puerto La Cruz presented a problem since Sarita didn't drive. What she did was write Cathleen every day. Cathleen was touched by Sarita's concern, but her letters never penetrated the shell she'd grown around her.

The sound of a baby crying would cause her to jump up with a start and run to the spare bedroom. Only to discover the empty crib staring up at her. Which made her feel she'd gone mad until she realized the cries were coming from next door. Numbly she remembered the Hardesty baby had a bad case of colic. She quickly turned on the record player to drown out the crying. And with shaking hands poured herself another drink. Until one day she couldn't stand it any longer, and running out of the house she made her way to the Hardesty kitchen door which she pounded furiously. Maruja just has to do something about that baby, she thought irritably. This has gone on long enough.

Maruja came running to the door.

"¡Llorando, siempre llorando esta niña!" Maruja burst out. "Nena does nothing but cry and I'm going out of my mind. Fred and I have been up all night, taking turns walking the floor with her." Maruja quickly opened the door.

"Oh, Cathleen," she cried out. "I'm so glad you're here. I just don't know what to do with Nena." Maruja burst into tears. "I've given her the medicine the doctor prescribed for the colic and yet she continues to cry. Cry, cry! She never stops!" The rings on her tiny fingers caught the afternoon sun as her hands flew into the air in a gesture of complete bewilderment. "And that stupid nursemaid I paid more money than she ever saw in her whole life has gone running back to Caracas."

Maruja in tears was something Cathleen never expected to see. Not the vivacious, delightful woman who could wrap the whole world around her finger and get whatever she wanted from life.

Then Cathleen put aside her shock and walked rapidly into Nena's bedroom. Automatically, without giving it a second thought, she reached into the crib and took Nena in her arms. The infant's red hair clung to her wet head, beads of perspiration ran down her splotched face. Cathleen whispered words of comfort to her, walking up and down the room, stroking her back so that the gas bubbles trapped in the infant's stomach would come up.

"Oh, that's a good girl," she murmured in Nena's ear when the first burp came up. She switched the baby on her back, cradling her in her arms, running her hand soothingly over the baby's distended stomach. Within minutes Nena's cries of pain had subsided and she fell into an exhausted sleep.

"Oh Cathleen, how clever you are," Maruja cried out exuberantly. Cathleen, still holding Nena, stared at the other woman. How many times had Maruja used that phrase? And she'd lapped it up, basking in the warmth of her words. Now she didn't care if she had Maruja's approval or not.

"I'm not the least bit clever," Cathleen snapped. She continued to hold Nena, hating the thought of putting her back in the crib.

"Oh Cathleen, don't be cross with me," Maruja pleaded. "Some women are born mothers, and you're one of them. While I am completely unequipped. I don't know what do to. Things that come naturally to you, I have to scratch my poor brain to figure out." Her manner and words were so beguiling that Cathleen found it difficult to remain angry.

"But how could you be so indifferent to her pain?" Cathleen persisted. "She has a stomach ache, that's what colic is."

"But, Cathleen, it's not that I am indifferent. No one knows better than me that my feelings toward Nena are not what they should be. I often wonder if I'm some kind of monster because I have no maternal instinct in me whatsoever. And then when she starts howling like that, *Ay Dios!* I just can't stand it, it gets on my nerves something fierce."

Maruja doesn't love this baby, Cathleen wept to herself, she doesn't want her, she has no interest whatsoever in her. The knowledge filled Cathleen's heart with an aching sadness. And a bitterness that a mistake had been made and the wrong baby taken. This is the one that should have been taken, she thought angrily, for she's not wanted. But no, mine was the one who died. What little faith she had left quickly evaporated and she doubted if she would ever believe in God and His wisdom again.

She put Nena in her crib and walked out of the house. When she got home, she grabbed a bottle of rum, splashing it savagely over the ice cubes, diluting it with very little water. All she wanted was the ache inside her to subside and the only way to deaden it was a drink. Certainly there was no consolation to be found in prayer.

The wrong baby was taken, the words kept repeating themselves like a litany in her brain, the wrong baby. Her thoughts turned to Fred. Fred had probably learned to live with the knowledge that Maruja didn't want their daughter. She felt bad for him, for he was such a decent guy. And then she realized he was still crazy about Maruja and would probably go to his grave madly in love with her. No matter how unfeeling she was towards their child.

Then the crying started again. She put her hands over her ears, throwing herself on the bed, hoping for the blessed escape of sleep. Pulled the pillow over her head trying to drown out Nena's cries. She's not my baby, she thought angrily, she's not my problem. But she got up and went to the bathroom, swigging her mouth out with Listerine. Then unsteadily she made her way out the kitchen door and across the yard to the Hardesty house. Where she silently picked up Nena and after soothing her, changed her diaper. It's not my problem, she kept telling herself, but she couldn't stay away. And all the while she held Nena, rocking her and soothing her tummy, she ached for the daughter she would never hold again.

....

Taking care of Nena sobered Cathleen for she was petrified of dropping her. But the time away from her, when the colic subsided or

Fred was home, she drank to dull the pain inside her. It was holding another woman's baby in her arms, remembering that hers was gone forever. Becoming more attached to Nena and knowing she wasn't hers.

One day after her daily visit to the cemetery, she found Pet Ford waiting for her. Sarita Maguire was in camp, Pet informed her. She'd come up with John just to see Cathleen and was waiting for her at Pet's house.

"Oh, Pet, I'm just not up to anything," she said evasively. "I think I'll go in and lie down." What she really wanted was a drink.

"You can't do that to Sarita," Pet insisted, "not when she's come all the way up from Puerto La Cruz just to see you." She shifted her heavy weight, fanning herself with a handkerchief.

Ordinarily Cathleen would have jumped at the chance to see Sarita. Not a day went by she didn't look at the house the Maguires had occupied and longed to walk through the back hedge to see her best friend. But looking irritably at her watch, she saw she was more than a half hour overdue for her first drink of the day. One of the *Mene Grande* supply trucks had broken down at the junction and backed up traffic, delaying her return home.

"You can't be rude to her," Pet persisted. She'd heard the rumors of Cathleen's drinking. "The sun may not be over the yardarm, but we're ready for a drink. Why don't you join us?"

"I've got to get out of this dress and into some shorts. You go ahead and I'll join you." She didn't enjoy drinking with people for it wasn't a social occasion anymore, just something which helped her cope and she preferred to do this in solitude. Slipping out of the *bolero* which matched her coral sundress she sat down in the chair opposite Pet. She'd discarded her white sandals the minute she got in the house, welcoming the coolness of the cement floors on her bare feet.

"No problem," Pet replied, resolving not to leave without her. "I'll wait for you." Seeing Pet's determination, she reluctantly agreed to go with her.

"*Mi querida*," Sarita cried out enveloping Cathleen in her embrace. "Every day you've been in my heart. Oh, how I wanted to come up to see you. But without a car, it's so difficult."

"Thanks for your letters," Cathleen smiled wanly. "That's awfully sweet of you to come all the way up here just to see me."

"Sweet?" Sarita's warm brown eyes swept over Cathleen. "Oh no, it's because I care for you so very much. So does John. Whatever we can do for you, just tell us."

"Bring back my baby!" Cathleen cried out.

Sarita and Pet exchanged anguished looks.

"Listen, girls, the bar's open," Pet's voice boomed.

"A martini will be fine," Cathleen said. She felt the need for the biting strength of gin.

"How is your husband?" Sarita asked gently.

"Fine," Cathleen shrugged her shoulders. "I don't see too much of him these days, he's busy at work."

"Four months and 22 days until vacation." Cathleen lifted the martini in a short toast, then put it to her lips where she took a large swallow. She was so thirsty and it was such an effort for her to be with people. She longed for the numb feeling which a drink brought her. Finishing off the martini she signalled to Pet she wanted a refill. Pet looked at Sarita across the top of her almost full highball glass, seeking guidance. But Sarita's face mirrored her uncertainty.

"Come on, girls. You'd better hurry and catch up with me," Cathleen's words came out slurred. The martini stronger than the rum and water she was used to sipping made her jittery. She had hopes a second one would calm her and give her that blessed tranquility she longed for. "Well, are you going to give me another drink, Pet?" she asked belligerently. Shocked at the sudden change in her, Pet went out to the kitchen where she mixed another martini, diluting it with water.

"You trying to put something over on me, Pet?" Cathleen remarked suspiciously when she sipped the second martini. Getting up, she weaved unsteadily in the direction of the kitchen. Pet and Sarita exchanging alarmed looks followed her.

"Let me show you, Pet my friend, how a real martini should be made." She dumped the contents of her glass in the sink but part of it trickled down onto the floor. Grabbing the gin bottle she filled the glass, waved the vermouth bottle over it and then attempted to drop an olive into the martini. But the jar slipped out of her hands and the floor became awash with little green olives. Shrugging her shoulders, Cathleen bent down. "What the hell," she laughed, retrieving two olives from the floor which she plopped in to her glass. Then she returned unsteadily to the living room.

Pet and Sarita started to follow, but Maruja appeared at the kitchen door with a plate of hors d'oeuvres.

"And not a moment too soon," Pet remarked. "Let's get some food into her."

"See what a good teacher you are," Maruja cried out hugging Cathleen. "Imagine! I was able to make these all by myself," she gestured towards the plate of canapes. "This is Cathleen's recipe," she informed Pet and Sarita. "Fred would have sent me packing if I didn't have such a wonderful cook next door to teach me."

Cathleen's head was whirling from the martinis. If she'd been home she would have slowly sipped a rum and water. Now she felt the way she did when she drank a rum punch. Except the gaiety was missing. And she felt annoyed and irritable. Why did Maruja have to be here and spoil things? She glared at Pet, convinced she had tricked her. Probably the whole damn camp would come traipsing in. Why couldn't they understand she just wanted to be left alone, that she couldn't handle being around people?

"I'll bet you're looking forward to your vacation," Sarita said softly. "Where will you be going?"

"I really don't want to go anywhere." Her words were becoming increasingly slurred and labored. "I can't leave her, Sarita. She's so cold."

"Leave who, *mi amor*?" Sarita asked, wanting to draw her out.

"Why, Sheila, of course." The dark circles under Cathleen's eyes highlighted their fatigue.

"What do you mean? She's so cold?" Sarita prodded her.

"Wouldn't you be, all alone in that coffin?" Her hand shook as she tried to light a cigarette. "Oh God, the nightmares I have about her."

"*Mi amor*," Sarita said soothingly. "Sheila doesn't feel a thing. That's not her in that coffin. It's only her body, a body which is completely empty of any life. Her soul is elsewhere and we all know she is happy with the rest of the angels. You must stop thinking that she feels anything in her body. She left it as soon as God called her."

"No, I don't think so." Cathleen shook her head insistently. "It never would have happened you know, if I hadn't left her with the maid." Her eyes, which had been pools of anguish, turned hard and cold. "It's all

Ryle's fault because he kept pushing me to get out."

"So you blame him?" Sarita felt she had to keep her talking.

"Yes I do. But I also blame myself, because I left her." She burst into tears. "But most of all I blame him. I'll never forgive him."

Sarita didn't say anything, but she put her arms around Cathleen, rubbing her shoulders and neck which felt tight and tense under her fingers. Sarita's hands are so comforting, Cathleen thought. That wonderful serenity of hers, which soothed everything it touched, flowed into her body.

"He feels this as much as you do," Sarita said in her soft voice. "I saw it in his eyes the day of the funeral. Oh yes, *mi amor*," she insisted when Cathleen started to protest. "Now listen to me, *querida*. Ryle is not a man who reveals his emotions, he keeps them to himself. But he loved Sheila very much. And he is suffering just as much as you. You must forgive him, just as you have to forgive yourself."

"I can't," Cathleen sobbed, all control completely gone.

"Maybe not now," Sarita continued consolingly. "But one day you will. And you know what, *querida*?" Her brown hands gently pushed Cathleen's hair out of her face, stroking her forehead. "When you make peace with yourself, then you will have it with him."

Cathleen shook her head vehemently, then reached for her cigarettes. The serenity which she momentarily felt from Sarita's touch had vanished. She'd never forgive Ryle, never. It made her ill to even think about it. And her anger at being dragged here to Pet's against her will returned. Why didn't people just leave her alone? She couldn't understand either why the martini hadn't helped her as a drink usually did. Instead of calming her, it agitated her. Everything annoyed her, she thought desperately, especially seeing Maruja here.

"Some mother you are," she lashed out at Maruja, the venom in her voice shocking everyone in the room. "Whaya do? Leave Nena alone, cryin' her eyes out, so you could come over here?" Her slurred words were running into each other. "I didna even wanna leave Sheila for that lousy bridge game."

"Of course I didn't leave her alone, *mi amor*," Maruja replied, alarmed by the change in Cathleen's manner. "Nena is taking her afternoon nap, sleeping like an angel. The laundress, who is a very responsible woman, is staying with her until I get back."

"Well, aren't you the lucky one," Cathleen snapped sarcastically, "to have such a wonderful laundress. Some people have all the luck." She picked up her glass, then seeing it was empty put it down with a loud bang. "It's not fair," she turned to Sarita. "It's not fair that she still has her baby and mine was taken away. She doesn't even want Nena."

Her last remark was greeted with silence. All three women looked at each other helplessly, then Sarita and Pet's eyes met Maruja's with sympathy, trying to ease the pain Cathleen's words had caused her.

Cathleen didn't give a damn what anyone thought. All she wanted was to go home and be left alone. Getting up she walked unsteadily toward the kitchen, bumping into the furniture, almost slipping on one of Peg's scatter rugs. Sarita, Peg and Maruja ran to her, terribly upset by the sight of Cathleen's feeble attempts to walk.

"Come on, honey, let me make you a cup of coffee," Pet said trying to get her back into the living room. But Cathleen resisted, pushing Pet away violently. She hadn't wanted to come here and now they were trying to stop her from leaving. Her arms flew out in protest.

"Just leave me alone," she lashed out.

"You can't go now, *querida*," Sarita said firmly. "You really must lie down for a little while. Those martinis were too strong for you." And the three of them struggled to restrain her. But the more they tried to stop her from leaving, the harder Cathleen fought them. She began to scream hysterically, her cries sounding like a trapped animal.

Pet hesitated for a moment, then her fist shot out, knocking Cathleen unconscious. Picking up Cathleen's limp body, Pet carried her into the spare bedroom, leaving Sarita to take off her sandals. Then quickly she and Maruja went back to the living room, flipping on the record player. The whistles and horns from a Spike Jones record blared through the room.

"I just hated to deck Cathleen, but it was the only way I knew to stop her hysteria, just put her out of her misery for awhile," Pet said. She went to her living room window, peering out. "I can tell you as sure as God made little green apples, this will be all over camp," she said quietly, "unless we make out like something else was goin' on. I just saw Sugar leavin' Wilma's bridge party. Oh shit," she cried out in disgust as she ran to lock the kitchen screen door. "Here she comes." Then her voice boomed out as she proceeded to tell Maruja one of her bawdy stories, screaming in laughter.

"Pet, is something wrong?" Sugar knocked on the screened kitchen door. "We heard the most awful screams comin' from over here." Finding the door locked, her voice became petulant. "I declare, I was just trying to be neighborly." She had to yell to make herself heard over Pet's voice and the Spike Jones record.

When Pet came to the door, she bellowed at Sugar. "Great balls of fire, just 'cause you're the super's wife do I have to tell you everything I do?"

"Something funny is goin' on here," Sugar said suspiciously. "Why else would you have the door locked?"

"Is it?" Pet asked innocently, unlocking the door. "Just playing my new Spike Jones record for Sarita Maguire who came up to visit me today. You remember her, don't you? She used to live in your house. Want to come in and say hello?" she asked slyly.

"No thank you," Sugar replied haughtily and turned away making her way back to the street.

"Shit in your hat, Sugar," Pet shouted, "then put it on your head and call it curls." She waddled back to the living room. "Damn meddlesome brat," she grumbled plopping down on the couch. "Well girls, I sure hope she believed it."

"You were marvelous, Pet," Sarita said as she returned from the bedroom. "Thinking as quickly as you did."

"I hope I didn't hurt Cathleen none, but it was the only way I knew to calm her down. That poor kid, she's going through a rough time. I know, I lost a baby when Pete and I were first married. And being here in hell's half acre so far away from home don't make it any easier."

"It hasn't been easy for my poor Cathleen, loosing Sheila," Sarita said softly.

"I've never seen her like she was today," Maruja cried out, still shaking inside from Cathleen's tongue lashing.

"It's because she was drinking those martinis," Sarita shook her head. "They're much too strong, especially if you drink them on an empty stomach, as I suspect she did."

"In Cathleen's frame of mind it don't matter what she was drinking," Pet insisted. "That's the way booze is, sometimes it makes you happy, other times it makes you go out of your head. The state she's been in, it made her flip. But she'll be better once she's slept it off a little."

"I'll wait until she wakes up," Sarita said, "and then take her home."

"Gal, you got a long trip ahead of you." Pet looked out the window. "In fact, your hubby's pickup is coming up the street. Don't worry your pretty little head, Maruja and me will hold down the fort."

Sarita hated to leave Cathleen. As she climbed into John's pickup she felt a great sadness. When John asked her what kind of a visit she had, her usually serene manner was gone. "*Muy mala*," she sighed. "Cathleen is not doing at all well." And she told him just how the afternoon had turned out.

"She'll be OK, Soogie," he reassured her. "In time she'll get over it. She's young and healthy and before you know it, she'll be pregnant again." Then his eyes twinkled and his mouth broke into a broad smile showing his uneven front teeth. "Maybe it will be catching."

Sarita looked at her husband, seeing him in a new light. Her *catire*, her blond *hombre*. How lucky she was to have him and what would she do if she ever lost him? He had given her so much and she continued to refuse him the only thing he ever asked of her, that they have children. Whether he stayed or abandoned her with a big belly, she couldn't deny him this any longer.

"*Sí Dios quiere*," she said trying to stifle the fear which still danced around inside her. "If God wants it, then so do I."

"Are you saying what I think you are?" His foot clamped down on the brake and he steered the pickup over to the side of the road. She nodded her head.

"I guess by now you believe me. That I'll never leave you." Then seeing the fear in her eyes which she tried not to show, Maguire took her in his arms. "You're stuck with me, *Señora*, for the rest of your life. Oh, *mi Sarita Linda*, we're going to have such beautiful kids and grow old together spoiling our grandchildren." He nuzzled his face in her hair, loving its sweet smell. He knew it was the Yardley Bond Street cologne she used, but he preferred to think it was her natural scent.

"They'll be beautiful if they look like you," Sarita smiled softly. "Blond and fair skinned."

"Then they'll be *feo*, very ugly if they do," he replied shaking his head. "No, I insist, they should be the spitting image of you, especially that sexy cleft in your chin."

"You want them to have dark skin?" she asked incredulously.

"It's beautiful, Soogie. Just like you are. My beautiful brown skin gal."

Oh, why did he have to call her that? "Brown skin gal, stay home and mind baby," the lyrics of the song went. "Brown skin gal, stay home and mind baby, I'm goin' away on a fishing trip and if I don't come back, throw way that damn baby." She felt a chill run through her heart.

....

Cathleen and Ryle continued to live in their two separate worlds, barely speaking to each other until he brought up her drinking.

"You really ought to put a lid on the booze."

"It helps me get through the day," she replied.

"Good God, Cathleen! The way you're going about it isn't right. You want to have a few drinks, fine, we'll go to the club or have some people in. But not the way you're doing it, all holed up here by yourself."

"I like it by myself," she snapped.

"I haven't said anything before because I figured you had to come out of your grief, and if this was a way of doing it, then so be it. But now it's getting out of hand. I come home and I can smell it on your breath. Each day it gets a little stronger, Cathleen. I grew up with a rummy father. I sure as hell don't want my wife turnin' into one." He stubbed his cigarette out, grinding it around and around in the ashtray.

"Do you want people talking about you?" he continued. "You know how it is here, everyone gossiping about each other. It just don't look good."

"The proper word is doesn't, not don't," she corrected him, sounding like a prim schoolteacher. She had become used to his slaughtering the English language as she called it, but she took great delight now in lashing out at him in the only way she knew. He gave her a startled look.

"Like I said, it don't look good," he persisted.

"I don't care how it looks, or whether you can smell it on my breath," she said wearily. "What am I supposed to do in this damn place? Do you think I can get on a train and escape to the city? Or pick up a phone and talk to my mother? There isn't even a radio program I can turn on. So I just cope the best way I know how, Ryle. And if the whole camp gossips about my drinking, I just don't give a damn."

But she did care. She still had enough pride left that she didn't want to become the topic of camp gossip, especially when it was started by the camp superintendent's wife.

"You just can't stay cooped up in this house by yourself," Sugar insisted one day when Cathleen had returned from the cemetery. Sugar never came in the house, not since the day Cathleen asked her to leave. But she called to her sometimes over the hedge which separated their houses. "You need to be around people. Maybe you ought to think about going back to the States for a short while."

"I'm fine," Cathleen replied. "If only people would just leave me alone."

"Well you're not fine," Sugar insisted, coming through the hedge and walking into the carport. "I really think you need to get away."

"So you can make a play for my husband?" Cathleen replied sarcastically. Not that she cared anymore about Sugar's obvious interest in Ryle. The two of them could run off together and it wouldn't bother her. But she couldn't resist the opportunity to make a dig at her. It was something she enjoyed doing these days, lashing out at people.

"See Cathleen, your nerves are really in a bad way when you start saying foolish things like that." Sugar's eyes rolled in feigned concern.

"Well, I'm not leaving. Sorry to disappoint you."

"People are talking about you somethin' awful," Sugar purred, making every effort to appear like a concerned neighbor. She leaned forward as if to impart a secret. "How you're havin' a love affair with the bottle."

Cathleen's hand flew out, slapping her. Sugar who was a good four inches shorter looked up at her in surprise. Then she backed away, walking slowly out of the carport, rubbing her face. "Oh wait 'til this gets around camp!" Sugar's drawl became more pronounced with each word. "Just you wait, Miss America, 'til I tell people how crazy you've gotten." She started laughing, as if she'd just heard the funniest joke. "Crazy with booze!" And then she ran towards the hedge.

Cathleen walked in the house and slumped down on the couch, angry with herself for letting Sugar goad her. There'd been so many other times when slapping Sugar would have been appropriate, but not now. Why did she lose control so easily these days? She knew how Sugar would tell the story, she'd certainly heard enough of her tales.

'Poor little thing, this has been too much for her, losin' that sweet baby.' Cathleen was certain that right now, at this very moment, she was embellishing the incident with her special brand of slyness. 'Now she's hittin' the bottle, and I declare it's affected her mind. Would you look at what she did to me?'

Cathleen could see her showing everyone her face, pointing to the red mark made by her hand, could hear her saying, 'Poor Ryle, he ought to send her back to her Momma until she gets over things.' Which was just the way the story came out, give or take a word or two.

To refute the gossip, Cathleen knew she had to show her face in public again. She decided she would go to the movies that night. But as the afternoon went by, she became increasingly nervous. Just a little extra one for courage, she assured herself, as she poured two shots of rum into a glass. Just to help her start feeling good about herself. Ryle would probably give her hell for slapping the super's wife, she thought despondently. Well let him, she decided defiantly. She forced herself to drink slowly for she remembered how the martinis she drank at Pet's had affected her. She didn't ever want to lose control that way again.

But despite her intentions, she went over her usual afternoon consumption, so by the time she and Ryle got to the club she was very drunk. But she didn't think she looked bombed, for she'd gone to great lengths to appear in control. Gargling and rinsing with mouth wash, applying her makeup carefully, steeling herself to walk steadily. She would have pulled it off, no one would have known she'd been drinking if she hadn't laughed at all the wrong times. During the movie when it wasn't funny, and afterwards talking to people.

By the time she and Ryle got home she didn't know where she was, for they'd joined the Ficketts for a few drinks after the show. She was so completely out of it there was a truce in her war with Ryle. He reached for her across the No Man's Land of their bed, and she didn't resist him. Her mind faded in and out of scenes of their honeymoon. She was back on board ship and she responded to Ryle's lovemaking with complete abandon. Then something in her brain clicked and she realized she was in Chacari. She fought him, screaming at him to stop. Then his lips covered hers, his tongue darting inside her mouth searching out her tongue. She wanted to bite him, she thought she might have, but her mind went blank.

When she woke up the next morning she wondered if it had been a dream, a companion nightmare to the ones she had about Sheila. Until she got out of bed and felt the unmistakable stickiness between her legs. Her head was splitting, she had the most awful hangover. She panicked, wondering if it was the wrong time of the month. She certainly didn't want to become pregnant. Not now, not with her hatred for Ryle. She swallowed three aspirins with a bottle of Coca-Cola. And struggled to remember whether she had been a willing participant or Ryle had forced himself on her.

The maid was waiting to clean the bedroom, and Cathleen became impatient for her to be done so she could have the house to herself. Then she looked at her watch and realized she hadn't gone to visit Sheila. She'd slept away the whole morning. Upset because she hadn't gone to the cemetery, angry with herself for not being able to remember what happened last night, she drove fast, hoping she wouldn't be stopped by the police at the outskirts of Maturín. By the time she got to the cemetery it was mid afternoon. As she stood before her daughter's grave, she told her how much she loved and missed her and asked for her forgiveness. And then feeling tired, she sat down and stopped talking to Sheila. She could tell by the waning light she'd been in the cemetery a long time. But she was reluctant to leave for she felt a strange sort of peace flow through her body, a peace not induced by a drink. It wasn't a joyous peace, but some of the aching inside her had subsided.

Maybe she would never get over Sheila's death, it would probably always be a sharp pain around the perimeters of her heart. But she had to accept it. She'd grown up with the acceptance of God's will drilled into her by the nuns. And all her life, in one way or another, she'd rebelled against it. She was going to live her life the way she wanted. She'd broken off with Danny and married Ryle, despite everyone's warnings that this marriage would come to no good. She had dropped everything to follow Ryle to Venezuela; wild horses couldn't have kept her from going off with him. Now that she had him, she didn't know if she still wanted him. For he wasn't the same man she'd fallen in love with. And neither was she the same trusting young girl who thought the sun rose and set upon S. J. Rylander.

She got up and blew a kiss to Sheila and then walked slowly to the

Chevy. All the way back to Chacari, the peaceful feeling inside her continued to grow. When she saw the camp fence, she didn't stop. It wasn't until the lights of Puerto La Cruz appeared that she realized where she was. She stopped at the El Gato cutoff for gas and headed back to Chacari. But she drove slowly for she wasn't anxious to get home. There was hardly any traffic on the road, her only companions the stars in the velvet sky.

But as peaceful as she felt, Cathleen realized she had to clean up the mess her life had become. Foremost was the realization that she'd gone and done it, just as Barry had warned her. Only it wasn't the boredom of camp life which started her drinking. Maybe, she reasoned, she wouldn't have gone off the deep end after Sheila's death if she'd been home, with her family and all the surroundings she'd grown up with to support her. But she was here, and she couldn't make any more excuses for herself because things weren't as they might have been. What was reality was getting so drunk she'd blacked out. Ever since Sheila's death she had been living in an alcoholic daze because it helped to blur the pain. But now whether her desire to survive had returned, or she feared there would be other blacked out times, she knew she had to take charge of her life, pick up the pieces, however scattered they were, and go on living.

Sarita was right. Sheila was gone and only the shell of her body remained. Suddenly Cathleen felt her baby reach out to her and she shivered because it was so vivid. She was holding Sheila again in her arms. Cathleen hugged her close and saw Sheila smile, as she'd done so many times in the past. But it was a different smile, for it seemed to contain the wisdom of the ages, as if she knew things Cathleen didn't. And then she was gone, Cathleen's arms were empty. But something lingered, she had the strongest feeling Sheila wanted her to know she was happy and safe. And that it was time for Cathleen to let go.

She took her time driving into camp for she was reluctant to face Ryle. When she drove into the carport, he came running out to greet her. "Thank God you're all right, baby. I've been worried sick about you." He took her in his arms. "Where were you?"

"I went for a ride." She pushed him aside. "I had to think things out."

He looked at her, sensing something was different. As they walked into the house, he asked her why she pushed him aside. "You wanted me last night."

"Last night I was drunk, I didn't know what was going on."

"Well I did, and I remember getting my wife back." His look had that old adoration.

"You may have gotten my body back, Ryle," she replied slowly, still upset with herself for blacking out last night. "I don't know about the rest of me."

Suddenly she realized how hungry she was. She hadn't eaten since last night. Going to the refrigerator she took out the remains of a roast chicken dinner, eating everything cold because she was so ravenous. Then she put on a fresh pot of coffee.

"Today I buried Sheila. I really buried her," she told him calmly. "I asked her forgiveness and I feel she gave it to me, because that horrible feeling of guilt doesn't seem to be hanging over me like it used to." Then she started crying, softly. "Oh God, I thought I was done with all these tears."

"I don't know if I'll ever get over losing her," she sobbed. "I can't bring her back. I have to accept that she's gone. But I realized something today. Our children are just loaned to us. We don't own them like some possession." She was finding it difficult to speak. "So we just have to be grateful for the time we did have Sheila and all the happiness she brought us."

Memories flooded her heart — Sheila in her playpen at the christening party taking everything in, sitting in her lap when she and Ryle ate, how she loved to crawl when she was in bed with them.

"I don't know if she knew how much I loved her," she said, her voice cracking. "I don't have the answers to anything. Not one damn thing! I only know I've accepted God's will. If there is a God. All my life I've had faith, but now it's gone. It sure would help if I could believe in something."

"Oh Cathleen, you can believe in us."

"I don't know about that," she replied evasively. "What I do know is I'm going to get a job."

"You're what? You've got a job, a full time one, supervising the maid, shopping, cooking. And being Mrs. S. J. Rylander."

"It's not enough. I'll lose my mind if I don't do something," she said with desperation. "I'd like to work as a teacher's aide, but school won't open until September. So I'll have to look for something in an office."

"But everyone stays home," he persisted. "Why can't you?"

"I'm not like everyone else, Ryle," she cried out. "Don't you know that by now? I have to do something with my life." What she didn't voice was her fear that if she stayed home, she might not be able to stop drinking. She had accepted what she had to accept. Now she had to change what she could change.

They argued far into the night. Finally Cathleen told him, "Take it or leave it, Ryle." But she was uneasy he might not go along with her decision. For in spite of her new found acceptance, she still wondered about her marriage. It might not be the best one, but she was unwilling to lose that too. She would take one step at a time. She'd said goodbye to Sheila. She'd forgiven herself and she hoped she could forgive Ryle. Now she had to face her drinking. It was such a comfort and it helped her cope so easily with things. She knew it would be sheer hell without it. But she had no other choice. She had to give up drinking. She must never, never lose control of herself again.

NINETEEN

The first thing Cathleen did every morning when she got to work was shake the rat turds out of her desk drawers. At first she was repulsed by the sight of the little black pellets. But just as she'd become accustomed to the bugs in the flour, she learned to go through this daily routine before starting work. She'd gotten a job in Chacari, and while it was only part time and not very stimulating, she was so happy to have a reason to get up in the morning. The administration office was housed in the front part of the warehouse, and at times she could hear the truck drivers shouting as they unloaded material. A far cry from the Palm Oil New York office in Rockefeller Plaza.

The easy camaraderie of the men was a beneficial balm to her depression. She was so efficient and businesslike they frequently told her to slow down; there was no need for her to rush everything. Except of course the drilling reports, which she typed every morning so they could be radioed to Caracas and then put in the daily pouch.

"You're looking swell, Toots," Murray complimented her. The color had come back to her face and the sadness was slowly leaving her eyes. Her clothes, which had hung so listlessly on her, now showed a body filling out as she gained back some badly needed weight.

Sometimes Murray danced by her desk singing Al Jolson songs, doffing an imaginary straw hat, or kidding about having danced the night away at the Glen Island Casino in New Rochelle. When she confessed she'd never been there, he looked at her in disbelief. She just shook her head. No sense telling him that aside from Danny O'Hara, Ryle had been the only man in her life.

That incredibly happy disposition of his has to be put on, she thought, no one could be that good natured all the time. But he was always the same. Cathleen found herself looking for him when she got to work,

251

needing his presence to get her started. And going along with his patter, she'd ask him how the Casino was last night. He made it so real that she hung on to his every word as he told funny stories about the characters he ran into. It was better than a radio show, something she missed terribly.

She had gotten her drinking under control, so she felt safe in having one or two at the end of the day. But no more. There were times though when she wanted one so badly she could taste it, especially when Sugar came to the office either to cash a check or drop off some mail. Cathleen could feel Sugar's eyes following her, taking in her every move. What can she possibly want with me, she wondered, shaking inside because she had come to loathe Sugar. It was bad enough having her as a neighbor, why did she follow her to work? Then when she saw her looking Murray over, she decided he must be the reason for her visits. Sugar must have the hots for him. Cathleen giggled to herself, she just loved that expression of Pet's. Her mother would be shocked if she heard it. But then she would be with a lot of things which made up her life now. Her best friend, a former prostitute. Jesus, Mary and Joseph, her father would blow his stack if he knew about that. It's another world here, she sighed to herself, light years away from the life she'd left in the States.

Sugar wasn't the least bit interested in Murray. But she knew he was infatuated with Cathleen, and now that she was working in the office Sugar wanted to see if Cathleen responded to him. To her it was the perfect opportunity to stir up trouble, for she still wanted Cathleen to leave. Especially after the humiliation of being slapped by her.

But she saw nothing. No matter how many trips she made to the office, she could never catch them in anything but harmless kidding around. Which is when she decided since nothing was going on, she would have to be creative and invent an affair. She was careful planting the rumors, going to great lengths to avoid incriminating herself, so no one would remember where they first heard that Cathleen Rylander was having an affair with Murray Bluestein. Since nothing of great interest happened recently in Chacari, the rumor received immediate attention.

Ryle was cast in the role of the unsuspecting husband, ignorant that his best friend Murray was carrying on with his wife. Most people didn't come down too hard on Cathleen, declaring the tragedy of losing her baby had made her go off the deep end. Others made Murray the villain. And then the pendulum swung the other way as the full force of Sugar's venom came out, courtesy of Wilma Wilcox who would do anything to curry favor with the camp superintendent's wife. Cathleen Rylander was always so aloof because she thought she was better than anyone else in camp. Why just look at those oddball fashions she wore, the long dresses she said was the New Look. How could anyone so stuck on herself be faithful to one man? What did she care about family and home? And she pretended to be such a good Catholic. You just wait and see, one camp gossip opined, when she goes to the States on vacation she won't come back. She just doesn't have what it takes for life in the oilfields. She'll go running off to California with that lover of hers, a voice whispered with great conviction, informing everyone of a conversation Murray had with Cathleen when he asked her to run away with him.

Sugar, listening to all the rumors now magnified beyond her wildest dreams, congratulated herself. Oh, yes, she thought smugly, all the ingredients were there. The friendship between Ryle and Murray giving him easy access to Cathleen, both of them now working in the same office. All she had to do was rearrange the recipe, and the stew cooked itself. She waited impatiently for the gossip to reach Ryle.

At first he didn't believe it. Despite his jealousy of any man who looked twice at his wife, he never regarded Murray as a threat. Even the fight they almost had in Rosita's, when he accused Murray of being in love with Cathleen had been forgotten. He still thought of Murray as the clown, the cocky, bantam weight guy who made everyone laugh. It was like finding out that one of the Three Stooges had wound up with the girl. Seeing the agonized adoration in Murray's eyes didn't bother him as much as the way Cathleen responded to him, her face lighting up whenever Murray was around. Almost as if Murray had the key to unlock her innermost thoughts and bring her to life. This is what filled him with jealousy. He wanted nothing more than to vindicate himself in the eyes of the camp. But he didn't want his personal life to be the topic of entertainment in Chacari, or Caracas. He had to settle this out of camp.

He knew at the end of the month Murray worked overtime getting monthly accounting reports ready for Caracas. Many times he returned to the office after supper and stayed there until 10 or 11. Sometimes some of the geologists or engineers were there, but most of the time the office was empty. The night Ryle sought out Murray he was the lone occupant of the warehouse/office complex.

"Let's go for a ride," Ryle told him.

Murray, looking up from the figures he was double checking, saw a strange look in Ryle's eyes. He hadn't heard the rumors, like most subjects of gossip he was the last to find out. But his antenna started sending him signals that something was wrong. He turned off the adding machine, stashed the reports in his desk, then followed Ryle out of the building. Where he climbed into Ryle's pickup. At first he thought they were going to the Looney Door, although he couldn't imagine why. Then when they drove past it and turned up a dirt road he knew Ryle was taking him into the woods to have something out with him.

"Okay, what's the story?" he asked impatiently. Ever since he'd gotten into Ryle's pickup, he tried to find out what was bothering him, but he came up against a wall of silence. "You obviously didn't bring me out here to admire the scenery."

"The story, you bastard," Ryle snarled at him, "is that I found out."

"Found out what?" Murray was more bewildered than ever.

"That you've been having an affair with my wife," Ryle cried out bitterly.

Now he understood. "No, I haven't," he shook his head. "I don't know what you heard, Ryle. Anything is possible in this place, but it's not true. And you shouldn't dirty Cathleen's name with such crap."

"What do you think I am? Some dumb Okie, as you're always calling me?" Ryle pointed to the door of the pickup. "Get out. Just because I'm not some smartaleck from New York, it don't mean I'm stupid."

"Ok, Ryle," Murray sighed as he slowly got out of the pickup. "Let's have the facts," he demanded. "If I'm going to be hung, I want to know why. Where's your proof?"

"I always knew you had a crush on her," Ryle snarled, "but I never thought you would take advantage of her vulnerability after she lost our baby."

"What proof do you have?" Murray persisted. "What concrete evidence do you have to support this asshole idea of yours?"

"The proof is the way you carry on when you're around each other," Ryle cried out. "God, I must have been blind not to see it. Don't deny that you're in love with her. Or come out with some cute remark like 'isn't everyone'?"

"No, I don't deny it," Murray replied, relieved in a way to have it out in the open with Ryle. "But it's one-sided."

"The hell it is," Ryle sneered. "She lights up like some dime store Christmas tree ornament anytime you're around."

"That's because I make her laugh," Murray said wearily. "Especially after all she went through over Sheila. I'm just the comic relief, playing the clown."

"Well, your clown playing days are over." Ryle grabbed him by the collar of his khaki shirt. "I'm going to beat the shit out of you, make you so beautiful she'll never look at you no more."

"What proof do you have?" Murray shouted wrenching himself free of Ryle's hands, pushing him away. "Have you ever seen us do anything out of line? Or caught us in bed? You just can't go around accusing people of something unless you've got something to back it up."

"What's the matter, city boy?" Ryle taunted him. "Afraid to fight?"

"Oh, listen to the big he man of the Old West," Murray cried out, dancing around on his feet. When Ryle swung at him, Murray dodged back and forth, then when he saw an opening his fist shot out hitting Ryle directly in the stomach, causing him to double over in pain.

"Come on, Lone Ranger," Murray goaded him. "Let's have a little action here." He aimed for Ryle's jaw, catching him in the mouth when he was still doubled over from the blow to his stomach. He was so fast on his feet, his hands flew around so deftly that Ryle never knew what hit him. Staggering, trying to stay up and ignoring the blood running down the side of his chin, Ryle went for Murray, hitting him in the eye and again in the mouth, finally having the satisfaction of seeing him go down. Until Murray lunged for Ryle's waist, his fingers hooking around his belt buckle. Pulling himself halfway up, he butted Ryle in the stomach, knocking him off balance, pushing him backwards until he fell. Immediately Murray was on top of Ryle, his fist aiming for his jaw. But Ryle's arms deflected the blow and his hands went for Murray's throat. Which is when Murray's gutter days in the Bronx took over and tearing Ryle's hands away, he squirmed away from him, until he was straddling his lower torso. Murray jabbed him over and over with his knee, following it with a knockout blow to his jaw.

When Ryle came to, Murray was sitting on the running board of the pickup. "You wanna go another round?" he asked Ryle. "Where I came from, we don't fight that way," Ryle groaned, his testicles throbbing with pain.

"Where I come from, when someone starts playing rough, we do." Murray threw up his hands in disgust. "Ah shit, Ryle, what the hell are we doing?"

Ryle didn't answer him, but struggled to get up. He was aching with pain, but he wasn't about to call it quits. It galled him that Murray had knocked him out. When he lunged forward, Murray decked him again. Murray knew that Ryle's pride was even more wounded than his body, and for a brief moment he was half tempted to let him win the stupid fight.

"It's a draw," Murray said putting out his hand. "Okay?"

"No fucking way," Ryle screamed at him. When he got up Murray decked him again, and this time when he went down he stayed there. Dragging Ryle's limp body over to the pickup, Murray hoisted him up into the passenger seat. Then going over to the driver's side he started the motor, keeping it in first as he drove slowly over the bumpy dirt road. When he reached the main highway, Ryle came to and asked him to stop.

"I want to drive," was all he said.

"Sure," Murray replied and stopped the pickup, getting out and walking around to the other side. But Ryle slid over and gunned the motor, leaving him stranded in the middle of the deserted road, almost sideswiping him as he sped away.

"Son of a bitch!" Murray called after him angrily. He started walking and a half hour later when he reached the Looney Door, he knew what he had to do. When Ryle and he showed up at work the next day with a fight written all over their faces, the tongues in camp would start wagging. He didn't have to wonder who started the rumors, he knew it was Sugar.

He walked in the Looney Door, going directly to the men's room where he assessed his injuries. The possibilities of a black eye, his cheek was cut and a split lower lip. What he planned to do might look like too much of a coincidence, but he couldn't think of any alternative. And he didn't relish the thought of coming out a loser; he'd never lost a fight. But it was the only way he could think to deflect the gossip away from Cathleen, give people something else to talk about.

Walking back into the bar he picked a fight with a burly driller. Afterwards the latest arrival in camp, a geologist newly graduated from Colorado University School of Mines in Boulder, slung Murray over his shoulders and brought him back to camp in his pickup. By the next morning the story was all over camp that Murray had gotten into a fight over one of the whores at the Looney Door. Where he had the crap beaten out of him by Tiny Worthington. The camp talked of nothing else for days.

Cathleen was appalled when she saw Ryle's face the next day. He refused to discuss it; his only words were that she had to quit her job, and under no circumstances was she ever to invite Murray to dinner again.

Shocked and puzzled by his antagonism towards Murray, she refused to even consider quitting. "You know I still haven't gotten over Sheila," she protested. "Can't you see how much better I am since I went to work?" Her life was beginning to have some order to it. She had her job in the morning and in the afternoon, because Maruja was still having trouble keeping a nursemaid, she baby-sat Nena while Maruja went out to the card parties. At first holding Nena in her arms stirred up too many memories of Sheila. But as her acceptance of Sheila's death became more and more a part of her life, so did her feelings for Nena grow. She knew Fred adored his daughter, but her heart went out to this small baby whose mother appeared so indifferent to her. Gradually all her maternal feelings which had been buried with Sheila came back to life with Nena.

Maruja for her part was delighted for it gave her so much more freedom. As for Fred, he was grateful, although he continued to make excuses for his wife, telling himself in time she would grow to love their daughter. Even the camp thought that Nena Hardesty was helping Cathleen get over Sheila's death. It was bringing her back to life. Until the gossip about her having an affair with Murray caused sly remarks about something else being the reason for the color returning to her face.

It took Cathleen several days to find out she and Murray were rumored to be having an affair. But no one would discuss it with her until she pinned Pet down. "Something screwy is going on," Cathleen insisted, "Ryle comes home looking like he's been in a fight, Murray gets into one at the Looney Door, but I can't get a word out of Ryle, except he wants me to quit working. And he's mad at Murray about something. Pet, what have you heard?"

Pet fidgeted uneasily in her chair, flicking imaginary dust off the coffee table. She looked towards the baby carriage where Nena slept peacefully. "I guess the kid's colic has straightened out," she remarked.

"You sure have the magic touch with babies."

"You're evading my question," Cathleen persisted. Her hand automatically went to the carriage handle, rocking it gently. Just as she had with Sheila, she took Nena with her wherever she went. Most afternoons though she was content to stay home, playing with her or putting her down to sleep in Sheila's crib.

Pet squirmed around in her chair. Then sighing as if all the weight of the world was on her shoulders she blurted out, "Well I don't know how else to say it, but the rumor is that you and Murray are having an affair."

"Oh, no," Cathleen moaned. "And Ryle believed it, believed it so much that he and Murray came to blows over it. That's the reason for Murray looking like he's been through a meat grinder. It wasn't a fight in the Looney Door."

"Oh, he got into a brawl there all right. Too many people saw it happen for it to be just a story," Pet said vigorously. "But who knows what went on before that? The rumors have been flying for weeks before the fight. And you can guess who started it all. Not that she hasn't covered her tracks. That brat wouldn't say shit if she had a mouthful," Pet snorted disdainfully.

Cathleen's stomach churned as she remembered Sugar's endless trips to the office. "Why didn't you tell me?" she asked Pet, mortified to be the subject of such awful gossip.

"Why, honey it wasn't worth wasting breath over," Pet replied making a face. "Everyone is gossiped about at one time or another." She affected a nonchalant manner hoping to ease Cathleen's anguish.

"What am I going to do?" Cathleen asked her.

"Nothing," Pet reassured her. "It'll blow over as soon as something else takes its place."

"But meanwhile everyone is talking about me," Cathleen cried out. "And it's not true." Her self-confidence, shaky at times, was rapidly evaporating with Pet's news.

"Honey, you just hold your head up high," Pet advised. "You know your skirts are clean. The truth will out, you'll see. Just ignore it. As soon as something more interesting pops us, they'll forget all about little ole you."

"No," Cathleen said stubbornly. "I refuse to ignore it. I'm going to put a stop to this right now."

She was shaking the next morning, feeling the butterflies nesting in her stomach. Over and over she rehearsed what she would say, feeling somewhat like she used to when she had to take part in a pageant in Assembly, the fear of standing in front of a group of people making her legs feel like mush. Right after putting the drilling reports in the daily pouch, she told Emmett she had to run home for fifteen minutes. She dreaded what she was going to do, but she felt she had no choice. Your name was all you had, wasn't that what Pa always said? You could be rich or you could be poor, but if your name was trash, you weren't worth a plug nickel. And her name and reputation had been trashed, along with Murray's and, for that matter Ryle's.

She didn't know where the coffee was, but she looked for the house with the most cars. And the voices spilling out through the windows confirmed she found the right place.

"Good morning, girls." She walked into the living room, declining the hostess' offer of a plate of sweet rolls. "Can I have your attention, please?" She felt foolish; as if she didn't have their attention already.

The minute she walked in everyone cried out, "Look who's here." Conscious of the sea of faces staring at her, she felt her resolution crumbling and all she wanted to do was bolt out the door.

"It's come back to me," her voice quivered and someone cried out, "We can't hear you."

"It's come back to me," and this time she wondered if she were shouting, "that a lot of nasty gossip is circulating about me." She looked around, she'd rehearsed this in her mind, how important it was to make the truth known. Then spying Sugar, looking bored and indifferent, she lost her fear and all she could think of was how angry she was. "I'm not having an affair with Murray," her voice grew stronger with each word. "I'm not having an affair with anyone. I don't know who started this awful rumor, only you know who you are. But I want it to stop!"

She hesitated, she wanted to tell them she'd had enough heartache, and she didn't need anymore. But she wasn't about to beg for their sympathy, only demand what was rightfully hers.

There was a hush when she walked out, then someone clapped. "Good for her," Nadine said. Other hands joined her in applauding. But for the most part everyone behaved like a bolt of lightning had struck the house.

While she had made her stand with the camp, she couldn't get through to Ryle. He continued to believe something had gone on between her and Murray. When Murray's two year contract ended, she pleaded with Ryle to make up his quarrel with him. But he ignored her. What upset her even more was the two of them would part estranged, for Murray wasn't returning to Venezuela.

"It's no good Toots, my hanging around here," he told her one morning at the office. "I can't go on like this, wanting you and not being able to have you."

She looked at him in disbelief. She just couldn't imagine life without him for he'd become so much a part of her. When she woke up missing Sheila and the anguish of her death hung heavy over her, she knew in a short time she'd see Murray who would make everything all right. He was her link to sanity, her knight in shining armor, who to protect her name had gotten himself beaten up in a whorehouse. He was the one constant in her life.

"We can't go on year after year in this triangle," he told her. "Maybe this will bring things to a head. For that's what I'm gambling on, Toots. That after I leave, you'll miss me so much you'll do something about it. I know you're not indifferent to me."

No, she wasn't indifferent to him. She cared a great deal for Murray, but how strong it was she honestly didn't know, and whether it was enough to make her leave Ryle. For no matter how strained their marriage was, there was still something there. Oh, maybe not the way it was in the beginning when she was so blindly in love with Ryle, and it seemed he was just as crazy about her. But it wasn't completely dead. When he reached out for her in bed, she didn't resist him. For then she felt traces of the Ryle of old, the one who had swept her so much off her feet that she was glad to leave everything she'd ever known and go off with him to Venezuela. Who, although he was difficult as hell to live with, from time to time gave her glimpses of another S. J. Rylander. And in those times when the layers he had built around himself were stripped away, he was more exciting than she had ever imagined. She could no more think of leaving him than fly away to the moon.

Ryle still refused to make up with Murray, although the camp was unaware of it. For at all the *despedidas*, the farewell parties for Murray, there was no sign anything was strained between them. They both pretended the friendship they once had. Then the night before he left for the States, Murray stopped by the house.

"I don't want to see him," Ryle told Cathleen, hastily picking up a magazine.

"Well, I want to see him and I'm not leaving until I do," Murray said walking into the living room. "Before you throw me out of your house, because I know I'm not welcome, I'd like you to hear me out. Let's just say it's for old times' sake."

Ryle ignored Murray, continuing to keep his face buried in the magazine. Cathleen asked Murray to sit down, but he shook his head, standing directly in front of Ryle's chair.

"Before I leave this place, you got to hear from my lips that nothing ever went on between Cathleen and me. It was just a bunch of dumb gossip started by someone who has nothing better to do. Don't you know by now how Sugar manipulates this place?" He put out his hand, pushing it over Ryle's magazine. "Let's say goodbye like a *mensch*."

Ryle put the magazine down, glaring at him. "Get out of my house."

"Okay, you dumb cracker, have it your way." Murray shrugged his shoulders and turned around. When Cathleen walked him to the kitchen door he turned to her, his mouth curved down in his lopsided, crooked grin. "See you around, Toots." It struck her then, seeing his feelings for her written all over his face, that she would never see him again. And she thought, 'Being loved by him would be so easy. There would be no walking on eggs trying to live with moody silences, no being told how to live her life, or wondering if he still cared.'

She wanted to reach out and grab him, stop him from leaving. Take the love he offered and run off with him up the Yellow Brick Road, straight on to Emerald City. Impulsively she reached over and kissed him on the lips. And then uneasy with what her emotions had done to her, she quickly pulled away from him.

Murray pressed a nickel into her hand. Cathleen watched him walk down the driveway towards his pickup. She held the coin in her fingers, rubbing it back and forth. She knew why he'd given it to her, a reminder that he would be waiting for her call. Oh, she didn't want to even think about it. She was married to Ryle and she would make it work, no matter how difficult it was at times. Looking at the coin she remembered the day they sailed from New York, she and Ryle throwing out streamers to her family on the receding dock. And when the wind tore them, how she clutched the small remnant of crepe paper in her hand, her last link to her family. Now she had only this coin with which to remember Murray. He's gone, she whispered to herself, he'll no longer be a part of my life. She started to call out to him. But as she stared at the dust swirling in the road from his departing pickup, she realized she had to let him go. A person can't ride two horses at the same time, Cathleen my girl, she reminded herself sadly. I'll always remember him for the happiness he brought into my life, she vowed, and the strength he gave me. People don't pass through your life without leaving their mark.

"You just lost the best friend you'll ever have," she told Ryle sadly. "And there was never anything between us but a very strong friendship."

"Well yeah, I believe you. You're too much of a straight arrow to ever fool around."

She looked at him, indignation flooding her insides. "Then how could you let him go off without reconciling with him? You owe him an apology."

He didn't answer her, didn't let her know how he felt. Probably because he couldn't sort out his feelings yet. That he had misjudged Murray, that his pride was hurt because he'd gotten his ass kicked in a fight which he'd instigated. I'll write him a letter, Ryle promised himself. What I couldn't tell him to his face, I might be able to put in writing. And he joined Cathleen in her regrets. Not that she knew, for it was just another thing they didn't share.

TWENTY

Fred and Maruja had an advantage over the rest of Chacari. They could escape the isolation of camp life. For with Maruja's large family there were constant invitations to weddings, engagement and christening *fiestas* in Caracas. The Venezuelans knew how to throw a party, not dull sit-around ones like the *gringos*, but lively affairs with music and dancing. And Maruja would have loved to attend every one of them. No distance was too far, for she'd grown up dashing off to a weekend at the family ocean villa in Catia La Mar or flying out to a cousin's *hacienda* for a few days. But while Fred loved to party as much as she did, he drew the line at getting on a plane every weekend to do so. So she learned to be selective in accepting the elaborately engraved invitations which arrived in the daily mail pouch.

Then they received one which had Maruja dancing with anticipation. Her uncle, Memo Alvarez, who'd built a resort hotel in Ciudad Bolivar, had invited them to its grand opening. It would be *fantástico* she declared enthusiastically. And with Cathleen taking care of Nena, they could finally have a honeymoon, even if it was only a few days. Fred wasn't too keen on going off without their baby, for the former carefree bachelor had turned into a doting father who looked forward to the weekends he could spend with his infant daughter. But because Maruja was so insistent, and it did sound like fun, he agreed. Mainly because he knew Nena would be well taken care of by Cathleen.

And it wouldn't cost them a cent to get there, Maruja declared fervently. Her cousin Paco, who was spending some time at his father's cattle ranch near Santa Rita, offered to swing by the Maturín airport in his private plane and pick them up. She had complete confidence in Paco's flying ability for he was a former *Línea Aeropostal* pilot. Now that he owned a Beechcraft, he and his wife, Pili, flew all over the country

263

together.

When Maruja brought Nena to Cathleen's house Friday afternoon, she was very affectionate with her daughter, kissing her several times before she left. Maybe she is finally growing to love her, Cathleen hoped. Knowing Nena had an indifferent mother saddened her. Then when Maruja was just as effusive with Cathleen, she realized nothing had changed. Only the excitement of going away for the weekend had made her generous with her affection. She danced out of the house.

Standing at the kitchen door with Nena in her arms, Cathleen watched Maruja's pink skirt whirl around her as she ran across the lawn separating the two houses. Maruja suddenly stopped running. She turned around and waved to them, her mouth breaking into a dazzling smile. Cathleen took Nena's chubby little hand in hers, waving goodbye.

And then the strangest thing happened. Maruja looked long and hard at her daughter and ran back to her. Grabbing Nena from Cathleen she cuddled her, then kissed her.

"¡*Ay! mi Nenita*, I was so anxious to dance away the weekend in Ciudad Bolivar. But now...." uncertainty creased her forehead. "I don't know if I want to go, for I think...." Maruja whispered in awe, her eyes taking in every feature of Nena's freckled face, "I think I'm falling in love with you." She started to laugh, joy and exhilaration rose up from her throat, but the main emotion was wonder. "*Mi chiquita lindita*," Maruja cried out, "your papa was right. He and I have created one sensational baby." Her voice cracked as she struggled with her feelings. "But why did it take me this long to realize it?" She hugged Nena fiercely, reluctant to give her back to Cathleen.

Cathleen swallowed hard, finding herself fighting tears of happiness. Then she joined Maruja in her laughter. "Oh Maruja, I'm so happy for you and Nena." She flung her arms around them, feeling a closeness she had given up hope would ever happen. The three of them swayed in unison, laughing and hugging.

Overhead the company plane roared as it climbed into the sky.

"¡*Ay Dios*!" Maruja cried out looking up at the plane. "I'd better hurry. Paco told us not to be late, he wants to land in Ciudad Bolivar before dark." She looked wistfully at her daughter. "Oh, how I hate to leave you, *mi amor*. But we'll be back on Monday and then I promise you, I'll be a good mother — we'll be a real family. I can't wait to tell

Fred."

As she ran across the lawn to her home, she turned once more throwing a kiss and waving. Maruja called out something, but the noise of the company plane's motor drowned out her words. Cathleen thought it was "*Hasta lueguito*" — "See you in a little while," but she was never sure.

....

Looking down from the Beechcraft's window, Fred admired the panorama. The trees and grasses of the plains were lush in their green finery and everywhere he looked he was reminded of a giant botanical garden. When they flew over the Orinoco River and he saw the long line of cars waiting for the ferry, he was grateful they hadn't driven.

"Nothing like going first class," he laughed, looking around in admiration at the interior of the small plane which Pili had upgraded and decorated.

"*Absolutamente*," Maruja agreed, her eyes lighting up like a child with a brand new toy. Oh, this flying in a private plane was so *divino*.

Tío Memo's new hotel was beautiful. Majestic royal palm trees lined the drive leading up to the hotel's portico. The newly landscaped grounds were a riot of colors, salmon colored bougainvilleas interspersed with others of deep magenta, *copa de oro* making bright yellow splashes against the waxy green leaves of the scheffleras, the crimson blossoms of the bleeding hearts framed by their white heart-shaped borders.

When they arrived the orchestra was playing a lively *guaracha* on the patio. And the large Olympic sized pool looked so inviting Fred wanted to dive in. But he was quickly distracted for it seemed that half of Caracas' high society was there. "There she is, the *Bruja*," people called out to Maruja. *Abrazos* and kisses were exchanged.

The women had left their elaborate hats in Caracas for this was a 'weekend in the country', as they all referred to their junket. But their dress wasn't casual. Their jewels sparkled while the Schiaparelli and Balenciaga gowns fluttered around the dance floor. And though the men started out in tuxedos, the heat made many of them change to *guayabera* shirts.

"*Ay, querido*," Maruja cried out to Fred. "Look at all this food."

Maruja's appetite never ceased to amaze Fred. He swore she ate more than he did. And she never gained an ounce. "*Camarones*! I haven't seen any since our last trip to Caracas." She popped one shrimp after another into her mouth, then spying the lobster salad, piled her plate high with it. Champagne flowed in an unending waterfall from a fountain in the middle of the buffet table. But a lot of people sipped scotch and soda. For while the oilfield people drank native rum to save money, the wealthy Venezuelans were avid consumers of Scotland's most famous export.

"This shindig must be costing *Tío* Memo a small fortune." Fred was very impressed.

"Don't worry, he can afford it," Maruja replied airily. "Anything *Tío* Memo touches turns to gold."

Which is the way the rest of the family felt. Although the region was rich in gold and diamonds and attracted its share of adventurers hoping to become instant millionaires, Ciudad Bolivar was still a sleepy little city. Originally called Angostura, its main claim to fame was as the birthplace of Angostura Bitters. But if Memo, with his talent for seeing wealth before everyone else did, built this hotel it must be for a good reason. And the early 50s proved his vision, for the region experienced boom times. U.S. Steel came in and developed the iron mines of Cerro Bolivar, building two cities in the process, while a hydro-electric plant, the Guri Dam, transformed the region. As always, Memo was there ahead of the crowd, staking his claim.

"*Que romántico* to be dancing under the stars," Fred whispered in Maruja's ear. Colored lights placed under the palm trees were the only illumination on the patio which circled the pool. "And you're the sexiest thing this side of the *Río Gran*," he added looking down at her in admiration. The material of her gold lamé halter dress curved with the swell of her breasts. Her straight skirt defied movement of any kind, but move she did as she danced along with him to a *merengue*. "I can't wait to see you take it off." He was relieved that the patio was in semi-darkness for an erection had started to bulge out from his pants.

"Oh, Fred," Maruja laughed as they danced around the patio. "Isn't this place wonderful? This is my kind of life."

"Well it ain't Chacari, that's for sure," he said. "Any regrets that you married this poor ole *petrolero* and are stuck out in the boonies?"

"*Nunca*," she replied vehemently. "Never will I regret marrying you, for I would follow you to the ends of the earth. Have I ever complained?"

"Nope, you never have. You're a real good sport, *muñequita*." No matter how disappointed he was in her lack of love for Nena, he admired how quickly she had adapted to life in the oilfields, a lot better than some of the other wives. A rich girl who was used to snapping her fingers to get anything she wanted, she'd quickly learned to keep house and cook. The rest will come in time, he kept telling himself, she'll be just as crazy about the baby as I am. She just had too much thrown at her too fast.

Later after they made love and were cuddling together she startled him for out of the blue she said, "I know I've disappointed you."

"Disappointed?" He propped himself up on his elbows looking down at her. "How's that?"

"Because I didn't feel anything for Nena." She paused, looking mysteriously up at him, for she still loved to engage in theatrics. "Fred, do you believe in miracles?"

"Why sure, baby doll. Didn't I meet you over the holy water font in church?"

"It's happened, like a miracle," she burst out, unable to keep the good news to herself. "This afternoon when I said goodbye to our daughter, all of a sudden I was filled with such happiness I thought I would burst. Fred! I fell in love with Nena. For the first time I felt like a mother, a real mother. I hated to let go of her, I wanted to stay and play with her, feed her, rock her in my arms. I looked at her for the first time as a mother should. And now, despite all the fun we're having — imagine we're on our *luna de miel*, our honeymoon after the birth of our daughter! I can't wait to get back so I can see her and the three of us can be a real family."

"Oh, darlin'," Fred looked lovingly at her. "I knew you could do it. Just give her time, I kept telling *Mamita* Isabel, just give her time. Next weekend we'll go to Caracas to tell your mother. Now the whole family will know *Maruja la Bruja* is the one who has been enchanted — by our daughter."

"*Ay Dios*," she cried out suddenly, her teeth chattering, "I'm freezing."

He pulled her towards him. "It's the air conditioning, baby doll." He'd flipped it on high the minute they got back to their room. "Wish we had air conditioning in Chacari. Don't worry, *muñequita*, I'm full of hi-grade Texas anti-freeze." As he held her close, her shivering gradually subsided. And the sorrow and disappointment which used to run all through his body, swelling his veins and lodging in his chest until he felt his heart would burst into a thousand little pieces, was put to rest. She loves her, he told himself over and over again, on Monday Nena will finally have a mother.

....

When they left El Encanto early Monday morning they all were in agreement Memo had given his hotel the perfect name, for it was an enchanting place. They drove off to the airport, more than a little bit tired for after the band had played the last piece, Paco persuaded them with a 200 *Bolivar* tip to play a few more songs. Songs which all of them were still singing as the plane taxied down the runway. Fred's high pitched laughter punctuated the music.

"Oh. Fred," Maruja cried out, flinging her arms around him. "Isn't life wonderful? I want to live forever."

"You will, baby doll, we all will." He had to shout for Paco had started up the plane. Pili had brought a thermos of black coffee but Paco told her to keep it for the others who might have hangovers. Which he didn't since he made it a rule never to drink the night before flying. The little plane wobbled and weaved as it climbed, making them even more giddy. Fred let out a Rebel yell, claiming this was the best damn roller coaster ride he'd ever taken. Finally the Beechcraft straightened out and they resumed their singing, Fred leading them off with his rendition of *El Rancho Grande* as Paco piloted them through the early morning mist. When the engine sputtered, they were singing so loudly no one heard it. But Paco felt it. His hands at the controls recognized the difference in rhythm immediately. Then over their singing he heard the engine skip a few beats, like a heart fading in and out. And he found it exceedingly difficult to keep the plane on a steady keel. Pili noticed it too. She cocked her ears, her forehead wrinkling in concentration as she tried to figure out what had happened to their plane.

In the back seat, Maruja and Fred were oblivious to what the occupants of the front seat were experiencing. Then the plane started to lose altitude and Maruja screamed. She grabbed Fred, her tiny fingers moving frantically across his chest, clutching in terror at his throat as the plane continued its downward plunge. Fred felt the blood rush to his head as he fought off her desperate hands.

The thermos of coffee flew around the cabin and because of the speed they were falling it hit Paco in the temples, temporarily stunning him so that his hands slipped from the controls. But it didn't matter, for there was nothing he could do to straighten out the plane. It continued to fall, going into a tailspin. The last thing Fred remembered was Maruja's cries of fear, her tiny fingers frozen around his hands. Then everything went black.

....

Charley Dawson, a derrickman working on the Monkey Board on Well #5417 near the Guanipa River, saw the plane going down. Or thought he had. He wasn't sure because one minute it was a fleck with the sun bouncing off it and the next minute his attention was claimed by the drill pipe coming up towards him. They were changing the drill bit and since they were pretty deep in the hole, there was a lot of pipe to come up. Working 90 feet above the drilling floor, it was his job to steady the drill pipe being lifted out of the well as it made its way up inside the derrick. And once it reached him, to stack the pipe vertically. Looking down he could see the tops of the pipe, looking to him like huge open cans stored neatly in rows.

After he stacked the last section, he looked out over the horizon. Funniest damn thing, he thought, it sure looked like a plane going down. It might have been a bird though, a silent bird plunging to the ground for he couldn't hear a thing above the noise of the rig's motors.

When he climbed down to the rig floor and was getting ready to go off tour though, he couldn't get the plane or what he thought was a plane out of his mind. He thought he just might go and mosey around to sort of break the monotony of things. He spied Joaquín Nuñez, the Venezuelan driller, also going off shift. Better have company, he decided, in case he found something. When he asked him if he wanted to come along, Nuñez nodded his head enthusiastically. He wasn't anxious to go home for he'd had a fight with his wife before leaving for work and he knew she'd be waiting to take up where they left off. They both agreed it was best to go together, no use thrashing around in the woods in two pickups.

They drove off in Nuñez's pickup in the direction that Charley thought he saw the plane go down. An hour later they found it. And what they discovered caused Joaquín Nuñez to make the Sign of the Cross over and over again. While Charley Dawson threw up all over his grease stained khaki pants.

....

The memory of the plane plummeting in the early morning light was the first thing Fred remembered as he shook his head and tried to focus his eyes. The back part of the small cabin rested in the lower branches of a leafy *Bucare* tree, and that's where Fred found himself when he came to. He was the only one in the cabin. Blood dripped into his right eye from a cut on his forehead, blurring his vision. He squinted out of his left eye, trying to extract his body from the cabin. When he finally squirmed free and fell a few feet to the ground, the dirt blotted dry the wound.

Rolling over gingerly, for every part of his body ached, his eyes searched for the others. Calling out to them brought no response, and then something caught his attention and caused him to look up. Where he saw Paco jackknifed over a limb of the *Bucare* tree, his dead body hanging like a broken doll. He stared at Paco's body for a long time, trying to make himself believe it was just a terrible dream.

Finally he stopped staring and moving his body slowly tried to sit up. But it was such an effort he kept slipping. Then he was able to prop himself up a bit on his left side where he forced himself to look back and forth searching for some sign of Maruja. Don't let her be dead, God, he prayed, all the while calling out her name. Then his eye caught some material billowing in the morning breeze. But all he could see was the material with no sign of Maruja. A cry of frustration, of fear that he wasn't able to move and look for her, lodged in his throat. Then he pushed himself completely over and that's when he saw the long, black hair. Crawling on his hands and knees he found Pili, her lifeless eyes staring up at him, the fear in them frozen in time. He passed out and when he came to a few minutes later he was down in the dirt, his teeth sunk into the soft ground. Spitting out the dirt, he started crawling again on his hands and knees, still calling out hoarsely to Maruja. It was a slow and tedious process for his right leg throbbed every time he moved it, and he mostly dragged it along while crawling on his left leg.

And then he saw her head, saw it move and he cried out a prayer of gratitude. She was alive. Thank God she was alive. He was so elated that when he started crawling towards her he didn't see the tree stump. He crashed into it losing his balance, his hands going out from under him. And as he tried to push himself up, he saw some pink material draped over the door which had been blown away from the plane by the impact of the crash. The door was wedged in some bushes and next to it were the plane wheels, over which a pair of legs dangled.

Fred was very confused. Maruja's legs and head weren't in the same place. Her body was near the plane, or was it? Hadn't he seen her head on the ground? He definitely saw her head moving. Frantically he started crawling toward her. She moved her head again. "I'm here, baby doll," he called out to her. "Just hang on, I'll be right with you." Then crawling towards her he watched as her head moved and rolled, it's movement caused by the animal pawing at it. And as Fred saw her head roll, he realized it was just her head. His eyes darted to the area below her mouth, that beautiful mouth he had kissed so many times. Her chin and throat were there, but nothing else.

He screamed when he realized his wife had been decapitated, and his cries continued as he crawled towards her head. Where he became a mad man as he fought off the dog which continued to paw at her head and was reluctant to relinquish it. Furious, he picked up a rock and smashed it down on the dog's head. Howling, the dog ran off. Then Fred picked up what was left of Maruja and cradling it in his arms, rocked back and forth. Which is how Charley Dawson and Joaquín Nuñez found him, clutching Maruja's head and staring at them with vacant eyes.

Joaquín Nuñez ran to his pickup and reaching for the radio, realized it was dead. It had been since the day before yesterday, and if it hadn't been for that stupid argument with his wife, he would have taken it into the shop.

"We'll have to take him in," Charley told him.

"But I don't think people who've been in an accident are supposed to be moved," Joaquín cried out, almost regretting he had agreed to come with Charley. The sight of Fred hanging on to Maruja's head was getting to him, and he was afraid he was going to start throwing up his guts. "Let's go back to the Santa Barbara Hospital and they'll come out with an ambulance."

"We ain't got no choice, *hombre*. It might be hours before an ambulance gets here," Charley insisted. Both of them struggled to get Fred to the pickup, no easy feat. For not only did Fred refuse to relinquish Maruja's head, but he was much bigger than both of them. Although Joaquín was on the corpulent side, Charley didn't weigh over 155 pounds. When they finally got him to the pickup and opened the tailgate, they half slid, half pushed Fred into the flatbed.

"I'd better drive," Charley told Joaquín. "You stay in the back with him. If he rolls over, you're big enough to hold your own. He'd crush me like a fly."

"*Carajo*," Joaquín cried out when they walked away from the Santa Barbara Hospital after having delivered Fred, "I've seen some bad sights in my life, but that was the worst. All the time driving here, trying to keep him from rolling over and the eyes in that head staring at me, *que mierda*!" His eyes kept swiveling to the back of his pickup as he relived the ride to the hospital.

"I heard the nurses say they only got that head pried loose after they knocked him out with an injection," Charley said. "They think it might have been his wife."

One of the nurses didn't think it might have been his wife, she knew definitely it was. As Fran Young plunged the hypodermic needle into Fred's arm, her hands trembled from the shock of what she had witnessed. Then the cold determination which had seen her through a war, had kept her going in the DP camp took over. Calmly and slowly she helped the other nurse peel Fred's hands away from Maruja's head.

I didn't want for it to happen this way, she thought looking at Maruja's head. I'm not that heartless I would wish this sort of thing on anyone, she continued her silent apology to Maruja. I thought in terms of something else. She remembered the night of the seismo barbecue and her determination that Fred's marriage to Maruja would end. Be careful what you desire, her grandfather used to caution her, you just might get it.

She pushed the thought from her mind and went over to the sink to wash her rubbed gloved hands. Over and over she soaped them, watching the blood and dirt slide off into the sink. That's the end of Maruja, she thought, seeing the last of the blood disappear down the drain. Then she noticed a few black hairs clotted together with blood which clung stubbornly to one of her gloves. She picked at it, pulling it off savagely with her other hand, and threw it down into the sink, moving it towards the drain with her finger and spraying the faucet over it. When it was gone, she felt a sense of elation. *Now he's mine*, she told herself with an icy calmness. *No one can ever take him away from me again.*

....

Miraculously Fred suffered nothing serious in the way of bodily injuries. What kept him in the back seat of the plane when it landed in the branches of the *Bucare* tree the authorities never could determine. What they did agree on was the others died on impact as their bodies flew out of the plane. The extent of Fred's injuries were several cracked ribs, a lot of bruises and a broken right leg.

While the doctors were satisfied with his physical progress, they were concerned about his mental state. For the shock of his wife's death and the manner in which she had died affected his mind. He either stared into space, or if he drifted off into sleep, he woke up screaming. His dreams always started out the same. He was back in Caracas reliving the first time he met Maruja in the Cathedral, their hands colliding in the holy water font. Then he was buying the white roses from the toothless old flower vendor in the Plaza Bolivar. But when he took the bouquet in his hands, it always turned into Maruja's head.

When he woke up screaming and calling for Maruja, Fran was always there. Even when she got off duty she stayed with him. Always ready to calm him when he woke up from one of his nightmares. Or take his hand as he reached out to her in fright. He held on to her, almost in a death grip, and only when his memories subsided did he let go of her. After awhile he began to know when she was there. In the beginning it was her cologne. Sometimes when his spirit was too tired, when opening his eyes was too much of an effort, he relied on his nose to tell him of her presence. For the scent she had on was the same one Maruja used, Joy. At times in his confusion Fred thought Maruja was still alive, that he was sitting next to her in the Cathedral, the soft scent of roses dancing in the air around them.

Gradually though, he came to realize it was Fran who was with him day and night. Sorrowfully he resigned himself to Maruja being dead, although he still called out to her in his dreams. The doctors thought that seeing family would help his recovery, but he didn't know his father who'd flown from Houston as soon as he was notified. Even Cathleen bringing Nena to the hospital every day elicited no response. He stared at his infant daughter as if she were a stranger.

....

And then one day he called out. Not for Maruja or Nena or his father, but for Fran. He pushed away the nurse on duty and firmly insisted he wanted to see Fran. The hesitant stammer which had taken over his speech since the accident wasn't as pronounced, nor was the blank look in his eyes. The doctors took it as a good sign, his father who'd kept a daily vigil at the hospital along with Fran was elated. His boy was back with the living. When Fran came running into the room, she'd gone home to take a shower and short nap, he called out her name again, reaching for her hand. He smiled wanly at his father, talking briefly with him. But Fran was the one he clung to.

Cathleen said a grateful prayer of thanks when she learned of Fred's recovery. Maruja's death had been a terrible shock to the camp. It was especially difficult for Cathleen. She kept thinking that now Nena would never know her mother loved her. The joy of Maruja discovering her love for Nena had come too late.

And it brought back memories of her own recent loss, making all sorts of thoughts run through her mind, causing her to brood, making her wonder if there wasn't some sort of curse hanging over all of them. First Sheila, then the Hardestys. Who would be next? If Murray were here, he'd scoff at the way her imagination was working. And he'd joke her out of it. But that was the trouble, he was gone and she ached for his good natured presence. She also realized she was becoming too attached to Nena. Sooner or later, she would have to give her up, either to Fred or Maruja's family.

Maruja's family was grief stricken by the news of the accident, as was all of Caracas, no one quite able to believe that *La Bruja* was dead. When her body was returned to Caracas in a closed casket, the church service was mercifully brief. For there were two other funerals — Paco's and Pilar's. Her family, normally very demonstrative in their emotions, were even more so now. Her two sisters' wails rose to the ceiling of the Cathedral. While the servants, especially Anselma the laundress, cried endlessly during the Mass. The only one who didn't, the one person who remained as lifeless as the statues, was Misia Isabel. Her heart was breaking, but she grieved for her dead daughter in silence. It was the only way she knew to keep the family together. Nor did her rimless glasses ever become stained with tears. For she felt if she ever lost control, it would be like a dam bursting and the whole family would go mad in their grief.

But Maruja haunted her heart. It didn't seem possible this free spirit who lived such a charmed life had been snatched from them so swiftly and in such a cruel manner. Over and over Misia Isabel tried to reassure herself Maruja hadn't suffered, that she died instantly and never felt the agony of her head being severed. This is what the authorities told her and she must believe them. When one brings a sweet little baby into the world, she thought hopelessly, one never dreams she might depart from it in such violence.

After the burial and the last person to pay his condolences had left the mansion, she still wouldn't allow herself the luxury of mourning. For Nena was on her mind, the child Maruja had been so indifferent to. She knew Maruja's friend and neighbor, Cathleen, was taking care of her. Probably better than Maruja ever did, she thought sadly. Now she must see about bringing her granddaughter to Caracas. But Fred's doctors advised against it, for they were hoping that seeing his child could bring him out of the mental shadowland into which he had retreated. As much as she wanted Nena with her, she realized she would have to wait.

"Are you sure Nena is all right, Alejo?" she asked her son whom she had sent out to the interior as the family emissary.

"She's in perfect hands," Alejo, the clandestine Communist reported back. As much as he despised the Americans, he grudgingly had to admit he was favorably impressed with Cathleen and the care she was giving his niece. "We just have to wait until Fred comes around. If he comes around, poor guy." His brother-in-law was in his thoughts a great deal and he feared he wouldn't recover.

Then the day Misia Isabel longed for so anxiously and Cathleen dreaded arrived. Fred was on the mend and the doctors said Misia Isabel could have her granddaughter. Would Cathleen mind making the trip into

Caracas, so Misia Isabel could have the pleasure of meeting this wonderful neighbor and friend of her daughter? If it weren't possible, her letter went on, she would immediately send one of her daughters out to pick up Nena. But if Cathleen would grant her this pleasure, she was enclosing plane tickets for herself and her husband.

Cathleen was positive Ryle wouldn't want to accompany her to Caracas. And was surprised when he said, "It's goin' be hard, baby, giving up that little girl. Don't think I'm not aware of it. Maybe it'll be a bit easier if I'm around." Just when she thought she had him figured out as being so wrapped up in his career he wouldn't take time to think of anything else, he turned around and revealed understanding and tenderness. She would never in a million years fathom this man, she decided. Maybe that's what kept her around, never knowing what he was going to do next.

Maruja's mother was sitting in the front patio when they arrived. A rush of people — Maruja's relatives and the servants — swarmed around, all of them wanting to take Nena. But Misia Isabel shooed them away, especially Maruja's sister, Lourdes, who kept popping in every minute or so afraid that she would miss one morsel of conversation.

"Like children they are," Misia Isabel's hands flew into the air as she talked, the gesture reminding Cathleen so much of Maruja. "All of them so anxious to take the baby. And none of them realizing how difficult this is for you. Maruja told me of your loss. I'm so sorry." She refused to take Nena, telling Cathleen to keep her a bit longer.

Cathleen held Nena close to her. The last time she would be able to do so.

"But you're young," Misia Isabel continued, " and in no time you and that handsome husband of yours will make another baby." Listening to her, Cathleen was grateful to Sarita for the Spanish lessons she had given her and for her insistence they speak only in Spanish so her ears would become attuned to the language.

"Please extend my apologies to your husband for not speaking English," Misia Isabel murmured. "There are times like this when I so wished I had taken lessons."

How gracious she is, Cathleen thought. And so full of compassion. Here she has lost a daughter and she is thinking of my loss. "I know you started taking care of Nena long before the accident." Misia Isabel leaned forward, her voice coming out in muted tones. "If it hadn't been for you, who knows how my granddaughter would have fared. Only God understands why my daughter had no affection for her child." She sighed, taking off her rimless glasses, cleaning an imaginary spot. Dark circles accentuated the sorrow and weariness in them. "I want you to know that we Venezuelans are not at all like that. I wouldn't want you to have a bad impression of our character. For we're very much a family oriented people."

"Please." Cathleen's heart went out to Misia Isabel and she had an impulsive urge to hug her and give her comfort. But Misia Isabel's aristocratic manner made her think twice about it. "You don't have to make excuses to me," she insisted. "I understand. Maruja was sort of a free spirit." And then because she wanted to ease the sorrow so evident in Misia Isabel's eyes, she told her of the last time she saw Maruja and how affectionate she had been with Nena. And Maruja's wonderful discovery that she loved Nena. A smile curved the corners of Misia Isabel's mouth and her eyes lit up with happiness.

"¿De veras? Was Maruja really that loving?" She clapped her hands together, bringing them up to her face just as Maruja used to whenever something delighted her. "Fred was right. He kept telling me she would grow into motherhood. Just give her time," he kept saying. She smiled affectionately at Cathleen. "How very perceptive you are, thinking of Maruja as I always have, a free spirit. And now you have given me something so precious. The knowledge that the last time she saw her baby she was caring and affectionate." She wiped a few tears from her eyes, the first ones she had allowed herself. "In the end she really did care for Nena."

But it's too late, Cathleen thought sadly, Nena will never know. Babies do sense when they're loved or when they are not. Why didn't God let Maruja live long enough so that Nena would know? To have given Maruja that grace and then to snatch her away before she could be a real mother was absolutely cruel. More and more she was finding it difficult to understand God's will. Life just doesn't make any sense at all, she thought wearily, maybe it's not supposed to.

She took off the little yellow sunbonnet she'd put on Nena for the trip and brushed her curly red hair. Tied the laces on one of her yellow booties. Get it over with. You can't hold on to her forever. She's not yours, only somebody God loaned you. That's all God seemed to do, she thought sorrowfully, loan her babies to love for a short while and then take them back. She listened to the placid splashing of the fountain and looked up when a bird alighted in it, watched it bob up and down in the water, warbling its song of happiness. Would she ever feel as carefree as that bird?

"Goodbye, my little pumpkin," she said, planting a kiss on Nena's forehead. Then impulsively she placed her on her knee. One last ride. Up and down her knee went, while she sang her the song about Wild Bill Hickock riding his horse. Then because she felt Misia Isabel's eyes on her, she became embarrassed and blushed. "It's just some dumb game, but she likes it," she said lamely, trying to explain the little game she always played with Sheila, and then Nena. "Sometimes it makes her laugh." And then as if on cue, when Cathleen sang ,"off fell Bill," and her knee shot out, Nena laughed.

Misia Isabel clapped her hands in delight. "My dear, you were meant to have children, a houseful of them."

Quickly now, Cathleen told herself. We've all had our last ride. She hugged Nena briefly and then walked over to Misia Isabel's chair. Felt her arms start to ache with emptiness the moment she gave her Nena.
Misia Isabel sensing Cathleen's feelings, reached for the bell sitting on the coffee table. "Let's get the family in here," she said understandingly. "Sometimes they can distract a person from thinking too much." The patio became noisy when the family and servants rushed in, all of them looking like they had been poised behind closed doors just waiting for Misia Isabel to ring for them. Cathleen was grateful for their presence.

"You are always welcome here," Misia Isabel told her when she and Ryle were ready to leave. Cathleen was reminded of Sarita when she added those age old Spanish words, "This is your house."

"Let's go back to the hotel and make mad, passionate love," Ryle said as they walked towards the Plaza Bolivar hoping to find a taxi there.

"Oh, yes," she replied, so grateful he had come with her. "Over and over again, Ryle." So that I get pregnant, she prayed.

"Did you ever see anything like that place?" Ryle marvelled when they got into the taxi. "It was a regular mansion. And the way all those servants came running whenever Maruja's mother rang that little bell. Now that's the way to live, baby. That's what you and me are gonna have one day. When I'm sitting in the president's chair of Palm Oil." He continued to rhapsodize over Maruja's house, and for a moment Cathleen wondered if it was the reason he offered to come with her. Just so he could see the wealth and luxury that had been Maruja's. Knowing how much store he put in having money, she thought it might be possible. But he was so tender and considerate, so like the man she had fallen in love with, she pushed aside her suspicions. She responded to him, feeling like a bride again, full of hope they would soon have another baby.

TWENTY-ONE

Fred's nightmares began to lessen. Gradually he stopped slipping in and out of consciousness and most of the time he was lucid. His father, seeing how much he improved, wanted him to come back to Texas.

"I can't do that, Daddy. I just can't leave this country," he said sadly. "It has too many memories."

"You can't live with memories, son," Frederick Hardesty III pleaded with him. Although his features were distinct from Fred who resembled his mother, the senior Hardesty had the same large, muscular body. Now that Fred's hair had lost its sandy luster and was turning grey, which the doctors attributed to the great trauma he had experienced, he was beginning to look more like his father's contemporary.

"I know that, but I can't let go of them," Fred replied morosely, "or they won't let go of me. I know I can't stay around this part of the country. It has too many memories. So I'm going to ask for a transfer out west to Lake Maracaibo. I've never been there with her." He couldn't bring himself to say Maruja's name. "I'll come back to the States, really I will. But right now, Daddy, I just can't make the break." He paused, looking off into space, as he did quite frequently. "And besides, I've got a daughter to think of."

"You could bring her back to Texas," his father persisted. "You know your sisters would love her to pieces."

"Yeah I know, Daddy." Fred smiled wistfully across the hospital room at his father. It would be so easy if he could just pick up and leave Venezuela with all its memories. In some ways he wanted to, just get the hell out of the country and try to make a fresh start. But he knew he couldn't for he had the strongest feeling that if he left, it would be like abandoning Maruja. He'd learned to accept her death, but he could still feel her presence. And he didn't want to let go of this.

280

"Let me try it my way, huh?" Fred pleaded softly.

Reluctantly his father made plans to return to Houston. But before he left he made one last try, reminding Fred that his two year contract was up, was in fact past due, and he was eligible for vacation.

"I don't plan on coming up to the States for it," Fred explained. "Maybe I'll go to the Andes in western Venezuela and do some hunting. They say it's real pretty up there in the mountains, nice and cool."

The thought of leaving Fran made Fred panic. The carefree, self assured person who'd been devoted to just having a good time out of life had turned into someone beset by a multitude of fears. Fear of going to sleep for he never knew what dreams he would have, fear of being alone and the memories which haunted his waking hours. Sometimes he felt he was just afraid to breathe. The doctors in Jusepin wanted him to see a psychiatrist which would necessitate trips to Caracas since there were none available locally, but he refused. He was sick and tired of doctors and hospitals. He just wanted to get back to work, hoping he could lose himself in his job. When his transfer to western Venezuela was approved he looked forward to the move, except for the anxiety he experienced when he thought of being away from Fran.

When he asked her to get a transfer and go with him, Fran didn't hesitate. He was a shadow of the man she'd fallen in love with, for he no longer had the gift of gab or joked around, throwing out compliments to people, endearing himself to everyone around him. His eyes, which once sparkled so mischievously, had an old look to them — they'd seen too much of life's dark side. But Fran still wanted him.

Fred discovered, though, that having Fran nearby wasn't enough. Not that he had much desire for sex, the need for a woman which had given him such pleasure was gone. But he couldn't stand being alone in the bachelor quarters at night. Only when Fran was around did some of the fear leave him.

"I have to be straight up with you," he told her one night. "I need you, Franny. And I care for you — as much of me that's left to care for anyone." He paused, for he was still trying to decipher his true feelings for her. He really didn't know. All he knew was he'd come to depend on her an awful lot. And he'd grown very fond of her. When he asked her to marry him he tried to be honest with her. "If what I have to offer you will be enough now — maybe it will grow into something deeper. I honestly don't know, Franny. I can't promise you anything more than that."

Well, Fran thought, it's not a movie love story. There's nothing very romantic about his proposal. But I want him, and I'll take him any way I can get him. Half a loaf is better than none. She didn't want to lose him this time, and gratefully she accepted his proposal.

The only thing Fred asked of her was not to wear the rose scented cologne. He hoped she didn't mind, he explained, but he really didn't like it, it gave him a headache. She suspected he wasn't telling her the truth. She was almost positive Maruja had also used Joy, and she seethed with anger when she had to give it away to one of the nurses.

He also indicated that as soon as they were settled, they would go to Caracas to pick up Nena. And because he knew what a caring person she was, he was positive she would be a good mother to his daughter. Fran wasn't too happy about that. To have lost him to Maruja the first time, and now to have to bring up her daughter, always a reminder of the great love they shared, oh no, that wasn't to her liking at all. She would have preferred that Nena continue to live with her grandmother in Caracas. But she masked her feelings and told him she would be delighted. She vowed to get pregnant as soon as possible and to give him a boy, several boys. And then as an afterthought, she decided a girl would also be good insurance.

They went to the Andes on their honeymoon where they spent more time hunting and fishing than they did making love. She wondered if all the wild and wonderful times they used to have in bed would ever come back. Most of the time she had to perform fellatio on him to get them started. Half a loaf, she realized, was exactly what she had. But only for now, she reminded herself. Just as she had made herself indispensable to him when he was recuperating, now she would make him absolutely dependent on her in marriage. Then when they drove into Caracas to pick up Nena, an unexpected bonus came her way. Misia Isabel wasn't too keen on giving up Nena, making all sorts of excuses for keeping her.

"The poor little baby had too many changes," she told them. "First losing her mother, then growing attached to Cathleen. And now after getting used to her grandparents, she would have to start getting used to Fran."

"She's just an infant," Fred pointed out to his mother-in-law, "less than a year old. Hardly at an age where she would know the difference."

"Ah, but children sense these things," Misia Isabel insisted. "Besides Nena is all I have left of my daughter," Misia Isabel cried out in her most cajoling manner, reminding Fred somewhat of Maruja. "Please don't take her away from me just yet. You've remarried and have your whole life ahead of you. Just let me keep her for a little while until I get over losing Maruja."

And because the fight had gone out of him and he found it easier not to make waves, he relented. But it broke his heart to leave Nena. Not only because she was his darling girl, but she too was all he had left of Maruja.

"I just couldn't allow Nena to be with that woman," Misia Isabel told Don Eugenio after they left. "There isn't an ounce of love in her except for Fred. No, my poor little Nenita would be *una huérfana*, truly an orphan if she were raised by Fred's new wife." It was bad enough, Misia Isabel thought morosely, that Maruja didn't want her when she was born. *Imagínate*, just imagine how she would fare with an indifferent and uncaring stepmother.

The uncaring stepmother though was a devoted wife. She made their house cozy and inviting, there was always a drink waiting for Fred as soon as he walked in the door from work. His favorite meals were served. Bit by bit his sexual drive came back. It wasn't firecrackers and cannons the way it had been with Maruja. Fran could never keep him in a constant state of feverish anticipation. Only Maruja had that power. But like Fran, he learned to make do with half a loaf.

From time to time he remembered his promise to his father to go back to Texas. But every time he thought about it, he became extremely upset. He just couldn't leave Venezuela and desert his *muñequita*. He had to stay close to her and her memory.

....

The days dragged for Cathleen. She missed her part time job which she'd given up to take care of Nena after Maruja's death. And she found herself missing Murray, longing for his unflappable, good natured disposition. But most of all she missed Nena. The crib which had been Sheila's and then Nena's was a constant reminder of the two babies. With

Nena gone it was like losing Sheila all over again. She put the playpen and bathinette in the other bedroom, along with the crib and kept the door closed. But just seeing the closed door seemed to reinforce her loss, and so in the end she had Ryle store them in the warehouse.

Meanwhile she hoped and prayed she would get pregnant. And walked around on cloud nine when her period was late and she experienced all the familiar symptoms — swollen breasts, lassitude taking over her body, queasiness. She just knew she was pregnant and was counting the days until she could go to the doctor with a urine specimen for the rabbit test.

Then one morning she woke up and her nightgown was stained with blood. Every month since Sheila's death it had been the same disappointment, but this time it overwhelmed her because she'd been so positive she was pregnant. The deep depression which she experienced after Sheila's death came back to plague her. Listlessly she walked around the small house, turning the record player on and off, trying to lose herself in a book. By ten o'clock she felt the old craving for a drink. And fought against it, she had too strong a memory of how it had dominated her life. Until menstrual cramps started, so strong and rough she broke out in a cold sweat from the pain. Which is when she decided one little drink couldn't hurt her if it would calm the cramps. She poured herself a shot of rum. Oh, what a lift it gave her. The blues left her, she felt serenity flowing through every pore of her body, her muscles went slack in blessed relaxation. She was tempted to have another one, but made herself wait until after lunch. By five o'clock she'd had three drinks, which she didn't consider excessive considering it was for medicinal purposes. It sure beats Midol, she decided, the thought making her break out in wild laughter.

The next morning when she woke up more depressed than ever, she reached for the rum bottle. Then shaking her head, she got into the shower. She wasn't going to fall into that trap again. I've got to be with people, she told herself, people who care for me and who'll get me out of these doldrums. She couldn't go to Pet's because the Fords had gone to the States on their long leave. How she missed Pet and her bawdy humor, which in anyone else would have shocked Cathleen's shy sense of decorum. But somehow the way it came out from Pet was just plain funny. Of course there was Nadine, who was the friendliest person in camp. But because her husband was Ryle's boss, she was still hesitant about getting too close to her.

Then her thoughts turned to Maruja, whose charm had beguiled the whole camp. Maruja who was gone now forever. That someone so young had died so horribly and the storybook romance between her and Fred over and gone, was still difficult for her to understand. Her heart went out to Fred for he was the one left behind with the memories, and his infant daughter who would never know Maruja had grown to love her.

Nena dominated her thoughts in another way. You should never have allowed yourself to care for her that much, she berated herself, you grew too fond of her.

I'll go insane if I keep this up, she told herself. The one person she could turn to was Sarita. But she was a two hour drive away. She went into the kitchen to make a cup of tea, resisting the desire to pour herself a shot of rum. As she waited for the kettle to boil she straightened out the spice cabinet and stared at a bottle of imitation brandy flavoring. It wasn't the real thing, but it just might make her think it was. She measured a few drops into the steeping tea. Then as she put the bottle back in the spice cabinet, it struck her how ludicrous it was. Lacing her tea with imitation brandy flavoring just so she wouldn't think about a drink. Angrily she dumped the tea down the sink and ran inside for her purse. She had to see Sarita, even if it was a long drive. She was the only one who could help her get through this. Her emotions pulled at her all the way to Puerto La Cruz and when she got there, she ran up the stairs of Sarita's house, throwing herself into her arms.

"We're both disappointed, *chica*," Sarita said in her soft and melodious voice. She also had been trying to get pregnant, she told Cathleen, with no results. "But of course I didn't lose a child, so my feelings can't ever compare with what you are going through." She insisted that Cathleen lie down in the *chinchorro* strung across the front porch. "There's nothing like that hammock to calm a person's nerves. You just rock gently with the breezes, back and forth. Isn't it wonderful?"

Sarita picked up some material and deftly cut it into the shape of a rabbit. She was making another one of her fabric pictures. "This will be Flossy Cottontail, I've already got Peter Rabbit sewn in." She held it up for Cathleen to see. "It's for the baby's room. One of these days I will get pregnant and so will you. Maybe it will be next month."

Sarita's voice was so confident Cathleen began to feel better. And Sarita was right about the hammock, it did soothe her nerves. She felt the tension melt away as the *chinchorro* swayed in the breeze. How she loved visiting Sarita in Puerto la Cruz. No matter how hot it was, and it was warmer and more humid than Chacari, there was always a breeze off the ocean. And the houses in El Gato were so spacious. The same basic two bedroom with connecting bath, but they were three times the size of the little boxes in Chacari and all of them had a huge front screen porch. They were built above ground so the air could flow underneath, adding to their coolness. Nor were they bunched together as in Chacari. The adjoining house was separated by a wide side lawn while behind them a small hill gave additional privacy. No chance of neighbors overhearing your conversation here, she thought. If only she and Ryle could live in Puerto La Cruz. But she knew there was no likelihood of that happening since there was no oil in the area. Only the men in transportation and materials could be based here. She started to feel drowsy. It was like being rocked in a cradle lying in the *chinchorro*. She could smell the salt off the ocean and as she dozed off she thought how nice it would be to go to the beach.

Which they did after lunch. A meal of cold lobster soup served with *tostones*, resembling potato chips but made from green plantains, fried *pargo*, and after the fried snapper, the fruit salad Cathleen had come to associate with Sarita, consisting of sweet pineapples, plump bananas, juicy oranges and papaya, which was called *lechosa* in Venezuela. With glasses and glasses of thirst quenching iced tea. Listening to John's stories — he had the most marvelous ability to mimic any accent, doubling them over with laughter as he described the people he ran into in his job — made her quickly forget the blues.

"Isn't it beautiful here?" Sarita sighed when they got to the beach at La Lechería. Located in a crescent shaped bay, it looked out to the hills of an outlying island named La Mujer because it supposedly was shaped like a reclining woman. To the left another island, El Morro, rose out of the water, its dark cliffs giving it its name. Later it would be developed into a luxurious resort with a cable car connecting it to the mainland. But when Sarita looked out, it was pristine with no traces of man. "I almost hate to leave, even though they say it is beautiful over in the islands."

"You're going away?" The news of Sarita leaving made her panic. Even though they were separated by a two hour drive, it was still a comfort knowing she was there.

"*Ay sí, chica*," Sarita exclaimed. "We had so many things to talk about that it slipped my mind. I suppose too because it's a last minute thing. John has vacation due him and he doesn't want to go to the States because it's winter there. You know how he despises cold weather. So when he found out the other day he could get away, we decided to go to Trinidad and Barbados where he can just laze around and do nothing. He's very tired, what with his job and laying the foundation for the trucking business he hopes to start up in a year or so."

"When are you leaving?"

"Oh, the end of the week," Sarita replied.

"That's three days away!" Cathleen burst out suddenly feeling very despondent. "Are you packed? There's so much to do getting ready for a trip."

Sarita shrugged her shoulders. "Just throw a few things in our suitcases, lock up the house and go to the airport. Fortunately I applied for a passport last year when we thought we were going over to the islands, but John couldn't get away." Then noticing the crestfallen look on Cathleen's face, she immediately stopped talking about the trip.

"You're probably feeling that everyone has gone off and left you which is only natural, *querida*. Life has dealt you an awful lot in a short time. Losing Sheila, then Maruja. Of all the people in camp it had to hit you the hardest, being her next door neighbor. I know it shocked us terribly and we didn't know her half as well as you did. And then giving up Nena after becoming so attached to her. But try to put away the past, think about good things you can look forward to. Like your vacation, seeing your family. When is it — next month?"

"Almost seven weeks away. Sometimes it seems like seven years. I just panicked when I heard you were going away. It's because you're my rock."

"But you're going to be just fine." Sarita assured her. "In no time at all you'll be back and then we'll get together and tell each other all about our vacations." She got up brushing the sand off her. "Come, let's go for a little walk." A short stretch of sand separated the ocean from a lagoon where the water was so placid it made hardly a ripple when it touched shore.

"That's what John always teases me he should do instead of starting a trucking business," she said pointing to a large building with a thatched roof located directly on the beach of the lagoon. It looked like something out of a Dorothy Lamour movie and was a restaurant owned by Jimmy King, an American married to a Venezuelan. But Jimmy did none of the work. He had his wife and her sisters and all of their children working in the restaurant while he spent most of his time on the beach.

"He kids me that since I don't have any sisters we'd have to make a lot of babies, so I guess I have my work all cut out for me," Sarita laughed. "And John claims the Irish always have large families, so both you and I have many children in our future. You see, *chica*, we both have a lot to look forward to."

Which is what Cathleen tried to remember when the wet season, which had tapered off came back in a fury, raining relentlessly day after day. Again the lawns between the houses became miniature lakes, where the frogs took up residence and commenced their nocturnal croaking, keeping her awake. Keeping her company, for Ryle was away on another temporary assignment.

And the old struggle inside her started up again, the yearning for the companionship of a drink. Some days she was able to ignore it. But the days she wasn't, when the yearning became a craving, a feeling that she had to have a drink, she went for the rum bottle which she'd hidden again in the linen closet, alternating between the blessed relaxation it brought her and hating herself for being so weak she needed this crutch.

TWENTY-TWO

Although Maruja's charm had managed to change Chacari's opinion of Sarita, there were still a few, especially Sugar Dalhart, who refused to regard Sarita as anyone but a former prostitute. John Maguire's transfer to Puerto La Cruz, therefore, brought him the one thing he wanted more than anything else for Sarita, escape from her past. While this was partially brought about by the physical set-up of El Gato, resembling more an international suburb than an isolated oil camp, it was firmly cemented by his friendship with the Schlumberger Company district manager, Jean Claude deMornay. If Jean Claude and his wife, Nicole, heard any rumors about Sarita's past life, they never acknowledged them. They were a well travelled couple who were much too cosmopolitan to give credence to camp gossip. In John Maguire they found someone with a sparkling wit and the ability to talk on just about any subject, while Sarita's serenity and quick intelligence were an absolute delight. Especially to Nicole who was a leading figure in local society. Anyone she took under her wing was assured of instant social acceptance.

Invitations to her parties were eagerly anticipated, especially the annual Bastille Day celebration on July 14th. This year Nicole outdid herself. Not only because the food was far superior to anything served by the other women, but she'd managed to find a trio of musicians who seldom took breaks and kept things going at a lively pace.

John appeared to be having such a wonderful time Sarita hated to spoil his fun. She was seven months pregnant and bothered by constant back pains, which only seemed to be alleviated when she was flat on her back. Slipping away from the festivities she asked Nicole if she could lie down in the guest bedroom. Which is where John found her an hour later.

"Come on Soogie, I'm taking you home," he said planting a kiss in her hair. "This is no fun for you."

"*No importa*," she protested. "It really doesn't matter to me if I lie down here or at home. You're having such a good time."

"Not if you're not around. I think every battleax in Puerto La Cruz has come up and asked me to dance. If nothing else, you have to rescue me," he grinned as he helped her up. "It's been a great party, but I'm ready to call it a night, Soogie."

Because the doctor had encouraged Sarita to do more walking, they hadn't taken their car to the party. As they walked leisurely homeward holding hands, he thought to himself how everything was falling into place now. Sarita was no longer ostracized as she had been in Chacari; in another year he would be able to swing things financially so he could start his trucking business and Sarita had finally gotten over her fear of getting pregnant. In two months the first of their children would be born. He was feeling so good about life in general that when they turned the corner to their street, he didn't notice the bedrooms of their house were ablaze with lights.

But Sarita did. "I don't remember leaving all those lights on," she remarked.

"Neither do I," he replied, his mellowness immediately evaporating. "Only the small light in the living room."

There had been a rash of robberies in camp the last month. Because the camp belonged to no special oil company, but had been leased out to various companies for their employees, security was lax. Sometimes the guardhouse was manned, other times it was vacant, a condition many felt was an open invitation to thieves. Requests to the Caracas offices of the various companies to beef up security had been lost in the red tape of the companies' indecision as to whose responsibility it was. The police had been unsuccessful in tracing any of the stolen articles, and everyone was convinced there was collusion between the authorities and the thieves. Two weeks ago when the Maguires went out to dinner with the deMornays, their house had been broken into and a camera was stolen. Now seeing the lights on they wondered if they were being robbed again. Despite Maguire's company car parked in the driveway, the thief seemed to know they were out. Remembering the theft of their camera, John swore profusely, "I'm going to get that son of a bitch."

"*Ay, no Juan*," she protested. "It could be dangerous. Let's call the police."

"The police! What a crock of shit." He was convinced the police were looking the other way. "A lot good that will do. No, I'm going to take care of the bastard myself." He went over to the car and unlocking it, reached under the driver's seat where he kept a gun under the floorboard.

"If you don't want to call the police, let's go back to the party and get help," Sarita pleaded with him.

"And what happens when we leave? The damn bastard could slip away." His face, which always got red when his temper was rising, became covered with splotches. "No, Soogie, I'm not leaving," he said stubbornly. "Besides, what could happen? I have a gun."

"Then I'll go back to the deMornays," she said. "But please *querido*, please wait until I come back with some help."

He looked at her protruding stomach and his first thought was to get her away from the house. "Yes Soogie, you go back to the party."

"No," she shook her head. "Darling, I know your temper. I don't want you going into the house. Promise me you will wait until I come back with help." She was close to tears she was so frightened.

"You want to help?" he snapped irritably. "Then get going. The sooner you go, the sooner we're going to nail this bastard." Whether she stayed or left, she knew he was going in. He thinks he's safe, she thought in despair, just because he has that gun. She started to run, but her wedgie shoes didn't give her much support and she turned an ankle. The sharp and persistent pain slowed her down. But knowing her husband was determined to corner the thief made her push away the pain and she started running again. Each house she passed she hoped to find someone home, but they were all empty, for everyone was at the Bastille Day party.

Maguire silently made his way to the side of the house. He saw that entry had been made through the bathroom window, for the screen had been cut and was dangling against the side of the house. The wooden jalousies, pried loose with a crowbar, lay scattered in pieces on the grass. He pulled himself up and looked into the bathroom. He couldn't see anyone, but he heard movement in the master bedroom. Crawling through the window, he slipped quietly into the bathroom. Through the half open door which connected the bathroom and bedroom, he could see the open closet reflected in the dresser mirror. Angrily he watched his slide projector being taken down from the shelf.

"¡*Manos arriba*!" he called out, pointing the gun in the direction of the closet. He heard the slide projector fall to the floor when he surprised the thief. Realizing it was probably smashed beyond repair infuriated him even more.

"I said, get your hands up," he bellowed, his face becoming beet red. "And come out of the closet — now!"

He stepped into the bedroom, the gun pointed in the direction of the closet. A young boy no more than ten years old walked slowly out of the closet. And because Maguire was concentrating on him, he didn't see the other occupant of the closet. Or the knife which flew through the air. When it pierced his chest, he dropped to the terrazo floor watching impotently as both thieves darted from the room.

The lousy bastards, he cried out in pain, more furious than afraid. Angry because the thieves had gotten away and he hadn't been able to nail them. He faded in and out of consciousness, his mind jumping around. And for some inexplicable reason he found himself remembering an incident during the war when he hitched a ride with a jeep full of other sailors. He couldn't remember the name of the island. What he did remember was they were headed for a depot where it was rumored a dozen cases of whiskey had been found. He was hanging on the back of the jeep and when the vehicle hit a pot hole in the dirt road, his Zippo lighter was knocked out of his hand. In lunging for it, he lost his balance and fell off. Cursing his bad luck he saw the jeep continue down the road without him, and then recoiled in horror when it hit a land mine and exploded. That's what he thought of lying on the floor of his bedroom. How he'd escaped death on a remote Pacific island. And now it was waiting just around the corner for him in a Venezuelan oilcamp.

Sarita's face was swimming in front of him and he found it difficult to focus his eyes.

"Soogie," he called out feebly. He wondered if she could hear him. "Guess I really screwed up this time." He knew he was dying and he had to make her understand. He tried to reach up and bring her closer to him. "When you find out, honey, remember the only reason I did it was because I was afraid of losing you." Every word was an effort, his breathing coming out strained and hollow. "I was trying to get it fixed, Soogie."

Sarita watched her husband slip away, her name the last word on his lips. She didn't quite understand what he tried to tell her and thought he was explaining the reason he had gone in after the thief without waiting for her to bring back help. It wasn't until John's brother·came to Venezuela to bring his body back to the States that she learned what he really meant.

She threw herself on him, his blood smearing her face and hair, trying to will him back, refusing to let him go. Sorrowfully she felt the warmth leave his body, that blessed warmth which had held her close to him every night. She clung to him, still not believing he had been taken away from her. When Jean Claude pulled her up gently, motioning to his wife to help him, she walked unsteadily with Nicole to the bathroom, hating to leave her *querido*. And she sat mutely when Nicole pulled off her red stained dress and washed her face clean of John's blood.

Sarita didn't cry, she was too stunned. But she numbly realized she had just lost the only man who'd ever given dignity to her life. He'd been everything to her — lover, mentor, husband, mother and father. And now he was gone. All because of his quick temper. And her worst fear had been realized, she was alone and pregnant. Grief flooded her body. But she still didn't cry. She wanted to, she wanted so desperately to give voice to her sorrow. But her first thought was for the child she was carrying. She mustn't do anything which would hurt or affect its wellbeing. She mustn't cry, she whispered to herself, or else the child in her womb would also cry.

She asked Nicole to bring her clean clothes, and after she changed, she told Nicole she wanted to be alone. She walked slowly out the front door, down the steps and into the front yard. When she got to the *Araguaney* tree heavy now with yellow blossoms, the moonlight filtering through its limbs in a lacelike pattern, she remembered another time when the tree had been bursting with life. And how she gathered up the flowers which lay like a golden carpet on the grass and placing them in pillowcases, brought them into the house. Where she spilled them out on the floor of the porch forming a thick bed. A bed where she and John made love under the stars.

Now standing under the tree she said goodbye to him. Whispering sweet endearments, she told John how much she loved him. And thanked him for the changes he had made in her life, the world he had opened up to her. She especially remembered his quick wit which made everything such fun. She brought her wrists up to her face, inhaling his after shave lotion, for she'd splashed a few drops onto her wrists, feeling this would keep him close to her. And then the realization that she would never see him again made something inside her snap.

"*¡Basta, ya!*" she cried out angrily to the night, "enough, no more!" Her mind ran around in circles and it always came back to the same thought. Fate had wanted a victim from each house on that corner in Chacari. First Sheila, then Maruja, and now her *querido*. *El destino*, she sighed.

Then to ward off her sad thoughts, Sarita began to sing the Latin American songs John loved so much. It was the only way she knew to express her longing for him. The Mexican *mariachis* and *rancheros*, the Cuban *guarachas* and the Venezuelan *joropos* — she sang them all. So softly only he could hear them. As the trade winds off the Caribbean rustled through the palm trees, Sarita said goodbye to John Maguire. But when she came to his favorite, *Adiós Maraquita Linda*, she couldn't go on. For it reminded her too much of another occasion when his parting words to her had been "*Adiós Sarita Linda*". Then it had been a temporary thing, for within hours he'd returned to Hortensia's and asked her to marry him. Now, he would never return.

Six weeks later when she gave birth to a boy, the first thing she did was look into his eyes. Brown like hers, they showed no sadness, and for this she was grateful. You will be a happy baby and grow up to be a good man just like your father, she vowed to John, Jr., for you were conceived in great love. As she held him in her arms, she saw that like her he had a cleft in his chin, just as John wanted. But the rest of him was pure Maguire. Dirty blond hair, a high forehead and fair skin. She looked down at Johnny and smiled. Her *querido* had left so much of himself with her. That's what she must always remember whenever she was overcome with loneliness, for already it had become her constant companion.

TWENTY-THREE

Caracas - 1969

The last time Cathleen woke up with this premonition was the day of President Kennedy's assassination. Now the same uneasiness hovered around her. She kept busy, hoping to convince herself if she didn't dwell on it, this sense of foreboding would disappear. Since Sarita and Johnny were arriving today to spend the Christmas holidays, she had plenty to do.

It seemed only yesterday she'd held Johnny in her arms at his christening, and now he was grown up and in college. And always starved for Venezuelan food whenever he got back from the States. She checked with the cook and after satisfying herself they wouldn't run out of *hallacas*, went out to the garden to select the flowers she wanted for the floral arrangements. Then determined to remain occupied, for the feeling persisted, she went upstairs to her mauve and white bedroom and tried on one dress after another, finally deciding on a yellow silk one with large white polka dots. Only to change her mind for something more casual. She turned on the radio hoping for the distraction of music and was grateful when the lilting strains of Tchaikovsky's *Capriccio Italienne* filled the air. Then the program was interrupted by an announcement that a VIASA plane from New Orleans had been hijacked.

Mother of God, it can't be Johnny's plane. Her hands shook as she struggled to pull the Peruvian silver belt through the loops of her designer pants. The announcer's detailed report dashed whatever hope she had. The premonition she awakened with hadn't been a fluke. It's going to start all over again, she thought in despair, all the bad luck which plagued our lives in the past.

She had to go to the airport to be with Sarita who was meeting

295

Johnny's flight. After buttoning the turquoise silk blouse, she reached for her leather shoulder bag and ran down the stairs of the large Spanish style house. Out the patio door, over the small bridge which spanned a shallow pond in the garden and into the garage. Damn, she fumed, the Cadillac wasn't there. She'd forgotten the chauffeur had gone for new license plates. Just as well, she consoled herself, one thing Julio couldn't do was move fast. She dashed across the garage to her green Bentley and quickly maneuvered it down the hill of the driveway, through the grounds of the *Valle Arriba* Country Club and on to the *Baruta-Caracas Autopista*, hoping a miracle might happen and there wouldn't be too much traffic.

What wishful thinking, the Bentley crawled along at a snail's pace. Several times when someone cut in front of her, she wanted to bang on the side of the car door and yell out in typical Venezuelan fashion, "*idiota*" or "*burro*," but ever since *la violencia* began and a lot of people started packing a gun, she was reluctant to engage in what had once been a favorite Venezuelan sport. The damn terrorists have taken all the fun out of driving in this country, she sighed. In the old days it was a challenge to see what choice insults one could think up. Why, it was practically an art form.

She wondered if *FALN (Fuerzas Armadas Liberación Nacional)* was behind the hijacking. The 60s had become a time of ferment and revolt, not only in the States, but in Venezuela as well, thanks to Fidel Castro who was attempting to export his revolution to Latin America. The Venezuelan terrorists, some highly educated and wealthy — doctors, engineers and lawyers, legislators — had kidnapped the head of Corning Glass, and bombed one of the oil companies' pipelines. Not content with that, they had formed guerrilla groups near some of the oil camps, so the armed forces had been called in to stop their attempts to sabotage the oil wells.

Martial law became almost a way of life in parts of Venezuela. She remembered taking Nena to the movies one afternoon and sitting behind the U.S. Military attaché, who had gun toting bodyguards on either side of him.

Maruja's family suffered another tragedy when her brother, Alejo, a longtime Communist, and one of the leaders of FALN, acknowledged his politics. How fortunate Misia Isabel is no longer here, Cathleen thought gratefully, at least she was spared that heartache. And the added one of

Alejo being gunned to death. She saw an opening in the traffic and cut through. Once she got out of the city and on the *autopista* to the airport, she knew traffic would move faster. She didn't know what she could do for Sarita once she got to the airport, but she couldn't let her wait alone for news of the hijacked plane. In the back of her mind was the fear that like his father, Johnny's life would be snuffed out by some stupid and senseless act.

When she arrived at the airport in Maiquetía she ran into the terminal, ignoring the *piropos*, the flowery compliments which slid off the lips of the Venezuelan men so effortlessly. Ordinarily she was amused by this custom, but not today.

"I came as soon as I heard," Cathleen said throwing her arms around Sarita. "They'll put the plane down in Havana," she reassured her. "Then in no time it'll take off and land here."

"*Claro que sí, chica,*" Sarita agreed. "That's the only reason these hijackings take place, some disgruntled Cuban."

How bravely we talk, Cathleen thought, when we don't really know who is behind the hijacking or where the plane is going. "Fred is here," Sarita said pointing to a huge bear of a man pacing up and down in front of the VIASA counter.

"But Nena's not due until tomorrow," Cathleen cried out. Fred turned and walked slowly in their direction.

"There was a cancellation so Nena took this plane," his eyes heavy with the anxiety he felt for his daughter.

Cathleen reached up to kiss him on the cheek, then threw her arms around his neck, wanting to comfort him. And at the same time wanting to be comforted. Be reassured this was only a bad dream which would disappear with the day's first light. That Nena, who had become like a daughter to her, wasn't on the hijacked plane along with Johnny.

"They want us to go in the VIP lounge," Fran Hardesty tugged at her husband's arm, her voice reflecting more annoyance than anxiety. Then acknowledging Cathleen's presence, she gave her a frosty smile. "How nice to see you again."

"Not under these conditions," Cathleen snapped, making no attempt to mask her dislike of Fran.

They walked into the exclusive lounge set aside to give privacy to the families of the hijack victims. The long vigil began, interrupted an hour later when the soap opera churning away on the TV was blacked out by a news bulletin. The hijacked plane now in Curaçao flashed across the TV screen and they learned that the hijackers were Venezuelan terrorists, the FALN. Six hostages had been taken — the president of Texaco Oil, his wife and two daughters, John Maguire, Jr. and Nena Hardesty.

Fred stared at the TV in horror. If any harm came to his daughter, he knew he wouldn't be able to handle it. Don't take Nena away from me too, he prayed. Memories of the plane crash which claimed Maruja flashed before him.

Fran, watching Fred, knew he was miles away from her. He's gone off to that other world in his mind, she fumed, where no one else can enter. He'll never admit it, but Nena is his favorite. Even though she'd given Fred two sons, Nena would always be the one he cared for the most.

Sarita's usual serenity deserted her. Apprehensive about what the hijackers could do to her son, she also experienced anxiety that the temper Johnny inherited from his father would make him do something rash and hasty. She struggled to push aside her fear. If I remain calm, she reassured herself, Johnny will too. I refused to cry when I was pregnant with him, even though I had such good reason. I can't give into panic now.

The craving for a drink nagged at Cathleen. It never leaves you, she thought nervously. One little shot of Scotch, or even a beer. It would help her so much. But of course it wouldn't. She bought a pack of cigarettes hoping it would take the edge off her anxiety. Around and around her mind went. Hostages, what an awful sound it had. The hijackers want something which they haven't disclosed yet, and they're going to use those kids as bait. Cathleen felt close to tears. And so frightened she could scream.

"You've been trying to get Johnny and Nena together for years now," Sarita said, smiling wanly at her. "The least you could have done was plan it a little better."

How like her to inject a little humor into a bad situation, Cathleen thought, giving Sarita's hand a squeeze. She's dying inside. I know that, but no one else would ever guess. Such is the inner strength she possesses, a strength which has enabled her to overcome a lifetime of obstacles. Why, she looks the same as she did when I first met her over twenty years ago in Chacari, Cathleen realized. She's hardly aged at all.

Her eyes turned toward Fred. Over the years he had become a subdued man. So different from the Fred she first knew in the oilfields, the fun loving young engineer who threw her over his shoulders in that wild jitterbug. In love with life before fate made him an old man overnight. When his high pitched, infectious laughter could fill up a room.

Her eyes travelled to Fran, taking in the dissatisfaction in her long, horselike face, the droop in her lips. She's thinking of Maruja. Cathleen would bet money on it. Maruja who will always stand between her and Fred. Maruja who enchanted us all.

And me, I guess I've changed too in the past twenty years. Her hands reached up to her short hair and remembering the reason she cut it, the old feeling of anger crept back into her heart. Mustn't think about it, she reminded herself. It's water under the bridge. Her thoughts returned to Johnny and Nena. Is there some sort of curse hanging over us, like the Kennedys, she wondered? One damn tragedy after another. Ah, don't think about it, she urged herself, because if you dwell on something long enough, it just might happen.

And in her effort to put the hijacking out of her mind, her thoughts turned to Ryle. She wouldn't be here today if it weren't for him. Looking around the lounge she noticed the Christmas decorations. The same time of the year, she realized, give or take a few weeks. When New York was ablaze with holiday glitter, and Ella Logan's big hit was *If This Isn't Love*. For a few moments her face softened with the memory of ice skating with Ryle under the huge Christmas tree in Rockefeller Plaza. Then she pushed it aside. She would drown in a sea of memories if she kept this up.

Her eyes looked with concern toward Fred. Of the two kids, Nena was the more vulnerable one. Despite Johnny's volatile temper, he had a lot of Sarita's inner strength in him. Cathleen sighed to herself remembering all the circumstances of Nena's life which had made her someone starved for love, and the more she searched for it, the more disappointment she encountered. But then we're all vulnerable when it comes to love, she reminded herself. She certainly was no exception, especially the year Sheila died. When she wasn't able to handle things and taking a drink was the only way she could cope with life.

The drinking stopped being a temptation when she and Ryle returned to Venezuela for their second contract. Not only was she full of hope she would become pregnant, but they'd been transferred from Chacari to Tucupido. Even having to live in town because there wasn't enough camp housing didn't dampen their enthusiasm. Ryle because he'd been promoted to chief geologist for the district, and Cathleen because she loved town life, despite its lack of conveniences.

Living in town meant no electricity during the day for the lights came on at six in the evening and went off at six the next morning. But there was a small 2-1/2 KW light plant in the back yard, although she seldom used it. Not only because the noise was deafening, it sounded like she was living under an airplane, but she had a difficult time getting it started. She soon got used to doing without electricity during the day. The maid heated the iron on a charcoal brazier, and Cathleen learned to keep the kerosene level in the refrigerator high enough so it wouldn't stop cooling and spoil their food.

The camp people looked down on the town people because they didn't have the conveniences of camp life, but she felt no hardship. After the identical little boxes in Chacari, she was thrilled with the house assigned them. It had an airy screened porch, at the end of which was the dining room and around the corner the kitchen, also screened. Although the living room was enormous, it was seldom used because the porch was so much cooler. The location of the master bedroom at one end of the house and the bathroom at the other end was the only oddity in its floor plan. Coral colored bougainvillea climbed over the front yard fence, while the back yard had shade trees and shrubs. No grass though. That was the first thing she noticed — the hard, brown dirt which nurtured everything except a lawn. The back yard also contained the light plant and the water tower which was replenished daily by a water truck, except on weekends when they learned to ration their showers.

What took some adjustment were the bats. The house had mud walls slapped on a framework of sticks and leaves which had been hardened to a dull finish by the sun and then painted a soft shade of yellow. Because the roof was thatched, the bats found it an attractive nest, and at night she and Ryle heard them moving above and screeching to each other. She was determined not to dwell on them, until the night one of the bats died and fell through the thatched ceiling onto their bed.

But she wouldn't trade her privacy in town when housing became available in camp, not even when a new camp with a bowling alley and swimming pool was built. She could walk to the *farmacia* and there was a general store where she could buy anything from dress material to hard, rock candy. There was even a dentist who countered the absence of electricity with a foot powered drill. The town had a church with a resident priest, but attending Mass held a few surprises. A brass band marched up the aisle with a great deal of flourish just after the Consecration and the priest had a notice on the church door that unless women wore long sleeved dresses he wouldn't serve them Holy Communion.

Gradually as she got to know the Americans in town she learned some of them preferred overseas life, hating to return to the States for vacation. At first she thought they'd missed too many boats, but as she nested into town life and her marriage became a constant source of contentment, she began to think of Tucupido as 'home'. When Ryle came home at night and found her reading in the *chinchorro*, the hammock they hung in the porch, he'd slip in next to her. It was a *matrimonio*, a double sized one, and they'd turn out the lights and spend hours rediscovering their love for each other. They never had to worry about neighbors, for no one dropped in uninvited as they did in camp. And because of this privacy, Cathleen looked forward to parties with anticipation instead of regarding them as a chore.

She'd never been happier. Later when her life was filled with wealth and position, she remembered the simple life she knew in Tucupido and wished she could somehow return. Go back again to the time when she and Ryle were expecting every month she would become pregnant. And his disposition was more consistent because he had ascended another rung of the Palm Oil ladder.

She'd only been there a few months when the news of John Maguire's murder came over the camp radio. Her first thought was that Sarita needed her. She threw a few things in an overnight case. It was a long trip to Puerto La Cruz, one that she'd never driven alone. But she figured if she left now, she'd get there by early evening. As she got into the Chevy, Ryle drove up.

"Oh honey," she said throwing herself into his arms. "How awful about John. I still can't believe it. Poor Sarita."

"Just where are you going?" he asked noticing her overnight bag.

"Puerto La Cruz to be with Sarita." Although she hadn't seen her since their return to Venezuela, they'd kept in touch with long letters.

"Are you crazy?" he demanded. "It's a long trip over lousy roads."

"I have to," she replied. "Sarita is alone, with no family." He doesn't realize this is what people do at a time like this, she reminded herself. Having gone to Oklahoma to meet his parents she understood even more how deficient his family life had been. If you could call them a family. His father barely spoke, while his mother never stopped talking because the poor woman was so lonely. They seemed to have no circle of friends. And such a depressing house. Despite the money Ryle sent to his mother every month, it was run down and shabby looking.

"She never spends it," Ryle said shrugging his shoulders in frustration. "She did without for so long maybe she's hoarding it. What can I do? Except keep sending it, so at least I know it's there." Oh no, he just can't understand about people reaching out to each other, not the way he grew up.

"She must have someone down there," he said stubbornly. "I don't want you going, Cathleen." As she saw the struggle going on in his face, she sensed his objections. He hasn't changed, she realized sadly, he's still all wrapped up in what people will think.

"Why?" she cried out to him. "Because it might hurt your image, Mr. Chief Geologist. Where's your compassion?" She got in the car, slamming the door shut and throwing the gears into reverse. And then her foot shot down on the brakes. "Did it ever occur to you that people get ahead in this company without worrying about their image?" she called out the window not caring who heard her. "John got promoted despite people like you thinking his wife wasn't an asset to him." And then she burst into tears. "Go to hell, Ryle, you and your damn job." The tires squealed, leaving him in a cloud of dust.

He was right about the roads though. There were times on the long, bumpy road to Puerto La Cruz when she wondered about her wisdom in making the trip alone. If she blew a tire, she hadn't the faintest idea how to change it. But she was too upset to dwell on any probable mishaps, still finding it difficult to believe John was dead. She turned on the radio and although it was full of static she kept it on, needing reassurance that life was continuing.

When she got to the funeral parlor she found Sarita sitting alone in front of John's coffin. Cathleen put her arms around Sarita and because she didn't know what to say, the two of them sat in a silent embrace. For a moment Cathleen wondered if the three couples who had lived next door to each other in Chacari were under a curse. Sheila, Maruja, and now John. But she pushed the thought aside. This is the way life is, she reassured herself. Some people sail through it leading charmed lives, while others seem to meet every misfortune the others have escaped. "In an hour they'll take John to church for the Mass," Sarita said softly. "Then my *querido* will be laid to rest."

But John Maguire was never buried, for his brother was expected in a few days to bring his body back to the States. This presented a problem since embalming wasn't practiced in Venezuela, burial being the same day, until Gulf Oil Co. offered the deep freeze in their commissary. It was the only time Sarita showed any emotion. She became extremely upset because John would be denied the dignity of a funeral and burial. That after the Mass, where she sat stoically with Cathleen, his body would be taken from her to be put in a freezer.

"Maybe this place has too many memories, Sarita," Cathleen said as she drove them from the church to Nicole and Jean Claude's house. "Why don't you come back to Tucupido with me for a few weeks?" Sarita shook her head, asking Cathleen to drive her to the beach.

"The ocean will always have a special meaning for me," she murmured, lost in her memories of meeting John and falling in love with him. "You know," she went on, "I still have the first bathing suit he bought me. It's turned yellow and lost its shape, but I can't bear to part with it."

"What are you going to do?" Cathleen asked hesitantly. Aside from showing emotion when John's body was taken to the Gulf Oil commissary, Sarita's face was like a mask. "Are you going back to the life you knew before you met John?" She knew it was a very indelicate question, but she was worried that because Sarita was alone and had no family, she would return to her former life.

"No," Sarita replied shaking her head. "The ladies took me in when I was homeless and for that I will be forever grateful. I'm proud they were my friends." She looked out to the ocean as if she were searching for someone, then she sat down on the sand, indifferent that it clung to her black stockings and shoes, or her black dress had become matted with it. "Now I have a child to think about," she sighed. Then the weariness left her face and her eyes became alert and determined. "You know that *maquinita* of yours, I'd like you to teach me how to use it."

Cathleen look at her blankly. "What little machine?"

"The one which writes letters," Sarita replied impatiently.

"Oh, you mean the typewriter."

"*Sí, eso*," Sarita nodded her head. "As soon as the baby is born, I have to get a job."

"Of course I will," Cathleen replied. "You could get a job any place because you're bilingual. Why, all the oil companies would be standing in line to hire you."

"No," Sarita shook her head. "Not the oil companies. John had this dream of starting his own trucking business. He said a lot of money could be made hauling materials to the oil camps. Well, this morning at the funeral parlor when Bustillo, the trucker came to pay his condolences, he asked if there was anything he could do. When I told him he could give me a job, he replied, 'of course'. But you know how we Venezuelans are. We say yes to everyone whether we mean it or not because we think it would be impolite to do otherwise, and we don't want to hurt anyone's feelings."

"Well, I mean to hold him to that," she continued. "He would give me a job out of respect to my husband who was very well liked by my countrymen. But I have to have something to offer. So now before the baby is born, if you could teach me how to type, then I wouldn't be accepting charity from Bustillo."

She stared out at the ocean again, lost in her thoughts. Then turning abruptly around she burst out, "John gave me so much. Why, do you know the day we were married, I didn't even know how to write? He took my hand and guided the pen over the paper!" And then she fell silent again. He did a lot more than that, she murmured to herself, he gave her a birth date and parents, then a home and security. But most of all, love.

When Cathleen took Sarita house hunting in the *barrios* the next day, she was appalled. "You can't live here," she protested looking disdainfully around the slum, aware more than ever just how much Sarita had lost.

"And why not?" Sarita replied. "Didn't I know poverty like this before I met John? It's just different from what you're used to, you being a *musiua*." Cathleen stiffened when Sarita called her an outsider for it made her realize they would be living in different worlds now.

"But you don't have to live in a place like this," Cathleen insisted. "You have John's life insurance from Palm Oil."

Sarita shook her head. "I can't touch it. That's to buy my first truck when I start the business."

But the trucks were denied her when John's brother arrived from the States. Seeing him, the both of them experienced a moment of shock. Although taller and heavier, he bore such a strong resemblance to John it was unnerving. Sarita offered him coffee and the three of them talked for a few minutes.

"I don't know what kind of laws they got in this country," George Maguire said slowly. "Maybe it's different down here," he paused and they could see he was uncomfortable about something. "Maybe Jack could marry you here."

"I don't understand what you mean," Sarita replied, a frown creasing her forehead.

"Well, you see, Jack . . . ." They noticed that he always called him Jack. He hesitated, squirming in his chair and fanning himself with his hat. "See, Jack's got a wife back in Pittsburgh." Sarita didn't say a word, but her hands flew to her stomach in a protective gesture. Cathleen's hands shook as she reached for a cigarette and her Zippo lighter crashed on the cement floor.

"Of course, Sally's not much of a wife," he went on. "She's been in and out of institutions for years now. More in than out when you come down to it." His words had a sad tone to them. "Oh, Sally was so vivacious and sparkling when he first met her. He couldn't resist her. Hell, none of us could, the whole family fell in love with her. Then when she got so bad and he had to commit her, he went through a real bad time thinking he was to blame. Until the doctors assured him that she was gone long before she met up with Jack. She's what they call a manic depressive."

"Does anyone in the company know this?" Cathleen asked him.

"No," he replied in the same husky voice as John's. "When he applied for the job he put down he was single. I think I know why. See, he was trying to start over, make a new life for himself. And he really was single in a way. Sally could never be a wife to him anymore."

Sarita understood now what John had been trying to tell her before he died. He told her it was because he was afraid of losing her, but she knew he married her to give her the protection of his name.

"The last time he came up to the States," George continued, "it was a real hurried trip, just a week or so. He was running from one lawyer to another, but they all told him the same thing. That it's not easy to divorce someone who can't contest it. And because of her condition, he'd have to stay up there a long time to see it through." Sarita remembered the trip. He'd told her it was family business.

As George spoke to Sarita he began to understand the reason for his brother's actions. When he first met her and saw the shabbiness of her surroundings, his first thought was his brother had really gone native. That like the wife he'd left behind in Pittsburgh, Jack had flipped out. But the more he talked with Sarita, the more impressed he was with her. The shock of her dark skin was forgotten and brushed aside by her dignity. And he stopped questioning why his brother had committed bigamy. This one took away the hurt, he realized, this one made him feel like a whole man again.

"George, the only thing I have to give our child is his name. Please don't tell me I can't," Sarita pleaded with him.

"Well, maybe you can," he said trying to give her some hope. "Maybe the law is different down here."

"No," she shook her head sadly. "Bigamy is bigamy. All I'm asking is that you don't say anything to the company."

"But I've got to," he protested. "I sure don't want to, but I don't have any choice. See, when Jack married you, he put you down as the beneficiary of his insurance. But that money belongs to Sally, to take care of her. Every month Jack sent me a check for her. But now that he's gone, what am I doing to do?" The perspiration trickled down his face and taking off his hat, he mopped himself with a soggy handkerchief.

"I've got a wife and family. I don't have the kind of money that's needed for Sally's trips in and out of the hospital. That was one of the reasons he came down here besides wanting to make a new life. It was for the money, so he wouldn't have to put her in a state facility." He shook his head vehemently. "You wouldn't put a dog in one of those state mental hospitals."

Sarita slumped in her chair. To find out she wasn't married, but had wound up like her mother, pregnant and no man around to give her child his name was the culmination of all her worst fears. She had succeeded in not giving into the grief of her husband's death. For her child's sake, she had refused to shed tears. But now she felt completely wiped out.

"I don't care about the money," she pleaded with George. "You can have it all." She'd manage to take care of herself and the baby, somehow she would save to buy the trucks. "I only care that no one finds out about his first marriage. Not for myself, I can live with it. But for his son, so he can grow up with his name and the knowledge that his parents were married," she cried out. This meant so much to her, and to be denied it was more than she could bear. She got up and walked awkwardly to the small table to get their wedding picture.

"How am I going to get the insurance unless I speak up?" George argued. Oh Jack, he thought looking at the picture Sarita thrust into his hands, you poor bastard. If only you hadn't let that quick temper do you in. He remembered sorrowfully all the times when his brother's short fuse had made him come out the loser. But none as final as this.

Cathleen had been a silent spectator through all this, but now she spoke up. "She'll send you the money as soon as she gets it. This way, you don't have to say anything, George. Sarita will still have her marriage and you'll get the money."

When she saw the hesitation in his face, she burst out, "You can trust her. Do you think your brother would have married her if he didn't have complete faith in her? Besides," she continued, furious that he had doubts about Sarita, "if you don't get the money, all you have to do is go to the company with proof of his first marriage." She hated to lash out at him for she understood that he was caught in the middle. But she couldn't stand by and allow the little Sarita had left be taken away from her.

"You've got all the cards, George," she said sharply. "Don't squeeze Sarita anymore than she already has been. Can't you see her back is up against a wall?"

Looking at Sarita and her swollen stomach, George was torn between the needs of his brother's two wives. He paced the floor, looking first at Sarita and then Cathleen. When he sat down, he took out his soggy handkerchief and mopped his wet head with it. Then finally he nodded his head. "It's a deal. As far as anyone here is concerned, he's married to Sarita."

"In my heart we were married," Sarita told him gratefully. "And I have our marriage certificate which says that we were. That's all I need for our child."

After George left Cathleen put her arms around Sarita, trying to give her some measure of comfort. "You two were so wonderful together. He loved you so much."

Sarita sat down trying to get into a comfortable position for her back continued to give her pain. "He didn't have to marry me, Cathleen. He could have just taken me to live with him as so many of the poorer people do here. In looking back, I can see that he moved mountains so we could get married. And before he died, he said he was trying to fix it. I can't ever blame him."

Cathleen nodded her head in sympathy. Then her practical nature took over. "How much money is there in your account?" Sarita looked at her blankly. She didn't know anything about bank accounts for John had always given her whatever money she needed.

"We've got to get you some money," Cathleen said with determination.

"I'll be getting his *Utilidades* at Christmas, plus two months salary now, so that will keep me awhile," Sarita replied. "And I plan to do sewing until I can go to work for Bustillo. But now you have to show me how to take care of a bank account, *chica*, write checks, things like that. John gave me such a wonderful education, but I'm so ignorant of everyday things. Imagine not knowing how to write a check!"

When she received the money, Cathleen took her to a bank and helped her open an account, showed her how to write checks and balance her checkbook, do bank reconciliations.

"What would I have done without you, Cathleen?" Sarita hugged her gratefully. "You've been like a sister to me."

"That's what sisters are for, Sarita," she replied kissing her goodbye, promising to come back when the baby was born.

She returned to Tucupido wondering what sort of reception she would get from Ryle. To her surprise he was very understanding. What she didn't know, because he never let on, was that someone of importance in Palm Oil had thoroughly approved of her actions. At the time of Maguire's murder, Wade Pearson, V. P. of Operations, was in Puerto La Cruz. When he went to the funeral parlor to pay his respects to Sarita, he was upset because no one from Palm Oil was there, for he thought of the company as one big family. When he found out Cathleen had driven all the way from Tucupido to be with Sarita, he was impressed. Just the kind of woman the company needs, he thought. In the course of his travels he contacted Ryle and complimented him on Cathleen. Wade Pearson had heard the rumors about Sarita, but as far as he was concerned they didn't amount to a hill of beans. Maguire had been one hell of a worker. And besides, he told Ryle, there were a few women in some of the camps who didn't have Sarita's reputation, but should have.

Six weeks later when Sarita went into labor, Ryle didn't object to Cathleen going to Puerto La Cruz. He arranged a ride with a toolpusher, but Wade Pearson was in Tucupido and gave her a ride on the company plane. After Johnny was born he brought flowers to Sarita, as well as a cash gift for the baby. Remembering how the women in Chacari had first scorned Sarita, Cathleen was very touched by his thoughtfulness.

"*Chica*, I think you have an admirer in Mr. Pearson," Sarita teased.

"That old coot! Why, he's old enough to be my father," Cathleen replied. "But he's a sweet old coot." She started to giggle, Sarita following suit, the two of them sounding like two adolescent schoolgirls. Laughing so hysterically that tears streamed from their eyes. Ah, we both needed this release from all the sorrow, Cathleen thought, life goes on and we have to keep in step with it.

TWENTY-FOUR

Caracas - 1969

Cathleen tried to make herself believe that Nena and Johnny being on a hijacked plane was only a dream and in a short time she would wake up in a cold sweat. Drenched, but relieved she had survived another nightmare. She reached for Sarita's hand and saw the half moons of her nails through the clear nail polish, felt her simple gold wedding ring. Glancing up she saw Fred run a hand through his white hair, his eyes reflecting his agony. Next to him Fran's hooded eyes displayed no emotion, her long nose accentuating her plain features. This was no dream.

But as much as her heart went out to Sarita and Fred, her main concern was Nena. The poor kid is probably scared out of her wits, she whispered to herself, she's had this terrible fear of flying ever since she found out how her mother died. Only by sheer will power has she been able to get on a plane. And now for this to happen. Be strong, my darling, she cried out to her. She searched her memory for the prayers which were once so much a part of her she could say them without thinking. Hail Mary, full of grace. She couldn't remember what came next. Feeling helpless she made up her own prayers, promising to go back to church, to say a rosary every day, if only Nena and Johnny would come to no harm. She tried to picture herself in the hijacked plane with Nena, to crawl inside her brain so she could give her words of love and encouragement.

....

In the hijacked VIASA plane Nena's mental state was just about what Cathleen imagined, except for spurts of hope brought on by the words of encouragement from the man sitting next to her. He was so confident the hijacking was just a temporary inconvenience there were moments when she began to believe he might be right. That once the FALN terrorists obtained the release of their leader from the *cárcel modelo* in Caracas, the plane would be on its way home to Venezuela. She was so grateful she wound up sitting next to him.

When she first got on the plane she couldn't help but notice him. Not only because he was tall, this being a must for her, but the part of his face not covered by large sun glasses revealed full and sensuous lips, while the cleft in his chin gave him an even sexier look. Dirty blond hair contrasted with his tanned complexion. He was so appealing she found herself stealing glances, hoping he would wake up. But the pillow he'd put behind his head indicated he intended to sleep away the trip to Caracas. Probably has a hangover, she thought. Either that or he's someone who does a lot of traveling and he's catching up on his shuteye. Maybe a travelling salesman who deals in oilfield equipment. For he definitely was an American. Then she decided he wasn't a salesman for he was dressed in jeans and a cotton plaid shirt. Ten to one he's a *petrolero* like her father. Or maybe, she debated with herself, he was a college student going home for the Christmas holidays.

She rather enjoyed trying to unravel his identity for it took her mind off her fear of planes. And somehow, this was really crazy she told herself, somehow she felt very safe sitting next to him. Isn't that wild, she giggled to herself. A stranger who hadn't said one word to her. She wondered if he was married. No ring on his finger, but of course that didn't mean a thing. It was when she was trying to decide if he looked like the married type (if there was such a thing) that she felt someone looking at her. Glancing up she saw a woman standing in the aisle, just a few feet from her. And what she saw startled and frightened her so much she had to bite her tongue to keep from screaming. For the woman's hands gripped a machine gun.

"You with the sunglasses," the woman snarled. "Take them off *ahora mismo*." She waved the machine gun in their direction. "And put those seats in an upright position right now." The menace in her voice was so unmistakable Nena's left hand trembled as she moved to adjust her seat. Which is when her hand collided with the blond stranger's hand.

She thought he'd been asleep, but she felt his hand take hold of hers and gently guide her fingers to the seat button. After the seats came up, his hand remained there for a few seconds giving her courage.

If only they would set this plane down in Cuba, she wanted to scream out, and let them go on their way. That's where all these hijackers wanted to go, wasn't it? *Ay Dios*, they could have made two round trips to Havana by now! What was taking them so long? "Cover the windows," the woman commanded.

"It's going to be okay," the man sitting next to her said softly. Encouraged by the strength in his voice she turned her head slightly to acknowledge his words.

"*Silencio*," the woman screamed. "No one is to talk. Eyes straight ahead."

Nena turned away with a sense of *dejà vu*. It wasn't the first time she'd seen his face. But where? In school, at a party? Or had she ever met him? Maybe she'd seen his picture in a magazine. Was he a TV or movie actor? Back and forth she went in her mind trying to remember. All the while looking straight ahead, afraid to move. And grateful she had this puzzle to keep her mind occupied, for she was frightened out of her skin, vowing to herself that once she got home, she'd never get on another plane. Flying was *mala suerte* in her family, just plain bad luck. Look what happened to her mother.

She felt her ears popping. Oh, thank God they were landing. Now maybe this nightmare would come to an end. But it wasn't Havana, only the airport in Curaçao. Not that they could see anything with the windows covered. They waited in the stifling plane where children cried out and people begged to go to the bathroom. Then after the plane was refueled, they were airborne again. The curtain separating First Class from Tourist was opened and the First Class section vacated.

"You," the woman with the machine gun prodded Nena. "Get up, and you too." She pointed the gun at the man sitting next to Nena. A couple with two teenage children joined them as they were roughly herded into the First Class Section.

"You Americans," a bearded man walked up and down the aisle, moving his machine gun every so often to punctuate his words, "are the guests of the *Fuerzas Armadas Liberación Nacional*. When our leader is released from the prison, then you'll be set free."

Ay Dios, Nena thought in panic, they're not Cubans, but the same group her uncle, Alejo, had belonged to before he was slain. How she loathed them and the terror they'd brought to Venezuela. Now she was their hostage. "*Pero Comandante*, I'm Venezuelan," the man sitting next to her declared.

The bearded hijacker glared at him. "You're not an American?"

"I'm Venezuelan, and American. I have dual citizenship." He showed them his blue American passport and the burgundy colored Venezuelan one.

"But he's still an American," the woman hijacker insisted. Nena found her voice, although she had to clear her throat several times before she could speak she was so frightened. "I'm also Venezuelan, and American."

"Your passports," the man screamed at Nena. "Give me your passports." Her hands were shaking so much she couldn't open her pocketbook and the female hijacker grabbed it, tearing the leather shoulder strap. When the contents spilled to the floor, she wondered if she should stoop to pick up everything. For she was hesitant to move, terrified their hostility might take the form of a bullet in her head.

"Pick everything up," the woman hijacker screamed, grabbing Nena by her long red hair and pushing her down to the floor.

"I know you're honorable people," the man whose identity still eluded her said in Spanish. "And your cause is just. This woman is so nervous. *Con su permiso*, I'd like to help her."

"Go ahead," the bearded terrorist snarled.

He helped Nena gather everything up, then handed her two passports to the hijackers.

"I told you to take only Americans," the bearded hijacker screamed at the woman. "And I told you to examine the passports first."

"Stop this fighting." A third man emerged briefly from the cockpit. "Get on with it." And then he returned to the front of the plane.

He's the one in charge, Nena realized, noticing how the other two deferred to him. The woman motioned for them to sit down. Gratefully Nena sunk into the seat. Again she sat quietly looking straight ahead, with only her thoughts to keep her company. So, he was the same as her, this blond whose face was so familiar, a mongrel. Oh, how that word used to anger her grandmother. But that's what they call me in school, she'd protested to Misia Isabel. A mongrel because she was half American. Something the Venezuelan girls never let her forget.

But then long before she left her grandparents' home for kindergarten, Nena knew she was different from the other children. Her cousins having heard the whispers of their parents were cruel in singling her out for their taunts, hinting that even before her mother died, she wasn't wanted. Hadn't her mother turned her back on her when she was born? Not wanting to hold her as any normal mother would. Why, her mother didn't even want to bring her back to the *campos petroleros*, but tried to dump Nena in Misia Isabel's lap. And would have succeeded if Nena's *gringo* father hadn't protested. They boasted of having parents, while Nena only had an absent father. When she fought back, pointing out she had grandparents who loved her very much, her cousins replied, so did they. But what about her mother? What about her father?

And look at her, they snickered, she doesn't even look like a Venezuelan. With those long legs and flaming red hair she looks like the rooster the cook fattens up every year to make the Christmas *hallacas*. All this because they were extremely jealous of the attention she received from Misia Isabel. It was no secret, though Misia Isabel tried to be impartial, that Nena was her favorite grandchild.

The first inkling Nena had of being different from the rest of her cousins occurred when she was around three years old. The family was returning from their annual Holy Week trek to the beach in Catia la Mar, where Misia Isabel and Don Eugenio had a seaside villa. Nena was glad to return to Caracas because the sun made her skin blister. While her cousins rode the waves or floated on old inner tubes, she had to stay in the shade of the palm trees playing with her pail and shovel. Only when the sun went down was she allowed to go in the water, but by then it was no fun because her cousins were inside and she had no one to play with. Feeling even more left out of things when she heard their laughter and shouts tumbling out from the villa onto the beach.

The white Cadillac hugged the highway as Claudio, the chauffeur, maneuvered the car around the curves of the narrow, winding road. Since the highway was a single lane each way, one never knew what was coming around the next bend. It was always exciting to barely graze the other cars. But Tulia, her six year old cousin, wasn't interested in the other cars. Popping a guava into her mouth, she sucked ferociously on the pulp, spitting out the seeds into her hand.

"Nena," she said softly, for she didn't want Misia Isabel to hear her, "why doesn't your father take you to live with him? Is it because he doesn't want you either?"

Nena thought for a moment. She knew a man came to visit her, brought her presents. But he was a shadowy figure whom she quickly forgot as soon as he left. As for her mother, hadn't her grandmother told her God had called *Mamita* Maruja to Heaven from where she looked down on Nena every day? But her father? She wasn't even sure what the word meant.

"¡*Epa*! Hey! Are you deaf or something?" Tulia poked Nena with a sticky, guava stained finger. "Why don't you live with your father?"

Confused, Nena pushed herself forward and tapped her grandmother who was in the front seat with the chauffeur. Ordinarily Misia Isabel sat in the back, except when they drove on the narrow, winding Caracas-Macuto road, claiming she could help Claudio spot any oncoming cars.

"*Mamita* Isabel," she asked, "what is a father?"

Misia Isabel groaned inwardly. A father, the child asked. The same as if she'd asked about an exotic flower. Or a strange constellation in the sky. It was said in such innocence Misia Isabel came close to tears. For a child not to know what a father was broke her heart.

"Tonight when I come to hear your prayers, I will explain. Right now let's see how clever you all are. Let's sing a song and I'll find out if you know all the words." She started singing. Of course they all knew the song. Hadn't they been singing it almost from the cradle when their nursemaids taught it to them?

Rice with milk
I'm going to marry
A cute little widow
From the Capital

Misia Isabel wondered what made Nena ask about her father. Looking in the rear view mirror, she spied the smug expression on Tulia's face. She must have put the idea in Nena's head. A busybody just like her mother Lourdes, Misia Isabel sighed to herself. She turned around and glared at Tulia, and Tulia seeing the angry look on Misia Isabel's face squirmed in her seat. That little snitch, Tulia thought maliciously, now she'd gone and made *abuela* angry with her. She plotted what she would do to the Rooster in revenge, for tormenting Nena was her favorite sport.

That night as Misia Isabel sat in the rocking chair holding Nena in her arms, she told her about Fred.

"You see my little treasure, when God called *Mamita* Maruja up to Him in Heaven, I was so sad and lonely. Your father wanted you to live with him, for he loves you very much. But I just couldn't bear to give you up because I too love you very much."

'Let Nena stay with me for a few years' I told him. And that's why you're here with me and not with him."

"But *Mamita* Isabel, what is a father?" Nena persisted. "You still haven't told me."

When Misia Isabel went into further explanations, she realized Nena was still confused for she thought her grandparents were her parents. And why shouldn't she? Weren't they the ones who were with her night and day? When she explained further that Nena's father came to see her from time to time, Nena said she remembered Fred, but only vaguely. To her he was just another relative.

As Misia Isabel rocked Nena in her lap, she wondered if she had done the right thing in keeping her. That despite Fran's total lack of interest in Nena, she would be better off with her father. The next time he and Fran came to Caracas, Misia Isabel was sorely tempted to turn Nena over to them. But she had only to look into Fran's face to see how unwanted Nena would be. Fran still only had room in her heart for Fred and their new baby boy. She certainly didn't want this child who was a reminder of her husband's first love.

But when Nena started school, Fred insisted it was time for Nena to spend her summer vacations with him. He'd been transferred from the Lagunillas District to an oil camp in Maracaibo. And while Maracaibo wasn't the big city Caracas was, he let Misia Isabel know it wasn't some primitive backwater as she was inclined to regard any place outside Caracas. It was the second largest city in Venezuela and even had a music conservatory. But aside from the amenities he could offer his daughter, he couldn't stand to be apart from her any longer. It was time she got to know him, and Nena spending her summer vacations in Maracaibo would be the start of her gradually living full time with him.

The first summer in Maracabo was quite an adjustment for her. Whenever her father was around, or Daddy as he told her to call him, Nena felt loved. Even though she had two half-brothers, Tommy and Fiver, Frederick Hardesty V, she didn't feel slighted. She was thrilled with the boys, ten months apart in age, and wanted to spend as much time as possible with them. But Fran resented her presence and was jealous of any affection the boys showed her. She was decent enough when Fred was around, but as soon as he left for work, Fran insisted she didn't want her hanging around the house. She had to go out and play with the girls. At first Nena resisted. It was her first time away from the security of her life in Caracas and her English wasn't good enough for her to feel at ease with the American girls. Eventually, though, she began to understand that Fran didn't want her around. She learned to stay with the neighboring children when her father was at work. But when she saw his car, which she looked for all morning, she knew it was safe to go home again.

It was an uneasy time for her. But whenever she felt that perhaps she really didn't belong with her father and his family, she had only to remember how he scooped her up into his arms when she came running into the house, lavishing affection on her. And the gentle patience he gave her, showing none of the brusqueness Fran displayed.

Nena knew Fran didn't like her and tried to exclude her from the family activities. One Sunday morning Fran brought the boys into bed with her and Fred. Nena, in her room at the other end of the house, heard the laughter and joking going back and forth between them. She left her room and headed towards their bedroom. Peeking through a crack of space, for the door wasn't completely shut, she saw the boys crawling over her father. She longed to be in there with them. It some ways it reminded her of when she went to the beach with her cousins and wasn't allowed to go into the water because the sun blistered her skin. She felt just as left out now. Pushing the door open she peered in, standing there with her hand twisting the material of her shorts. Fran looked up and stared at her with frosty eyes. But as intimidated as she was of Fran, she stood her ground. Surely her daddy would be glad to see her. When he did, he called out to her.

"Why, darlin', what are you doing standing out there like Little Orphan Annie? Get in here with us. These wildcats are plumb wearing me out." And he patted a place for her in bed. As she ran into the room and climbed on the bed, she felt Fran's eyes on her, the anger churning just below the surface. But Fred didn't notice. The boys howled with pleasure because they had a new body to crawl over.

Fiver's laughter, high pitched like his father's had been, squealed with delight when Nena joined them. He had his father's personality, or rather the personality Fred had before Maruja's death. And he also had his father's affectionate nature, for Fiver was forever hugging and kissing Fran. And now that Nena had joined the family, he wanted to include her in his outpouring of affection. Actually Fiver loved all females. He was friendly enough around men, but let a woman enter the room and he came to life. Nena was delighted with him. Now she felt as her cousins did with their brothers and sisters, only more so for she felt there was no one quite like Fiver.

By the time she returned to Caracas at the end of the summer, she was full of stories about her newfound family. Misia Isabel was pleased to see how Nena had blossomed, but she noticed she never mentioned Fran. When she questioned her, Nena's reply was 'Oh, she's okay.' But it was never said with enthusiasm. Which is exactly what Misia Isabel expected. It was for this reason Misia Isabel pleaded with Fred to let Nena stay with her a little longer. "Of course Nena would go there every summer," she assured him, "and most surely at Thanksgiving, a holiday which meant absolutely nothing to the Venezuelans. But for the time being, let her live in Caracas until she gets used to you and her other family."

What Nena didn't tell her grandmother was that despite Fran's hostility, she had another reason for liking Maracaibo. For the first time in her life she didn't stand out like a sore thumb because of her red hair and long legs. She was just another American girl.

But each summer became more difficult as Fran's antagonism grew. The summer Nena was ten the maid quit. And until Fran got another one, she made Nena's life miserable.

"Just because you have maids all around you in Caracas to pick up after you, don't think you can get away with murder around here," Fran informed her. "We're just regular people, not high society." She gave her a dust cloth and ordered her to clean all the bedrooms. "I don't suppose you even know what to do."

Nena really didn't. She had seen Aurelia, the inside maid for the second floor, do cleaning. When she was a little girl she used to follow her around, so she had some idea how it was done. But it was a game then, imitating Aurelia as she dusted and cleaned. She wanted so badly for Fran to like her. She used to lie awake at nights trying to figure out what she could do to gain her love. Maybe, she thought in desperation, this will do it. She put her heart and soul into dusting. She got down and cleaned all the table and chair legs, which the previous maid hadn't touched. She took her time, for that was the way Aurelia had worked. But even though she did a thorough job, Fran fussed at her for being so slow. Dusting faster, her hand knocked a china bell off Fran's desk. When it hit the terrazzo floor it broke into three even pieces and could have been easily mended. But Fran became hysterical and started screaming. It upset Nena for no one in Caracas had ever shouted at her. Not even her cousins who tormented her so endlessly. She covered her ears in fright and ran to her room. Fran went after her in hot pursuit. Picking Nena off the bed she proceeded to shake her violently, boxing her ears.

"Don't you ever put your hands over your ears when I'm talking to you," she commanded.

Nena stared up at her, fear written all over her face. She rubbed her ears and it was this gesture which made Fran stop. She saw the red marks on them, and her first reaction was she didn't want Fred to know she'd hit his daughter.

"Go wash your face," she told Nena. "And then comb your hair."

"Why don't you like me, Fran?" Nena asked in a pleading voice.

"Who said I didn't like you?" she sputtered. The American accent which she had cultivated so diligently disappeared and her European enunciation slipped back into her speech. "I'd do the same to the boys if they misbehaved." But Nena knew differently for she'd never seen Fran hit the boys.

That night she wanted to tell her father what happened, but she was afraid of another confrontation with Fran. Maybe she wouldn't be allowed to come to Maracaibo anymore. She didn't know what kind of power Fran had, but from all that she'd seen she knew Fran pretty much ran the show. Whatever she wanted, her father went along with it. If Nena could never be with her daddy or the boys again, she would die.

Besides, they might never take her to the States on vacation again. Last year they'd gone to Texas and she met her grandfather and aunts for the first time. The Hardestys laughed and joked a lot. There was so much good natured, boisterous talk going on it was hard to follow them at times, for they all talked at once. Fran ridiculed them, insisting she could never understand a word they said. But Nena adored them for they all had such a good time together.

When Fran and her father went to New Orleans to visit friends, his sisters begged them to leave Nena with them. She visited back and forth, but the one she especially felt close to was her Aunt Rita. Rita had two boys and a girl who made her feel as if they'd been waiting all their lives to meet her. Her cousin, Patty, especially liked to brag about her, telling her friends to come over and meet her Venezuelan cousin who looked just like a Texan. When it was time to return to Venezuela, Aunt Rita took her shopping. "Don't ever be ashamed of your height, darlin'. Wear it proudly like a badge," Aunt Rita told her. "And wear lots of pink and lavender, they set off us redheads like the cat's meow. Oh, I'm so tickled there's somebody who looks like me. You can't imagine what a thrill it is. None of my kids do, they all take after your uncle Roy."

Nena was ecstatic that she favored her aunt. "Sometimes I don't know where I belong," she confided to Rita. "I love my grandparents and I like living with them. But at times I feel like such an outsider because I don't look at all like a Venezuelan. And then when I go to Maracaibo, I feel like a visitor. Aunt Rita," she burst out, "what was my mother like? Oh, I know what she looked like, I've seen enough pictures. But what was she really like?"

"Oh darlin', I really didn't know her too well. I only met her when we went to Caracas for their wedding. But what I do remember was she was tiny and cute as a button. And what a personality! That one's a real pepper pot, I told Daddy. She's going to keep Fred hopping. She must have been real special 'cause we never figured he'd get married so young. He liked to flit from one gal to another. I don't think he'll ever get over losing her." Her eyes crinkled in sympathy.

"That's probably why he and Fran got hitched. She nursed him real good after your mama passed away. And she takes good care of him now. Maybe she's not easy to like," Rita said knowingly. "We all know how possessive she is of Fred, but Daddy said she got him out of his sickness. She pulled him back from the dead to the living, and for that we'll always be grateful." Rita put her arms around Nena, stroking her hair. "Anytime, baby, she's not easy to take, and I know it ain't no hill of beans for you, just think on that."

Which is what Nena did the day Fran hit her. Remembered her Aunt Rita's words and tried to understand her stepmother. If Fran made her daddy well after her mother's death, then she didn't want to do anything which might make him sick again. She had lost a mother she never knew. She couldn't take a chance losing her daddy. In her ten year old mind she only knew she mustn't do anything which could upset him. He might be angry because she ran away from Fran. He might even agree with Fran that she needed to have her ears boxed. So she never said anything to him, but continued to walk tenuously on the emotional tightrope Fran placed her. She tried to help as much as possible around the house, becoming more confused as Fran continued to berate her.

"How many times do I have to tell you to use the vacuum cleaner before you dust?" And then the next day she would tell her the opposite. When a maid finally appeared and stayed, no one was more grateful than Nena. She went back to her routine of staying out of Fran's way until her daddy came in from work. She didn't ever want to be slapped and shaken again.

And she never was. Until the plane she'd taken to go home for Christmas was hijacked. And she was slapped around by one of the hijackers. Then it all flashed before her, that awful summer when she was ten and Fran made her life hell. As she looked up into the guns of the hijackers, she wondered if she would ever see her father again.

....

Fred refused to leave the airport until Nena landed in Venezuela. Fran pleaded with him to check into a hotel so they could take a shower and a short nap. But he wouldn't budge. He knew Nena's fear of planes and while to some his vigil might seem a futile effort, it was his way of prodding the airline into doing something. After the first 24 hours the other waiting relatives joined him in demanding the government release the prisoner or mount a rescue attempt. Everything that could be done was being done, they were informed. Fred and the others continued to wait.

While Sarita experienced the same anguish as Fred, she held hers in check, refusing to give into it. If she worried and fretted that Johnny might be killed, then it could very well happen. No, she had to believe he would come home safely to her. And hope the volatile temper he inherited from his father wouldn't jeopardize his chances and shut out a lifetime as her husband had. She remembered what a beautiful baby he was and how she hated to leave him. But of course she had no other choice, she had to go out and make a living. Because she couldn't afford to hire a nursemaid, she took in one of the waifs from the streets. Like Sarita, the twelve year old girl, whose name was Crisanta, was so grateful to have a home and enough to eat she never wanted to leave. Sarita cleaned her up, instructed her in personal hygiene and the care of Johnny.

Bustillo, the contractor, gave her the job he promised her. She knew he wasn't keen on hiring her, and only did so out of respect for his friendship with John. He had a Spaniard who did the payroll, typed the invoices and shipping lists. At first the Spaniard resented Sarita for he saw her as a threat to him. Sarita went out of her way to make him realize she wasn't after his job. Whatever menial tasks he gave her to do, she did. She was there for one reason only, to learn the trucking business. She helped the Spaniard whenever English was required and encouraged him to think about becoming a *caporal*, a foreman, so in time he might wind up becoming Bustillo's right hand man.

At night and on weekends she did sewing. The women in the oil camps flocked to her for she could sew without a pattern, duplicating any fashion magazine page they brought her. Now they didn't have to wait for stateside trips to have new clothes. When her clientele increased, she taught Crisanta to sew and then took in another street urchin to replace her as nursemaid. In a few years she had a very profitable cottage industry going and could have moved to a larger house in a nicer neighborhood. But she didn't, for she was saving for the trucking business.

When Johnny was old enough to start school she had the money for a truck. Bustillo was shocked by her plans. He never dreamt she would attempt her own trucking business. He knew about the dressmaking and thought it was admirable she was so industrious. Dressmaking was something many women did. But trucking? Never. "It's all right *compadre*," Sarita reassured him. "There's enough work for both of us. *La India* won't be in competition with you."

La India, the name John had chosen, wasn't in competition with any company in the beginning. Because she'd bought a used truck, it frequently broke down. She knew if she didn't deliver material when promised, there wouldn't be any future work coming her way. So whenever the truck broke down she was forced to rent another one which ate into her profits. Sometimes she felt so discouraged she was tempted to just stick with the dressmaking business. But the thought of letting John down, of giving up his dream kept her going. When she finally found an Italian who was a genius with motors, she struck a deal with him. If he kept the truck running, she would give him a percentage of the profits. Despite her burgeoning success, she was concerned about her son. Not only because he was growing up in an all female household, but he had inherited John's temper which got him in one scrape after another. She realized the only place for him was a boarding school where he would have discipline and male companionship. When he was seven years old she took him to Caracas and placed him in a Jesuit school, where he cried and howled when she left. All the way back on the plane to Puerto La Cruz, she agonized over her decision. Only Cathleen's assurance that if anyone could straighten Johnny out, it was the Jesuits, eased her troubled heart. But her emotions were always torn between wanting to raise her son, more so because he had lost his father, and the economic needs of her situation. Only when he came home after his first year did she know she'd made the right decision. He talked continuously of his friends and proudly showed her the scratches on his knees from soccer.

The last thing Sarita did before she went to bed was sit before her wedding picture and talk to John. It was a conversation no one heard for her thoughts flew silently into the frame where she felt her husband understood her. She couldn't go to sleep without telling him about her day. And when she had something on her mind, she talked it over with him. The time she was beside herself with worry over the truck which continuously broke down, she felt that he told her to find a good mechanic and offer him a cut of the profits.

There wasn't a night when she didn't ache for him. She kept his pillow next to her, burrowing into it where she could still smell traces of his scent. Sometimes when she fell into bed exhausted but unable to sleep, she whispered into the pillow, voicing her fears and frustrations until bit by bit they left her. She remembered how he used to hold her when they slept and she tried to imagine he was there beside her. She thought about taking a lover to ease her physical frustrations, but the idea of another man touching her repulsed her. Whenever life became too much for her, she escaped into her memories. Tonight, she whispered into the pillow, I am going to remember our vacation in the islands. The hotel in Barbados and how the ocean lulled us to sleep.

By the time Johnny was nine she had her first profit from the trucking business. With Crisanta, the first girl she had taken into her home, she had expanded the dressmaking so she now had a small business specializing in very distinctive sundresses. The oil company wives snapped them up for although they had one basic design, she gave them different looks by the materials she used. Some could be worn casually in daytime, while others with a matching stole could go to any cocktail party.

As she became more successful the gossip about her past receded until no one spoke about it anymore. Women who ignored her in the past now boasted of having been close neighbors when she was the wife of a *petrolero*. Of the two oil camps Sarita lived in and the handful of women who befriended her, it was interesting how many claimed to be in those ranks. Nor was there a lack of suitors. Their invitations though were always turned down for her life revolved around business and her son.

As soon as she learned to drive and bought a car she headed for the beach, for it was the one place she could unwind. Swimming became her escape from the pressures of her life. And she felt especially close to John there.

One day when she was swimming back to shore an Emily Dickinson poem ran through her mind. It was years since she had time to read poetry, so she was surprised she still remembered it.

> *If you were coming in the fall*
> *I'd brush the summer by*
> *With half a smile and half a spurn*
> *As housewives do a fly*

As she tread water and looked back to the beach she thought about John. Oh yes, she told herself, if I only had to wait a few months to see him again, how easy it would be.

> *If I could see you in a year*
> *I'd wind the months in balls*

And put them each in separate drawers
Until their time befalls

Even a year, her heart cried out. A year would disappear on wings if I knew I could see him again. She felt the mask she wore for the world slip off and all the feelings which she'd buried in the deep recesses of her heart spring out. How easy it would be, she thought, to stop swimming and just let the water take me to John. The desire to see him was so strong she completely forgot about her son. She stopped treading water, letting her body sink downwards. She welcomed the darkness. It was such a relief not to have to struggle anymore. The longing for John would be over. Once more she would be in the arms of her *catire*.

Then she heard his voice, as she often did when she held their wedding picture and talked to him. She saw him smile at her. He was just a few feet away and she swam eagerly towards him. Where he took her in his arms and she melted in the blessed feeling of being close to him again. The years faded away and she was once again with her *querido*. His hands caressed her face, his finger lingering in the cleft of her chin as he had done so many times. "Soogie," he murmured before he kissed her.

Then she felt him being pulled away from her, saw him smile wistfully, heard him say, "*Hoy no, mi amor.*" Saw him shake his head as he repeated, "But not today my love." He started fading. She swam quickly toward him. Exhausted herself trying to reach him, but he continued to be pulled away from her until he was completely gone.

She wondered if she really had seen him, if it hadn't been her imagination and her longing to see him again which made her hallucinate. She reluctantly kicked her way to the surface. When her head broke clear of the water she hated the thought of living. She had so wanted the ocean to take her to John. She was weary of going on without him, of pretending her life was full enough. Then she remembered her son. She swam toward shore, terrified she wouldn't make it back for she felt completely depleted. From time to time she stopped swimming and turned on her back to float, looking out to where she'd been, hoping she would see John again. When she emerged from the water she threw herself down on the sand and thought back to what she had almost done. It had been such a powerful desire, for the passage of time had done nothing to ease her longing for John. She was afraid she would give into the desire to let the ocean claim her.

The next day she flew to Caracas and brought Johnny back to Puerto La Cruz. She knew she had to have him with her, or she just might go swimming one day and not return. She sold the dress factory and concentrated on the trucking business. Then she bought a house, a house her son would be proud to bring his friends to, and enrolled him in the American School. His English was spotty and he spoke with a decided Venezuelan accent. Time for him to learn his American heritage, she decided. And time for her to be a real mother, something she had missed out on in her struggle to be the breadwinner of the family.

When he went away to college at Tulane, she didn't think she would be able to take his absence. She kept busy with the business and the *muchachitas*, the girls she took in from the streets. That was something which would never change, she always took in the homeless. It was her way of keeping John's memory alive. Just as he had changed her life and taught her to read and write, she wanted to do the same for other girls. If the girl showed enough intelligence for further education, Sarita offered it to her. If she didn't, then she saw to it that she was trained to make a living as a servant. She always felt sad when a girl was ready to move out and make her own life, even though she knew there would be another to replace her. They all had become like daughters to her.

Now it was her son who might be taken away from her. She tried not to dwell on what could happen. That like his father he might try and be a hero or take matters into his own hands. And like her husband, because of his temper, cancel his future.

TWENTY-FIVE

There were moments when Nena could almost forget she was being held hostage on a plane. For the woman hijacker no longer walked up and down the aisle waving her machine gun, while the bearded hijacker had suddenly become less menacing.

"Please make yourselves comfortable," he urged. "We're not unreasonable people. All we're asking is that they release our leader from prison." He walked to the curtain separating the Tourist Section and called to the other hijackers. "Have the stewardess bring some cold drinks," he commanded. And when she brought them in, he hovered over the six hostages like a maître d' in an elegant restaurant. The change in him threw them all off guard, especially when he told them they could read, giving each of them a magazine. But Nena's hands shook as she turned the pages.

The man sitting next to her raised his hand deferentially and spoke to the bearded hijacker. "She's so nervous, let me talk to her a little to calm her down."

The hijacker waved his hand. "But no whispering," he warned. "Or I'll forbid you to talk."

"I still don't know your name," the blond sitting next to her said warmly, "Even though I have the craziest feeling I've either seen you some place or met you before."

"But that's exactly what I've been thinking," Nena exclaimed when she told him her name.

"That explains it. I've seen your pictures in my godmother's house," he smiled. "She has them all over the place, at least one in each room."

"And so are all your pictures," she replied, forgetting for a brief spell the horrible circumstances under which she was meeting John R. Maguire, Jr. Cathleen had told her so much about him, had even intimated that she wanted her two godchildren to meet. But with Nena living in Maracaibo in western Venezuela and John at the other end of the country in Puerto La Cruz, it never came about, although a few times their paths had almost crossed.

"Isn't it weird," he remarked softly, "that after all these years of growing up seeing each other's pictures we finally meet. But," he continued dryly, "I can think of better ways to do it."

Nena nodded her head and smiled, feeling the tension melt away for the first time since the whole horrible business had started.

"God, you have a gorgeous smile," Johnny said looking intently at her. "That's probably why I couldn't place you. In all the pictures you were laughing and smiling." He took her hand and pressed it warmly. "It's going to be okay, Nena. Soon we'll be home in Venezuela." He shook his head. "I still can't believe it. Nenita, little Nena, sitting next to me. But not so little any more."

Nena suddenly felt very self-conscious as he continued to look at her in frank admiration. She found herself wishing she had worn something different. Her jeans and matching jacket, always a favorite for travelling because they were so comfortable, now seemed old and faded. Nor was she satisfied with her new striped yellow T-shirt. She looked down at her sandals, noting with relief that the nail polish on her toenails wasn't chipped.

But Johnny saw none of this, continuing to look warmly at her. "You know I went to boarding school in Caracas until I was twelve," he said naming the school. "I wonder how far it was from your grandmother's house."

"*Ay Dios,*" Nena cried out. "That was four blocks away. All my cousins went there as day students," and she rattled off their names.

"That little bully," Johnny remarked, referring to her cousin, Memo. "Oh, how I remember him. He made my life miserable until I beat him at soccer."

"He could do that," she agreed. "But his sister, Tulia, was even worse. She always made my life miserable." Tulia, who loved to torment her and started calling her the Rooster, a name her other cousins quickly picked up. The childish nightmares she suffered because of this came back to her, when she went to bed wondering if she would wind up like the rooster the cook was fattening up for the Christmas Eve *hallacas.*

"Didn't you hate it when you started going to the American School?" Johnny asked. "In the beginning I felt like such an outsider."

"Oh no," Nena replied. "I finally felt like I belonged."

"You're whispering," the bearded hijacker screamed shrilly at the American couple sitting in front of them. "Now you leave me no choice but to revoke the privilege I granted you. ¡*Silencio*! And eyes straight ahead."

Startled, Nena turned away from Johnny taking comfort from the small squeeze he gave her hand. I'd die if he weren't here beside me, she thought struggling to remain calm. Think about something else, she told herself, anything but this awful hijacking. What was the last thing they talked about before that flaky hijacker started yelling at them? Oh yes, going to the American School. She remembered what a job it had been convincing her grandmother. "*Mamita* Isabel, I may be a Venezuelan to you, but I don't look like one," she had cried out. "You know the only time I feel that I really belong, that I'm not a mongrel, is when I'm in Maracaibo or in Texas with Daddy's family." She didn't have Maruja's cunning to get whatever she wanted out of people. But because Nena was her favorite Misia Isabel agreed, though not without some misgiving. All her daughters had been schooled by the nuns, she didn't believe in mixing boys and girls together in a classroom. Fred, of course, agreed she should go to the American School. And to placate him because he continued to press for Nena's custody, Misia Isabel gave in.

Every morning Claudio drove her to the Campo Alegre school in the eastern suburbs of Caracas, and every afternoon he picked her up. No more dowdy school uniforms with the hated black stockings and high necked, longsleeved white blouses over pleated navy blue skirts. She was free to wear whatever she wished.

A lot of the Americans were fluent in Spanish, and there were quite a few Venezuelans in the school so she soon started talking Spanglish — half English, half Spanish. She thought it was the most delicious way to converse, for one could always choose the best word from each language. Whenever her friends from school came to the house, nothing delighted her more than for them all to jabber away in Spanglish, making her cousins feel completely out of things. She got hysterical seeing them become thoroughly baffled when she and her friends switched back and forth to English. By the end of the year she had lost her accent and spoke like a typical American, and more important, she gained a lot more self-confidence. Which pleased Misia Isabel no end, as did the English lessons Nena gave her. What didn't please her was the custom of going out Trick or Treating on Halloween.

"You're going out begging, like a common street urchin?" Misia Isabel threw her hands up in the air as if the sky had fallen. "¡*Ay, no, señorita!*"

"But, *Mamita* Isabel," Nena pleaded. "It's an American holiday. And it's not really begging because people expect us. Why, some mothers have been baking cookies and candy for days. And Debbie's mother will drive us from house to house. So you see, I just have to have a costume. And if you don't want the dressmaker to sew me one, I'll go out as a ghost in a sheet!"

"In a sheet?" Misia Isabel gasped.

"Yes, in a sheet," Nena replied hotly. "It's an old American custom. Remember I'm also an American!"

The way she said it was like hearing Maruja assert herself. And it brought back memories of the time Maruja declared she was going out at Carnival dressed as a boy. Reluctantly Misia Isabel agreed and she pulled Maruja's Boy Robin costume out of the closet. Although it was too small for Nena, she kept it because it was something which had once been her mother's. She hugged it to her, running her hands over the fabric, trying to visualize how her mother looked. And asked Misia Isabel all sorts of questions, most of which she couldn't answer. Impatiently she waited for Thanksgiving so she could ask her father.

When she told him Misia Isabel had given her Maruja's costume, his quiet, deliberate manner disappeared. He started laughing in the same high pitched tone she associated with Fiver.

"You got her costume, that Boy Robin outfit?" His eyes lost their lackluster paleness, while his face shucked off his age and became almost boyish. "Well I'll be, if that ain't something." Nena watched the transformation in her father, knowing intuitively that another man had stepped into his body. "I thought she was the smartest *señorita* this side of the *Río Gran* when she dreamt up those costumes." His grin spread from ear to ear and he ran a hand through his grayish white hair, and for a moment Nena could picture how he looked when his hair was sandy and his eyes sparkled with a zest for life.

"Geez, how we danced during that Carnival," he continued. "We started out at her cousin Pilar's house and kept cuttin' a rug from one party to another, sometimes even out in the street, until we wound up at the Club Internacional. She looked so danged cute in that costume."

Nena continued to look in fascination at her father. His face and eyes were alive with enthusiasm. He was in another world, she could see that. As young as she was, she knew he had left her and taken a journey to a time which no longer existed. And instinctively she understood his reluctance to return. She plied him with questions, wanting to know how he and Maruja met, when they got married. Listened with a sense of reverence as he recounted his life with her mother, making her feel that she and *Mamita* Maruja and her father were together in a loving, warm family circle.

"I kept lifting her mask so I could kiss her." His words tumbled out. "And then I said to her, 'Since we're dressed as a team, Batman and Robin, does this mean we're gonna be a couple who will be going out to Carnival parties the rest of our lives?' And she answered like she always did, 'But of course.' Like I should have known all along." He continued to grin like a lovesick boy.

"But, we only had a couple of Carnivals together," he said quietly. "Oh, how I miss her. A day doesn't go by that she ever leaves my thoughts." His words came out in such anguish that Nena became frightened by the sudden change in him. His voice which had been so lighthearted and happy turned hoarse. "Why couldn't I have gone with her?"

"But Daddy," Nena cried out, uneasy with this strong show of emotion which had turned her father into a complete stranger, "then I wouldn't have anyone."

He stared at her vacantly. Then slowly his eyes came back into focus. "Oh darlin', I didn't mean it that way. Of course I'm glad to be around for you." But she had the strongest feeling he would trade anything in this world to be with her mother in the next.

"It sure wouldn't have been fair for God to have taken both of us, would it now?" And when he took her in his arms to comfort her, she understood what Aunt Rita meant when she said Fran had brought him back to the living. As it was, he was barely here now.

"Someday, darlin'," he whispered softly, "I hope you'll find someone who makes you as happy as your Momma did me. Then you'll really be rich."

But Nena wasn't so sure she wanted what her father had known with her mother. His spirit flew like a plane breaking the sound barrier. Why, even his skin had taken on a rosy glow. To know such happiness and then have it end. No, she didn't think she'd wish for that kind of love, not when it could be stolen so quickly and so cruelly.

Maybe I should never talk to him again about *Mamita* Maruja, she thought later. She was frightened by the memory of his vacant eyes when he was in that distant land of his mind, almost as if he'd gone away and would never return. It probably upsets him to remember *Mamita* Maruja. And she mustn't do anything to disturb him, no matter how difficult things were with Fran. She couldn't stand it if anything happened to him. She had to be good so God wouldn't take her father as He had her mother.

She continued to shoot up so by the time she started high school at the Colegio Americano, she was 5'9". It was difficult for her to feel she should wear her height like a badge, as her Aunt Rita had counseled her, when she towered over most of her classmates. She kept hoping the genes of her tiny mother would win out over the Hardesty genes.

Then in her fifteenth year her life turned upside down. "It's time for you to go live with your father," Misia Isabel pronounced one day. Claudio had driven them to the park in El Pinar, mainly because it was the only place Misia Isabel could think of where they would have some privacy. At home there were people constantly under foot, and if they took a stroll through the Plaza Bolivar, they would run into half of Caracas.

Nena received the statement with mixed feelings. "But why?"

"Because I've been a selfish, old woman all these years," Misia Isabel replied. "I've had you all to myself, just as I wanted. Now it's time to share you with your father."

To live with her father and the boys would be heavenly, except for Fran. She hesitated about trading her life in Caracas. For no matter how miserably her cousins treated her, she had been living in the old house on the corner ever since she was born. It was the one part of her life which had been constant.

Misia Isabel saw the confusion in her eyes. "Of course it will take a little adjustment on your part. But ever since I can remember, your father has been wanting you to live with him . . . ."

"*De veras, Mamita* Isabel?" Nena interrupted her. "Is that really the truth? Has Daddy always wanted me with him, or was he like *Mamita* Maruja who wanted to leave me with you when they went back to the *campos petroleros*?" Her cousins' innuendos had brainwashed her so thoroughly she'd grown up always wondering just what the truth was. Not only about her mother, but why, if her father loved her so much, she'd always lived in Caracas with her grandparents. It had taken this surprise announcement to bring these feelings to the surface.

"Of course he wanted you with him. From the very beginning. What nonsense you're spouting." Misia Isabel's normally soft voice had become strident. Now to tell a little white lie, she whispered to herself, what harm can it do now? I'll carry it to my grave where no one can contest it.

"If you must know, *señorita*, it was my idea that you stay with me after you were born. I had no idea what it was like in those *campos petroleros*. I thought it would be like living in the wilderness, so I insisted your mother leave you here with me. And I told her that as soon as you were a little bit older, past the stage where a lot of babies get infections and things like that, then she could have you. But your father wouldn't hear of it. He fell in love with you the day you were born. And so they took you out to the oilfields much against my better judgment. Naturally after your mother was gone, your father was in no condition to take care of you. He was sick for such a long time. You have no idea how bad he was."

Nena, remembering the way her father acted that Thanksgiving, could well understand how grief stricken he'd been. But she still wasn't convinced.

"And when he married Fran your father wanted you with him," Misia Isabel continued. "But by then I had become so attached to you, I couldn't bear to give you up. I had lost your mother, how could I live without you? So you see, it really is my fault. I am the reason you have lived here in Caracas rather than with your father." Reaching for Nena's hands she held them tightly.

"But now I can't keep you any longer, *mi amor*," Misia Isabel sighed. "Your father has always been after me to let you live with him, and now it's time. You're fifteen, you've had your *quinceañera* party just like your mother did. Now *es tiempo* for you to become an American, a Texan as you're always telling me you are." Her words had run into each other, so eager was she to get them out. Her breath was coming out in little spurts and she had to remind herself to stay calm. She mustn't become upset for it sapped her already low vitality.

"I'll come and visit you on vacations," Nena said, stroking her grandmother's tiny hands, putting her arms around her. She suddenly noticed how frail Misia Isabel had become.

"*Mamita* Isabel, what's the matter? You've lost an awful lot of weight," Nena said suspiciously. "Are you sick?"

"Of course not, *mi amor*. Just getting on in years. You see, what happens to women in their old age is they get thin." She laughed putting her hands on her hips. "All my life I've had to *guardar mi línea*, watch my figure. Now I'm getting slim and I'm delighted. Why, I can eat all the sweets I want." Traces of Maruja came through in her attempt to be flippant.

"Now that you're leaving my house, my little Nenita, just remember what I've always told you," Misia Isabel looked lovingly at her granddaughter. "Remember how special you are, always remember."

"Oh *Mamita* Isabel how could I forget?" Nena cried out hugging Misia Isabel. "You're always telling me that. But I don't think I'm so special, I'm just like anyone else."

"No you're not," and Misia Isabel's voice again became firm. "You were special the day you were born." To make up for Maruja's lack of love at Nena's birth, Misia Isabel had always tried to make Nena feel she was a cut above the others. "It's true what your cousins say," Misia Isabel admitted. "You really are my favorite. I can't help it! I love them all very much, but you're the one I love the most." She reached for Nena's hands again, holding them tightly and bringing them up to her lips.

"*Ven*," she said getting up, for the park bench suddenly felt cold under her. "Let's go for a little stroll. And then we'll get in the car and have Claudio take us to the Confectionaria Avila, where we'll have hot chocolate and lots of sweet pastries." They walked together in the afternoon sun which filtered through the tall pine trees. The tiny elegant Caracas matron with not a hair out of place, her long sleeved silk print dress worn with a single strand of perfect pearls. Next to her the granddaughter who towered over her in her American styled clothes, a denim skirt and wool sweater, and who had to pace her steps to her grandmother's diminutive walk. Like lovers they walked with their hands clasped together. Lovers who have that special bond which needs no words, the only sound in the secluded park the crunching of the fallen pine needles beneath their feet.

"How do you get in touch with your father?" Misia Isabel asked her a few days later.

"I write him a letter and bring it over to the Palm Oil office where they send it out in the daily pouch. Sometimes I call him, but you know how the phones are." Nena rolled her eyes. "Honestly, I think it would be quicker to get on a plane than try and reach him long distance."

"Well, write him a letter and tell him I want to see him," Misia Isabel said. "Now that I'm going to send you to live with him, I must do it in the proper way. I have to tell him what vaccinations you have had, what the dentist has done to your teeth — very little thank goodness. Things like that. So get a letter off to him today. Perhaps Claudio can drive you over to the office."

Now what's the matter with her, Nena wondered. She knows the office is only six blocks away and I always walk there. Why the sudden rush?

"*Mamita* Isabel, you really are in a hurry to get rid of me, aren't you?" she said feeling suddenly like all the familiar props in her world were being pulled out from under her.

"Don't be silly," Misia Isabel laughed. "But you see, once having made up my mind, I have to get on with it. Don't you know how difficult it is for me to let you go? You've become so much a part of me. Tell me," she said in an attempt to divert Nena, "once you start living with your father, are you going to be a real Texan and wear boots like he does? Be a . . . . What do you call it? A cowgirl?"

"Of course not," Nena laughed. "Oh, *Mamita* Isabel you are so comical. You think all Americans, especially Texans, are without *cultura*, don't you? We're quite civilized!" Nena didn't know how pleased Misia Isabel was with the emphatic way she said we, or the fact that she had become so thoroughly Americanized. Nena didn't know that her time with her grandmother had run out.

Fran was desperate to get some sleep, she longed to stretch out in a bed. Not cat nap in the airport VIP Lounge as they'd all been doing. But nothing would budge Fred, he was determined to stay until Nena's plane returned to Venezuela.

Leave it to that girl to get on a plane which gets hijacked, she fumed to herself. Not that I don't want her to return safe and sound, she thought hastily. But it's just typical of Nena to mess things up for the rest of us. When she thought of the Christmas party at the American Embassy they had missed, she became even more irritated. Taking out her compact she looked worriedly at her face, noting how her pores were oozing with oil. It's all this stress that's doing it. Sighing in resignation, she patted her face with powder then ran a lipstick across her mouth. She wished she'd worn a dress, her beige pants felt like she'd been wearing them for a week. Smoothing down her brown and white striped blouse, she took a small atomizer out of her purse and spritzed her wrists with Ma Griffe.

But she still felt grubby. Oh, how she wished she could take a shower, wished the damn plane was landing right now in Venezuela so they could all go home. And while she was wishing, she decided irritably, she might as well make a wish Nena got married and moved to Siberia. And then, she reminded herself, they'd all have to pull up stakes just to be near her, the way Fred doted on his daughter. No, don't wish for Siberia. You have to be careful what you wish for, she thought, for you just might get it. Hadn't she wished for Fred? Well, she'd gotten him all right. The trouble was he wasn't the same man she'd fallen in love with. And she'd long ago given up hope the happy go lucky Fred would ever return.

Oh, he still had a courtly way about him, paying her compliments, but his boisterous good nature and ready conversation had disappeared, along with the joy he used to have in life, the fun loving streak which shone out of his eyes. All the wonderful qualities which brought her back to life had evaporated. He didn't like to party anymore and when they went to a dance, she always had the feeling he was just going through the motions and his heart wasn't in it. Ole Man River, that's what he's turned into, Ole Man River.

While she was glad his looks had matured for she was always conscious she was older than him, she longed to see the Fred of long ago who called her a statuesque goddess and begged her to play doctor with him, Fred whose every move was calculated to get her into bed with him.

Now when they made love there was none of the youthful passion she remembered from their single days in Santa Barbara.

Not that he ever looked at another woman, she knew he'd never been unfaithful to her. He just didn't seem to be with her all the time, almost as if his spirit had wandered to another planet. And no matter how many years had gone by, she still had the feeling she was competing with Maruja's ghost.

But he was a wonderful father to their boys and a good provider. Despite his relative youth, he'd risen very rapidly in the Palm Oil ranks. But no wonder, she thought, he eats and breathes his work. And then her face softened when their eyes met. Even though she only had half a loaf, she was still madly in love with him. And wouldn't trade her life with him for anyone else. Fred smiled wanly at her. "You look beat, Franny," he said reaching for her hand. "Why don't you go check into a hotel on the beach and get some shuteye. You don't have to wait here with me." She shook her head. There was nothing she wanted more than to crawl into bed and sleep. But she wouldn't leave. Fred might think she wasn't interested in Nena's fate. No, she had to stay and play the role of the dutiful stepmother. She dropped her head on his shoulder and when he put his arm around her, she felt all the tension melt away. The contentment of being in his arms soothed her and in a few minutes she drifted off to sleep.

Fred's mind was elsewhere. Other than being concerned for Fran's welfare — he realized what a strain this was for her — his thoughts were with his daughter. He prayed for her, saying a Rosary by counting off the decades in his head. You wouldn't do that to me God, he pleaded, take her away from me too, would you? He looked around the airport in anguish, the fear of Nena coming to any harm almost smothering him. He'd waited so long to have her with him, and then in a few years she went off to college in the States. One minute they're cute little babies, he agonized, and the next they're all grown up.

Sometimes he blamed himself for being too pliant in allowing Maruja's mother to raise her. But there were times when it just seemed easier. Everything was such an effort after Maruja was taken from him, he frequently walked away from a confrontation. It was a struggle enough to get up and face each day, to put one foot in front of another. So every year when his mother-in-law pleaded with him to allow her to

keep Nena for a little while longer because she still was grieving for
Maruja, he gave in to her. Then when Nena started coming to Maracaibo
to spend her vacations with him it seemed like the ideal compromise.
Until finally he got the letter from Nena saying that at last Misia Isabel
thought it was time for her to live with him. He remembered how he flew
to Caracas with such eager anticipation.

But then he always looked forward to visiting his in-laws' home for
he felt close to Maruja there. Her spirit hovered everywhere, and
whenever he entered the enormous colonial mansion he felt her presence.
And for a brief spell he was young again, full of the incredible wonder
of life, with the world spread out before him and Maruja by his side.

When he sat in the sun drenched patio with Misia Isabel, listening to
the fountain's murmur, he always felt Maruja was just around the corner.
And any moment she would open one of the doors in the *galería* and walk
out to greet him, the high heels of her shoes clicking on the highly
polished tile floors, the scent of roses from her perfume following her
footsteps.

"You sat in that chair the first time you came for Maruja's hand,"
Misia Isabel reminisced as she looked at the bird cages swaying in the soft
breeze. "And now I'm going to give your Nena back to you." She spoke
to him in English, she explained, so the servants wouldn't be able to
eavesdrop as they frequently did. Nena and the rest of the cousins were
in school, their parents out at social engagements, so she and Fred had
the house to themselves. She would have preferred going out for a drive,
perhaps to El Pinar park, but Lourdes had the car and chauffeur today.
She spoke slowly, for despite the lessons Nena had given her, she still
wasn't comfortable speaking English.

"*Mamita*, I appreciate the good job you did with Nena," Fred told
Misia Isabel, mystified as to why there was this urgency on her part for
them to be alone. "She's beautiful not only on the outside, but inside as
well."

"Oh, yes," Misia Isabel responded smiling, "she is an absolute joy.
I'm so glad that her. . . . What is the word I want? *Bueno*, what I mean
to say is . . . . she is no longer *flaca*, skinny. She's filled out. And her hair
has turned to a beautiful shade of red. *Y los freckles*, well there's not much
one can do about them, is there?"

"Freckles are cute," Fred insisted.

"Of course they are," Misia hastened to reply. "I was only making a *chiste*, joking. We all look so much alike in this family, small and dark haired, she always stood out so. I'm afraid it was very hard for her, poor child, looking so different." She sighed, fidgeting with the floral arrangement on the coffee table. "Maybe I was wrong to keep her with me all these years. Her cousins made her life miserable at times, always with the talk about Maruja not wanting her."

"It's because she was so young," Fred replied rising to Maruja's defense as he always did. "She became pregnant as soon as we got married and not only that, she had to get used to life in the oilfields. I kept telling you, she'd grow to love Nena, and . . . ." his voice faltered with the memory of his last night with Maruja, "and she did. I remember it as clear as if it were yesterday. Fred," she said to me, "this afternoon when I left Nena with Cathleen, all of a sudden I fell in love with her. And for the first time, I felt like a real mother. I wanted to stay with her, and play with her, feed her, rock her in my arms. And now I can't wait to get back to her so I can see her and the three of us can be a real family."

"*Ay! Dios Mío*," Misia Isabel cried out. "I know. You told me, and so did Cathleen about the love Maruja felt for Nena. I was so happy that before she died, she realized it. And at the same time, *absolutamente* heartbroken that God took her before she could show her daughter this love." She reached into the pocket of her skirt for a handkerchief.

"Oh, *Mamita* Isabel," Fred said softly, "it will haunt me 'til the day I die, the way she kept saying she couldn't wait until we got back to Chacari so the three of us could be a family." He got up and walked slowly over to the bird cages, looking sorrowfully at the canaries, trying to keep the ache in his heart from turning into tears.

"*Ay, mi hijo*," Misia Isabel called out to Fred. "This talk of the past is not good for either of us. We both know the truth about Maruja, that her love for her daughter bloomed a little later than other mothers." She threw up her hands. "But, that's not why I wanted to see you. I think it's time your daughter lives with you. Just as you've wanted all these years." She brought the delicately laced handkerchief up to her eyes. "Though I shall miss her every day."

"But *Mamita*," Fred remarked consolingly, "she can come and visit you anytime you want."

"No," Misia Isabel replied sharply. "She's not to come back to this house after she leaves."

Fred looked at his mother-in-law in bewilderment.

"*Mi hijo*," she said softly, "I've been going to the doctors these past couple of months. And they all come up with the same diagnosis, so I have to believe them. In a few months I'll be gone, some sort of stupid cancer. "No," she said reaching to take his hands when she saw the shock on his face. "No words of condolence. We all have an allotted time on this earth. And mine is almost up. But, that's not what concerns me," she continued. "I'm not too worried about my husband. It will be a loss for awhile, but Eugenio has a new mistress who will keep him consoled." She nodded her head knowingly. "Maruja was the smart one. She didn't want to marry a Venezuelan for she wasn't about to tolerate their mistresses." She shrugged her shoulders. "But that was the way we were brought up. How were we to know any different? I've often wondered what it would have been like to have a man all to myself," she remarked.

Fred, his heart broken, looked at her in admiration. *She's one helluva lady.*

"Oh, I'm wandering in my conversation, forgive me. Put it down to *la vejez*, old age." She moved forward in the wicker chair, her hands holding tightly to its white arms. "What I wanted to say before I started on this *camino tortuoso*, is I'm not too worried about what will happen here when I go. My children and grandchildren will miss me for awhile and then go on with their lives. The one I am concerned about is Nena. We have been so very close and I won't be here to protect her anymore."

"Protect?" Fred shook his head in confusion.

"Yes, protect," she said firmly. "You see, in spite of all the love and attention Eugenio and I gave to Nena, it hasn't been easy for her here. Her cousins all felt — they still feel — that she got more love and attention than they did. And no matter how much I tried to bridle their tongues, they were always taunting her with the gossip of how Maruja turned her back on her when she was born and didn't want to take her back to the oilfields with her. Even though you and I know that Maruja changed."

"They got this, of course, from their parents," she explained. "I suppose it really started with Lourdes, she's always been such a busybody. And then too, Maruja's sisters were always a little bit jealous of her. She was so different from them. Not so much in looks, but in other ways. She was so full of life, so utterly enchanting that she far outshone them."

She sighed for this was so difficult for her, trying to make Fred understand how things really were in her family.

"So when Maruja committed her only big sin, when she showed that flaw in her character — such total lack of maternal feeling when Nena was born — they were all quick to pounce on it." Her hands flew out to emphasize just how strong this feeling had been. "You know in every family there is always talk about one member or another. It's sad, but it's one of the facts of life. And not even the sorrow of Maruja's death could still that gossip." She reached in the pocket of her navy blue skirt for a pack of cigarettes.

"¡*Mamita*!" Fred cried out shocked because she was smoking. But then the whole afternoon had been one surprise after another.

"Oh, yes," she said seeing the look of astonishment on his face. "It's one of the things I have allowed myself since I don't have too much time left. I always wanted to smoke, but you see I never had the courage to do so. Of course it's bad for me, but what difference can it make now?"

"Oh, *Mamita*," Fred said struggling to keep his voice from breaking, "if only there were something I could do for you."

"But there is," she replied. "You can make sure that Nena is out of the house before I go. I can control things when I'm here. Hush the whispers, put a muzzle on Lourdes' mouth and Tulia's. But after I'm gone, there will be no one around and Nena will be at their mercy." She inhaled quickly on her cigarette. "I know this sounds very dramatic, but that's the way it really is."

"I never dreamt it was like this," Fred said shaking his head. "Then why didn't you let Nena come to me sooner?"

Misia Isabel didn't answer him right away. "It's not easy to raise another woman's child."

"You're talking about Fran? But *Mamita*, she's a wonderful mother."

"I'm sure she's wonderful with her own children." She wanted to say more about Fran but didn't. What good would it do to be so frank about things? "It hasn't been easy for her I guess, being the second wife, Fred. I don't know much about this marriage, but I don't believe it's at all like your first one."

"Oh no, *Mamita*," Fred replied firmly, "nothing could ever be like what Maruja and I had together." He finally was able to say her name. "Fran knew that. I was completely above board with her. But I do love her. Oh, not the way I did Maruja. I'll never feel that way again."

"That's what I mean, Fred. Perhaps Fran is a little jealous of Maruja, just as her sisters were, so naturally she would resent Nena." For the first time Fred saw confusion and uncertainty in Misia Isabel's eyes.

"Oh, I don't know what is the right thing to do," she cried out in frustration. "I've gone over this so many times in my head. Perhaps it would be better to send her to her Aunt Rita. From all that she tells me, she loves it in Texas."

"No, *Mamita*," Fred said firmly, "she's my daughter and she belongs with me. And I'm sure you're exaggerating about Fran. She's really a very good woman."

Good with you, good with her children, Misia Isabel wanted to cry out. How blind you are, Fred. Don't you see how things really are? But she kept her thoughts to herself. She was beginning to get tired. So very tired and all she longed for was her bed and the luxury of crying. She was so weary of putting up a big front, of keeping everything inside, exhausted from trying to put everything in order before she died.

"*Bueno*, then it's settled," she said getting a grip on her emotions. She had done all that she could, the rest was up to God. "Now here are her medical reports, the vaccinations she's had, and a letter from her dentist with her charts. That was the reason for this visit, or so I told Nena. *Naturalmente* she doesn't know about my illness, nor does the rest of the *familia*." She shook her head wanly. "Fortunately no one is concerned about the weight I lost. I told them it's a natural occurrence of old age and they all believed me. Only Claudio, the chauffeur knows. But then, he's been the keeper of so many secrets all these years. Every time he took me to a doctor, we told everyone I was out visiting friends. And I insisted the doctors keep their silence. In due time, the family will know. But for now . . . ." Her voice trailed off.

"Of course *Mamita*," Fred said feeling helpless and sad. "When do you want me to take Nena?"

"Why don't you come back in a few weeks, *mi hijo*. Go home and prepare your wife for this and then come back for her at the end of the month." Her voice had become brisk and businesslike as she tried to move things along and get the visit over. "It would be better of course if Nena could leave at mid-semester, but we don't have the luxury of time on our hands. She'll just have to transfer to another school in the middle of the year. Hmph! I don't suppose the schools out there in Maracaibo are any good. Those *Maracuchos* don't have the *cultura* we *Caraqueños* have."

"Oh *Mamita*, they have good schools," Fred assured her. "Why, the boys go to Bella Vista, the American School, and it's a fine one."

"Well, *mi amor*, now we must take leave of each other." She just couldn't say the word goodbye. Looking fondly at Fred, she smiled softly. "You've been a wonderful son-in-law, even if you are a *musiu*." She tried to make light of him being a foreigner, an American. She so wanted to inject a little bit of humor into their conversation. "I'm proud to have you in our family." Oh dear God in Heaven, she must control herself, or pretty soon she would burst into tears. She got up from the wicker chair, her every movement an effort and took Fred's hands in hers, looking up at him and feeling dwarfed by his height.

"As we Venezuelan say, '*hasta luego*'," she smiled trying to be brave. "Not *adiós*, that's so final, just *hasta lueguito*, until a little while when we meet again."

"Oh, *Mamita*," Fred said tenderly, bending down to hug her to him and kiss her. Her skin felt like parchment and her body so frail he was afraid she would crumble into pieces. "You've been such a good mother-in-law to me, the best." The thought of her dying was like losing another piece of Maruja.

He gently released her from his embrace, then looked around the patio. "I really love this house," he sighed. "The way it's laid out, shut off from the world with all the beauty inside. And I always feel so close to Maruja when I'm here. There was no one quite like her, was there *Mamita*?" His eyes darted around as if he might find Maruja in some secluded corner. "*Maruja la Bruja*, you were in a class by yourself."

"*¡Maruja la Bruja!*" the parrot squawked, "*¡Maruja La Bruja!*"

"Hush you stupid old bird," Misia Isabel cried out. Now what made that old *lorito* suddenly come to life? "*Cállate*," she commanded the bird, "shut up, shut up!"

But the bird ignored her, continuing to call out, "*Maruja la Bruja*."

"Oh Fred, do something with that stupid bird," she pleaded. "Make him say something else." She felt close to tears. All the talking and dredging up of old memories, the anguish of giving up Nena. And now that stupid *lorito* repeating Maruja's name like a litany.

In spite of Fred's cajoling, the parrot continued to cry out Maruja's name. Even when he unhooked the cage and carried it back to the servants' patio, it's voice could be heard faintly in the front part of the house. Calling out Maruja's name, sounding like a record which had become stuck with no one around to change it.

Fred walked into the vestibule and out to the street, pausing for a minute to look up at the second story balcony. Then he blew a kiss. She was there, in his mind he could see her. Black hair framing a heart shaped face smiling down at him, her eyes flashing with life. The years slipped away and he was twenty two years old again, madly in love and completely under the spell of *La Bruja* whom he'd never been able to forget. And the yearning, which had stayed with him ever since she died, gnawed at him stronger than ever. Oh, what he wouldn't give if he could just go back in time and regain those brief years they had together.

TWENTY-SIX

Nena knew the plane was descending because her ears started to pop. Maybe now, she thought hopefully, this nightmare will come to an end. Because the window shades were still down, she had no idea where they were when the plane hit the runway. No reassuring captain's voice came over the intercom, only the sharp words of one of the hijackers warning them not to do anything which would provoke their captors.

She felt a gun in the back of her neck. With shaking hands she undid her seat belt as instructed, then struggled to get up as the gun burrowed deeper into her skin. She wasn't alone, Johnny was also pushed and prodded to the exit. Where the hijacker whispered sarcastically, "Welcome to Barbados," and the sunlight blinded them as it streamed through the door. The gun moved from her neck to her temples and she heard a clicking sound as the woman hijacker spun the barrel of the gun. And more lights from the flashbulbs of photographers who had been summoned to record this moment. So when her picture flashed around the world on TV and in newspapers, the first thing people saw was the fear in her eyes because she expected to die right then and there.

But she wasn't fated to die, not yet, the hijackers informed the waiting press. Neither was the other *gringo*. If their leader wasn't freed by the time they landed at their next destination, then one of these two hostages would be shot and the body thrown out of the plane. Did you take enough pictures, the hijackers politely asked the press, so everyone understands just how serious we are?

Nena and Johnny were pushed back to their seats. "You did very well," the woman hijacker sneered. "Yes, very well indeed. Now people will see we're not a bunch of amateurs. Okay, you can relax now." She laughed when she said the words.

Nena couldn't stop shaking, positive she was going to throw up. I

345

wonder if anyone will mourn me if I die, she thought sadly. Oh, Daddy will and the boys, especially Fiver. Certainly not Fran. But Cathleen, her adopted godmother, would. She thought about her other family, the Venezuelan cousins and their parents, her grandfather. Would they go into *luto*, mourning, for her? The women wear black dresses and the men black armbands? Not go out to parties, stop playing music in the house? Put aside their card games? She doubted they would go to those lengths. Probably the black clothing for awhile, but that's about all. For she knew from experience how mourning can be a perpetual thing in Venezuelan families as there was always some relative dying. And she remembered how they all chafed at having to continue the *luto* for any length of time for the way it disrupted their lives, especially when it was some distant relative. No, she didn't want them to go into a long *luto* for her. She did hope, though, they would remember her for a little while.

She felt Johnny's hand give hers a reassuring grip. She squeezed his hand back. If she knew Morse Code she could tap out a message. Wasn't that what prisoners did sometimes? Do you really think they'll kill us, she wanted to ask him, or are they bluffing? She wished she could stop trembling; she still felt like she was going to vomit.

As Nena hung on to Johnny it occurred to her that they'd met just as her parents did — when their hands collided. Except a hijacked plane was hardly a Cathedral. She cried inwardly when she thought of what the hijackers might do to them. Keep your mind occupied, she reminded herself. Think of anything but the gun to your head, try to forget that you might be killed by these hoodlums. Even if it's only a fantasy, think of something else. Her thoughts turned to Johnny and how identical their past was. Both Venezuelan/Americans losing a parent at an early age.

By now she'd grown a little leery of ever finding happiness in love because it seemed determined to elude her. Despite the great affection her grandparents gave her, she'd grown up always wondering if her cousins' innuendos about her mother were true. She'd done everything she could to make Fran care for her, but had failed miserably there. When it came to men, she'd struck out every time. She used to think it was because she towered over most of the boys in high school. Stop growing, she'd tell her body every morning, stop growing. And when her body finally heard her and she stopped at 5'11", she thought her luck would change. She remembered how her height was the one thing she had in common with

Fran. People not knowing she was her stepmother often thought they saw a resemblance there, since Nena didn't look like her father. Nena didn't know what Fran's reaction to this was, for her hooded eyes never revealed what she was thinking.

In college she lost her virginity to an engineering major who showered her with attention. She was wiped out emotionally when he went back to his former girlfriend, and she realized it was nothing more than love on the rebound for him. After that, she dropped out of college for a year and went to work at the perfume counter of Neiman Marcus because she couldn't concentrate on her studies. Then just when she felt that she'd gotten her head together and made plans to return to college, she met a musician buying perfume for his sister. That relationship led to a marriage proposal, something she wanted very badly. To have a home of her own with a man who loved her and would give her lots of babies. She almost made it that time, but all she was left with was a wedding gown and another broken heart when he got cold feet and called off the marriage. She went back to college determined to graduate no matter who came into her life. If she couldn't find happiness in love, then she would find fulfillment in an exciting career. And she vowed to never trust a man again.

Until this nightmare started and Johnny gave her courage. She felt she'd known him all her life. And her self-esteem, which had taken a nose-dive from her two past love affairs, felt it might return. With my luck, she thought despondently, I'll never see him again. Either he'll lose interest after this is over or we'll be killed. No, she refused to even think that something would happen to him. Or to her. But although she tried to think positively, her body started to shake again with fear. And then she felt she would die of shame for she'd wet her pants. Oh God, she hoped it hadn't gone through to her jeans. She raised her hand, hoping the hijackers would allow her to go to the bathroom.

....

"No whispering," the woman hijacker threatened, her shrill voice filling the First Class section.

"But you can still talk," the bearded hijacked said condescendingly. "Just don't be secretive." Looking at his smug smile Johnny wanted to smash his face in. He was fed up with the games these bastards were playing with them. He'd bent over backwards to kiss the hijackers' asses because he didn't want to antagonize them. He knew he had to keep his feelings hidden and his temper under control. His mother kept entering his thoughts and he remembered all the times she had pleaded with him not to fly off the handle, but to try and reason things out. He especially remembered the year when he'd broken another boy's nose in a fight at school. That was when she told him how his father died. "Only so you learn that he would still be with us if he hadn't lost his temper and gone in after those thieves." He made a promise to her that day he would never let his temper propel him into situations he would later regret.

But this last indignity with Nena, playing Russian roulette with a gun against her head, made something inside him snap. He had to do something now. But what? He racked his brain trying to come up with a plan. He thought of tackling the sickening psycho who could turn in a second from an obnoxious thug to a smiling, fawning son of a bitch. But he knew the looney tunes woman hijacker in the back would make history of him. It always boiled down to the same thing, they had the guns and he had nothing.

So the first thing he had to do was somehow get a gun. Maybe pretend he wanted to go to the bathroom. One of them would undoubtedly accompany him, probably the woman. And in those few seconds he could turn around and disarm her. The odds were against him, but he couldn't sit around impotently anymore. He also had to come up with an alternative plan so he had something to fall back on. He was so lost in his thoughts he didn't realize Nena was talking to him until she nudged him.

"Talk to me, Johnny," she begged him. "Say anything, but please talk so I won't have time to think." Her hands shook and to steady them, she gripped his arm.

"Sure wish I had a joint now," he replied, although he didn't do drugs. But now a few hits might stimulate his brain to come up with a good plan.

"Me too," she agreed, although she'd only smoked pot a few times. In high school she had the reputation of being a *zanahoria*, a carrot, the Venezuelan slang word for someone who didn't do drugs. She was petrified Fran would find out and throw her out of the house, even though she suspected Fiver did more than experiment. She also didn't want to disappoint her father because he didn't talk down to her as Fran did, but somehow made her feel doing drugs wasn't the coolest thing to do.

"It's funny how our paths missed each other for years," she remarked when the silence between them became unbearable. She could see Johnny was miles away in thought, and if they were going to have a conversation, she would have to be the one to keep it going.

"Yeah, how about that?" he replied distractedly. She knew he wasn't responding to her, but she was so nervous she continued to chatter away.

"Cathleen isn't my real *madrina*," she explained, "but I call her that because she's been like a true godmother to me." More like a mother, Nena thought, remembering how Cathleen came back into her life in Maracaibo.

"I knew you when you were a baby," was the first thing Cathleen said when they met the summer after her twelfth birthday. She remembered how those words delighted her.

"Really?" Nena replied looking in awe at Cathleen. Now that's the way she wanted to look when she grew up, she vowed to herself. She envied Cathleen's straight blond hair pulled back in a French twist, wishing she could do something to control her red, curly mop. And Cathleen's lime green sundress worn with white hoop earrings and matching necklace made her look crisp and cool, something almost impossible to achieve in Maracaibo's hot and humid climate.

"I used to take care of you," Cathleen's eyes danced with enthusiasm. "Whenever your folks needed a baby sitter, I helped out. We were next door neighbors."

"Then you knew my mother!" Nena cried out.

To meet someone who knew her mother and remembered Nena when she was a baby was like getting a piece of her life back. She was further surprised when she discovered pictures of herself around Cathleen's house.

"Your grandmother gave them to me when I came to Caracas," Cathleen explained. "You don't remember me coming by?"

Nena shook her head. How could she have forgotten someone so interested in her?

"Well, it's not surprising, you were awfully small."

Having Cathleen in Maracaibo was the nicest thing to happen to Nena that summer. Whenever life with Fran became too rough, which it invariably did for she could never seem to please her, Cathleen was there for her. Cathleen's home became the place where she brought her friends. There were always freshly baked cookies and cool drinks set out on the kitchen table. And she seemed to have time to sit down and talk to the girls, for everything about them interested her.

"I wish you were my mom," one of her friends declared one day. "You're always home, not out playing bridge all the time like mine."

"Yeah," another girl piped up. "Your son is lucky. Is he away at camp for the summer?" In every room there were pictures of a boy they assumed was Cathleen's son.

Nena remembered the pain in Cathleen's eyes when she replied she didn't have children, it was her godson in the pictures. It wasn't until weeks later Nena found out Cathleen's baby, who only lived six months, had been born three months before she was. As the weeks went by, she began to think of Cathleen as her *madrina*, somewhat envious of the boy in the pictures who could legitimately call her his godmother. But Cathleen became more than a godmother when Nena found out the truth about her mother's death.

Fran was in between maids again, and for a week Nena was back to cleaning. One morning when she was dusting Fran's desk some yellowed newspaper clippings with her mother's name in the headlines caught her eye. The newspapers were so carefully spread out on the desk she couldn't help but notice them. The Caracas Journal, the English language paper, didn't go into details. But she did have to get out the dictionary to look up the word 'decapitated.' The other papers were more explicit, sparing none of the details of her father being found with her mother's head in his hands. Sick to her stomach, she ran out of the house and headed for her father's office. She just had to see him, but when she got there, she remembered he was away in Caracas attending a seminar. She wandered around camp in a daze until she found herself standing outside Cathleen's house and then sobbing, she ran inside.

She didn't go home for two days. Two days of trying to forget the horror of her mother's death. The nightmares stayed with her long after she went home, Cathleen couldn't stop those. Ultimately when she returned to Caracas, therapy with a psychologist was required. And it was years before she could get on a plane again. But initially, when her father was out of camp and the shock of the newspaper stories and pictures were still fresh in her mind, it was Cathleen who was there for her.

"Your mother never knew what hit her," she reassured Nena as she brushed her hair. "She didn't suffer for even a moment." The soft strokes of the brush on her scalp had a calming effect on her. "Of course your father took a long time to get over the accident, but he's recovered now. And gone on living, as your mother would have wanted him to. Just as you have to, baby." Cathleen stopped brushing and bent down and hugged her. She was so warm and loving, the opposite of Fran who doled out her affection only to the boys and her father.

"When your father gets back you'll feel a lot better," Cathleen said encouragingly. "That's the way it is with the women in this company," she smiled. "The guys are on the road so much we have to make do the best we can." She was thrilled Cathleen considered her a young woman, not some awkward child as Fran did. "You'll never know the happiness you've brought me, Nena, coming back into my life," Cathleen told her refilling her glass with ice cubes. Nena noticed she was never without a drink, but she didn't give it a second thought. For Maracaibo was so muggy a person was always thirsty. She never dreamt Cathleen had a drinking problem. Didn't even know what a drinking problem was until she heard her father and Fran arguing.

Her father had returned from the seminar in Caracas, and just as Cathleen promised, Fred helped her get over the shock of her discovery. He never went back to the office, but spent the day with her. And stayed with her that night until she was able to fall asleep, reassuring her he would be with her in a second if she woke up with nightmares. But when she did wake up, she was too upset by what she overheard to call out to him.

"How could you have been so careless as to leave those damn clippings around?" she heard Fred say. His words were sharp and angry, so different from his usual slow, deliberate manner of speaking.

"I didn't leave them out," Fran replied shrilly. It was her voice which had awakened Nena, Fran's high pitched shriek which always set Nena's teeth on edge. "I swear to God, Fred. Nena must have been rummaging through my desk."

That's not true, she cried out, and she wanted to run out and deny Fran's accusations. But then her father started talking again.

"What I can't understand is why you kept the damned clippings in the first place. Who the hell needs them?" His voice was full of anguish. "Did you think I wanted my daughter to know all the horrible details? Christ Almighty, Franny, I've spent half of my life trying to forget that day."

"I certainly don't know how they came into my possession," Fran continued to protest. "Maybe your mother-in-law sent them. After we got married there were a whole bunch of papers in your things which I just put away in my desk. And then promptly forgot about them."

"I'm sure she didn't send them," he said wearily. "Anyway, no matter how they got into this house, I don't ever want to see them again. I'm burning them right now." Nena heard him go out to the back porch where the grill was kept. Through her bedroom window she saw the flames leap up as the clippings caught fire. "Thank God Cathleen was home when this happened," she heard him tell Fran. "She's been just wonderful with Nena."

"Oh, I'm sorry I was out playing bridge," Fran said apologetically. "If only I had been here for poor Nena."

"Fred darling," she heard Fran continue, "I know Nena has become very attached to Cathleen, but do you think it wise to allow her to go over there so much? You know, on account of as lovely as Cathleen is, she does have a drinking problem."

A drinking problem? What did Fran mean? Nothing must ever come between her and Cathleen, Nena whispered to herself, suddenly afraid that the only person in camp she could turn to besides her father might be declared off limits.

"Cathleen — a drinking problem?" She heard her father's snort of derision. "Honey, that's just a bunch of camp gossip. Besides, when would she find time to hit the bottle? She's always doing some kind of charity work. Either teaching English to the slum kids, or working with the blind. Naw," he scoffed, "that's nothing but idle oil camp talk."

"Oh, I hope you're right, darling," Fran continued fervently, and listening to her Nena began to despise her. Didn't her father know what a *mentirosa* Fran was, couldn't he see how she twisted things around so the truth was never there? Lying in bed with the moonlight making murky shadows on the back porch outside her window, Nena realized Fran had purposely left those horrible newspaper clippings on her desk. She wanted Nena to know how her mother had died. If only her father realized what Fran had done. But she knew he never would. For Fran had him wound around her finger. Why, tonight was the first time she'd ever heard her father lose his temper with Fran. And then, it didn't last. The wind off Lake Maracaibo became gusty and the shadows of the palm trees danced grotesquely across her window, creating patterns which made her agitated imagination think she saw a plane crashing. And when the silhouette of a coconut swayed back and forth, it so resembled a head that she ran in fright to her father. It took her a long time to forget that night, sometimes she felt the memory would always be lurking in a corner of her mind, ready to pop out and torment her.

Now ten years later as she sat in a hijacked plane frightened she would be killed, she kept remembering that her mother had died in a plane. And she wondered if she would share the same fate.

"Fasten your seat belts," the woman hijacker snarled prodding her and Johnny with her machine gun. "We'll be landing very soon. Let's see how seriously they've taken us. If not," and there was no mistaking the anticipation in her voice, "one of you dies."

....

Despite her display of serenity, Sarita's insides were churning with the memory of her son's face flashing on the TV screen. For Johnny's eyes had that same look of anger her husband's had the night he was murdered. So much for the environment versus genes theory, she thought. He's never known his father, yet I see so much of him in Johnny. Don't do anything impulsive, she called out silently to her son, don't lose your temper. Don't try to be a hero or think you can take care of a situation yourself, as your father did. It can mean the difference between living and dying.

TWENTY-SEVEN

In the airport Cathleen fought her craving for a drink. The cigarettes she smoked did little to calm her nerves, and she felt she was close to caving in. If this kept up, she knew she had to get help. If you can't handle it alone, she reminded herself, all you have to do is make a phone call. It's no big deal. What would turn into a disaster was the alternative. She would give it one more hour, she decided. Maybe she could cope with the emotional roller coaster they were all on.

She didn't know when she started having a drinking problem. In looking back she couldn't pinpoint the one incident which pushed her over the edge. Sometimes she thought it began with Sheila's death. Or maybe it was the false euphoria of becoming pregnant. Of praying that this baby would take away the void left by Sheila. Only to have all her hopes come crashing down when she miscarried. There were times when she thought it might have been the year she went seven months, learning afterwards it had been a boy. And the feeling she'd let Ryle down again because he so wanted a son. Each miscarriage chipped away at her ability to live with the way her life was turning out.

Watching the other babies in camp grow up only heightened the disappointment of not having one of her own. She was the dependable baby sitter whenever anyone was without a maid, and nothing gave her greater pleasure than to take kids on a day's outing. But when she brought them home and then walked into her empty house, the letdown was so strong the first thing she did was make herself a drink.

And whenever Ryle was away on business she wondered if he was with another woman. That because she hadn't given him children he might find her inadequate and turn to someone else, someone who didn't have her impediment, as she'd come to look on her failure to have a baby. Too often a drink became her companion.

Nor could faith sustain her. She envied her sister, Beebe, whose belief in God and His Grand Design never wavered. After awhile when she did get to Mass — the strong need to go every week had eroded over the years — she prayed for one thing only, that she would get back her faith. She'd given up praying for children, for God didn't answer her prayers, nor any of the saints to whom she made novenas so diligently. She began to think He'd forgotten her existence. And whenever she experienced the futility of belief, a drink helped push away her disillusionment.

When they were transferred to Maracaibo, she vowed she would cut down on the drinking. The move was such a promotion for Ryle he was easier to live with. Even the camp was a new beginning, so totally different from the isolation of Chacari and the primitiveness of Tucupido.

A transfer to Maracaibo was a move to the big city. The Palm Oil camp was right in the center of things. While it didn't have the magnificent location of the Mene Grande camp which overlooked Lake Maracaibo, it wasn't far from the breezes off the water. The camp had a huge swimming pool and clubhouse with a beautiful lounge and bar. On movie nights people sat under the stars next to the pool. They'd come a long way from Chacari and its tinned roof clubhouse. The spacious houses, built off the ground, which made them cooler, all had back and front porches — big open decks just made for parties, or old fashioned American barbecues.

And whenever anyone wanted to get away from camp, Maracaibo was right next door. It wasn't a cosmopolitan city like Caracas, but in 1958 it was growing in all directions. There were a few good restaurants as well as nightclubs featuring imported bands and acts. And the resort hotel, the *del Lago* (so named because it sat directly on the lake) was a mecca for everything going on in the city. Toastmasters and the Rotary held their meetings there. Its nightclub, the Caroni, featured the most unique shows in town. The Caroni outdid its previous triumphs though when it brought in the Ice Show.

Like a circus coming to a small American town, the Ice Show brightened everyone's lives with its color and spectacle, as well as in a few other unexpected ways. But unlike the circus, it didn't pull up stakes after a short time and go on to the next town. The Ice Show stayed for several months because people came back again and again. The rink was so ridiculously small, it was always a wonder to everyone how the skaters could maneuver in such a small amount of space.

Perhaps it was the sight of ice in Maracaibo's sweltering heat which mesmerized the Venezuelans. Or maybe it created nostalgia for the expatriates so far from home. More likely it was the skaters, beautiful long legged and mostly blond American showgirls in brief, exotic costumes. Suddenly everyone's lives were a little less drab. The kids who aspired to be ice skaters, the women who envied the skaters' glamorous life and the men whose hormones took on a new vigor. When the Ice Show finally moved on, Maracaibo was never the same.

When Cathleen and Ryle saw the show they both felt the same stirrings of remembrance, the magic of their falling in love at the ice rink in Rockefeller Plaza. Afterwards when Cathleen took Nena to the show it still held her interest. She lost track of the times they went. Nena had brought so much happiness into her life. For the first time, the ache of being childless wasn't as acute. That was the added bonus which Maracaibo brought her. Finding someone who needed her mothering as much as she needed to express her frustrated maternal feelings.

Every Friday night, she and Ryle took Nena to the *Rincón Boricua*, an open air restaurant which served the coldest Polar beer, the best hamburgers and steaks in town and garlic flavored fried yucca. The *Rincón Boricua* also had a movie screen where Abbott & Costello, the Three Stooges and Charlie Chaplin played to an adoring young audience. There were movie theaters in Maracaibo where the latest Hollywood releases were shown, but the *Rincón Boricua* with it's old comic movies never failed to draw a crowd. And for the smaller kids who became restless there were swings and slides. It was the perfect place for families, and with Nena, Cathleen felt she and Ryle were finally a family.

Before Fred brought Nena to her house, she'd heard the rumors of Fran's behavior. Remembering Maruja's indifference to her daughter when she was first born, Cathleen's heart went out to Nena. Then when she met Nena, she began to think her sister, Beebe, might be right. Maybe God did have a Grand Design. Nena had come back into her life because they needed each other, especially the day Nena found those horrible newspaper clippings. Cathleen suspected Fran had purposely left them out. She was furious and wanted to confront her, but she realized she couldn't go barging into their home accusing Fran. There had never been any great friendship between them, but after that their relationship became strained. And knowing things might get even worse for Nena if she confronted Fran, Cathleen swallowed her anger. Bit her tongue and was grateful for the time she and Nena had together.

It was Nena who noticed one of the skater's resemblance to her. "She looks just like you, not as pretty of course. But she could be your sister," Nena insisted.

"Another addition to the Grace Kelly look-alike club," Cathleen replied dryly. People were forever telling her she could be the double of the movie star who'd recently married royalty, but she always shrugged it off. She'd been looking the way she did long before Grace Kelly came on the scene. But she could see her similarity to the skater. Except she had a youthfulness Cathleen no longer possessed. When she got home she looked in the mirror, and Cathleen was shocked by what she saw. Her face was starting to become puffy, and she had to use a lot of makeup to cover the blemishes in her once flawless skin. Faint red veins could be seen in her eyes.

Oh God, she was turning into a tropical rummy. Despite all her attempts to keep busy, there was still too much time on her hands. Time when she took a drink to cool off, or chase away the blues. She had to cut down, really start limiting her consumption. She could do it. She could do anything she put her mind to. And besides, who needed the stuff? Nena had given her a whole new lease on life. Cathleen felt her spirits sag though when she remembered Nena would be returning to Caracas at the end of the summer. Don't think about it, she urged herself. Be like Scarlett O'Hara and think about it tomorrow.

Which is what she did. Put off thinking about the end of the summer, reminding herself Nena would be back at Thanksgiving. Be happy with the time you can have with her, she told herself, always have that thought to keep you going.

As a result of all the matinees she and Nena took in at the *del Lago*, Nena struck up a friendship with the manager's daughter, Annie Rogers. Nena and Annie became inseparable and Cathleen was only too glad to drive Nena to the hotel or pick up Annie to bring her back to camp. Fran was indifferent to this friendship, except to insist Nena be home on Thursday afternoons to look after the boys since this was the maid's day off.

One afternoon when Cathleen stopped by the hotel to pick up Annie, she saw the skater whom Nena seemed to think resembled her. They stared at each other for a minute, and Cathleen had the eerie feeling this woman was no stranger. That somehow she knew who Cathleen was. Dressed in an aquamarine bathing suit and matching wraparound long skirt with her blond hair cascading down over her shoulders, the skater resembled a beautiful young mermaid. Suddenly Cathleen, who was pushing 30, felt incredibly old. The skater continued walking across the lobby and then disappeared through the glass doors to the pool area. Cathleen stood there trying to sort out her feelings, wondering why she felt so threatened.

"Hello, young lady," a voice broke into her reverie. "I swear every time I see you, you get prettier." Looking up she saw Wade Pearson, the former V. P. of Operations and now president of Palm Oil.

"Mr. Pearson, how nice to see you again," she replied. His wiry body dressed in a blue and white seersucker suit always reminded her of Murray, but there the resemblance ended. For Wade Pearson's grayish blond hair was cropped in a crew cut and his eyes which looked at her behind horn rimmed glasses were blue green. Almost the same aqua color as the skater's bathing suit and skirt, Cathleen thought, still unable to forget her.

"Would you join me for a cup of coffee, Cathleen?" His western twang had a solid sound to it which always made her feel that he could right every wrong in the world. Despite Sarita's teasing she had an admirer in Wade Pearson, she never thought of him that way. To her he was the benevolent authority figure of the company.

Cathleen murmured her regrets at not being able to accept his invitation, explaining she'd come to pick up the daughter of a friend. As they chatted a few moments Cathleen thought of Ryle and how desperately he wanted to be president of the company. When she shook Wade Pearson's hand she pressed it firmly, hoping some of his success would rub off. And, as her grandmother often theorized, she could pass this success on to Ryle.

When they parted, Pearson came out with the same joke he'd been making over the years. "You tell that husband of yours he'd better take good care of you. And if he doesn't, I'll beat his time."

That old coot, she laughed to herself. But he's a sweet old coot. And he always makes me feel like a million dollars. Sort of the way Murray used to. Oh, how she missed him and how she looked forward to his Christmas cards. She was so glad Ryle had made his peace with him; otherwise she'd never know Murray had finally married in California and was the father of twins.

That afternoon she went to special pains with her makeup and clothes. She wanted Ryle to feel she was worth coming home to. And later, when they made love she put her heart and soul into it, hoping to recapture the magic they had in the beginning of their marriage. Wondering to herself if perhaps things between them had grown stale. And hoping if she became pregnant, this time fate would be generous and give them a child.

"You've still got the prettiest hair, baby," he murmured when they cuddled together afterwards. "I remember the first time I ever saw you — it knocked me for a loop. It still does. Promise me you'll never cut it."

He would be forty next month. His mustache had become salt and pepperish, just as it looked from the snow the night they fell in love. They had a ten year anniversary coming up the beginning of next year. Even if he wasn't the easiest person to live with, she couldn't imagine life without him. He still was the only man who made her motor race. Sometimes she looked at other men, studied the latest arrival of bachelors, wondered if any of them could make her feel as he did. Whenever things became sticky between them — either because of his moods or her feelings of inadequacy because she hadn't given him children — she'd panic and think she had to find someone else. But it always came back to the same thing, she didn't want anyone except S. J. Rylander.

Which was the first thing Cathleen thought when she saw him with the blond skater. The mermaid who Nena said could be her kid sister. That she never wanted anyone but him.

She'd gone to the *del Lago* to drop off Nena for her last visit with Annie. Summer was drawing to a close and the day after tomorrow Fred would drive her back to Caracas. Cathleen decided to stop and visit the manager's wife, Ellie, who was confined to a wheelchair with polio. Whenever Cathleen felt despondent her life hadn't turned out the way she wanted, she only had to look at Ellie Rogers to realize how fortunate she was.

She was turning the corner into the corridor leading to the Roger's apartment when she saw them walking in front of her. Actually she saw

Ryle first. She'd seen him walk too many times — when he left in the morning or when he was going into the shower — not to know his distinctive gait. The slow lazy way his hips moved, the easy strides his long legs made. The sight of which always made her heart beat a little faster. His arm was around a slim blond and without seeing her face, Cathleen knew it was the skater who looked so knowingly at her that day in the lobby. The skater was laughing at something Ryle whispered in her ear, and then Ryle pulled her into his arms for a passionate kiss.

A sob escaped from Cathleen's lips as she called out his name. Ryle and the skater turned around. For several seconds he looked painfully at Cathleen who stared back in disbelief. This isn't happening, she cried to herself. It's just a dream, like the awful nightmares she used to have after the well blew up and he was burned. When she woke up in the middle of the night drenched in sweat and terror. Missing him in bed beside her, afraid she'd lost him.

Looking at him now, she knew it had finally happened, she had lost him. She turned and fled down the corridor and didn't stop running until she got to the lobby. There she composed herself and walked steadily across its marble floor, into the west wing corridor which housed the offices of Occidental Petroleum and various oil contractors. And then out to the parking lot where she walked hurriedly, almost ran to her car. After dropping her keys a few times, she was finally able to open the door of the green Oldsmobile 98. Her hands were still shaking when she lit a cigarette. She didn't see Ryle come out of the hotel until he opened the passenger door and slipped in beside her.

"You bastard," she gasped, wanting to hurt him the way he had demolished her. "Flaunting your infidelity at the *del Lago* where everyone goes. Couldn't you at least have found some out of the way hotel to screw your showgirl?"

"Ah, it was stupid, baby . . . ."

"Don't you ever call me baby again," she cried out, struggling to keep back the tears. "I'm not especially thrilled by it — not anymore. Do you call her baby, too?"

"Of course not," he shook his head.

"Why, Ryle?" she cried out. "Because I couldn't give you any children?"

"No," he shook his head again. "I don't know how the hell it all got started. Maybe because she reminded me so much of you," he said lamely. "One day when I was here at the Rotary luncheon I saw her, and it was like finding you all over again."

"Finding me again?"

"You know," he hesitated, fumbling for his words, "the way you were when I first met you," he replied.

"Have I changed that much?"

"I guess we've all changed," he replied lamely.

The memory of him with the skater, his arm around her, whispering intimately into her ear, kept flashing in front of her eyes. It was like a knife twisting inside her. "How was I when you first met me?" she asked him, dreading his answer, yet knowing it. Young and untarnished, wasn't that what he told her that night in Rockefeller Plaza?

"Oh, I don't know how to explain it," he said, his words slow and labored. "Like you were before all the problems set in."

The problems? Ah yes, the problems. Before she got into the *say goodbye to the babies* business. And *say hello to have a drink, Cathleen, it'll ease the pain* occupation.

"Have there been others?" she asked, knowing even as she spoke what the answer would be.

"Yeah, well . . . . Maybe one or two. But they didn't mean anything to me."

Brick by brick she felt the walls of her marriage crumbling. "So, it was like that," she said sorrowfully, feeling she had walked into a street with no exit. "I just wasn't enough for you."

"Sure you are, baby," he said softly, his eyes filled with pain.

"Then why?" she cried out. "You're just not making sense."

"Because they were there," he sighed. "That's all, no more or no less a reason. Maybe that's the way I am. A no account pussy chaser." He stared moodily out the window. "We both got problems. You've got to get a handle on the drinking, and me? Hell, maybe there's a Pussy Anonymous."

"You rotten bastard," she said coldly. All the sadness and regret had dissipated and instead she felt an anger so strong she thought she would choke on it. Maybe she could forgive him the fling with the skater. Maybe it was her drinking which had driven him to her. But she couldn't swallow the knowledge there had been others, she absolutely couldn't live with it. When she remembered the nights, sometimes weeks on end, when he was away and she'd been alone, always missing and trusting him, she wanted to destroy him.

"It's over — no more," he shook his head. "I'm through with all that stuff. I promise you, baby. I'll never hurt you this way again."

"You're dammed right you never will," she said calmly, her voice becoming icier with each word. "Now get out of my car, Ryle. Just leave me alone."

"Let's go home," he begged her. "Let's get away from this dammed parking lot and go home where we can talk in private." And he'll get me into bed and think that one, two, three he can make me forget what's happened. Too much milk has been spilled, she thought, too much sour milk.

"No," she shook her head. "I'm not going home with you."

"Then let's go somewhere else," he pleaded with her. "Let's take the ferry across the lake. Yeah, the ferry, baby. Let's go for a boat ride where we'll have some privacy and can talk."

"I don't want to go for a ride," she snapped. "I've just been taken for the biggest ride of my life." Her aquamarine eyes resembled polished gems, flashing with a cold brilliance. "If you don't get out of this car, I'm going to make a scene." She pointed to a group of people, several of whom they knew, going into the hotel. She started the car, gunning the motor. Slowly he opened the car door. "I have to stop off at the office and then I'll be right home," he said before walking to his company car.

"Don't hold your breath," she snapped. He wasn't going to make a fool of her again. She drove fast, much too fast, weaving in and out of traffic. She didn't know where she was going, all she knew was she had to get away from Ryle. She thought of taking the first plane out except for all the rigmarole she would have to go through getting an exit permit to leave the country.

When she got home, she pulled one of the suitcases down from the closet, throwing clothes in it indiscriminately. As she closed the mirrored closet door, she looked at herself, gazed with glazed eyes at her long blond hair which was combed in an upsweep. Then she pulled out the hair pins savagely, watching it cascade down her shoulders and back. Her beautiful blond hair which Ryle said he'd fallen in love with the first time he met her. And which over the years he'd asked her not to cut.

Angrily she searched for her scissors and when she found them, she whacked away at her hair, cutting off large chunks of it, not caring how uneven it looked. Then she went over to their bed and placed her hair on Ryle's pillow, along with her wedding ring.

And then Cathleen Rylander walked out of her house and her ten year marriage.

....

She headed for downtown Maracaibo and the ferry. Standing on it's deck watching the city become smaller and smaller Cathleen stifled a sob. She couldn't break down here, not in front of all these people. But she couldn't shake off the memory of sailing with Ryle from New York and the confidence she felt then that the world was her oyster and she could hardly wait to pry it open. She walked around to the other side of the ferry and looked vacantly at the small town of Palmarejo coming into view.

A tropical afternoon shower poured down on the shores and then just as quickly dissipated, the sun coming out stronger than ever. A brilliant multicolored arc sprawled across the horizon. Looking at it, she thought ruefully, 'Love is like a rainbow. You're dazzled by all the beautiful colors in it, but if you tried to reach for one, you'd find out it's only an illusion.' Just as her marriage to Ryle had been. She fought to keep back the tears. Only after the ferry docked and she had the solitude of her car and the road did she break down. She cried all the way to the Andes.

She didn't have any itinerary; all she knew was she had to get away and try to find some peace of mind. If such a thing is possible, she thought bitterly, for a woman who's found out her husband cheated on her. Because it was there, was the reason he'd given her for his sordid little affairs.

At first she found the peacefulness of Trujillo soothing. Although it was a state capital, it had a small town atmosphere with its quaint 42 room hotel. The cool, crisp air 3,300 feet above sea level was a welcome change from the heat of Maracaibo. But after a day she became restless and drove higher into the mountains to Merida. The colonial city was so far removed from any other place she'd been in Venezuela that she felt she had found the perfect hideaway, the hole she could crawl into to lick her wounds. If she wanted to, she could have gone skiing at Pico Bolivar, but she was content to wander around the city. Sometimes the mountain tops were obscured by a cover of clouds the city was so high up, and she could imagine Heaven was but a step away. Except she'd lost her trust in God, for she felt like a boxer hanging on the ropes after receiving the final knockout punch. Her trips to the exquisitely designed cathedral were a disappointment for she found no solace there, no help. This time, she decided, God had gone out for a very long lunch and who knew when He would return.

She felt more at home in the park in the central plaza. There she found the peace denied her in church. The morning sun relaxed the tight muscles of her neck, and she was grateful for the quiet solitude of her surroundings. She spied a majestic Royal Palm rising almost to the top of one of the cathedral's cupolas. It looked so out of place in the mountains, palm trees to her way of thinking belonged on tropical beaches. Just as she was out of place with Ryle, she thought, struggling to suppress her tears. Despite her efforts to push Ryle out of her thoughts, she couldn't forget the mockery he'd made of their marriage. There was only one thing she wanted now, and that was to destroy him. Just as he had wiped her out.

She got up and started walking and when she found a beauty parlor, she had her short hair shaped and frosted. Now she didn't look at all like her old self, which suited her fine. For that person was gone. She had died in a corridor of the Hotel del Lago. Time to celebrate the new Cathleen, she decided, and what better way than a drink. She walked briskly back to the hotel, lost in her thoughts as she crossed the lobby. So much so that she didn't hear her name called out.

"Hello Cathleen. It is you, isn't it? For a minute or so I wasn't sure. You look different somehow — ah, you've cut that beautiful hair of yours. But you're still pretty as a prairie flower."

Startled she turned around and stared at the president of Palm Oil. "Mr. Pearson, what are you doing here?" she gasped. Damn it to hell, couldn't she ever get away from that blasted company?

"Cathleen, I was about to ask you the same thing," he laughed genially. "For me, Merida is the closest thing to being back home in Colorado. Whenever I want to run away from all the traffic and noise of Caracas I come here." He stopped talking and squinted his eyes at her. "Something's wrong, I can see that. You look like someone who's run away, too. How about we two fugitives go in and talk it over a cup of coffee?"

Coffee? God, she needed a drink. "I'm about coffeed out," she replied, hoping he would get the hint. Which he did, except while she drank Scotch and water, he sipped slowly on a Pepsi. "I did run away," she blurted out, not caring what he thought or how it would reflect on Ryle and his damned career. In fact she hoped it would damage him. Throw a monkey wrench in his finely laid plans to ascend to the presidency of Palm Oil. She was through with him and when she got herself together, she would take off for the States and get a divorce. And she wouldn't go back to New York and eat crow either. She was a far different person from the timid 21 year old who'd set such store in what her family and friends thought.

"That bad, huh?" Wade Pearson remarked.

"Yes, that bad," she replied. "I don't seem to be enough for my husband," and she said these last two words derisively. "He likes more of a variety in his diet." She gulped the Scotch down and stared at her empty glass. "No special reason, he claims they don't mean anything to him, but just because they're there. Like why do some people climb mountains."

"I know the saying," he said gently picking up her lighter when her shaking hands reached for another cigarette. "He's a damn jughead, Cathleen."

"Jughead?" Her laugh was bitter. "Oh, you're so polite. I call him worse than that."

"I'm sure you do," his eyes crinkled. "And with very good reason. My daughter's ex-husband had the same problem and he was a jughead too." He shrugged his shoulders. "You might say it's my hobby, trying to find a polite way to curse some one out. I figure anyone can swear, it doesn't take a whole lot of imagination. So whenever I get boiling mad. I like to think about what word I can use. And by the time this ole tired brain of mine figures one out, I've simmered down." He smiled at her, looking suddenly very boyish. "Corny, huh?"

"No," she smiled faintly. "I like words too, Mr. Pearson. I guess you might say I love words. Seeing as I'm such a bookworm."

"All my friends call me Wade."

"Oh, I don't know if I could . . . ."

"Sure you can," he said firmly.

Cathleen looking at him hesitated, then slowly she saw him in a new light. An idea began to swirl around in her head for the most wonderful way she could completely destroy Ryle. "Okay Wade," she replied, feeling very sure of herself. Cutting her hair was nickels and dimes compared to what she planned to do next.

....

"I know you did it to spite Ryle," Wade told her after they made love. "But this old codger thanks you for the privilege." Not so old, she thought, not so damn old at all. Oh, it sure wasn't like it was with Ryle. But Wade Pearson did elicit some sort of feeling in her. Maybe he didn't make her motor race, she was past that. But Wade Pearson was a tender and consoling lover and that's what she needed now. And knowing. "You didn't have to seduce me, you know," he said as he got up to open the window. The cold mountain air rushing into the room felt deliciously clean and beautiful. "I would have made the first move. Not that I'm complaining. At my age, it's quite a compliment to be desired by someone as beautiful as you."

"Was I that obvious?" Cathleen replied, inhaling deeply on her cigarette and feeling very embarrassed. "I haven't had that much experience in this sort of thing." Oh, but I plan to, she thought, I'm going to screw everything in pants. But going to bed with the president of Palm Oil was such a wonderful coup, it was the piece de resistance. She could hardly wait to throw that in Ryle's face.

"Does this bother you?" she asked pointing to her cigarette, suddenly realizing he didn't smoke. She was so used to sharing a cigarette with Ryle after making love that she lit up without thinking. "I notice you don't smoke or drink."

"But I ride a bicycle," he winked at her. "It's okay, the smoke I mean, the window's open." He flashed that boyish smile at her again. "I know you haven't had much experience in seducing men. I guess you're just a pixie who's been through the wars."

Why, the old coot has a bit of poetry in him, she thought. "A pixie?" she asked.

"Yep," he said running his hands through her tousled hair. "Your hairdo is so cute, it made me think of a pixie." And then he took her in his arms, arms so strong they made mockery of his age. "You know, I always regarded New Yorkers as wise guys and phonies, but I guess I ran into the wrong ones. But I still think there are very few pixies around with New York accents."

Cathleen had never been aware of having an accent. But in thinking about it she guessed she did, that to a Southerner or a Westerner whose accents she thought of as cute and sometimes quaint, she sounded just as strange. And maybe not so cute. The first time she'd gone home from Venezuela, she noticed how jarring New York accents could be.

"You mean I say Toity Toid Street and Toid Avenue?" she demanded in an exaggerated nasally tone, screwing her face up in an imitation of a New York cab driver with a cigar hanging out of his mouth.

"No," he laughed hugging her again. "Oh, pixie, you have the most wonderful quality of being urbane without being jaded. Don't ever lose it. Right now you're feeling angry and hurt and you're out to bamboozle the whole world, but time does heal things."

"Really, Wade?" Her voice became hard and all the bitterness was racing through her veins again. "I can hardly wait."

"Sometimes it doesn't seem possible, especially right after you've had a low blow. Something you were totally unprepared for," he said sighing as if remembering his own private sorrows. "And you think you'll never get over it. But you do, believe me, you do. We survivors are too tough to hang it all up."

Cathleen was finding him easier and easier to be with. And as she listened to him, a thought began to formulate inside her head. She wondered if he were married. And if he were, she decided, who cares? So I've committed adultery — big deal! What would really be the icing on the cake as far as pushing Ryle's face into her sleeping with the president? She still wanted to hurt and destroy him. She smiled to herself when she came up with the answer. And, she decided, I don't give a damn how many people get hurt in the process. Nice guys finish last.

But she didn't have to scheme or use any trickery. Or protest her conscience wouldn't have bothered her if she had broken up a marriage. Wade Pearson's wife had been killed in a car crash thirteen years ago. And when he asked her to marry him and she accepted, the first thing he said to her was, "I guess I fell in love with you when you drove all the way from Tucupido to Puerto La Cruz to be with your friend, Sarita. It's like I told you, if Ryle didn't take good care of you, I'd beat his time."

"I don't flatter myself as to your real reasons for saying yes, Cathleen," Wade said when they were getting ready to leave Merida. "I know I'm getting you on the rebound and there's probably a strong desire for revenge on your part. But I'll make you happy, I think you just might even fall in love with me."

"Sometimes you make me feel so naked," she said, embarrassed because he could see right through her. "Then why do you want me, knowing all these things?"

"Because finding you was such a wonderful gift. I'm being given another chance." Again that look of sorrow in his eyes. "You're not the only one who's lucked out in the matrimonial sweepstakes, Cathleen." For the longest time she didn't know what he meant about being given another chance.

"Are you going to be okay when you get back to Maracaibo?" he asked as they lingered over coffee their last morning. Cathleen played with her *arepa*, breaking it into little pieces, taking tiny bites. Ordinarily she was crazy about the corn cake, but today she had little appetite.

She nodded. Wade would take care of everything, her exit permit, plane ticket. They had agreed she would say nothing to Ryle, other than to inform him she was divorcing him. As soon as her decree was final, Wade would fly up to the States and they would be married in Denver. She would have stepchildren older than herself and she knew that would take some getting used to.

"I can't give you any children," he'd told her apologetically as she sipped her coffee. "I had a vasectomy a few years back." For a moment she wavered in her hasty decision for revenge. She put the *arepa* down and reached for her water glass. What she really wanted was a drink. "Then we'll make the perfect couple," she replied flippantly. "I won't have to be disappointed by any more miscarriages." Reaching for the coffee pot she poured them both another cup. "So, what do you do in Caracas besides run Palm Oil and fight the traffic?"

"I don't fight the traffic. My chauffeur does that. I told them I wouldn't take the damn job unless they gave me one. Man, the taxi drivers there get crazier every day." His middle finger pushed up his glasses which were always slipping down his nose. "Having a chauffeur gives me a chance to catch up on my reading."

"What are you reading?" she asked delighted she could share her love of books. That's another thing he has over Ryle, she told herself smugly.

"Well, in the mornings I've been reading Bruce Catton's book on the Civil War. I'd tell you the ending," he said dryly, "except I wouldn't want to spoil the book for you." She loved his droll sense of humor.

"And in the afternoons," he continued, "after a hard day in the corporate jungle I relax with something translated from the French."

"I'm very impressed," she said.

"Well, I don't know if you really would be," his mouth broke out in a wild grin. "It's something called *The Amorous Adventures of a Gentleman of Quality* which causes even me to blush," he chortled. "It makes *Tobacco Road* look like a Tom Swift story."

"You read dirty books!" She shook her head in mock disgust.

"Yeah," he smiled, "but I promise to reform — except I might learn something to make you happy."

Cathleen felt pangs of nostalgia remembering all the wonderfully erotic things she and Ryle had done together in bed. Lovemaking she would never experience with Wade Pearson. But you don't want that anymore, she had to remind herself, not when you know he's been doing the same things with God knows how many others. Maybe it won't be so exciting this time, she thought, but don't ever forget the reason you're doing this. It will kill Ryle when he finds out, just kill him, and that is exactly what you want. It was that thought which kept her going during the two days she got ready to leave for the States. Ryle begged her to forgive him, vowing never to look at another woman, offering to quit his job and go back to the States. Anything to keep her, he promised.

I despise him, yet I still love him, she admitted to herself. And I wonder if I will ever get over him. If one day I'll be able to wake up and say to myself, 'I don't hurt anymore, I'm free. And he'll never have the power to break my heart again.'

But she couldn't wait until her return in two months to tell him of her future plans. And more important she might never know his reaction when he found out. The very best part would be denied her if she didn't tell him to his face.

"You're marrying that old man?" he sputtered.

"Not so old," she replied smugly.

"You've been to bed with him!" he said accusingly.

"Of course I have. And he's very, very good in that department, I might add." She smiled again as she continued to pack her clothes.

Ryle grabbed her wrists, so tightly she thought her bones would crack. Who knows what he would do to her, she panicked. Mother of God, she'd been so foolish to tell him.

"You'd better let me go, or I'll scream and make a scene the whole camp will hear," she said, her heart feeling it would jump out of her chest any moment now. "And then everyone in Palm Oil will know that in addition to being an adulterer, you're also a wife beater." She looked at him coldly, calmly, while underneath she was frightened out of her wits.

"But why him, baby?" he asked, his hands slipping away. His eyes were two pools of pain, she could see that and it made her feel just glorious. "You and me, we were going all the way to the top together."

She shrugged her shoulders indifferently. "Because he was there," she replied mockingly. "I guess I just didn't want to wait, just like you couldn't wait to jump every skirt you saw."

"You're just doing this to spite me."

"If the shoe fits, wear it," she replied indifferently. But inside she was gloating. She wouldn't be satisfied until she destroyed him.

Over the years she had that satisfaction. He quit Palm Oil just as she knew he would. The humiliation of her leaving him for the president of the company sent him back to the States, then overseas to Libya where his indiscretion with the general manager's wife became much too obvious and he was asked to resign. The same thing happened in Saudi Arabia, and again in Colombia. Pretty soon everyone knew that S. J. Rylander had a thing for the wives of executives. And then she heard he was back in Venezuela with one of the large oil companies. The one thing he said he'd never do, go with a big oil outfit. The reason he always wanted to stay with Palm Oil was because it wasn't that mammoth he'd get lost in the shuffle. But when a man gets bounced from one company to another, Cathleen thought disdainfully, he can't be that choosy. He's lucky he has a job. But she knew it wasn't only luck, he was a workaholic who was tops in his field. When Fred told her he'd run into Ryle and he had never remarried, her heart started beating like a teenager. But no one was aware of her feelings. As always she covered them with the cool, detached mask she'd been hiding behind all her life. And caustically remarked to Fred it was just as well he hadn't remarried, as one woman would never be enough for the likes of a man who couldn't keep his pecker in his pants.

"Oh, Cathleen," Fred replied, shaking his head. "Hardness doesn't become you. You're still in love with him, darlin', and so is he with you. The years you've wasted because of this bitterness. Years I wish I had."

He said these last words with such emotion that for a moment Cathleen stopped dwelling on her unhappiness and realized Fred had his own heartache.

"You've never gotten over Maruja, have you?" she asked him softly.

"No," he said quietly, and that one word was packed with such power, she felt his sorrow as if it had been hers.

"Love is not love which alters which it alteration finds," she murmured to herself in wonder, suddenly remembering the Shakespearian sonnet. How many years ago had she read that? Coming home from work, studying for a final exam on the train. She remembered how utterly romantic it had sounded to her then. "We're going to last forever," Ryle had promised her on their wedding night and, romantic fool that she was, she believed him. Just as she believed because she felt so safe in his arms, their love would grow into a ripe maturity. And the sexual excitement they had together would only get better. That's the only thing that did remain, she thought bitterly, the passion which haunts me, clings stubbornly to my heart, always tormenting me. That's all our marriage was, she realized sadly. Her passion for Ryle and children. And Ryle's passion for power and sex.

"At least Maruja didn't cheat on you." Cathleen burst out.

"When you're hurt, you're hurt," Fred replied quietly. "What the reason is really doesn't matter. It's still the same heartache." He looked at her with pleading eyes. "I could be so angry with God, with fate, for taking Maruja away from me. But what good would it do? I'd just be consumed with anger, that's all. It wouldn't bring Maruja back. Learn to play with the cards you've been dealt, Cathleen. It's the only way you're gonna survive. Most important of all though, let go of your anger, darlin', or it'll just eat you alive."

"So what am I supposed to do?" she asked him bitterly. "Leave Wade and go back to Ryle? If Maruja were to come back to life, do you think you could just walk out on Fran and the boys?"

Fred's eyes clouded up with pain. "Fran needs me. She depends an awful lot on me. In the beginning it was the other way around, I couldn't have made it without her."

"Oh, you think she's so wonderful, Fred. How could you?" she cried out. "Knowing the way she's treated Nena."

"Because it hasn't been easy for her, living with the ghost of another woman. And that's why she takes it out on Nena," he said gently. "Don't be too hard on her, Cathleen. She's had it rough in a lot of ways, what she went through during the war. Losing her family, her country."

"Oh, spare me the hearts and flowers, Fred," she snapped. "You're a regular goody two shoes."

"Not so good," he insisted shrugging his shoulders. "I just try to see all the parts of a person. Everything's not black and white, darlin'."

"You didn't answer my question, Fred," she persisted, still uncomfortable with the way he rationalized things. "Just what would you do if you ever had to choose between Maruja and Fran?"

"I guess I'd be more in Hell than I already am," he replied. And seeing the pain in his eyes, Cathleen regretted she had ever brought up the hypothetical question.

"Fortunately, it's a decision I'll never have to make." He paused, getting that faraway look he sometimes had when he seemed to be in another world. "Or unfortunately," he sighed.

"Oh, Fred, I should never have thrown all that stuff at you," she apologized, feeling guilty for the wounds she'd opened up in him. "Jesus, what a bitch I've become." She got up and went to the bar to refill their glasses. He followed her. "It's so wonderful to see you again. Every time you're in Caracas you always come and visit me. And what do I do? Throw crap in your face!"

"Don't be so hard on yourself, Cathleen," he said patting her gently on the shoulders. "I understand."

"There you go again," she cried out. "Acting like some damn saint. St. Ulysses the Understanding!"

"Let it go, Cathleen," he pleaded with her. "Just release all that bitterness inside you, it'll wipe you out, darlin'. Believe me, I know."

Cathleen clung to Fred as if her life depended on it. She didn't know what had happened to her, she seemed to be falling to pieces so quickly these days. He was right, she had become bitter. Hard was a better description. As if to match the changes she'd made in her physical appearance. Her short hair which was frosted because she never wanted to have long, blond hair again. The clothes which were no longer soft and feminine, but mini-skirted and tight so every man noticed her. After the hurt of Ryle's infidelity she wanted every man to go crazy with longing for her. She wanted to have sex with all of them, doing all the exquisite things Ryle had taught her, then leave them high and dry, hurting as Ryle had hurt her. But flirting didn't come easy to her, so she always took an extra drink or two for dutch courage when she and Wade went to parties. Flirting though was all she could do. Whenever she was ready to step over the line, she remembered the decent man she'd married. Somehow she just couldn't do to Wade what Ryle had done to her.

But a few extra drinks did make things easier for her. It loosened her inhibitions in other ways, so she soon acquired the reputation of being a very funny lady at parties. The quips which sent people into gales of laughter, the one-liners which masked the hurt inside her. It was her way of coping with her unhappiness, come out with some self-deprecating joke. Or her view of the absurdities of life, something flip and funny, so that no hostess in Caracas would dare have a party without Cathleen Pearson who was always guaranteed to keep things lively with her brittle wit. The trouble was she kept things lively for everyone but herself. For her marriage to Wade Pearson brought her no great happiness other than the satisfaction of destroying Ryle and his dreams of making it to the presidency of Palm Oil. Gone was the hope that one day she would have a baby. And as good as Wade was to her, she missed Ryle more than she dared admit. She just couldn't seem to let go of him, sometimes questioning whether it was some imperfection in her which had driven him into the arms of other women. That despite his admission of guilt, it really was her fault. Around and around she went, drinking more and feeling less peace of mind as time went by.

But while her personal life was at the poverty level, her outer life wasn't. "If you have to be miserable," she'd console herself, "it's better to be miserable with money." And money she had. From her custom made clothes, no off-the-rack reproductions for her anymore, to the jewelry Wade showered on her, as well as the palatial house he bought for her in the Valle Arriba Country Club, she had all the trappings of success. Especially the pear shaped solitaire with the emerald and diamond wedding band, rings which Ryle had wanted to give her.

There was one bright spot in her life and that was her nearness to Nena now she was living in Caracas. Cathleen became a frequent visitor to Misia Isabel's old mansion in the heart of downtown Caracas. And the weekends Nena came to visit brought her some of the happiness and peace of mind so lacking in her life. Cathleen shooed her cook out of the kitchen, preparing all the American food Nena loved. She arranged tennis lessons for her at the club, and nothing pleased her more than for Nena to bring her new found friends from the club back to her home. "This house was meant for kids," she smiled, remembering too well its emptiness when only she and Wade rattled around in it. For other than the times she entertained, it was much too silent, too large, too barren.

Then when Misia Isabel sent Nena to live with Fred and Fran, and there was no hope of Nena ever returning to Caracas, Cathleen couldn't cope any more. Her drinking got to the point where Wade suggested she seek help.

"But I don't need help," she shot back. "Do I ever get messy or sloppy? So I have three Martinis before dinner. Big deal! Did I ever embarrass you at any company or government function?"

"No, you haven't, sweetheart," he replied. "Never. But it's the other times I'm concerned about. I've been there — I know what I'm talking about."

"Just because you're an alcoholic doesn't mean that I am," she insisted. And then she wanted to bite her tongue. She'd never called him that before. "I'm sorry, that was out of line."

"No, it wasn't," he replied calmly. "I am an alcoholic, just as you are, sweetheart. That's why I want you to go to AA."

"Why did you marry me, if you knew I was an alcoholic?" She walked over to the mirror above the bar in the patio, studying herself, pushing her bangs down on her forehead.

"Because I love you and I hoped in time you'd realize just what you're doing to yourself." The boyish grin which took years off his face was nowhere to be seen, and he looked intently as her, pushing his glasses up his nose.

"That's the thing about being an alcoholic, Cathleen. We never realize it, until it's too late." He went up to the mirror, taking her by the shoulders, turning her around. "Who do you think killed my wife? Did you ever stop to wonder who was driving? She wasn't alone, goddamn it, Cathleen. Some sorry drunken son of a bitch was driving her car — me."

His words shocked her. He'd never talked too much about his late wife, never once told her the details of her death. But looking now into his eyes and seeing the sorrow in them, she threw her arms around him wanting to comfort him. He was so good to her. It was really for this reason she agreed to go to AA. Not because she felt she needed to. She still kept insisting she wasn't a sloppy drinker, she did know what was going on. There was no comparison to the way she'd been after Sheila's death.

If she had to count on one hand the worst times in her life, going to AA would have been on a par with Sheila's drowning and discovering Ryle with the skater. To walk in that room, even with Wade beside her, made her feel naked and ashamed. Looking around she couldn't see herself. Not in any of the people there could she see any resemblance. Her hands didn't shake like the man sitting next to them, nor did her breath reek of liquor like the woman in front of them who chain smoked one Alas cigarette after another. And when the meeting began and each one got up and said their name, she just knew this was the one thing she couldn't do. Especially when each name was greeted with applause. Jesus, Mary and Joseph, why had she agreed to come? How could Wade subject her to this? She was under no obligation to stay, she would just get up and leave, that's all. She told him she would come and she had. Now she'd come, she'd seen and she was going to leave. But when she made the move to get up, she found herself slumping back into her seat, feeling Wade's eyes upon her. Turning and seeing the expectation in his eyes, remembering the promise she'd made to him.

It was her turn to introduce herself. She took a deep breath suddenly feeling her heart would jump out of her chest. She opened her mouth, but no words came out. Mother of God, she needed a drink. She felt Wade's hand in her's, reassuring her, urging her forward.

"My name is Cathleen," she said, her voice so faint even she had trouble hearing herself. My name is Cathleen and I am not an alcoholic, she wanted to cry out. This perfectly groomed woman in the custom made clothes who is a leader of Caracas society is not about to get up and admit to a room full of strangers that she's a drunk.

But even as she said the words to herself, she knew she'd been chasing shadows in denying what she'd become. She took another breath. Oh God, I just want to get this over with, she cringed inwardly. "My name is Cathleen," she said again in a stronger voice. For a moment she was back in time, getting up at Assembly in school and reciting a rehearsed piece in front of the nuns. Feeling shy and frightened, as naked as when she'd emerged from her mother's womb. Get on with it, Cathleen, she pushed herself irritably. "And I am an alcoholic," she admitted. And when her words were greeted with a round of applause she stood her ground, although she wanted to crawl into the woodwork. Oh God, it sure wasn't anything to be proud of. She could think of a lot of other things that deserved applause, but not this. To tell the world you were a rummy.

Nine years, she'd celebrated her ninth birthday of sobriety two months ago. And now the shame was gone, and she felt proud. Proud that she'd finally admitted she was indeed an alcoholic. So now she couldn't blow it, she kept reminding herself, not even if all around her the world was breaking up into little bits and pieces.

One day at a time, she repeated to herself, one hour at a time, she thought looking over at Fred and Fran, reaching for Sarita's hand and gripping it. We're all in this together. Nothing bad is going to happen to Nena and Johnny, she said the words over and over like a novena prayer, those terrorists are just bluffing to see how far they can get.

"*Mira, la televisión*," Sarita cried out nudging her out of her thoughts. Cathleen's eyes turned to the TV. The plane had landed in Jamaica. And the words of the terrorist made her heart sink.

"We are not fooling around," he declared ominously. "The world will see just how serious we are. In one hour if our demand is not met, one of the hostages will die." He paused, shaking his finger at the camera, then continued. "Either the redheaded girl or the blond *gringo*."

With these words Cathleen lost what little faith was lingering in her soul. It's going to happen just like it did with their parents, she cried to herself, their lives are going to be snuffed out. There really must be a curse hanging over all of us, she thought despondently. A curse that's followed one generation to the next. Just like the Kennedys, one goddamned tragedy after another. But unlike Rose Kennedy, Cathleen couldn't accept God's will. She wanted to curse and rant at whoever was pulling the strings in this mad dance of death.

TWENTY-EIGHT

"They're going to kill me," Nena whispered. "I just know I'll be the first one."

"No, they're not," Johnny insisted. "You've got to keep a positive attitude, Nena." But inside he had the feeling the hijackers would make him their first victim.

For over an hour they'd been sitting in the plane in Jamaica. Shades still covered the windows so they had no idea whether they were in the capital, Kingston, or on the north shore in Montego Bay. Nena remembered nostalgically the welcoming rum punch served on past trips to the island. It always helped her get back on the plane, for the runway at Montego Bay, smack in the middle of two sheets of water, was an intimidating one and she never breathed easy until the plane was airborne. If that were her only worry now.

The air in the plane was so humid her jeans stuck to her like sheets of paper plastered with glue. Was it yesterday this awful nightmare began, or the day before? Her mind was so numb it seemed a century ago when she boarded the plane in New Orleans. The only thought which hadn't been deadened was the conviction that just as her mother had perished in a plane, so would she. Nena struggled to remember something Cathleen told her she'd learned at AA. Something about the strength to change the things that could be changed and the serenity to accept the things that couldn't. If this was her destiny, to be shot by hijackers, then she prayed she would meet her fate with dignity.

"Our leader still hasn't been released. The fools!" the woman hijacker screamed. "Now your time is up." The bearded hijacker nodded in their direction.

Nena looked at Johnny with resignation in her eyes. All she could think of was that she wasn't experiencing what people about to die were supposed to feel. Her past life wasn't flashing in front of her. Only what might have been if she and Johnny had met in a different place, for their lives and backgrounds dovetailed like two pieces of a missing puzzle. And realizing this, the resignation to her fate receded, and in its place came such a strong desire to live she was overcome with a cold fury. How dare these thugs play God, destroy lives because they couldn't get their way? She glared at the bearded hijacker, so filled with hatred she knew she could kill him and not feel a bit of remorse. She was not going to her death without a struggle, she would fight these *asesinos* all the way.

But they ignored her, pulling Johnny out of his seat, shoving him roughly up the aisle to the exit. So quickly she never had a chance to tell him of her newfound courage. Nena watched in agony as he resisted them, refusing every couple of steps to move, until a blow to his back made him cry out in pain and dance forward like someone hit with a charge of electricity. Even when they got him to the door, he fought them despite the handcuffs which had been snapped on him, pinioning his hands behind him. His knees shot out and up as he tried to catch the bearded hijacker in the groin. And when that failed he used his feet, kicking in and out in every direction.

"Bastards," he roared at them. Nena wanted to run and help him. He was resisting so bravely and it tore her up to see what they were doing to him. She started up from her seat only to feel the hard, cold muzzle of a gun against her neck. "Not so fast," snarled another hijacker who had come in from the tourist section. "Your turn will come soon enough," he remarked slyly. She slumped back in defeat, indifferent that the gun was no longer pressed against her flesh.

She watched in anguish as the woman hijacker smashed her gun down on Johnny's head, saw his blond hair catch the light when he was pushed savagely out the door. Then flinched as she imagined his body hitting the runway. The woman hijacker raised her gun and aimed it. One shot rang out. When the second shot went off a second later, Nena's body jerked involuntarily. As if she were the one who'd been shot.

Then not a sound. In the row in front of her, the American couple and their two teenage daughters shifted uneasily in their seats. Nena stared at the door through which Johnny had been pushed. Her eyes never blinked. Then something inside her snapped and she started to scream. And she didn't stop until the woman hijacker rushed down the short aisle and hit her, so harshly she felt her jaw was broken.

It's just a matter of time, she thought in despair, feeling the life inside her drain away. The hijackers have all the chips. They killed Johnny, so now maybe their demands will be met. And if not, then she would be next. Somehow she didn't care anymore. Her desire to survive was gone. It seemed that all her life she'd been fighting, and with very little success. Fighting to get a toehold in her grandmother's house with her cousins and their sly innuendos about her mother. Struggling to win Fran's approval and love. And always coming out the loser with men. She'd gotten to the point where she was positive there was something wrong with her because the men in her life always dumped her.

But with Johnny, although they'd known each other for only a few days under the most horrendous conditions, she had the feeling things would have turned out differently. She cried great silent tears, not only for what might have been, but for the unjust murder of a good and caring man who deserved better than the violent death he received.

"In an hour, if they still haven't met our demands, you'll be next," the woman hijacker sneered.

Nena closed her eyes, wanting nothing more than to avenge Johnny's death. She longed to leap up and tear out the woman hijacker's eyes, scratch great welts across her face, but realized it was just wishful thinking. She looked at her watch from time to time and said to herself, 'Forty-five minutes to live,' 'Thirty minutes to live.' Somehow the thought didn't frighten her.

If this is it, she decided, I mustn't let these thugs know I'm afraid. The determination not to give them any satisfaction was uppermost in her mind. *Mamita* Isabel was in her thoughts a lot. She remembered her saying how special she was. A sigh escaped from her lips. So special that I'm going to be bumped off by a bunch of gangsters. Oh *abuelita*!, how wrong you were. Such a short time left and somehow she must say her goodbyes. No one would ever receive them. Not in the usual sense, but she did want to believe that somehow they would get through to the people who mattered. So that her daddy would know how much she loved him. And her brothers, really half-brothers except she never thought of them that way, would know she remembered them in her last minutes. Then the person who'd made such a difference in her life, Cathleen. 'You are the daughter of my heart,' Cathleen had told her so many times. And now that she was going to die, Nena regretted she never told Cathleen just how much those words meant to her. Hadn't let her know how strong was her love for her. All the things Nena had hungered for, Cathleen had given her. The greatest of which was being loved as a daughter. You must know, she cried out silently to Cathleen, somehow after I'm gone, you must realize just how much I treasure the love you gave me.

"You're next," the woman hijacker broke into her thoughts, pulling her up by her long red hair. Like a dog on a leash the hijacker pulled her up the aisle by her hair. I will not cry out, she vowed, not let her know how much it hurts and how undignified she is making me feel. She started to say an Act of Contrition, praying she would die with courage. Her last thought was she would now see *Mamita* Maruja. Her hunger for her real mother would finally be satisfied.

As they approached the exit door, the brilliance of the sunlight blinded her. She closed her eyes. And she heard the bullet she knew the hijackers had been saving for her. So loud it sounded like a charge of dynamite going off and the last thing she remembered was the certainty that her body had exploded in a million pieces.

The other four hostages huddled down in their seats. One of them, a fifteen year old girl with a bad case of acne, screamed, then her head swiveled to the left from the impact of a random bullet which killed her instantly. The inside of the aircraft took on the look of a 4th of July celebration. Brilliant lights illuminated every corner of the plane, so bright they blinded everyone. While the noise sounded like the explosion of a million firecrackers. The hijackers, a moment ago so thoroughly in charge, now stumbled back in confusion, completely disorientated. Taken by surprise, only one of them had time to use his gun. It was his bullet which killed the fifteen year old girl. And this was no more than a reflex action, a brief moment before he, like everyone else, became dazed by the chaos breaking around him.

Which is exactly how the Special Forces team planned their operation. The grenades they'd thrown in the open door, the "flash bangs" — a stunning mixture of fulminate of mercury and magnesium — looked like a million kleig lights had been turned on, while at the same time the noise of explosives detonating added to the confusion. It gave them the time they needed, just a minute or two, to penetrate the plane and disarm the confused hijackers. The woman hijacker, the one who had tormented

Nena from the very beginning, felt an arm slip around her neck. Looking down she saw a khaki sleeve. Then the grip became tighter and she realized she was being used as a shield. It all happened so fast she never had a chance to fire her gun, for at the same time her wrist was brutally twisted until she screamed in pain and the weapon slipped out of her hands.

In the tourist section the rescue operation didn't go as smoothly. Before they could throw in the flash bangs, two of the Special Forces team were killed as they broke open the emergency doors. In that exchange of fire a pregnant woman, trying to shield her two year old child, cried out when she was hit. The child, despite the protection of his mother's arms, died without knowing what hit him. His mother suffering only flesh wounds survived, but miscarried a week later.

Nena was found in a seat curled in a ball. At first she couldn't believe she was still alive. When the explosion went off, she was sure she'd been shot. Even after she found herself in the seat, she just knew she had been mowed down by a bullet. And that in a short time she would be dead. She didn't remember diving into the seat to take cover. After that everything went blank. All around her lights were flashing and the plane was rocked by loud sounds. But Nena knew none of this, for by now she had passed out.

....

Sometimes she slept peacefully, other times she struggled to wake up. For she wanted to escape from the dreadful feeling that she was dead. If she could only wake up, open her eyes which felt as if they had been sewn shut. The times when she succeeded in waking up, she let out a cry of relief and then staying awake became too much of an effort. She slipped back to sleep. One time she woke up and saw her father. Felt him bury his face in her hair, and she thought she must have been dreaming for he quickly disappeared. She called out to him, begged him to come back, and then things went blank again. Other times she dreamt she talked to Cathleen, but she was never sure. Everything was so blurred and indistinct she wondered if she were looking at herself from a distance.

And then one afternoon she woke up, and it wasn't an effort anymore to stay awake. She felt refreshed and alert and she couldn't wait to bound out of bed and see the world again. She was alive, through some miracle she still didn't understand, she was alive. Then she remembered Johnny, and her newfound happiness slithered away. And she wondered why she had been allowed to live and he hadn't.

"Are you up to a little ride?" the nurse asked in her lilting Jamaican accent, pushing a wheel chair into her room. Nena shrugged her shoulders indifferently, but the nurse seemed to take no notice. Instead she busied herself combing Nena's hair, suggesting she might like to add a little color to her face with some lipstick. And rummaging through Nena's luggage she brought out her favorite perfume.

"You've been in this room for two days now!" the nurse fussed. "Time to get out on the patio and get some fresh air in your lungs." All the way to the patio the nurse kept up a non-stop monologue, most of which Nena didn't hear. She couldn't forget Johnny and the horrible way he had died.

"One of your fellow passengers is in this room," the nurse said stopping at a semi-closed door. "Wouldn't you like to go in and say hello?"

"Sure," Nena replied listlessly. She was so depressed about Johnny she felt little enthusiasm. But if there was another survivor of their horrible nightmare in the hospital, then she guessed she owed whoever it was a visit, even if her heart wasn't in it. As the nurse pushed open the door, her first thought was that she was looking at a mummy, or at least half a mummy. One leg wrapped in a cast hung from a pulley suspended over the bed, an arm was also in a cast. A turban like bandage was wound around the patient's head. Since she didn't have even a Band-Aid on her, Nena guessed she should consider herself lucky. Except it would take her a lifetime to forget what she'd gone through. She knew one thing. She wasn't ever getting on another plane. If she couldn't find a cruise ship, she would go home by freighter.

"Well Nena, aren't you going to say hello?"

It couldn't be. Jumping out of the chair she ran over to the bed. He had a black eye and his cut lip had stitches, but he looked positively gorgeous to her. Huge tears rolled down her cheeks. She reached for his left hand and, bringing it up to her lips, kissed it. Then she bent down and kissed him on the mouth. Carefully because of his stitched lips, but her mouth lingered there, hating to pull away from the warmth of an alive

Johnny Maguire.

"When I heard the second shot," she told him, "I felt like I died along with you."

"Oh, you're sweet," he grinned up at her. "I thought I had died too. There I was on that runway, waiting to fade away. I knew I had been hit, because my ear was bothering the hell out of me. I was positive it was just a question of seconds before the bullet would reach my brain. Then I heard the explosion and I thought to myself, this is it, your brain and head are exploding like a bunch of *triquitraqui*. But when I heard all the yelling and screaming going on, I couldn't figure why if my head had blown up like a bunch of firecrackers, I still knew what was going on."

"It seemed like an eternity," he continued reaching for her hand, "lying on that runway, afraid to show that I was alive. I thought it was the hijackers blowing up the plane. It wasn't until it was all over and one of the soldiers came over to me and said, 'This poor bastard is dead,' that I had any inkling of what had gone on. I remember looking out of the corner of my eye and seeing a khaki uniform, high laced boots, and then it dawned on me. These guys weren't hijackers, they'd come to rescue us! Which is when I yelled, 'This lucky bastard is alive.'" He shook his head slowly, as if he still couldn't believe his good luck.

"Despite all her toughness, that woman hijacker couldn't shoot straight," he grinned again. "Thank you, Dragon Lady!"

"*Lo más importante* is that you survived, just as I did," she said gratefully. "Even though you broke your arm and leg when you landed on the runway." Her eyes travelled to his bandaged head. "Does your ear hurt an awful lot?"

"Yeah, it really does," he replied. "But the bullet lodged there, and didn't travel any further, so I'm very grateful. They had to remove almost all of my ear. It'll probably be gross to look at."

"No, it won't," she reassured him. "You can wear your hair long, like a rock star."

"Try telling my mother that, she hates long hair." And then without missing a beat he said, "She's going to love you, Nena."

"Really?" she asked, almost afraid to believe the promise in his voice.

Standing outside the door, Sarita and Cathleen shed tears of happiness. Their kids were safe. Her sister, Beebe, was right, Cathleen cried out to herself, there really was a God and his Grand Design. All her prayers that this generation wouldn't be snuffed out as their parents were had been answered. Nena and Johnny had been pushed into the Valley of Death, but emerged victorious on the other side.

EPILOGUE

December, 1975

Cathleen stepped over a tricycle in the driveway, then realizing she'd never be able to get the car out, went back and slowly pushed it aside, careful not to make any noise. She also picked up a small wagon and set it on the grass, pleased so far it was turning out to be a silent operation. Between the cars and the toys, the house had a well lived-in look to it. It's the way a house should be, she thought. Brimming over with people, especially children. She loved coming to Puerto La Cruz, for all her favorite people were here, the only people who really counted in her life.

"*Tía* Catalina," Juanchito came running out of the house, his red hair glistening in the early morning sunlight. "Let's go for a ride! *Nos vamos en el carro.*"

"Not this time," she laughed. The little devil, how did he know? She'd been so quiet, at least she thought she had. Nena and Johnny swore their first born had a built-in antenna as far as automobiles were concerned. So much so that whenever any of them had to go somewhere, it became a cloak and dagger operation to outfox Juanchito. Rule Number One was never let him hear keys. Pick up a set of keys firmly so as not to jangle them. Rule Number Two was slip out of the house as stealthily as possible. And Rule Number Three was make a godfather getaway, as Nena called it. Get out of the driveway burning rubber.

"Chito, Mommy is making pancakes," his younger brother by a year, Alfredo Alejandro, called from the patio door. Cathleen always thought it curious that Fredo, who was a carbon copy of Sarita, was the more American of the two, speaking mostly in English, while Juanchito who had Nena's coloring and an all American look was the consummate Venezuelan.

"Why isn't the cook making them?" Juanchito asked suspiciously.

He just knew this was a trick to get him in the house. He adored *panqueques*, except when Octavia made them. As wonderful a cook as she was, her pancakes always tasted like rocks. His mother was the only one who made them so light and fluffy he could never get enough of them.

"Because it's her day off, dummy," Fredo declared.

"Come on, Fredo, Chito." Nena appeared in the doorway, a spatula in her hand.

"¡*De veras*!" Juanchito cried out. "You really are making *panqueques*," and, forgetting completely about going for a ride with Cathleen, he bounded into the house.

"Hey, little Nena," Johnny called. "I'm going to be late for work. Are you going to feed me?"

"Little he calls me," Nena remarked patting her extended stomach. "The man is demented." She waved to Cathleen. "I just hope this one is a girl. I'm so tired of seeing the toilet seats always up." She started to walk back into the house, then turned around. "Drive carefully, *mi amor*. There are a bunch of tapes in the car so the trip won't feel like it's taking forever."

"Thanks, darling." Cathleen blew her a kiss. "I'll be fine. See you tonight."

"Are you sure you don't want company?" Sarita asked coming out of the house. Now that Johnny had taken over the trucking business, she only went in a few days a week. In her hands were a large bouquet of freshly cut flowers. "Here, I've wrapped the stems in wet cotton. With the air conditioning on, they should last."

"Oh. Sarita, they're beautiful," she exclaimed, giving Sarita a quick hug. "Thanks for the offer, but I want to go by myself."

"I understand, *chica*," Sarita replied picking up some toys which Juanchito had dropped in the driveway. "I just didn't want you getting all upset and having no one around."

"But I'm not going to get upset," Cathleen replied impatiently. Then her voice softened. "Thanks for being so thoughtful."

"It's such a long drive," Sarita remarked hesitantly. "You could fly up so much quicker."

"I think I'd rather drive," Cathleen replied firmly. "Sometimes people need to get off by themselves. I'll see you tonight, so don't worry. Besides, this car needs a good long trip to break it in."

She got into Nena's white Buick stationwagon which had very low mileage and quickly checked where everything was since the dashboard was so different from her Bentley. Whenever she came to Puerto La Cruz to spend the Christmas holidays with Sarita and the kids, she usually flew out. Between Sarita's Cadillac and Johnny's two cars — his old Jeep which he refused to part with even though it had no air conditioning and his red Mercedes convertible — and Nena's stationwagon, it was always a hassle getting in and out of the driveway.

She had hoped to slip away before anyone was up. But because she hadn't slept well last night, she didn't hear the alarm go off. It was a trip she wanted to make; yet it was one she dreaded for all the old memories it would stir up.

It would be a pleasure though driving on these roads. For they were regular highways now, right down to the green overhead signs. Almost like driving in the States. Nothing like the rutted washboard affairs she and Ryle had travelled on. Even Puerto La Cruz had changed from the sleepy little port she knew 28 years ago to a resort city with all sorts of enticements for the tourists.

The pipeline was still there. Of course it would be, she reminded herself. Some things don't change. They're still pumping the oil to Guanta to be refined and put on tankers. Seeing the continuous line of piping reminded her of Sugar Dalhart and that awful ride on the pipeline road. The memory of that day still remained with her. Every once in a while her path crossed Sugar's in Caracas, and they nodded cool hellos to each other. Cathleen had lost track of how many husbands Sugar had gone through. The only marriage she remembered was the one which came to a screeching halt when Sugar's affair with an American ball player became the talk of the town. Until the winter baseball season came to an end and he went back to spring training in the States and Sugar moved on to someone else.

She and Ryle would have made a good combination, Cathleen decided. It would have been interesting to see who chalked up the most affairs. They could have had one of those open marriages. Oh, why did she dwell on things like that, she wondered. She was over Ryle, he didn't have the power to hurt her anymore. All the dreams she used to have about him, waking up feeling that he'd just made love to her. They were gone now, she was free of him.

But things had turned out well for Nena. She'd finally found the love which had eluded her all her life. She and Johnny were crazy about each other and their children were absolute delights. No problem having babies like she did. And what was it Sarita said about the two of them fulfilling the love which she and John had known before his sudden death? Well for that matter, they were fulfilling the love which all three couples who had been neighbors in Chacari had lost. Strange how things turned out. Almost like a novel or a movie, except that it had all really happened. Unfortunately.

She was getting nearer to Chacari, there was the fence and the familiar palm tree logo. It wasn't the first time she'd made the drive, but somehow this trip evoked a lot more memories. She pulled the Buick over to the side of the road and turned off the motor. How many American brides inside that fence are being initiated into oilfield living now, she wondered. Not too many more. This year *Accion Democrática*, the same party which had decreed in the late 40s that the oil companies had to share their profits and give *Utilidades*, had won the national election again. Now the new President elect, Carlos Andres Perez, was going to make good on his campaign promise and give Venezuelans an even larger share of the industry which accounted for over fifty percent of their country's income. Next year in 1976 the foreign owned oil companies, as well as the steel companies, would be nationalized. Cathleen sometimes wondered at the coincidence in dates — if the government hadn't chosen 1976, the same year as the American Bicentennial, to declare their independence from the foreign companies which had developed their resources. Oh, what the hell, she thought, if I were Venezuelan I'd want them nationalized. And if I were Venezuelan, I also hope I would realize that without the foreign owned companies, none of this would have been possible. She'd been in Venezuela for so long she almost looked on it as her own country. And had come to love it, not only for the diversity of its physical beauty — the snow capped mountains, the lush warm seacoast areas, even its lonely barren plains. But she also was very proud of its political growth and maturity. After 1958 when Perez Jiminez, the dictator, was ousted and Romulo Betancourt came back from exile — the Americans always regarded him as a Communist, but soon learned he was a very socially progressive visionary — she watched each election with great interest. As the years went by with no more military coups, and

Venezuela became the model showcase of democracy for the rest of strife-ridden South America, she grew more and more attached to the country. She never forgot she was American, but she felt something very strong for Venezuela. Sometimes when she heard the stirring strains of *Gloria al Bravo Pueblo*, the national anthem, she got a lump in her throat. You missed too many boats, she would chide herself, embarrassed at her emotions. She thought it might have been because of her closeness to Sarita and the kids. But she tended to think it was because so much of her life had been spent in the country and it had become home to her.

She saw a car drive out of Chacari; for a moment she thought she had gone back in time. The woman driving the Ford resembled Maruja so much, Cathleen had to look twice at her. But then she realized it was just a fleeting resemblance. Ah, Maruja, if only you could have lived to see your daughter, she thought, wiping at the tears which moistened her eyes. To have grown to love Nena, and then not be given the chance to show that love. Cathleen shook her head. It just doesn't make sense, she thought sadly, but then she learned long ago that some things in life weren't ever meant to make sense.

She started up the car for she still had around an hour's drive to Maturín. Time to visit my other baby, she thought. It's just a ritual, she knew that. Sheila was no more in Maturín than she was. But for the past week, ever since she'd been in Puerto La Cruz, she had the strongest desire to visit her grave. Something had been pulling her into making the trip today. It was almost as if her dead daughter had called out to her to come and place a few flowers on her resting place and tell her how much she loved her. As if she didn't know, Cathleen thought, haven't I told her every day I've never forgotten her? She would be 26 years old now, and I'd be hugging her kids as well as Nena's.

She drove by Sheila's grave twice before she found it. Not that she had forgotten its location, it would be engraved in her mind for eternity. But this time it looked different. The most gorgeous coral colored bougainvillea bush, almost a tree really, shaded the gravestone. Sarita must have put it up, Cathleen decided. Sarita whose incredibly green thumb could make a stick in the ground blossom. She'd done this and hadn't said a word to her. How like her, the best friend a person could ever have. And this is why she had felt Sheila urging her to make this visit. So she would know Sarita had made a garden of her daughter's resting place.

She placed Sarita's flowers in a pottery vase she'd brought with her and stuck it in the ground. They would be dead by tomorrow, but the bougainvillea wouldn't. It would last a long time. Just as Ryle had said their marriage would last. Ah Cathleen, she scolded herself, nothing lasts forever, just remember that.

> *With rue my heart is laden*
> *For golden friends I had*
> *For many a rose-lip maiden*
> *And many a lightfoot lad*

Recalling A. E. Housman's words, she felt the breath catch in her throat. How many years had gone by since the impressionable young girl she once was had read those lines? Too many, she realized. She probably couldn't remember the rest of the poem. But the second verse rippled through her mind as if she'd just finished reading it.

> *By brooks too broad for leaping*
> *The lightfoot boys are laid*
> *The rose-lips girls are sleeping*
> *In fields where roses fade*

Suddenly she felt so alone, as if they'd all run off and left her. She still missed them. Sheila, Maruja and John Maguire — all cut off in the bloom of their youth. Even the person who left after a full life — her second husband, Wade, who went to bed one night and slipped away peacefully in his sleep. And the two people who were still alive, but were no longer a part of her life. Murray who would always occupy a special place in her heart. And Ryle. It always came back to him! She knew she was over him and the grand passion she once had for him was finally gone. But there was still a rue in her heart for him, a regret for all that might have been. Ah, put your memories back in the closet where they belong, Cathleen, she urged herself, way back in a corner on the top shelf. Get in that car and start driving. Go back to reality where there are no ghosts, only flesh and blood people.

The afternoon sun, which had been strong, shifted as if covered by a huge cloud. She'd better start back before daylight faded into dusk. As she got up, for she'd been kneeling, she saw it wasn't a cloud which had blocked off the sun, but the shadow of someone standing behind her. When she turned around she jumped back in fright, momentarily disorientated by the sight of the man who had invaded her solitude.

"Hello Cathleen."

She stepped back a few more steps, her heart pounding and thrashing around in her chest. Fred had told her Ryle was with Creole Petroleum now, somewhere in eastern Venezuela near Caripito. But she had paid no attention to his news. Whenever he mentioned Ryle, she deliberately ignored him.

"How are you?" the man asked. Mother of God, it really was Ryle standing before her. His black hair had turned to salt and pepper while his mustache was silver white. His eyes shocked her. They were empty and sad. Defeat was buried deep in their corners.

"What are you doing here?" she demanded, the old anger boiling up inside her.

"The same as you," he replied softly in that slow drawl which had intrigued her when she first met him. "Visiting our daughter. I come here quite a lot."

"Do you now?" She glared at him.

"Yeah well," he shifted from one foot to another. She'd almost forgotten how he always started off his sentences with those two dumb words.

"Yeah well," he said again. "I'm workin' out in the East now and I figured you being so far away in Caracas, it was up to me to do the visitin'. And keep things spruced up."

"Spruced up?" she demanded shrilly. "Just what in the world are you talking about?"

"The bougainvillea. When I saw it, it reminded me so much of the one we had in Tucupido and how much you loved the color."

"You planted it?" She couldn't believe it. It was Sarita who planted it. She just knew it was Sarita, and now he was trying to steal her thunder.

"Well yeah, I did," he replied. "A person brings flowers and they don't last in this heat. But a plant or a tree — that'll last a long, long time. I plan to put in a few more little plants, some that can be shaded by the bougainvillea. I was just waitin' for it to grow enough."

"Well, how wonderful," she remarked sarcastically. "You're turning into a regular gardening enthusiast, aren't you?" She was furious he was here and completely unhinged at learning Sarita hadn't planted the bougainvillea.

"Oh Cathleen," he pleaded, "let's not quarrel, not here. She deserves better than that."

At the mention of Sheila she gasped. It just didn't make sense, that feeling she'd had. That her daughter had been calling her, urging her here. For what? To see Ryle again and stir up all the old bitterness between them? But he was right. They shouldn't quarrel over her grave.

"That was very nice of you," she said, trying to be gracious to him. Only for her daughter's sake, she told herself. "It does make it prettier, not so barren and lonely looking."

"I'm so glad you think so," his smile had a shyness to it which almost made her feel sorry for him. He shifted from one booted foot to another, turning his hat around and around in his hands. He still dresses the same, she thought. Like some cowboy in a Grade B western. Some things never change.

"I thought maybe you'd go back to the States after your . . . ." he hesitated and she could see he was having trouble with the word.

"After my husband died?" She took a malicious enjoyment in saying the word he couldn't. "What? Go to Florida like so many people have done and buy a beachfront condo?" She shook her head. "I'd miss the mountains. Venezuela has become home to me." She reached down to fix a flower which had slipped sideways in the vase, deliberately flashing her pear shaped solitaire and emerald band, hoping he would remember he had wanted to give them to her. But that Wade Pearson had done it instead.

"What about New York?" he asked. "Don't you ever want to go back there?"

"I'm not welcome anymore," she replied frostily. "Having to divorce you took care of that. Things have been strained with my family ever since I dropped that bombshell on them." She wasn't being entirely truthful with him. Her brother, Bubba and her sister, Beebe were still close to her. Beebe wrote her every week with the family news. And her mother, however much Cathleen had broken her heart with her divorce and marriage to Wade, had finally forgiven her. It was her father though, who, until the day he died, regarded her as an outcast and refused to allow her to come in the house. So when she did go to New York, it was in Bubba's home where she saw her mother and the rest of the family.

"Fred's not going back to the States either," he said after an awkward silence.

"Yes, I know," she replied. Now that they were on neutral territory it was easier to be pleasant to him. "When the government nationalizes the oil companies, he's going to work with Maraven. Everyone's happy about it, except Fran. She wants to pack it all in and go to the States. It's the dollars she'll miss the most. She hates the fact the foreigners who do stay on with the Venezuelan companies will be paid in local currency."

"Yeah well, that's something to think about," he agreed. "But it's not going to stop me — I'm staying." Why did she have the feeling he'd just made up his mind?

"You are?" she said, some of the belligerence returning to her voice.

"Yeah, I am," he replied. "The government needs people who know the business the way me and Fred do. I'll probably go with Lagoven — in an executive position. We've been doing some talking back and forth."

"Well, congratulations, Ryle."

"Oh, but you're the one to be congratulated, Cathleen."

"Really?" She looked at him warily. What was he going to pull on her now?

"The way you kicked the sauce." For the first time since this incredible encounter began, she saw the heavy, unhappy look in his eyes disappear. "Oh, baby, I'm so proud of you going to AA."

"It was my husband who was responsible," she insisted, completely at a loss as to how to handle this conversation with him. They were becoming too civilized, too polite. She didn't ever want to forget how he had ridiculed her and their marriage. "He was a very good and understanding man."

"Well, yeah, I guess he was a better man than me."

"In many ways," she replied coldly. "How did you know about AA?" she asked him suspiciously. "Fred?"

When he nodded she wasn't surprised. Fred had been bringing her news of Ryle over the years.

"He asked me to come to Puerto La Cruz and have a New Year's Eve drink with him," Ryle said hesitantly. "Are you going to be with him and Fran?"

"Heavens no," she shook her head firmly. "Sarita and I will be home baby sitting while the kids go out New Year's Eve."

"But you do go out, see other men," he blurted out. "I've seen your pictures in the newspapers at all those society parties and balls."

He really was keeping tabs on her, she thought. And the knowledge made her suddenly feel giddy. Like a teenager who finds out her crush isn't one sided. The excitement she felt when she first met him came rushing back, in company with the tug of war playing havoc with her emotions. The swarm of butterflies which invaded her stomach when he winked at her in Barry's office so long ago. She reached up to the chain around her neck, half expecting to find Danny O'Hara's class ring so she could hold on to it for dear life. But her fingers wrapped themselves around the gold heart Wade had given her one Christmas. What am I going to do now, she cried out to him. You were always there to point me in the right direction, Wade, what am I going to do now? Mother of God, I've lost all my marbles, she panicked. I can't allow myself to ever care for him again. He's probably got a string of women in every camp. Jumping them all like some goddamn jackrabbit. That's probably why he never remarried. Having a wife would cramp his style. And then before she was even aware of what she was doing, she felt so rattled, the question popped out of her mouth.

"I just couldn't remarry," he replied, and she could see how difficult the words were for him. "I guess I was too afraid I would fuck up someone else the way I did you."

We both screwed up, she realized sadly. Me with the booze and him with his women. She wanted to push back the clock and undo all the things they had done wrong, rewrite the script so this time it would all come out right. But it's just wishful thinking, she realized sadly. You can't go home again, she knew that, you just can't undo the past.

She looked around in panic, feeling she must leave right now before she lost her head completely. "Do you still carry that beat up old Swiss Army knife?" she asked him. She wanted to take a cutting of the bougainvillea with her. She tried not to watch him as he carefully cut away a branch of the bush, for the sight of his hands and his long fingers still had the power to do things to her. How typical of him, she thought, he could drive her crazy with his moods and sharp tongue and then he would turn around and do something so incredibly sweet. Like remembering how she loved that coral colored bougainvillea in Tucupido, and making a garden for Sheila. And the time Sarita was having so much trouble with Johnny, when Ryle went to Puerto la Cruz and brought Johnny back to spend the summer with them because Ryle decided Johnny needed to be around a man. She sighed to herself remembering that summer and the change he'd made in Johnny. As if reading her thoughts, he asked, "How's Sarita's boy doing?"

"Not a boy anymore," she replied smiling. "He's a father now and they're expecting a third child."

"So I heard. He's a good kid."

"You had a hand in that, Ryle."

"Naw," he replied shrugging his shoulders. "His mother did that. I just sort of hung out with him, took him fishing, a little bit of hunting. Tried to give him some of the things my old man never gave me."

"Maybe that's what he needed," she said remembering that summer when they'd all felt like a family.

"Sure you won't change your mind about New Year's Eve?" he asked as he continued to slowly cut the bougainvillea wood.

"No," she said, every minute near him driving her crazy. He finally made the cut and was wrapping the branch in his handkerchief when he looked up at her.

"You could be proud of me too, Cathleen, if you gave me a thought or two."

"I really have to get going, Ryle. You know what a long trip back it is, even with these good roads they have now." She didn't know what he was talking about and she didn't want to hang around to find out. She must get away from him and stop feeling like some ridiculous lovestruck teenager. Act more like the woman she had become, someone who was in control of her life.

"I've grown up too, Cathleen. I really have, so much so I even surprised myself," he said laughing in a self-deprecating manner which momentarily stunned her. "You're not the only one who got her act together."

"Oh please, Ryle, don't say anything else. Not one more word because I just don't want to hear it." She reached for the branch and in her haste to snatch it out of his hands, the thorns ripped the tips of her fingers.

"Oh, baby, here let me," and he took her fingers in his mouth, sucking away the blood. She closed her eyes and swayed back and forth in a wave of dizziness. She wanted him to take her in his arms, those strong arms she still missed so much.

"Please," she begged him. "Please, let me go," and pulling away from him she ran to the Buick stationwagon.

"It's still there between us," he followed her to the car putting the bougainvillea branch down on the back seat. "Did you ever stop to think what Sarita and Fred would give if they had the chance we still have?" he asked, blocking the door so she couldn't get in the car.

"It's over for them, baby. John Maguire is gone and will never come back." His hands were pressed against the side of the car, hemming her in. "And neither will Maruja. They're both history. But you and me — we're not." She could smell his after shave lotion and she tried to block the memory of how it had intoxicated her so long ago. "We still got tomorrow, we still have time to make it right."

For a few seconds, minutes, she didn't have any conception of time anymore, she almost believed him. Believed the two of them could wipe out the past, erase all the things which had driven a wedge between them. Start all over because life hadn't robbed them as it had John and Maruja.

"Oh, baby, it's going to be so good this time. I really will cherish you," he promised.

"Bullshit!" she cried out unable to forget the cheapness he had made of their marriage. "You ran around on me before, and you'd do it again." She struggled to get in the stationwagon.

"Oh, Cathleen, I don't blame you for feeling that way. I was a damn fool. I didn't realize what I had in you. The best, that's what you are, the best. And I had to screw it up by acting like some damm alley cat." He looked at her with pleading eyes. "I'd give anything if I could have you back."

She hated herself for what he was doing to her, making her feel weak with desire. And when he took her in his arms, she didn't resist him but clung to him, returning his kiss, feeling the years, all sixteen of them, slip away. Almost believing, as he did, they could make a go of it this time.

But her memories were too strong. Pushing him away, she opened the Buick's front door quickly and sank down on the front seat, pulling the door firmly shut. Oh, it would be so easy to give in to him, be thrilled by his promise that he had changed. But she mustn't, she told herself, she mustn't ever give him the opportunity to hurt her again.

"Goodbye, Ryle," she said putting the key in the ignition. "Lots of luck in '76."

"It's going to be such an exciting year, Cathleen. Share it with me," he begged. "This will be a whole new era for Venezuela. We were a part of all the changes that made the country what it is today. Let's see what the future brings — together." He paused, then hoarsely whispered. "Oh, how I need you. I never realized how much until it was too late. Give me a chance to make it up to you."

She shook her head. "It won't work, Ryle. Too much water under the bridge."

"We had almost ten years," he said urgently. "Let's try for another ten and ten after that." He reached in through the window and kissed her gently. Cathleen felt herself weakening. If I don't leave now, she cried out to herself, I never will. She pushed him away and turned the key in the ignition, driving off in a cloud of dust.

She searched for one of Nena's tapes and slipped it in the tapedeck. Good old rock and roll, she thought. None of that sappy music they used to play in my day. A person took all of it at face value, at least she had. Believed it when Harry James' horn had wailed *You Made Me Love You*, when Helen O'Connell surrendered with *It Had to be You*. Or when Frankie Laine promised a lifetime together.

How very *apropos*, she thought when Linda Rondstadt's voice filled the inside of the car. Only the kids of today had the smarts to pen a song like *You're no Good, You're no Good*. No one wrote a song like that in her day. Oh no, only things like *My Man* and words to the effect that no matter how badly a man treated a woman, she'd go on pining away for him. Her feet beat time to the music, feeling they were playing her song, that it was her personal anthem. She kept hitting the rewind button, playing it over and over again. When she passed Chacari, she raised her middle finger in a salute. And felt so good about it, she waved goodbye to the last link of fence with the same greeting.

Then the tape stuck. She slowed down, pulled it out, reinserted it, and heard the same pattern of repeated music. Disappointed she inserted another tape. But this one didn't have the same go to hell quality of the first song. She turned off the tapedeck, suddenly wanting silence and solitude.

The reddish, blue lights of the flares from the wells lit up the evening sky. A trailer truck carrying casing passed her going in the other direction. She saw the logo on the side, *La India*, one of Sarita and Johnny's fleet of trucks. How proud John would be to see how his dream had flourished. And remembering John, Ryle's words came back to her. How Sarita and Fred would give anything to have the chance that she and Ryle still had.

No! Push it aside, she told herself. Ryle was just playing on her emotions, trying any way he knew to get her back. And if she did go back to him, he'd hurt her again. All that hogwash about giving him another chance. Probably because he's getting on in years. If she was pushing fifty, then he was going for sixty. He's just slowing down, she sighed to herself, getting lonely now because he's no longer young. It happens to the best of them, even an old stud like S. J. Rylander.

If only she hadn't gone today. Maybe yesterday she wouldn't have run into him. Suddenly she felt chilled. It certainly wasn't the weather. Even though the air was less humid, it still hadn't cooled off that much. Nor was it from the air conditioning for she'd turned it off to get some of the night air. Then why did she feel so cold, and why was she shaking?

And then she understood. Sheila had wanted her there today. It was as simple as that. But why? To see Ryle again after all these years? Stir up all the old anger and bitterness? No, that didn't make sense. Cathleen didn't think it strange to feel her daughter had called out to her, urging her to make the trip. So many times in the past she carried on conversations in her mind with her baby.

Ah, Sheila Mageila, she asked her daughter, calling her by that silly little nickname she had used so many years ago, why? Why did you want your father and me to see each other after all this time? You know I won't go back to him, I can't go back to him.

She remembered his words, how exciting it would be to share the new era when the oil companies were nationalized. She would ride that one out alone, thank you. She would have a box seat in Caracas for that ballgame. So he'd grown up, had he? Well, it was about time. That's what life was all about, growing. But just because they'd both gotten their act together, it didn't mean they could get back together again.

And then Cathleen forgot all her words of recrimination, and all she could remember was the look in Ryle's eyes when she first saw him. She wasn't the only one who had suffered. If she had wanted revenge for what he'd done to her, she'd gotten it. Not only the surface satisfaction, the knowledge he'd bounced around from one job to another because he hadn't been able to take the humiliation of staying with Palm Oil after she left him for its president. But today she'd seen the look of defeat in his eyes. And somehow the feeling of how sweet it was didn't feel so good anymore. In fact, it gave her absolutely no pleasure.

Let it go, Fred had been urging her all these years, let go of the anger and bitterness which had clung to her heart. Slowly she realized it was time to let go. Maybe that's why Sheila wanted her there today, so she would do just that. Just as she'd found peace of mind at Sheila's grave so many years ago when she'd resigned herself to her death. Cathleen felt a warmth surrounding her. She was free now, happier than she had been in years. Finally at peace with herself. And she wished the same tranquility for Ryle.

But that's all, Sheila Mageila, no more. I've made my peace with your father. So, don't try any more of that Irish witchcraft on me, she told her daughter sternly.

She put another tape in the deck. It wasn't a song she'd heard before, but listening to Janis Joplin's raspy voice with its bittersweet rendition of *Me and Bobby McGee*, she felt an immediate sense of recognition.

From the coal mines of Kentucky
To the California sun
Bobby shared the secrets of my soul

She nodded her head as if discovering some great truth. From Chacari to Tucupido to Maracaibo — from one end of Venezuela to another — she and Ryle had shared so much. The memories of those days flooded her mind. But it was the next verse which twisted her emotions into such a tight knot she had to pull the car over to the side of the road.

I'd trade all my tomorrows
For a single yesterday
To be holdin' Bobby's body next to mine.

Hearing the yearning in Joplin's voice, identifying with the pain the lyrics depicted, Cathleen's head slumped down on the wheel. She remembered Ryle's words, that Maruja and John didn't have a tomorrow, but he and she did. Her hands shaking, she pushed the stop button, then slowly took out the tape, curious to know who wrote the song. Well, Kris Kristofferson, she thought sadly, you've been there too. Only you were able to make a beautiful song out of such regret.

She reinserted the tape, listening knowingly when Janice Joplin sang.

I'd trade all my tomorrows
For a single yesterday
To be holdin' Bobby's body next to mine.

Struggling with her emotions, taunted by the haunting music and lyrics, Cathleen cried out to her daughter.

"Ah Sheila, don't push me toward tomorrow, I'll get there soon enough."

T H E   E N D